# Praise for Helena Coggan

'The next J. K. Rowling'
**Today Programme, USA**

'Vivid and intense. Helena Coggan had me on the edge of
my seat, wondering who would betray, who would kill, and
who would survive to the final page of this gripping new
YA fantasy'
**Amanda Bouchet,** *USA Today* **bestselling author of
The Kingmaker Chronicles**

'A phenomenal achievement . . . assured, frightening,
action-packed'
*Observer*

'Fast-paced and action-packed . . . Truly thought-
provoking. Featuring strong female leads, and firmly
ditching the 'love will conquer all' trope, [Coggan] presents
women as sidekicks-turned-heroes, damsels-turned-
warriors, and children-turned-leaders'
*Happiful Magazine*

'A pulsing, labyrinthine, emotionally visceral plot'
*Metro*

'Exploding with life, ideas and passion'
*Daily Mail*

Helena Coggan is a writer from London. Her first novel, *The Catalyst*, was published when she was fifteen years old, and was named as one of 2015's debuts of the year by the *Guardian* and Amazon and featured on BBC Breakfast and NBC's Today. She is currently a student of physics at the University of Cambridge. *The Witchling's Girl* is her fourth novel.

Also by Helena Coggan

*The Catalyst*
*The Reaction*
*The Orphanage of Gods*

# THE
# WITCHLING'S
# GIRL

## Helena Coggan

HODDER

First published in Great Britain in 2021 by Hodder & Stoughton
An Hachette UK company

This paperback edition published in 2021

1

A CIP catalogue record for this title is available from the British Library

Paperback ISBN 978 1 473 62945 5
eBook ISBN 978 1 444 79475 5

Typeset in Sabon MT by Palimpsest Book Production Ltd, Falkirk, Stirlingshire

Printed and bound in Great Britain by Clays Ltd, Elcograf S.p.A.

Hodder & Stoughton policy is to use papers that are natural, renewable and
recyclable products and made from wood grown in sustainable forests. The logging
and manufacturing processes are expected to conform to the environmental
regulations of the country of origin.

Hodder & Stoughton Ltd
Carmelite House
50 Victoria Embankment
London EC4Y 0DZ

www.hodder.co.uk

*To Cat,*
*without whom*
*everything would be different*

# THE
# WITCHLING'S
# GIRL

# CHAPTER ONE

My first memory is of resurrecting the cat. I was seven years old. I was sitting in the kitchen of my mother's house, and the cat was sprawled unmoving on the floor. I had one hand in its fur, mid-stroke, feeling the warmth leach slowly from the body. Its eyes were open and unblinking. Somewhere above me the baby was crying, and my mother was trying to calm it.

I hadn't seen death before. I know that because in the memory I'm not afraid. The cat had stopped purring. I just watched it. I thought it must be angry with me, like the time I'd stroked its fur the wrong way. I took my hand away, cautiously, in case it tried to bite me again.

The cat did not move. It stared blankly at the wall behind me, its tail curled slackly on the wooden floor.

I have a lot of questions about this memory. Where is my father? Did I ever *have* a father? The baby upstairs was newly born, so if he died or walked out, it must have been recent. You'd think I would remember. But I don't. All I remember is the cat, and its glassy yellow eyes.

I knelt on the floor, still watching it curiously. The silence was starting to drag at me, like the pull of river water.

I lowered my hand. Certainty settled over me very slowly.

After perhaps five minutes, I realised it wasn't going to move again.

At last, for want of anything else to try, I drew the cat into my lap. I settled its paws on my knees and arranged its back legs awkwardly beneath its tail, as it had liked to sit when it was alive. Its head lolled onto my leg, grotesque. I propped it up gently. I thought, with a quiet, happy certainty: I need to warm it up. When I warm it up, it will move again.

Above us, the baby had stopped crying.

We sat like that for a while, in silence. I was almost sure now it wasn't going to scratch me.

I started stroking it again with the tips of my fingers, from the little crook behind its ears to the fold of its shoulder joints, the way I knew it liked. I was very careful not to press too hard, in case I disturbed it and made it slip off my lap and onto the floor. I could feel my human warmth seeping into it, like the dribble of honey into a teacup, and a little of its death-cold moved into me. I could feel it, but I wasn't scared. Like I say, I was very young.

At last, I heard footsteps on the stairs. My mother, coming to find me. It is so strange, this memory, what it blurs and what it preserves. I can remember so clearly the absent-minded way she patted the baby's back, the way she shifted her weight to rock it back and forth – and yet I have no memory at all of her face, or whether the baby was a boy or a girl.

She stopped short at the doorway of the living room, peering in at me. 'Haley, sweetheart? What are you doing?'

Then she saw the cat.

Her eyes went wide. She stopped dead and pressed the baby closer to her chest as if to keep it away from the cat, away from me. I think she already knew.

'Oh, no,' she whispered. 'No, Haley, put it down – come on, get away from it now— '

And then the cat's milky eyes flickered. It blinked, once and then twice, and stirred in my lap. It tried to get up, stumbling. I had never seen a cat unsure of its own balance like that. It was normally so graceful.

My mother started screaming.

*

Later, I was lying in her arms. My mind was sleep-slow and my eyes and ears were dulled, but I knew her feel, her smell, instinctively. I would have known her blind. Now, of course, I wouldn't know her at all.

The world was faded and blurry, like a bad dream. She must have given me something. I know there were cupboards in the house I was never allowed to open. I don't always remember the house – it comes back to me in flashes sometimes when I try to sleep. Sometimes I can smell the pouch of lavender my mother kept on the pillow of her double bed, see torchlight on the cedar wood of a kitchen wall, hear the echo of the baby crying up a flight of stairs. Sometimes there's nothing at all, as if I came from darkness.

It was raining and dark. I could feel the water trickling down my face, the empty-air smell of it. We were outside. The drugs had dampened my understanding, made it dribble like mud down the surface of my brain, but still I was sure this wasn't our street. My mother was holding me delicately against her body, one hand underneath my back and one supporting my head. I know that position very well now, from my work. It is the way you carry someone when you don't really want to touch them.

She was waiting for a door to open. I could see the edge of it through my swooning vision. I saw the wood swing over the carpet. The darkness within smelled odd, like burnt rosemary.

There was a silence. Then a low voice.

'Lysa?'

For years, this was the only reason I knew my mother's name.

My mother didn't say anything. I could feel her shaking.

'Lysa, what—'

'I have a girl for you,' said my mother.

Marian did not say anything. I know the look she must have been giving her, those unreadable grey eyes.

'Your girl?' she said at last.

'Yes – yes, of course.' My mother seemed slightly affronted, although she had no right to be. If she was willing to give up her own daughter to a witchling, I don't know why it was so unreasonable that she might sacrifice someone else's. 'Mine. Haley.'

'Haley.'

Marian said it slowly. I know she was looking at me. A raindrop ran down my scalp, and I remember thinking, through the haze of drugs, that I was so warm and sleepy, that it must be night-time now. I remember wanting my own bed, wanting this to be over.

My mother said, with a good attempt at righteous impatience, 'Can we come in?'

Another pause.

'Of course you may,' said Marian at last.

The door swung wider and my mother carried me into the darkness. I felt the gentle sway of her footsteps, the sudden dizziness when she lowered me onto the kitchen floor. It was hard and uncomfortable, pressed against my ribs.

A scrape of chairs from above me.

'Are you hungry? Have you come far?'

'No, just from the house.' My mother sounded distracted. 'Laura's with the baby.'

There was a silence. I watched an ant climb up the wall, my eyes unfocused.

When Marian spoke, her words floated over my head.

'You understand what—'

'Yes, yes. I understand.'

A pause.

'You understand,' said Marian again, 'what this means.'

My mother took a deep breath.

'Yes.'

'You won't see her again.'

'I – I know.' My mother's voice trembled slightly. 'I don't have any choice, do I? If I keep her, you'll come after me, right? She's one of you. She belongs to you.'

Another dreamlike silence.

'What did she do?'

My mother hesitated. 'She, uh . . . It was the cat.'

'She raised it?'

'Yes. It died, and she – I mean – it kept walking around for hours. I thought it—'

'You're sure it was her?'

'Of course I'm sure, who else? She was *hugging* it.'

'Calm yourself, Lysa,' said Marian quietly. 'I believe you.'

Another long silence. I could feel eyes on me.

'Well, then,' said Marian at last. 'You can leave her here.'

'Just—' My mother sounded startled. 'Just like that? I just leave, and—'

'Yes.'

'There's nothing I have to—'

'No,' said Marian. 'Leave.'

A silence. Nothing happened for a long time, or maybe a few seconds. Words I didn't understand yet lay at the base of my skull, waiting.

'I thought – I should go back and get things from the house. Her things—'

'She doesn't have any *things*,' said Marian, her voice as cold as I have ever heard it. 'She's not your child anymore. The sooner you understand that, the better. Leave.'

A pause. Then the scrape of a chair. My mother had got up.

'Sweetheart,' she whispered, and her voice broke at last.

I could not move or speak. I stared at the ant, almost at the ceiling now.

'Don't go any closer,' said Marian. 'Leave, Lysa.'

There was a long, long silence.

Then, at last I heard footsteps down the corridor. The door clicked shut. I heard no dread finality in it. I was seven years old, and had no idea what was going on.

Marian didn't move. I could hear her drumming her fingers on the table, a halting, leaping rhythm, an old song of praise to our Lord Claire. This was before we lost the war, of course.

Another chair-scrape. Nails on chalk. I would have winced at the sound, had I been able to move. There were no footsteps. Marian just stood there, above me, for a long time.

I watched the wall, half-asleep. I wondered where the baby was. The quiet sank slowly over me, and my eyes drifted closed.

I woke up hours later in a dingy upstairs bedroom, and from that moment on I was the witchling's girl.

# CHAPTER TWO

One of the first things Marian taught me, or perhaps just the first I remember, is that I would die young. Witchlings live our whole lives steeped in death-magic, and after a few decades it seeps into our bones, makes us sick and frail and old before time. 'You won't live fifty years,' she told me, with perfect equanimity, and she herself died at forty-five, looking closer to seventy, blue-veined and emaciated.

But I'm getting ahead of myself.

We lived in our House of the Dead. There is one in every town in the living world, built and kept for the resident witchling and her girl, although in those first years it did not feel like much of a home to me. And it was more than that to Marian. It was woven into her, bone-deep, a part of her mind. I feared it, and tried desperately to avoid its unblinking, tireless gaze, thinking that she watched me through the walls.

The house is at least eight hundred years old, built from the gnarled roots of an ancient tree that twines around the house like a lover, so that branches stretch across rooms and sprout up through floors. I always knew exactly how tall I was by the branches I had to duck under. It has absorbed the tree's gnarled, aged look; every room is slightly dimmer than it ought to be, the windows dusty, and in winter without the fire it is cold enough to kill. You have to master the house to live there, and you have to grow up there to master it.

The house has a dozen rooms, although in those days we only really used five: the hallway, the kitchen, the underground storeroom with its trapdoor into the tunnels, Marian's bedroom, and my own. Marian's room was always locked. I didn't set foot in it until many years later, tending to her as she lay dying. When I was a child, I imagined monsters hidden within it.

Marian did not speak to me much in those first months, but I know that she must have felt for me. Once, a long time ago, what was happening to me had happened to her. She had been a child, once, born to a family who loved her, and they had surrendered her to their witchling at once when they saw she had the gift of death-magic.

She told me that she didn't fight, when she was given up. I don't believe that for a moment.

*I* fought. I held out for nearly two months. I didn't understand where I was, what was happening; I wanted my mother back, I wanted the baby, I wanted my home, I wanted to escape. I tried everything I could. Marian locked me in my room, and I screamed loud enough that I knew she could hear me downstairs. The window was barred, so I clawed at the walls – there are still scratches in the windowsill where I tried to dig my way out with my fingernails. I wept until I thought my eyes would dry and fall out.

One day when Marian came with food I hit her, pounding my fists against her stomach. She picked me up, carried me back to the bed, sat me down, walked out, and locked the door. I sank to the floor and wept.

The next time she came, I tried to charge past her onto the landing. I don't know what my plan was; I don't think I had one. It was pointless, of course. Marian caught me by the waist, picked me up as I kicked and flailed, and put me back down on the bed. She sat there looking at me for long minutes, silent and unyielding, until my sobs faltered. I could not read her expression.

Then she slapped me across the face.

The shock of it hurt me more than the actual blow. I had

never been hit before. I stared at her, my eyes welling with tears again. She looked at me, then turned and walked away. In the silence I heard the lock click.

She only had to do it once. I think she was counting on that. In that moment, the fears that had gripped me ever since my abandonment were given shape and form. Everything seemed very clear to me then. I could be hurt, here – and if I could be hurt like that, what else would she do to me? She was a witchling, a creature of the dead; my mother used to twitch with unease when she heard her name. Could she kill me? Did she want to?

I stopped scratching the walls. I stopped screaming. I stopped trying to draw her attention in any way at all. When she came with food I crawled into my bed, covered myself with the blanket as she set the food on the ground and left. I did not want her to look at me and see all the veins and bones in my neck, all the things she could use to hurt me. I closed my eyes and prayed for my mother to hurry. Soon, one day soon, she would come back and rescue me.

Downstairs there was always movement. The voices crept into my dreams and took root and grew faces; I imagined monster friends of Marian's plotting to eat me. Later I found out they were just townsfolk, the same people I had known before I was given up. They were sick and injured and grieving and dead, and so they came to Marian, wanting healing, consolation, resurrection, or passage for their loved ones to the underworld through the tunnels beneath the house. Marian soothed them, set their bones, stroked their heads, gave them the rites and laid their bodies in the cellar under shrouds. She was a very good witchling. Everyone who came here needing help, even those who were terrified of her and of death-magic, emerged believing in some part of themselves that she loved and cared for them, and after that they could not hate her. It was a great gift.

I knew very little then about what a witchling did, about healing and childbirth and corpse-rites. I was seven years old, and sickness and death were not yet real for me. But I could *feel* the death-magic here, pooled in the shadows at the corners of my bedroom, seeping from the tattoos on Marian's arms. I felt the bodies cooling in the basement, and I was afraid. The witchling was a creature of the dead, she raised them and she carried them. She wanted to make me one of them.

At night I pushed chairs against the door and pulled blankets over my head. I counted the hours till dawn. I believed firmly that she could not kill me in daylight, and I treasured the first grey light through the barred window.

It would be over soon, I thought. If I could just hold on long enough, fight hard enough, I would be freed. My mother would come for me. I knew the tales. Children held captive by monsters were always rescued and returned to their loving homes. I would tell this story for the rest of my life.

There are few things stronger and more durable than the trust of a young child in her parents. Perhaps, had things been left as they were, I would have stayed like that for years. Perhaps I would have turned ten or eleven still believing that my mother was out there, holding my face in her heart, still fighting for me.

Instead, seven endless weeks after I had first woken up in that dim, musty room, I was enlightened. I was sitting on the windowsill, staring out at the trees, nursing my hate for Marian and wondering for the thousandth time whether there was anything in the room I could use to shatter the window.

And I saw my mother.

She was standing on the other side of the street, staring up at the house. The baby was in her arms. Her eyes roved hungrily over the windows. She was rocking back and forth, her lips moving in whispered song, but she didn't look down at the baby in her arms. She stared up at the House of the Dead, sheltered under the tavern porch.

And then she saw me.

Nothing sparked in her eyes, or maybe I just couldn't see it from fifty yards away. She went very still. Her mouth had stopped moving, frozen in mid-note.

We looked at each other. Later I tried to deny it, and could not. I saw her, she saw me, and we stared at each other across the street, through soft autumn air and dirty glass and the bars on my window.

My hand went to my chest. Hope and joy had lit up inside me, the kind of explosive blast that sucks all the air out of you. I pressed my hands against the window.

The baby started to cry. I could hear the thin strain of it through the window. My mother turned and slipped between the shops, cradling the baby to her chest, into the shadows and out of sight.

I stayed there staring, unable to breathe, hands still splayed on the cold glass. I had gone mad. My eyes were tricking me. This could not, *could not* be real.

But I was not stupid. The words my mother had said to Marian lay in my head, calm and waiting. I could not ignore them anymore. I turned them over and over in my mind. I considered what they were, what they meant. She had meant to give me up. She had laid me on Marian's floor and left willingly. There had been no trick, no misunderstanding. She had come to catch a glimpse of me, but she would not try to rescue me. Doubt wrapped strangling tendrils around my heart, and at last my spirit was broken.

For hours I stayed there, staring through the glass at the space where my mother had vanished. I refused to eat for days. I took to my bed with fever and a lethargy too deep for sleep. Marian left food by my bedside and did not try to speak to me. It took me years to recognise this as kindness.

I lay facedown, the musty sheets pressed against my cheeks so that I wouldn't have to look at the room, at the house, at the branches of the trees that stretched through the ceiling like gnarled fingers. I could talk myself into delusion – that I was back in my own home, that the rising whisper of the wind was the baby crying, that my mother had not left me, that I was anywhere but here. I was in a dream, and all I had to do was wait for dawn. But it was impossible to mistake the House of the Dead for my home, or anyone's. The house at night was coated in a thick, greasy silence. Sometimes I could hear people coming through the door, their thudding footsteps, weeping in the kitchen, and once, the unmistakable, wrenching screams of a woman in labour. I pulled the covers over my head and refused to listen. I was not here.

One night, I tried to escape.

I woke in the hour before dawn. The house was quiet. I could hear Marian's breathing from the next room. I remember exactly how I felt: very still, as though the inside of my mind was preserved in diamond. New courage had settled upon me in the night.

I slipped out of bed and got to my feet. I was still small, four feet tall, maybe not even that. I could move through the house without being heard. Or so I believed. My mind was airy and bright, and doubt did not poison it. Now, I would call this *transcendence,* the witchling's name for such super-natural clarity of thought and purpose. All I knew then was that somehow my fear had left me. I was no longer waiting for my mother. Nothing kept me there, and so I ran.

I expected the house to lay traps for me, so I thought to outwit it. I did not go to the kitchen, pull food from cupboards, haul blankets from my bed. I did not even put on shoes. I looked straight ahead, slid open the door, walked across the landing and down the stairs. I could have been sleepwalking.

The floorboards did not betray me. Nor did the front door. And then I stood on the cold doorstep, a child in a nightshift, staring up at the fading stars. The sky was lightening to grey in the east.

I felt no ecstasy, no rush of freedom. Everything was quiet inside my head.

Where would I go? Not to my mother's house, I understood that now. But who else had ever sheltered me? Who might keep me beside their fire and defend me from the witchling?

The wind creaked in the hinges of the front door of the House of the Dead. I pulled it hastily closed in case it slammed and woke her.

Maybe I should run from this town altogether. Maybe that was the only way out. I considered the vast bleakness of the empty world. Beyond this town were the hills and the river, and eventually the sea, and across the sea lay the lands of Lord Jonathan, with whom we were at war. They would not protect me. Lords, beautiful and undying, did not concern themselves with witchlings and kidnapped children.

And then, standing in the dark, I remembered Daniel.

Yes. Daniel would help me. He had been my friend, before all this. We had played at being lords together – he had been Jonathan and I had been Claire, clashing with wooden swords in the fields behind his house. It was a terrible risk, then, close to blasphemy, to take Claire's name and dirty it. But Daniel had done it, he had dared me to do it, because he had not been afraid. He did not fear lords or their men. He would not fear Marian.

I turned with sudden purpose and walked down the street. Daniel lived far away from the river, far from my mother's house. Marian would not think to look for me there.

I was worried I would not remember the way, but I could hear the river through the dimness and its distant murmur guided me. The gathering sunrise gave me east and west. I walked, shivering, until the twisting streets became familiar and the windows lit up gold in the dawn. I walked faster. I did not want to be seen, to have voices raised in alarm, to have word of where I had gone carried back to Marian.

And then the streets parted, and I was there. I stumbled at the sight of Daniel's doorstep. It was like warmth and firelight, like the release of an in-held breath. I had not known until that moment how terribly homesick I had been.

I half-ran to his door and rammed on it, the unmistakable hummingbird knock of a child in danger. It opened at once.

'Haley?'

I blinked at her. I had expected Daniel. Instead, his sister Niamh stared down at me, wrapped in a blanket and wiping the sleep out of her eyes. Niamh was fourteen, which so far as I was concerned made her a grown-up – loyal to the witchling, not to me. I could not ask her for help.

I turned away, but she caught my shoulder. 'Haley! What's wrong? What's the matter?'

Angry instinct made me wrench myself from her grip and I slipped on my numb feet. The fall was hard and then I lay breathless in the dirt. That supernatural calm had left me, and I was cold and frightened. I tried to get up.

I felt Niamh at my side, her hands on my shoulder.

'Haley,' she said, softly. 'Haley. Come on. Look, you're hurt.'

She was right. There was blood on my right hand, a scrape from the fall. She pulled me to my feet, and helplessly I let her guide me inside the house. Their father was a tailor, and there were piles of woollen blankets in the corners of every room. I was still trembling. Niamh draped a shawl over me and sat me down at the table. She opened my hand, gently, and wiped away the blood.

'Haley. What's wrong? Has someone hurt you?'

There were no words for it – the house, and Marian's hard

face, and my mother disappearing into shadow. I stared up at her mutely. After a second, grim understanding seemed to settle in her face. It occurs to me now how young she was, a child herself. It was nothing at all to me then to put this on her, to seek her asylum.

She got up and called Daniel's name. I heard his footsteps on the stairs. Niamh turned back to me. 'Our parents are away,' she said. 'In the next town over. Our aunt's having a baby. We can keep you here for a while. If your mother comes looking for you, I might not be able to keep her out. You get that, right? You'll have to hide.'

I did not know how to tell her that my mother would not come for me. I watched her in silence and after a while she turned away.

Daniel came running into the kitchen. He looked delighted at the sight of me – I treasured that memory later – and then confused at my blood-stained hands. 'Haley? Are you okay?'

I opened my mouth to try to answer, but nothing came out. Daniel, too, seemed to understand after a moment. He was a clever child – eight years old, with clear dark eyes. He could see the terror in my face.

He turned to his sister. 'Is Haley staying here?'

Niamh glanced at me and I looked down at the floor. I could not speak.

'Yes,' she said. 'Yes, I think she's staying with us.'

They did their best. I never blamed them, then or now. I overheard Niamh murmur instructions to Daniel not to ask me too many questions before he took me upstairs and tried to play with me, to keep me happy and distracted. I pretended not to hear her, and was grateful.

I was shivering, unable to eat or sleep. I could only imagine the terrible things Marian would do to me now, the stupid hopelessness of my attempt to escape. I thought wildly that it was not too late to run, steal a boat and float downriver to the sea. I could be a fisherwoman, a merchant sailor. I could be a new person. Not my mother's daughter, not the witchling's girl, not anyone or anything. I could escape this terrible village where no one wanted me.

But I was seven years old and scared. I stayed in Daniel's bedroom, under his confused, encouraging gaze. He tried to teach me card games, like he'd promised to do the last time I'd seen him, before all of this. My hands shook too badly to hold them. The sun rose in the window, and its glare was low and blinding. I wanted to hide from it under the bed. I could no longer make myself believe daylight would protect me from the witchling.

And then, at last, from below, I heard a knock at the door.

I sprang to my feet in panic. I had not told Niamh not to answer. Marian might hurt her if she thought she was hiding me. She might hurt Daniel, too. I had been so stupid to bring her to them. I clung to Daniel's wrists, terrified.

He seemed bemused by my terror. 'Haley, it's okay, Niamh will talk to her—'

He thought it would be my mother. I heard the door creak open. Niamh's voice, high and calm, and then another, lower. This house did not have the glass-clear acoustics of the House of the Dead, so I could not hear the voice, but I did not need to. I knew it was Marian.

We stood there together, hands clasped – me too frightened to move, Daniel confused and scared, trying to assume a man's courage, to tell me with his eyes that it would be all right.

Then we heard Niamh's voice on the stairs, sudden and clear. 'Daniel? Daniel, come down here for a moment.'

I clung to him, desperate. 'Don't go,' I whispered. 'Don't. Please. She'll kill you.'

I saw his eyes widen, saw him swallow.

'Daniel?'

'Don't go – please, don't go—'

He glanced at the door, and I knew it was over. He had to protect his sister, and if that meant leaving me alone upstairs, so be it. Like I say, I don't blame either of them.

He pulled his wrists from my grasp. 'I'll be back in a moment,' he whispered. 'It'll be okay. Stay here, Haley—'

I tried to plead with him, but he turned from my anguished gaze and left, closing the door carefully behind him.

I heard his slow footsteps on the stairs. Three voices at the doorway. I waited, cowering in the corner, listening. The voices changed; surprise in Niamh's tone, then sombreness. Footsteps in the house, in the kitchen. More voices at the doorway.

Then, beneath me, I heard the door close.

I sat there for a long time. Daniel's window did not overlook the front door, so I could not see what was happening. I sat with my arms wrapped around my knees, trembling, waiting for them to come back in.

Five minutes passed. Ten. The house was silent.

After half an hour I slowly got to my feet and opened the door a crack. Part of me expected to see Marian on the landing waiting for me, but there was nothing.

I descended the stairs as quietly as I could. No one. The rooms were empty. They had left me alone in the house.

I waited there until darkness fell. Eventually I grew hungry and I checked the cupboards. No food. Nothing in the pantry except a pail of water. They had taken it all with them when they left with Marian.

I stayed there another day and night, but after that I knew they weren't coming back.

After two days I went back to the House of the Dead. I never tried to escape again.

## CHAPTER THREE

In the last days of the war in the east, just before the terrible loss at Airan the year I was nine that broke our left flank and forced us back over the mountains, our soldiers used to go out on raids to kill the enemy's witchlings. Once a town has no witchling, it is doomed. There is no one to heal their broken bones, to cool their fevers, to ease wet blue cords out from around the necks of babies as they are born. There is no one to carry their dead down to the underworld for judgement, and their ghosts rot in their bodies after death. By staying in a town with no witchling, you risk your health, your life, your afterlife, your chance at eternity in the world of the blessed, or of leaving that world to return to this one and become a lord. You give up everything.

Of course, nobody did. They gathered their things and left, sought out larger towns and cities, further from the front, and tried to build new lives. It could not work. There were famines, overcrowding, riots. We heard of them even in our tiny town in the south, far away from the border.

Niamh and Daniel were only children, and these stories had not yet drifted back to us from the front. But they knew a little about what happened when you died. They knew you were brought to the House of the Dead, and that if you did not want to be resurrected the witchling would carry you down to the underworld. They knew that there you might choose to be judged, and if you had lived your life well, you would be sent to the world of the blessed. And they knew none of it could happen, for anyone they loved, if Marian died without a girl to inherit from her. They understood what they would be destroying by protecting me. I had been born marked and unlucky, and that was not their fault, any more than it had been my mother's.

Would I have done the same if Daniel had been born with death-magic? If he had come to me needing my help?

I cannot imagine it anymore.

One morning weeks later, I woke to hear Marian's voice through the floorboards.

'Ira. Ira. Calm down, now. Listen to me.'

Her tone stopped me; I had not heard her use it before. It was soothing, almost tender. It confused me. I had not known she could be kind, this woman who kept me in a bedroom and raised the dead.

Slowly, I rose through the stiffness of sleep and dried tears and walked out onto the landing. I was still in my night-things. I stood at the banisters, listening. Below, I could hear a woman crying, and Marian's low voice, soft and reassuring in the absolute silence of the house.

'Ira. Listen to me. You can choose, here. You have a choice.'

'No, I don't,' whispered the woman called Ira. 'I don't. I need him back.'

'Ira. You know what this is. It isn't *life*, not like that. He'll have a few years, and then he won't be able to work, or to—'

'To work? You think I care about his *job?*'

A silence. I edged onto the top step, wanting to hear better.

'You delivered our children,' said Ira. Her voice was hoarse from weeping. 'Elior's only fourteen. If Michael dies—'

'He *is* dead, Ira.'

'I know that!'

A rough, sobbing cry. The clatter of wood. Ira had started to weep again.

Under cover of her sobs, I took the steps two at a time, trying to keep my footsteps as quiet as possible. I peered around the banister. I saw the two of them, half-silhouetted by the sunlight through the kitchen window; Marian, with her short, greying hair, her arm around the shoulder of a young woman hunched in a chair, her face in her hands. And at their feet—

A body.

Michael. Ira's husband. I knew without having to be told. I knew from her sobs, from the way she turned her body slightly away from him when she wept, so as not to catch a glimpse of him through the fingers pressed over her eyes. I thought, absurdly, of the cat, a hundred thousand years ago. I had never seen that deep stillness in a human. I found myself drawn to it, a thin wire in my chest. I stayed where I was.

'Ira,' said Marian quietly, when the woman's sobs faltered at last, 'you understand what this means?'

The words stirred something in my head. She had said that to my mother, when I had been brought here. Years later, after she died and I became the witchling in her place, I said those words so often I stopped hearing them. *Do you under-stand?* Of course, nobody ever did. Only when you live surrounded by death, steeped in it, as a witchling does, can you truly understand its gravity. When you live a normal life, death comes for you like lightning, too sudden and painful to look at. It isn't like that for us. Our eyes adjust to it.

Ira looked up at Marian with tears in her eyes.

'Yes,' she said, at last. 'Bring him back.'

Marian nodded slowly, though I could sense her dismay. 'Do you mind if Haley watches?'

The sound of my name, which part of me believed had been left in Daniel's house, sent a jolt of terror through me. I stood frozen, clutching the banister as though it would protect me. Ira looked around at me, wiping her eyes.

'You have a girl now?'

Marian nodded. Ira looked at me and tried a smile. It didn't work. 'Hey, little one,' she said.

I shrank away from her.

Marian said, 'Haley, come here.' Her voice was soft, but I dared not disobey her. Perhaps now she would finally dole out punishment for my trying to escape, set some monster on me, like the ones that lived in the underworld and ripped your body apart to judge you. Daniel had told me about them. I moved slowly forward into the light. The kitchen was colder than my bedroom upstairs, the wood hard against my bare feet.

The closer I got to her, the taller Marian seemed to become. She looked rough-hewn from stone, with the black scar-tattoo marks twining over her hands and arms, like the strangling tentacles of poison ivy. The tattoos were intricate and concentrically woven, hundreds of them, so dense her skin seemed ash-black.

Marian saw me looking. She did not smile.

'Sit at the table,' she said to me. 'Ira, come away from him. Drink your tea. I'll work.'

Ira nodded, wiping tears from her cheeks as she sat down. I took the chair opposite her, trying not to look at the chair my mother had occupied on the night she had abandoned me. The tea was still steaming. Marian placed a mug next to her as she knelt on the floor beside the corpse. She had a system, I would learn later: camomile for the grieving, lemon and honey for the sick and for herself, black tea for laying the dead to rest, and green for raising them. Even now, I smell green tea and shiver.

Ira watched Marian light the fire in the grate with horrified fascination. 'What are you doing?'

Marian glanced up from where she sat, polishing a short knife with a cloth, and did not answer.

I watched, too, but I did not speak. I was drawn to what

she was doing, pulled by that same taut silver wire of fascination that had drawn my eyes to the body on the floor. I watched hungrily as Marian got to her feet, walked into another room, and came back with a flask of a thick, reddish-black liquid that had left dark crusts where it had dried on the glass. *Blood-ink*. I knew without having to be told.

'I want to leave,' Ira said suddenly. She got to her feet so abruptly the chair skidded back on its legs. She was not looking at the flask but at the knives, lying in their cloths at Marian's feet. 'I don't . . . I don't want to see.'

Marian's eyes moved slowly over the woman's face. She set the flask down on the counter.

'Of course,' she said. 'Haley, see our guest into the living room and then come back.'

I didn't even know where the living room was. I got down from my chair, trying not to look at Ira or the body, and walked out of the kitchen into the hallway. Dusty sunlight spilled through the glass windows in the door. I stopped, so suddenly that Ira nearly walked into me. The feel of the sunlight on my face was so strange, clean and warm and airless. I had not been outside in days.

There was a door to my left. A slight, scared push with the tips of my fingers and it swung open with a slow creak. Inside was a dim, warm room: two faded armchairs, curtains half-drawn across the dusty glass windows, books cluttered on shelves along the walls. It looked more homely than anywhere else in the house. I knew instinctively that Marian had never willingly set foot in it.

'Thank you,' said Ira, and walked slowly past me, her fingertips trailing against the walls, dreamlike. The wooden mug of camomile tea was still in her other hand. I left her there with the door open.

When I got back to the kitchen Marian was waiting for me, drinking her green tea, twirling a knife absent-mindedly in her hands. The body was still on the floor, facedown. I sat on the chair opposite the one my mother had sat on and waited. It was still a shock when Marian spoke to me.

'Have you ever seen a dead person?'

I shook my head mutely.

'I want you to watch me,' she said. 'Just watch. You can ask questions later. Stay quiet and learn. You understand me?'

I nodded. She could see fear in my face, I knew, so I stared down at my hands. I heard her chair scrape back, saw her feet in their leather boots move over the timbered floor. The fire was blazing gold in the grate now.

'Watch,' she said, and I looked up.

Marian pulled a cloth bag down from a shelf on the wall. From it, she drew out a handful of dried herbs and threw them into the fireplace. Greyish, choking smoke blossomed at once and filled the room. I coughed, but Marian seemed quite unperturbed by it.

'You know what they are?'

I swallowed, trying to catch my breath. I knew this was a test.

'Rosemary.' That was always the easiest. My voice sounded small in the quiet of the kitchen. 'Sage. Lavender.'

'Two more.'

I was too scared to look away, but I had no answer.

Marian nodded slowly, then picked up her knives from the floor. She sat cross-legged beside the fire, holding the blades in the flame until they glowed. The heat didn't seem to bother her at all. She pushed her hair out of her eyes.

'What were the other two?'

She didn't look up at me.

'Tomorrow,' she said, 'you're going to go out into the woods around the back of this house and find them for me. Pay attention to the smell. Then, when you come back, we'll see if you can name them.'

She got to her feet. I was astonished – she was letting me out of the house, alone! How did she know I wouldn't run again? – before I remembered, with a sickening thud, that I had nowhere to run to.

'I'm not allowed in the woods on my own.' It was a stupid thing to say, but it was all I could think of. My mother had expressly forbidden it.

Marian glanced up at me. 'It's winter. The wolves and bears are asleep. They won't come near you.'

'No, but— ' I remembered my mother's face, her fear. 'Men hide in the woods. Strange men.'

'No one will hurt you.' Marian took the knife out of the fire, holding it by the wooden hilt, which was smoking. She got to her feet and looked at me. 'And if anyone tries, tell me.'

'And you'll hurt them back?'

She looked at me, tilting her head slightly. I felt I was being examined.

'Perhaps,' she said. 'Or perhaps I'll just remember. Perhaps one day they'll come to me sick or dying or with child, in need of my help. Perhaps they'll bring me someone they love, a dead person, and ask me to raise them or carry them down to the underworld. And then I will remember that they tried to hurt you.'

I considered that for a while, staring at the dead man on the floor. I was unfamiliar with patience, with the slow taking of revenge. It struck me as odd that she would be willing to hurt someone for me.

'Haley,' she said. I looked away from the corpse at last, to Marian's face. She was watching me gravely. 'You're safe. No one will harm you. People need witchlings. They don't hurt us.'

I stared at her, shocked out of my fear. I was no kin to her. 'Us?'

'Witchlings.'

'*I'm* not a witchling!'

Marian considered me, and crouched beside the corpse, her head still slightly tilted like a bird's. Her fingers were entwined between her knees.

'You will be,' she said. 'After I die. You understand that, don't you? You know why you're here?'

I thought of the cat, its milky eyes, and my mother's screaming. Panic rose in me, and with it a fierce, childish denial. 'I'm not like that! I'm not like you!'

'You are,' said Marian. 'Or you will be, with time and learning.'

The thought was so horrifying I could not speak.

Marian looked away at last. She took one of the cold steel knives from its cloth and picked up the flask of blood-ink. The smoke was starting to make me dizzy. I clung onto the table, white-knuckled and sweating. There were deep black burn marks in the wood.

She ripped open his shirt, took the knife and made a cut – three cuts, four, using a twisting dexterity I'd never seen before – and then dropped the blood-ink into the flesh, whispering under her breath, murmurs too soft to hear. No blood welled in the wound, because he was dead. The simple, obvious strangeness of that captivated me.

Marian put the flask down, took the other, still-glowing knife, and traced the mark again. The *hiss* and the smell of roasting flesh made me gag. Her face remained impassive.

The smoke cleared slightly and I could see the wound: healed and clean, a black-line tattoo, intricate and elegant as the ones on Marian's own arms. It looked like it had been made years ago.

I just stared. All I could think was: I could never do that. I would never do that. I could never, ever be a witchling.

She made five more scars like that, on his stomach and

chest, at the base of his throat, and on his palms: first the cold knife, then the ink, then the cauterising knife, and the hiss and the stench. I nearly threw up, but I controlled myself. I knew this, too, was a test, that she was watching me.

At last, Marian was done. She lay the knives down on the cloth and got to her feet, went to a cupboard in the kitchen and pulled down a dirty glass bottle, took a gulp from it and threw the rest onto the fire. She was sweating. There was a long *hiss* and a gulf of dark steam.

I sat there in the chair, clinging to the table, terrified. I could hear Marian's footsteps in the wet, white dimness. I didn't move. Then the footsteps stopped.

Something was moving, out there in the steam. I could hear spasmodic thudding and a rough rasp that wasn't quite breathing. I drew my legs up onto the chair, pressing my knees into my chin. A monster had come from the under-world to eat me. Marian had summoned it. This was it. I wondered wildly if I was close enough to grab one of Marian's knives.

And then at last the steam cleared, and I saw the dead man sitting up.

*Michael*. I remember his name, still. I remember his blood-shot, wide-open eyes, and Marian's low, reassuring whisper; his arm, spasming and thudding against the floor where the heart attack had deadened it; his open mouth, his yellow teeth. The look of bemused shock on his face as he stared at me, a strange child in a house full of smoke. I think he was afraid of me.

Above all I remember that he didn't blink. The dead go blind quickly when they forget to blink; their eyes dry out. His chest did not rise and fall, either. The process of resur-rection binds a soul to a corpse and animates it with magic, but the heart is dead within the flesh. All instincts vanish – to blink, to breathe, to recoil from heat or shiver in cold. Slowly, over years, they rot away to nothing, soul and body and mind. But I did not know that then.

I stared at the dead man, and he stared back at me, and I did not scream.

Once I knew I could do that, everything was a little easier to bear.

The day after the resurrection, Marian let me out, as she'd promised.

I was happy in the woods, in their deep, leafy silence, with the sunlight, pure and clear through the canopy. I twined my fingers through the wild herbs, trying to smell them. I felt like a child in a way I hadn't done since my mother had left me.

I had asked Marian the date and been told it – another sign of unexpected trust – and knew I was two and a half weeks away from turning eight. I wondered if I should tell Marian, if she would care. In my mother's house it would have meant celebration, a gift. I didn't expect that, of course, but I wanted there to be something. I didn't want to lose track of time again. If I knew where and when I was, then maybe I could survive this.

A mouse lay curled in the frost-tinged roots of a sycamore tree, dead of the cold. I picked it up and held it in my palm. It was freezing, of course, and I wondered why that felt strange. My brain told me quite clearly that it was dead, but some deeper part of me fought back, wanted living warmth, the slow stirring of breath. I felt the trickle of my own life-heat move slowly into the mouse. I felt its death-cold seep into me.

This time I was expecting it. I knelt slowly, so as not to disturb it, and felt a struggling within my closed palm. I opened my fingers. The mouse moved stiffly, hesitantly, stunned by its own reanimation. I laid it gently onto the ground and watched it scurry away into the leaves.

I stayed there for a while, crouched in the frosty grass, looking at my own hands.

# CHAPTER FOUR

Two months later, a girl named Eve came to us, screaming. She was not due to have her child for another three weeks, but as Marian said, babies were mischievous, they liked to try you even before they were born. The father was with her, smooth-cheeked and smooth-palmed, grey-faced with terror. I had heard of them, the seventeen-year-old newlyweds – they had been married the week I was given up, and my mother had talked of them derisively. 'They're too young,' she had said, rocking the baby in her arms as she poked at the fire. 'It won't last the year. I just pity the child.' Because, of course, everyone in our small town knew Eve was pregnant.

The father's name was Jorah. He came to us half-dragging, half-carrying his wife, who was between pains and short of breath. He rattled the door instead of knocking on it, and Marian came running down the stairs to meet him, tight-faced. Together, they helped Eve into the kitchen and laid her down on the blankets where my mother had deposited me months ago. We tried to make her comfortable, but her breaths were still quick and pained. She was swearing viciously as Jorah wrung his hands. 'It's too early,' he said. 'We thought we had weeks.'

'Never mind,' said Marian briskly, rubbing willow-bark soap into her hands. 'We'll make do. Eve, do you mind if my girl helps?'

Eve glanced at me distractedly, panting. I was sitting on a chair in the corner of the kitchen, my knees pulled up to my chin. 'If she wants to.'

Marian nodded. 'Haley, put some water over the fire.'

I moved slowly, my eyes on Eve. I had never seen a child born before. Part of me was scared. I knew women died this way. I didn't want to be here if that happened— I didn't want to hear the bleak silence, Jorah's sobs. But Marian had told me to stay.

Eve's breaths were rising again, rough and agonised. She rolled over and grasped Jorah's hand. He kissed her head.

'Have her waters broken?' Marian said to Jorah.

He looked up at her blankly. 'What?'

'Yes,' said Eve, 'yes, they— '

But her breath hitched again, her chest convulsing, and she screamed. Jorah cradled her head, his face full of her reflected pain. Marian crouched beside them.

'Where's her mother?' she asked Jorah.

Jorah shook his head. 'She doesn't speak to us.'

'I'm sorry to hear that. Briony always was an idiot.'

Eve had stopped screaming at last. She took a long, rattling breath and managed a tight smile.

'Hold her hand,' Marian said quietly to Jorah. He nodded and grasped her fingers; her knuckles were white. Marian knelt down beside Eve and spoke to her gently, hands sure on her ankles.

'I'll be here the whole time. You were born right here on this floor. Eighteen years ago, almost.'

'Did you do it?'

'I helped,' said Marian, with half a glance at me. 'I wasn't the witchling then. Bite down on this, here, and open your legs for me.'

She held out a strap of leather to Eve, who stared at it. 'Is it that close?'

Marian peered between the girl's legs. 'I'd say so, yes. I can see the head. Haley, come and look.'

I crawled forward uncertainly. Marian didn't seem to think

it was indecent and Eve was past caring, but I was young and deeply uncomfortable in this smoky room, looking at a soft, bloody part of Eve's body I didn't recognise. Jorah gave me an uneasy glance.

Eve started screaming again. She had dropped the leather. Marian knelt beside her. The calm of her expression was stranger and more fascinating to me than anything else in the room.

'All right, girl, hold on,' she murmured, adjusting her grip on Eve's leg. 'All right, now – push for me.'

And then, suddenly, a knock on the door. I jumped. Marian looked up. Her hands were covered in blood.

'What—?' she muttered.

'*Help!*' The man outside hammered on the door again. '*Help! Please! My sister – she's hurt—*'

I saw the whip-quick movement of Marian's eyes over us to the door and back. She glanced at me. Then she got to her feet.

'No!' Eve looked up at her, panting, aghast. 'No – stay here—'

'Haley,' Marian said quietly to me, 'hold the baby's head, now.'

A horrified pause.

'No,' said Jorah, 'no, I won't let— She's a child—'

Marian gave him a look, level and considering, and he fell silent. The man was still hammering on the door. I was frozen with terror and could not speak. No more could Eve: she screamed again and something slipped further from between her legs. I bent to grab it and found blood and slime, soft bone and wet skin.

'Give her a moment to breathe,' said Marian from above me. 'When she wants to push, let her.'

I could not even look up. The man at the door was still screaming, loud as Eve. '*Please! Help! Help her, please—*'

Marian turned and strode down the corridor. I was left there, absurd and terrified, holding the child's skull. Jorah was staring at me. I had to say something.

'Breathe,' I told her earnestly. It was what my mother had said to me when I woke from nightmares, gasping with terror. 'Breathe slowly.' I found out much later that this was terrible advice, but I said it with authority and they knew no better. I imagine they thought me invested with unearthly wisdom.

'Push,' I said, and Eve screamed again, and without warning the baby slid out into my hands. It was that simple. I was so surprised I almost dropped it.

Jorah gasped and clutched the table. Eve let her head fall gently against the floor, breathing slowly through clenched teeth. I stared down at the baby in my bloody hands, at its open red mouth.

'What is it?' said Jorah, excitedly.

'What?'

'What *is* it?'

'Oh.' I looked back down at the baby, tilting it slightly. 'I think it's a girl.'

Jorah smiled, the widest smile I'd ever seen. 'Grace,' he said. 'That's what we said, right, Evie? Grace for a girl.'

Eve was breathing very slowly. 'Sure,' she said. 'Yeah. Grace.'

'Can I hold her?' Jorah asked excitedly, but the baby was kicking in my trembling hands, and was still attached to the deep unseen parts of Eve by something veiny-bluish and very alive-looking, and I was trying to think of a way to explain all of this to him without running into any words I didn't know when Marian came back into the room, her hands still bloody. She took in the room, looking over Eve, and then at me, and then at the child, quiet and warm in my hands.

'Has she cried?' she said to me, over Eve's head.

*Cried?* Was it meant to cry? Crying was bad, wasn't it,

crying meant it wanted something it didn't have. But the air in the room had gone cold.

Marian said, more sharply, 'Haley, answer me. Has she cried?'

I shook my head.

'All right,' said Marian. 'Give her to me.' She was so calm; later I would remember that more clearly than anything else. The baby had stopped kicking, and her skin was slowly darkening. Her eyes had not yet opened. Cats did that too, I remembered, they were blind when they were very young.

Eve could not speak. She was shaking, and her face was grey again. Jorah was panicking, his eyes on the baby.

'Marian, is she – is she all right? Is she – is she alive?'

'She's alive,' said Marian. 'Give me a moment.'

'But she's not—'

'Be quiet, Jorah,' she said, and he fell silent. Eve's eyes had not left her child.

Marian knelt beside me again. The baby was still not breathing, and her face was turning a dark red. I expected Marian to issue orders, to ask for herbs and salves and hot water. But she just said to me, 'Watch.'

There was a little divot in the back of the baby's head. I had forgotten they had those. Marian held the baby very carefully, like she was offering it up to something. The cord still wound slickly back between Eve's legs.

Marian touched the centre of the baby's chest, a mess of blood and mucus and new skin, and something passed from her into the child. It was a pulse, a soft shimmer in the air, and I know Eve and Jorah could not see it, but I felt it deep within myself and shivered. Something changed – a click in the air – and then the baby coughed, and stirred, and started to wail.

Jorah started to laugh wildly and raucously, and Eve fell back as if all the energy had been drained from her. Marian gave the baby gently back to her mother. 'Grace,' she said, 'right?'

Eve nodded, too faint to speak.

In the centre of Marian's left hand, a tattoo burned hot and black. I felt its heat from where I sat. Marian saw me looking and held it up for me to see. There were new shadows under her eyes.

'This is what the runes are for,' she said. 'You take your own strength, you put it into them. You see?'

I nodded.

'She just needed to be jolted,' she said to me quietly. 'A push, to clear her airways. If she'd been born with a bad heart, or a hole in her lung, she would have needed a tattoo to keep her alive. Something permanent. But this wasn't permanent. You understand?'

I nodded again, trying to look as though I was calm too. Behind her, Eve cradled the baby, and Jorah started to cry. Marian looked at me very intently.

'Do you want this?'

Did I want to be the woman who made babies breathe again? I was too proud to answer that; I had been enchanted from the moment the child slid into my hands, and we both knew it. Instead I asked, 'What happened to that man's sister?'

Marian hesitated for a moment, watching me.

'She died,' she said at last. 'Now, watch how to cut the cord.'

That night I dreamed, for the first time since I had been delivered to the House of the Dead. I went to sleep full of trembling joy at the sight of the baby's screwed-up face and Jorah's smile and Eve's delighted exhaustion. I had been trying very hard not to think of my mother or the baby, but now, in my sleep, they came back to me. In the dream my mother left me here over and over again, turning and walking into the alleyway as I ran after her, the baby fading in her arms until she held only a bundle of rags. I cried after her at first, but after a while I realised she couldn't hear me, and so I just watched, trapped and helpless. The alleyways she walked through weren't paved with cobblestones but with varnished oak timbers, like the House of the Dead, and finally one splintered beneath her foot with a crash like breaking glass. She stumbled, and I woke with a start.

Not *like* breaking glass. Actual breaking glass, downstairs.

I sat bolt upright in my bead, breathing hard.

Movement to my right, through a wall. It was a soft wooden *creak,* barely noticeable if you did not know the silences of the House of the Dead. I got slowly to my feet, padded across the room to the door and peered out into the landing.

Marian was standing at the top of the stairs. She was deathly still, staring down into the darkness, her hand on the banister. I stayed where I was, unsure whether or not to be scared.

Then everything happened at once. Something flew at her from the shadows, a huge winged shape like a bird, and everything was thuds and grunts and commotion. Marian was knocked back, struggling on the staircase against the creature on top of her. She unbuckled her belt and got it halfway round the thing's neck, but it growled and wrenched itself free, clambering over her to the top of the stairs, where he stumbled and straightened up—

*Him.* The man who had knocked at our door. I had seen him crying in the living room over his sister's body. I could see him clearly now, cloaked and hooded, and the face beneath still streaked with tears. He saw me standing in the doorway and howled.

'*Witchling!*' His voice was cracked. '*You let her die!*'

Marian was on her feet, on the stairs behind him, her belt in her hand like a whip. He glanced back at her – half-crouched and wary, on her guard now – and then at me, and a terrible smile broke across his face. Marian's eyes widened. Too late, I realised what was going to happen, and could not move to prevent it. He lunged for me.

I tried to run, to slam the door in his face, but he barrelled past it just as he had run down Marian. I glimpsed her struggling up the stairs, one hand to the ribs he had bruised, before he tackled me. The blow knocked the thought from my head, and then I was trapped between his weight and the hard floor, a bone-cracking pressure too powerful for breath.

He grabbed my shoulders and slammed my head into the ground. Once, twice, three times, four. By the third time all pain had left me and everything was swooning dizziness.

'You – let – her – die!'

Out of the corner of my eye I saw Marian walking up behind him. He heard her too and leapt to his feet. I gasped, spluttering, and tasted blood. He rounded on her, drew a smooth thin knife from nowhere.

She did not try to defend herself. The blade went in, once, twice, and blood spattered my face. She was grabbing for him, not the knife. Then, at last, she managed to get a hand around his wrist.

The effect was sudden horror. I saw him sicken before my eyes. His bones stood starker in his face, his eyes sank into their sockets, and his skin stretched tighter, greying. He seemed in those instants to age ten years. Then he swayed, staggered, and fell. He hit the ground with a *thud* I can still hear, if I concentrate.

Marian's head fell. She had one hand pressed to her chest; it was there, in the shoulder and upper arm, that he had stabbed her. Her shirt was soaked with blood. She drew her good hand across her forehead, exhausted. Everything was quiet.

'Haley,' she said faintly. 'Haley, are you all right?' Then her eyes fluttered and focused, and she saw me. 'Oh, no—'

I was bleeding, I realised. I could feel it trickling slowly down my cheek. *Haley,* I heard my mother say sternly in my head, *you're drooling—*

The world flew up and away from me, and I fell into darkness.

I woke on the floor of the kitchen. Everything was acrid smoke and dimness. I could taste burning dandelion and sage, and feel the stitches in my head. I could see Marian out of the corner of my eye at the kitchen table, biting down on a strip of leather, sewing up the cut in her arm. I was not quite sure I was not still dreaming. *You're bleeding,* she had said. I raised a hand to my face and found it clean.

She saw the gesture and half-rose from her chair. 'Haley,' she said, hoarsely. 'How are you feeling?'

I didn't know how to answer that. When I tried to speak, it felt like the inside of my mouth was bruised.

'Did you kill him?'

That made her pause, taken aback. 'No, I didn't kill him. I don't kill people.'

'What did you do to him?'

'Nothing,' she said shortly. 'Next to what he did to you, nothing at all. Can you sit up?'

'Where is he?'

She put down the needle and thread she was using to sew up her arm and looked at me again. 'In the basement,' she said. 'I didn't want to lay him next to you. I thought he might frighten you when you woke up.'

The basement was where she kept bodies. She had taken the man's sister down there that afternoon. Everything was still blurred in my mind, a pulsing haze of fear. 'Are you sure you didn't kill him?'

She stared at me. How many children had lain on this floor before me, asking for reassurance? But they had had mothers and fathers to reach for, if she couldn't soothe them; I was hers alone. Some part of her must have been frightened and overwhelmed, too – maybe not then but in some earlier moment, when I had been screaming inconsolably in my locked bedroom. But if she was distraught, she never showed it to me.

'No, Haley,' she said gently. 'I didn't kill him.'

I stared at her, my eyes slightly unfocused, unsure whether to believe her.

She knelt beside me, wincing slightly, to examine my head. 'It might scar,' she said. 'But if you grow your hair out, it'll be almost invisible.'

My voice felt thick in my mouth. 'Why did he hurt me?'

She sat back on her knees and looked at me. I had the sense she was choosing her words with care.

'His sister died. He wanted to blame someone. He chose us because I couldn't save her.'

'But why *me?*'

'He wasn't . . .' She seemed lost for words. She looked up at the front door, considering. 'He expected me to save her, and when I couldn't, he got angry. He wanted to hurt me like that. So he hurt you.'

I considered that for a moment. The world spun slightly beyond the singular, steady point of Marian's face, and I tried not to look at it in case I threw up. 'Why couldn't you save his sister?'

'She had a tumour.'

'What does that mean?'

'It means . . .' I saw her reach for the right words again. 'Something grew in her brain. It had been there for years. By the time he brought her to me it had done too much damage. She was half gone already.'

'So what did you do?'

'I made her comfortable,' said Marian gently. 'I took away her pain. I calmed her down. Death isn't the worst thing in the world, Haley.'

I didn't understand that at all. 'Won't they punish you?'

'Who would punish me?'

'The Lord's men.' There was a court in the centre of town. I had seen a man dragged there by soldiers of Lord Claire for beating his wife. He was put on trial, sent to a prison in the city in the north. 'If you let her die—'

'No, they won't,' she said softly. 'I'll be fine.'

'But she *died*.'

'People die in my house all the time,' said Marian. 'They die of old age and sickness and injuries too deep for healing. Everybody dies, Haley. I can't change that. If the Lord's men came and asked me, I would tell them that, and they would understand.'

I stared up at the ceiling. I still did not understand why Marian could not save the sister. Eve's baby had been dying, and Marian had saved her. I thought of the hole in the baby's skull, the blood that had slicked my hands when I held her. I had not expected so much blood.

'Did you ever have a baby?'

Marian looked at me almost absent-mindedly. 'What?'

'Before you were the witchling. Did you have a baby?'

A slight pause.

'No,' said Marian at last. 'I became the witchling when I was twenty.'

That seemed impossibly old to me. 'Did you ever want one?'

'No. We're not allowed to.' She had picked up the salve to rub into her arm again. 'If I had a child I would have less time to spend looking after my patients. Less time to look after you.'

'I don't need looking after.'

She looked down at me and gave me a swift, tired smile. She had never smiled at me like that before, maybe not at all. 'I know.'

'Are you married?'

'No. That's against our vows as well.'

'Why not?'

'Think about it like this.' She put the salve down and started winding bandages around her arm. 'Let's say two people come to me needing help. One just needs medicine to be well again, and the other is very injured and near death. Who do I treat first?'

I knew this. 'The sicker one.'

'What if I'm married to the other one?'

'You still treat the sicker one first.'

'Of course, that's what I *should* do. But maybe I don't. Maybe I'm more worried about them, and so I treat them first, and the other person dies when they didn't need to. Love works against good healing.'

I thought of my mother. I did not think I understood how love worked.

Marian looked down at me, sighed, and stopped winding the bandages. I knew from her expression I was about to be told something I did not want to hear.

'Listen to me, Haley. I didn't decide these things. When you become the witchling, you take vows. They're written down in a book at the court, and if you break them there are punishments.'

'It's a crime? Like stealing?'

'Yes.'

'It's a crime if you have a baby?'

'Yes. There are five vows you take.' Marian showed me her splayed hand and counted them down on her fingers as she spoke. 'You treat the patient in front of you without reservation or judgement.' One finger. 'You do not favour one patient over another.' Two. 'You don't love or hate, or hold grudges against anyone who comes to you for treatment. That means you have no family. You have no husband or wife, parents or children. You never demand payment or favours in return for treatment.' Four. 'And unless it will hurt them, you do what the patient or their loved one asks of you. If someone asks you to resurrect a loved one, you do it. If they're very sick and in pain and would rather die than be kept alive, unless they're too young to ask for it, you have to do it. Those are our vows.'

'Have you ever broken them?'

'My vows?'

'Yeah.'

Marian looked at me. She put her hand against my forehead as if to check for a fever, and was silent for a long moment, and then she lied to me.

'No,' she said.

The world was blurring again. I was still frightened and confused. 'The lord's men won't come for you? You're sure?'

'Yes, Haley,' she said softly. 'Go to sleep.'

Everything was blurring again. There were bandages under her shirt. I reached towards them, curious and unthinking. She flinched, and for a moment we both looked at each other.

'He hurt you.'

'Yes,' she said. 'But I'll be okay.' She lay her hand on my head, careful to avoid the tender skin she had sown back together. 'Sleep, Haley. He'll be gone in the morning.'

Many years later, after she was dead and I was the witchling, the grieving brother's body was found rotting in the woods beyond the river after a two-week disappearance. It was too thoroughly decomposed for me to take him down to the underworld, and his ghost had dissipated into the air. He must have known that would happen, how long it would take the search parties to find him. He had not wanted to survive death.

He had been dying of a cancer growing in his leg, I found out eventually, too frightened to come to me for treatment, more frightened still of being taken down to the underworld.

There he would face an eternity of wandering, or burning in the world of the damned if he was stupid enough to choose to be judged, for what he had done to Marian and me. He had been clear-eyed enough to know that, at least. So he had chosen oblivion.

If I had known, I would have told him not to worry, that I was bound by the same vows as Marian had been. By law I could not hold a grudge against him. I would have healed him, carried him, offered him my counsel.

I wonder if he would have believed me.

I hope his sister chose to be judged. Sometimes I imagine her wandering around the twilit forests of the world below, all these years later, still waiting for him.

## CHAPTER FIVE

One day, about five months after my abandonment, I was lurking at the end of our street when I saw three children playing in the shadow of the alleyway. I did not approach them at first. I never strayed far when the house was empty of patients. I needed to be close enough to hear Marian's call, or to be able to shout ahead if I saw someone approaching the house. I felt safer within range of her voice.

Since the grieving brother had attacked me I had been wary of the outside world, of people who might aim their anger at me for deaths I had no part in. Marian would not hurt me, not like that. She had not struck me except that once, when I had tried to escape, and when she became angry it was for reasons that made sense to me: neglected chores, disobeying orders, a messy room. The anger of other people did not obey any rules I understood. So I watched the children in the alleyway and stayed within a few yards of our front door.

They were older than me, maybe ten or eleven, and they had not seen me yet. They had two sticks they were using as swords, and two of them were beating the other – not gently, but with real and vicious force. The other child tried to fend them off, spinning and swiping with her stick, until at last one boy got her arm behind her back and the other hit her hand with such force that she yelped and dropped it. She growled up at them.

'Surrender!' said the first boy, panting and pressing his stick against the girl's throat. 'Surrender in the name of Lord Jonathan!'

The girl bared her teeth. 'Never! I'll die for Claire!'

'Then die!'

He poked the stick into her throat. They both giggled, and the spell was broken.

'No,' said the other boy, 'come on, Bea, you're dead, you have to lie down.' She settled obediently, splayed on the cobblestones.

'Right,' said the boy who had defeated her, looking up at our house, 'now we have to bring her to the witchling. You have to go down to the underworld, right? 'Cause you're dead.'

The girl sat up indignantly. 'I don't want to go! You go!'

'No, no, you're the best at lying still. It has to be you.'

'But how do I get back up? What if the monsters eat me?'

'Then they eat you,' said the boy indifferently. 'I don't know, ask the witchling.'

'Yeah, but . . .' The girl looked properly scared now. 'What if she doesn't believe I'm not dead? What if she doesn't let me out?'

The boy shrugged. 'She's a witchling, right? They can tell the difference.'

'If we died right now,' said the other boy, as though they were discussing whether or not to go swimming, 'would we go to the world of the blessed?'

'I can ask her for you,' I said, more loudly than I had intended. They all whipped around to stare at me.

'Who are you?'

The girl scrambled to her feet. 'That's the witchling's girl. Get away! Go!'

'I can help you,' I said. 'If you want to get down to the underworld.' I had no idea if this was true. I was, I think, desperately lonely; so lonely I had no name for it as a single emotion. It was just the way I lived.

'Go there yourself,' said the boy. 'Get away, dead girl!' He spat at my feet. The girl threw a stone at me and they turned and ran. Their laughter faded into the murmur of the river, and they were gone.

Everything was quiet. I did not move, watching their sticks forgotten on the ground. I was remembering Daniel, who had held my hand and then left me alone in his house. I thought of my mother, who had carried me as though I were diseased and then laid me down on the floor and walked away.

After a while I wandered back inside. Marian was sitting at the table chopping fennel – half to eat, half to distil for healing. I almost went straight upstairs to sit on my bed, but something stopped me. I walked into the kitchen and curled up on the chair opposite her. She glanced up at me but did not speak.

Eventually, after five minutes with my fingers pressed to my own wrist, I said, 'Am I dead?'

Marian did not answer for a moment. Then she put the knife down.

'That,' she said, 'is a very strange question.'

'I can't find my pulse.'

'Where are you looking?'

I held up my wrist.

'Touch where you think your pulse is.'

I pressed my finger to the centre of my wrist, as I had seen her do.

Marian shook her head. 'A little lower and to the left. Look.' She demonstrated.

I tried to copy her and pushed, and there – *there*, stronger than I had imagined, the jumping beat of my own heart. Relief flooded through me.

Marian was still watching me. 'Why would you think you were dead?'

I stared mutely at the table. Marian put the knife down

and leaned across the table. 'Haley,' she said, 'I think both our purposes would be served best if you told me the truth.'

I hesitated. 'There were people outside.'

'What people? Sick people?'

'No. Children. They said I was dead.'

'Ah, yes,' said Marian with a slight smile. 'I remember that story. That's very old. Even older than me, if you can believe it.'

'Why do they think that?'

'Because witchlings work with death, and people don't understand death. They fear it.'

'But dead people aren't scary.'

'Maybe not to you. But most people aren't that wise.'

I looked up, startled. She had never given me a compliment before. I decided to push my luck. 'Can I go down to the underworld?'

'No.'

Marian did not seem at all angry that I had asked. I was so used to my mother's irritability that it took me a long time to realise I could ask questions about most things in the House of the Dead without fear.

'Why not?'

'Because it's very dangerous. You need to have protection before you can go there.'

'What kind of protection? From the monsters?'

'What monsters?'

'The ones that eat you to judge you.'

There was another silence. Then she said, 'No. Not from those. From the air.' She laid her right arm on the table in front of me, her ink-black tattoos swirling and unreadable. 'The tattoos have magic in them. It's my magic, but the runes store and direct it. This one –' she laid a finger on her elbow '– is for strength. This one –' she pulled her shirt aside to show me one at her collarbone '– is for quick healing. I have others for wisdom, and good memory, and sure hands.

And there are some that keep me safe from the air in the underworld.'

'You could tattoo me.'

'No, I couldn't.'

'Why not?'

'Well, you're too young, for one thing. And for another I wouldn't know how. The tattoos that give me strength won't work on you. You have to come up with the runes yourself.'

'How do I do that?'

'When you're older.'

That was always the answer. I hated it so much I wanted to scream. 'Can you make me older? With magic?'

Marian smiled a little. 'No. I can't do that.'

What was the point of her magic, then? 'What would happen if I went down there without protection?'

'You would forget,' said Marian. She seemed to have forgotten her distillation and was watching me intently. 'The air is not meant for the living. You would forget why you were there. Then you would forget your name. Then you'd forget how to breathe. You'd be a shell – alive, but with no ghost. It's not like dying in the living world. It's more permanent. There'd be nothing left of you at all. No memories, no conscience, nothing.'

I thought about that for a while. Marian did not pick up the knife again. She was waiting for the next question.

'If I died now—'

'You're not going to die now.'

'But if I *did*.'

Marian sighed. 'Haley. Listen to me.' I could not look away from her. 'Keeping you alive is the most important job I have. More important than anything else.'

'So I can be you when you die?'

'So you can be *you* when I die. But yes, so you can be the witchling.'

'And I won't be able to get married, or have babies, or friends, or anything?'

Marian was silent for a moment. 'You can have friends,' she said. 'So long as you treat them the same as everyone else when they're sick, you can have friends.'

'But I can't *love* them. You said it was in the vows.'

She was quiet again. I tried hard to hide my impatience.

'Love is complicated, and . . . hard to define. It's not easy to prove either. I wouldn't worry too much about it now, Haley.'

'I can love them if I lie about it?'

'What you can do,' said Marian, 'is be careful. What were you going to ask?'

I didn't understand that at all, but it was less viscerally important than my question. 'If I died now, would I go to the world of the damned?'

She hesitated again. She always considered what she told me very thoroughly, so as not to have to frighten or lie to me.

'I don't know,' she said. 'Nobody can tell you that with certainty. I can't, you can't. But I think, for an eight-year-old . . . I think you would have to have done something truly, truly evil to deserve that.'

'Like lying? Or stealing?'

'Worse than that. Maiming or killing.'

'What's *maiming*?'

'Injuring, very badly.'

'Oh.' I thought about it very carefully; I too wanted to be sure of what I was telling her. 'Like throwing something at someone?'

'No, I mean an injury that causes permanent harm. Stabbing someone, or beating them. Although – Haley, look at me.' I did, reluctantly. 'Throwing things at people is very wrong, you know that?'

'I know that.'

'All right.'

There was silence for a few moments.

'Have you ever been to the world of the damned?'

'No. Nobody living has.'

'There aren't tunnels there, like there are to the underworld?'

Marian thought about it. 'I don't know. Maybe there are. I know it's below the underworld, like the world of the blessed is above the sky. But I've been to the underworld and never seen holes in the ground.'

'Are there holes in the sky? For the lords to get down from?'

'I don't think so. Maybe there are and they're too small for us to see them.'

'We should go check.'

'You would have to learn to fly for that.'

'I can do that.'

Marian smiled and nodded, and we were quiet.

'What's the underworld like? Is it bad?'

'It's not good or bad. It's nothing.'

'Why would you go there?'

'Nobody *wants* to go there,' said Marian. 'People don't die thinking they're going to stay in the underworld. They think they're going to ask to be judged. But when it comes to it, they all worry about being damned. They think, *I'll ask to be judged in a little while.* They put it off. Sometimes they put it off for hundreds of years. Sometimes they put it off forever.'

'So the ones who stay are cowards?'

'Not always.' Marian got up from her chair and poked at the fire to raise it. I watched the smoke rise in the grate. Her voice sounded low in the darkened house. 'I knew a couple when I was the witchling's girl. They were about twenty-five, they were just married, and they had an agreement that if one of them died they wouldn't ask to be judged. They didn't want to risk being separated forever. Whichever one of them died first, they would stay and wait for the other.'

'Did they?'

'Not yet. They're still alive.' She heaved the kettle over the fire and sat down, deep in thought. 'The underworld is huge. There are billions of ghosts there. It would take a very, very long time to find someone. And you wouldn't know when they died, or where, or if they changed their mind about you. You wouldn't . . .' She hesitated. 'I suppose . . . you couldn't know if you'd still love them, if it took a thousand years to find them again.'

I thought when you loved someone you loved them forever, unless they turned out to be the witchling's girl. 'Will you ask to be judged?'

'I don't know. Death changes you. It changes what you want. But . . . yes, I hope I would.'

'Why?'

She paused. 'Because I would want to know.'

'Even if you're damned?'

'Well, I hope I wouldn't be,' said Marian, with a slight smile. 'But I would rather know, I think.' She turned to me, away from the fire. 'What would you do?'

'I don't know.'

'Good answer. Anyone who tells you they know for certain is lying.'

There were a lot of lies to tell apart. That was one of the skills of a witchling, to know when they were being lied to so they could best treat someone. 'If I was dead and you had resurrected me, would you tell me?'

'You're not dead, Haley.'

'Do dead people have heartbeats?'

'No.'

'All right.' I put my fingers to my wrist again. There, at last, was a way of knowing for sure what was real.

Marian sat and watched me for a while, and about a week later she started to teach me to heal.

*

We began with easy things. She tried to show me anatomy textbooks and make me learn the names of various body parts, but that only lasted a few minutes until she discovered I could not read. Then we spent months on that, tracing letters with pigeon-feather quills, ink-stains seeping into my finger-tips, a nub rising on the middle finger of my left hand. I asked if it was blood-ink we used and Marian gave me a long look and said it was iron-gall. But I saw how it dried brown, and never quite lost my suspicion.

I never asked whose blood was in the ink she used to raise the dead. I was too scared of the answer. I had so little faith in her, in those days.

Marian also began to take me with her when she went to the market for food, herbs or parchment. The market was a sprawling wooden labyrinth on the banks of the river, teeming with people, and no one there recognised me as my mother's daughter. People grew quiet when we approached, lowered their eyes, backed away. If Marian went up to a stall, everyone standing in line hastily made way for her. Their wariness was hard to read. With some people, like Ira, it came from respect; with others it betrayed fear and disgust. No one showed their distaste too obviously, of course. They needed her too much. She healed their children, delivered their babies, cared for their sick and their dead. But they had no such fear of me. Adults were polite enough, but children shrank from me, and older ones threw stones at me in the street. I learned to run, to dodge sticks, to fight if I had to. It was its own kind of education.

There were a lot of children at the market in those years. In the east, the war was blazing, the last terrible conflagration before the end, and parents and older siblings were summoned in their thousands to the great front over the mountains. The war had not yet touched us in the House of the Dead. We did not even know we were losing; no information was allowed to seep back from the front. All we had were hymns to the Lord Claire, the tales of her glory, her return from the world of the blessed and the establishment of her indestructible empire.

Occasionally, one of her descendants would pass through our town. We would kneel and worship them, and they would leave with more of us, gone to fight for the honour of our deathless lord. They told us we were three months from victory, that the army of the Lord Jonathan was crumbling and would soon retreat, and then their great eastern lands would be ours. I was a child, and believed them.

I never saw Daniel or my mother at the market. I was glad of that. I don't think I could have borne the look on their faces. I tried not to think about them at all. My world was the House of the Dead now; I buried them all with the baby, deep in the silt of my brain, and pretended they had never lived.

Once I could read the tight, curling script of the books on Marian's shelves, we went back to anatomy, until I could name every bone and every muscle in the human body. I lay awake at night, muttering names until I could pronounce them, tracing the lines of sinew under the skin of my arms. Marian tested me. I answered without a single error. We moved on.

I learned how to take blood from painless cuts, how to listen to the whisper of the heart and lungs, how to test nerve and brain to see if they worked: poking needles into deadened flesh, holding lit matches to glazed eyes. I memorised from Marian's books the symptoms of every disease the people of our town sickened with. I learned quickly, because if I studied, I was doing something: I was getting better, I was becoming cleverer and more useful, and that was good. The child my mother had abandoned had been stupid and illiterate. The more I knew, the less like that girl I would be. I would heal the sick and deliver children. I would be the watchful soldier who stood between this town and oblivion. If I stayed stupid, if I did not study, then I would not learn how to carry the dead to the underworld, and when I became the witchling they would rot away to nothing in their corpses and have no afterlife at all. Whether the townsfolk survived death was down to me. That was why I had been born, and marked, and abandoned. That was the reason I was alive.

Marian watched my progress, and I could tell she was pleased. I learned her too: the way she talked, the little tired quirk of her smile, the way the lines between her eyebrows creased, the colours and shades of her silences. When she cooked for us, she'd make me stand beside her to watch the crisp of meat over a fire and the simmer of oil and tomato in a stew. 'One day you'll need this,' she would say, and she meant, *when I'm dead*. She was not yet forty, but looked much older. She must have known she didn't have that long.

When she realised she was dying, years later, she told me that she used to worry she'd go while I was still young. Not just for my sake, but for the town's – for who would bring their labouring wife to a child? Who would trust a young, untrained girl with the corpse of their mother, to ensure their afterlife? Jorah's disdain had taught me that I was too young to be useful. I hated my own childhood, my small weak body.

My memories of Marian in those first years are mostly of the evenings: her sitting at one end of the kitchen table with a scroll of open parchment and a quill in one ink-stained hand, working on who knew what. I sat at the other end with my books of healing, reading feverishly. Occasionally she would put down her quill, get up and walk into the parlour behind the kitchen, bring something out of a cupboard and set it on the table in front of me.

'What's this?'

One time it was a poppy flower, dried and shrivelled but still recognisable. I'd seen a picture in one of the books. I told her so.

'And what's it for?'

I squinted, trying to remember. 'Insomnia.'

Marian smiled grimly. 'Not exactly. Look at the seeds.' She picked one small black one from the centre and gave it to me. I peered at it.

'Crack that open,' she said, 'scrape it out and let it dry. Then dissolve it in as strong a wine as you can find. A few drops will stop a sick man feeling pain. A few more and he won't notice you sawing his arm off. A few more than that, and he'll die.'

I stared up at her in horror. 'Why would you use it?'

'Because sometimes you *do* need to saw his arm off. Do you remember the man Kavana brought in last week?'

I remembered. He had fallen asleep drunk outside a tavern, and a horse had stood on his hand. He was too stubborn to seek Marian's help, and by the time Kavana had dragged him to us he had paled and grown feverish; his hand was swollen and black, oozing blood and pus.

Marian had sent me upstairs. 'Not yet,' she had said quietly at the sight of his hand. 'You're too young, I think.' I had sat on the landing and listened, but heard no screams.

'You took off his *hand*?'

Marian nodded. 'It couldn't be saved. Some things can't. You understand me, Haley?'

I nodded, although I didn't, really. There was a silence. My mouth was dry. *I don't kill people,* she had said to me the night we were attacked, but I had been delirious and injured and couldn't be sure of anything.

'Have you ever killed anyone?'

Marian twirled her quill slowly in her hand. She was staring at me with those hawk-like grey eyes. I did not look away. I was still a little afraid of her, but there was no anger in her expression, only grave contemplation.

'Yes,' she said at last.

My heart was tripping over itself. I considered my next question carefully.

'Why?'

'Because it was the right thing to do.'

'Were they dying anyway?'

Marian nodded, slowly. 'Something like that.'

I wanted to ask more, but there was a new hardness in her gaze and I didn't dare go further. I looked back down at the book. Everything was quiet but for the crackling of the fire. I was awed and horrified. I remembered the man she had sickened, turned into an emaciated half-corpse, just with her touch.

If a knock came in the evening silence, Marian would rise to answer it and I would retreat up the stairs to my bedroom, listening to the soft voices through the floor, waiting. Eventually, Marian would ask them the question: 'Do you mind if my girl watches?' The words had a rhythm that I knew by heart, even through the floorboards. Nobody ever did mind, and I would descend the stairs again and watch as she healed the sick, learning from the impassivity of her face, the deft movements of her hands. If it was a corpse, Marian would not bring me downstairs, not after that first resurrection. I was still too young, she said. Instead, I would wait in my bedroom with a book, or sit at the window watching the street, waiting to learn the arts of the dead.

The leaves turned again and again. My body changed, lanky and awkward. I turned nine and then ten. And then Michael returned to us.

The most important decision of your existence will not be your own. It will be made by whoever brings your body to us – your husband, your mother, your grandson, or your daughter. They will knock on our door and we will bring you inside, lay you down on the kitchen floor and make your loved one the camomile tea of the grieving, hold their hands until they are dry-eyed and they have stopped shaking.

Then, gently, we will ask the question: what would you like us to do?

There are two choices: resurrection or burial. Of course, there are no guarantees – this all assumes that your loved ones find you and bring you to us. Maybe you'll be unlucky and die in the woods, or fall into a river and drown, and your undiscovered body will rot to nothing with your ghost trapped inside it. This is the eventual fate of the resurrected, too, but they at least get a few years of half-life before that. You will get nothing – no afterlife, no corpse-life, nothing at all.

Let's say you are lucky, then. Resurrection or burial? I'll say this: no one willingly chooses resurrection. You do it because you have to – because without your dead wife to help provide for your children, they will starve; or because you yourself are a child, with three terrified younger siblings, crowded around your dead father.

To choose resurrection over burial is to choose a few years of almost-life over an eternal afterlife in the under-world. Resurrection is the greatest sacrifice you can make for those you love – although of course, *you* will not make it. Your loved one will make it for you, holding a mug of camomile tea in trembling, white-knuckled hands, tears running slowly down their cheeks.

So Ira had decided for Michael, with Marian at her side, because she had no choice. And then, three years later, he came back to us with his son.

Marian had begun to allow me to answer the door, so I saw him first. The boy was older than me – fifteen or sixteen – yet Michael carried him in his arms as if he were still a baby. Michael blinked at me. His eyes were rotted, milky and half-blind. He wore a bandage to hide the terror of them, but I knew what lay under it. I had seen it before.

'Marian?'

He had been lucky. For two years after his resurrection he had been as close to alive as anyone could have hoped for – young, strong and handsome, unscathed by death. Unless you touched him, you couldn't know that he was cold, or that there was no pulse in his wrist. He and Ira hid it from the world. He would have lost his job, his friends, his life; once his neighbours knew he was a living corpse, he would have been feared and shunned. He wore gloves in summer, and powder to hide the blue pallor of his skin, and every week he or Ira came to the House of the Dead to collect the medicines Marian made for him to stave off decay. There were whispers about him, of course – it was a small town – but nothing concrete until the day his time suddenly ran out and he woke up with a vein of rot running up his neck, spreading across his cheek like the roots of a tree.

After that, there was no hiding it. He stayed alone in the house while people threw rocks through their windows and Ira grew thin with work and anxiety. Everyone knew why he came to the House of the Dead; his children were jeered at, called half-things, corpse-bastards. Michael bore it all while his body rotted away beneath him. And now he was here, with his son.

'Marian?' he said again. His voice was soft and furred with mould.

'She's inside. It's Haley.'

He shook his head wildly. 'Please. Marian. I need to see Marian.'

I opened the door. He heard the creak of wood and stepped forward but nearly tripped on the doorstep. I held his wrist. I was used to the dead by then, but still found the moist, clammy cold of his skin odd; my brain and heart fought each other, wanting to find life where I knew there was none.

I guided Michael into the sitting room, steadying him. As

we walked, I looked at the boy in his arms and saw that there was bloody foam at his mouth. I tried to decide whether he was dead or not.

Marian got to her feet when she saw us in the doorway of the kitchen. There were open books on the kitchen table, a flickering candle. 'Michael? What's wrong?'

'My boy,' he said, hoarsely. He searched for the doorway with his blind, grasping hand, trying to steady himself, the boy draped over his other arm. 'He got sick, and Ira was at work – Please—'

'Lay him down,' said Marian at once. She put the back of her hand to the boy's forehead, and the gesture struck me as oddly motherly in a way I didn't like. She swore. 'He's cold. Haley, get the blankets.'

The blankets were old sheepskin rugs, smelling slightly of damp. I stoked the fire so that it blazed brighter, illuminating the cracks in the skin of Michael's face, the veins that had hardened beneath the thin skin of his hands. He looked, in that light, like the dead thing he was.

With my help, Marian wrapped the blankets around the boy. She knelt beside him, pushing her hair out of her eyes, and examined his face. 'What happened?'

'He was fine. He was – he was *good*.' Michael seemed completely bewildered. 'He was visiting his girl here in the village, and he – he came back home, and he was strange. He started speaking in . . . tongues. None of us could understand him. He wasn't moving right, jerking about. And then he just . . . collapsed. Like this.'

'When?'

'Ten minutes ago. I brought him straight here.'

Marian glanced up at him. 'Good. Haley, put the kettle over the fire and bring me—'

The boy coughed, suddenly and violently. Marian and I froze. For a second it seemed to be over. Then he jerked, and the movement came from the stomach, not the shoulders. More blood dribbled from his mouth and his eyes opened, rolling. He kicked at the floor, his hands clenching and unclenching as if trying to grab something that wasn't there. His breaths were rasps now.

Michael clutched blindly at the table. 'What's happening?'

'Haley,' said Marian levelly, 'help me hold him down.'

I grabbed his wrists. I could feel something in him struggling – all the muscles in his chest were rebelling, contorting against his heart. I heard the crack of ribs as he struggled. Marian was forcing the strip of leather into his mouth to stop him biting off his tongue. He was like a horse, spooked and rearing.

'*What's happening?*' Michael cried desperately, and Marian was saying to me, low-voiced and urgent, 'Haley, get the essence of rue, it'll help him,' and I started to scramble to my feet—

And then, suddenly, the seizure stopped, as quickly as it had started. The boy shuddered and laid still, his head lolling back on the blankets.

Marian leaned back, looking at him. After a moment, she put two fingers to the base of his throat.

'What happened?' said Michael, tremulously. 'Is he—?'

'He's not dead,' said Marian. She got to her feet, still looking down at the boy, a strange expression on her face. 'He's still cold, though. Haley, make him the tea.'

I boiled the kettle, but when I had sliced the lemon and dripped honey into the mug I looked up to find Marian standing beside me. Michael was still sitting at the kitchen table. She took the mug silently from my hands, reached up to the top cupboard and pulled down a flask I hadn't seen before. The liquid inside was a slightly viscous golden-brown, like watery honey. She poured a little into the mug and stirred it.

'Brandy,' she said at my questioning look. 'It'll warm him. And this, you know what this is?' She was holding up a vial of clear liquid. I squinted.

'Laudanum.'

'Very good. And why?'

'For the seizures. It slackens the muscles.'

'Let's hope,' she said. She added a single drop to the mug of tea and handed it back to me. 'Give it to the boy. Not too fast or he'll choke on it. A sip at a time. And remember to raise his head.'

When we came back into the living room, Michael was staring around, his hand still clenched on the table. 'Is he going to be all right?'

Marian hesitated. 'I'm not sure. You say there was nothing wrong with him before this?'

'Nothing. He was fine. He hasn't been sick since he was small.'

'Speaking in tongues, spasming, and then a collapse? All in the last two hours?'

'Yes. Yes.'

'All right,' said Marian. She raised a hand almost unconsciously to the back of her neck. 'Michael, I'm going to ask you to leave him with us.'

'No,' he said at once. 'I'm staying with him.'

'It's just tonight—'

'I'm his *father*.'

'I know that,' said Marian gently, 'but the magic that keeps you alive is very delicate, Michael, and I don't want to risk interfering with it.'

'You mean . . .' He was confused, helpless. 'You'll use magic on him?'

'If I have to.'

'Doesn't that—' He raised a hand to his stomach, where years earlier I had seen Marian carve the black tattoos into his skin. 'Doesn't it leave marks?'

'He would have to be very ill,' said Marian, and put her hand on his. He jerked around to look up at her, unseeing. 'With any luck, it won't come to that.'

Michael nodded at last. I had one hand supporting his son's head, pouring the tea in a slow trickle down his throat. I heard Marian guide Michael to the door, her soft reassuring voice, the click of the lock, and her footsteps as she came back into the living room. She stood in the doorway with her arms folded, looking down at the boy.

'His name is Elior,' she said. It was important to find out the names of our patients, she had told me. It made us care more, helped us to work better and harder. 'Haley, look at me.'

I put down the mug and sat back on my heels. In the light from the window her tired face looked greyer than usual.

'You've read every book I own,' she said. 'Do any of them talk about an illness like this?'

I shook my head. She considered me.

'What do you think?'

What did *I* think? She had never asked me that before. I was ten years old, still untrained, and most of my knowledge came from the books on her shelves – many of which, I knew, she had written herself. I chose my words carefully.

'I don't think any sickness could make you speak in tongues.'

'Are you sure?'

I'd seen fever and drugged delirium. I knew people murmured nonsense in their dreams. But none had ever spoken a different language, not if they hadn't known it before. Elior was Ira's son, born and raised in our town, and spoke no tongue but ours.

'Yes,' I said. 'I'm sure.'

Marian nodded slowly and kneeled beside the boy. I expected her to correct me. Michael did not lie; if he said the boy had spoken in tongues, then the only question that remained was why. But all she said was, 'He's still cold. Put more wood on the fire.'

I went to the front of the house where our logs were piled

beside the stairs. They were a gift, of sorts; Marian had delivered the woodcutter's baby daughter a few weeks before. I
carried three logs into the living room and fed them method-
ically into the roaring fire.

'I've never seen this before,' Marian said at last, from behind
me. I didn't reply; I knew sometimes she talked to herself, or
to the sleeping bodies at her feet. 'It doesn't make sense.'

I drew another blanket out of the cupboard and draped it
over Elior. Marian shifted slightly to allow me room, still
staring at the boy. Then I stood, uncertain, waiting for more
orders. There was a pause before she twisted around to look
at me.

'If I weren't here, what would you do?'

I stared at her. 'Are you going away?'

'One day I'll be gone forever,' she said. 'And then you'll be
alone in this house. Tell me what you'd do.'

I swallowed. 'I'd keep him warm. Keep giving him the tea
you gave him.'

Marian folded her arms. 'And just hope he wakes?'

A flicker of frustration: she never usually tested me like
this. I was ten years old, and she was the one with the answers.
'What else should I do?'

She sighed, and looked down at the boy. 'I don't know,'
she said. 'I don't want to give him anything more than this.
I don't know what's wrong with him, so I don't know what
will heal him and what will kill him. Even the laudanum is
a risk. With some sicknesses even a drop can kill you.'

She rubbed her eyes. I was fascinated. She had never shared
her thoughts with me like this before. I watched her.

'One of us has to watch him,' she said at last. 'In case the
seizures return.'

'I'll do it.'

She hesitated, and then nodded.

'If anything changes, you call me, all right? I'll come down after midnight. Keep giving him the tea if he doesn't warm up. And keep him close to the fire.'

I nodded back. She walked past me towards the door and climbed the stairs to her room, and I was left alone in the kitchen with the sleeping boy. It had started to rain.

The night lasted a thousand years. I sat beside him and watched him shiver. Living in that house, I knew the quality of certain silences: the tense, strung-wire silence that meant Marian was angry with me, or I with her; the warm, curled-cat silence of summer; the smoky suspension of resurrection, and the dead grey silence that meant I was alone in the house and Marian had gone through the trapdoor in the basement to lay the dead to rest. This was different. I could hear Elior's hoarse breathing, and as the night went on my thoughts acquired the lamplit sheen of sleeplessness. I was too alert, my senses too bright, and the patter of the rain seemed to crush my ears. The world dissolved in steam and reformed as I made mugs of tea every hour for the boy, my instructions stark words in my head: lemon, honey, brandy, more wood on the fire. Laudanum added to every third cup, so as not to drag him into a sleep he could not wake from. My hands shook on the stop of the vial.

The windows yielded only darkness. I poured kerosene into a cup from the barrel at the back of the house to fuel the lamps, and still the boy did not warm. His skin was clammy and cold, his breathing too shallow. He was wrapped in so many blankets he looked like a newborn, but inside there was just stillness and pallor. *Some things cannot be saved,* I remembered Marian saying as I sat beside him, staring down at his sunken face, and at last I thought I understood what she'd meant. I was sure the boy would never wake.

And then at last, an hour before midnight, he did.

It was very sudden. The rain had died away by then, and

so when his breathing hitched I heard it from where I stood in the kitchen and ran at once to kneel beside him. It did not occur to me to wake Marian. I could see the muscles stark in his throat. I shook him, one hand underneath his head. 'Elior,' I said, clearly. 'Elior, wake up.'

His eyelids fluttered. His fingers twitched, and one hand found my wrist and clutched it. He took a long, rattling breath and his eyes opened.

'Elior.' I could see his eyes trying to focus. He did not know me. 'Elior—'

'Yara,' he whispered, staring at me.

'I'm not – I'm Haley. Tell me what hurts.'

'Yara? Yara, I – please—'

'Elior—'

And then it was over. His chest arched, his muscles contorted, and he gasped in a way I had heard before in the dying. His eyes rolled back in his head. I shouted Marian's name in panic and heard movement from upstairs, but it was already too late. He was jerking around in his blankets, his spasms violent. His grip on my wrist was iron. I couldn't move. I tried to hold him down but he was stronger than me.

Footsteps thundered on the stairs and Marian burst into the room, but before either of us could do anything he took another long death-rattle breath and was still.

Silence.

After a while I realised his grip on my wrist had slackened. I withdrew it slowly, shaking. There were sharp little cuts where his nails had pierced my skin.

'Is he dead?' said Marian, quietly.

I put two fingers to his neck, as I had seen her do so many times. I nodded, my throat tight.

Marian rubbed her face. She looked exhausted. 'All right,' she said at last, 'all right. Let's move him downstairs.'

We carried him together, still in his blankets, down to the

basement. It was colder than the rest of the house, stone carved. In the slats of grey light through the floorboards Elior looked scared, in a way corpses rarely did. Most people, Marian had told me, died in their sleep, and felt no fear at the end. I thought of Ira, his mother, and something hurt deep in my stomach.

'Should I go and get them?'

'Who?'

'His family.'

Marian looked down at him again, and sighed. 'No. Let them sleep. I'll get them here in the morning.'

We looked down at the thing that had been the boy. I made the distinction carefully in my head. This was not Elior; Elior had left us very abruptly some minutes ago.

I realised I was shivering.

'Why did he die?'

'I have no idea,' said Marian. 'Does that scare you?'

I wasn't sure what the right answer was. I just hugged myself, looking down at the face, the staring eyes.

'It scares me,' said Marian. 'Everyone who has died in my care has died because I made a mistake. I chose the wrong medicine, I gave them too much or too little, I misremembered my books, or I didn't see their illness until it was too late. But I never made the same mistake twice. This . . .' She rubbed her face. 'He's dead and I still know nothing. *Nothing*. The next person who comes to me with this sickness will die in the same way. Because I don't know what I did wrong.'

There was nothing I could say. Marian stood for a long time looking down at the boy, until at last she turned and ascended the stairs. I followed her carrying the gas lamp, and we left him alone in the dark.

In the morning, I woke to Michael's choked, dry sobs through my bedroom floor. I lay there listening until I heard the door click shut, then I descended the stairs into the grim silence.

Marian was sitting at the kitchen table, holding a mug of tea. 'I made eggs,' she said when she saw me. 'They're in the kitchen.'

I ate the eggs slowly, with salt fish and tomatoes, watching her all the while. She looked exhausted, as if she had lived a hundred years since last night, and she wasn't eating. The mornings after deaths were always bad, and Elior had only been sixteen. I tried to imagine telling Ira and Michael their son was gone. One day that would be my job. I couldn't imagine being able to do that.

When I had finished eating, I said, 'Do they want to bring him back?'

Marian gave a short, barking laugh. 'Of course they want him back. But not as a corpse. No child deserves to live like that. They said to take him.'

I looked down at the stairs in the parlour, the darkness of the cellar below. Marian was watching me.

'I know you don't believe me,' she said, 'but one day this won't scare you anymore.'

'I'm not scared,' I said, very quickly.

We sat in silence. After a while Marian got to her feet and stretched.

'I'm going to take him down there,' she said at last. 'I'll be back in an hour or so. Go and get caraway and iodine from the market, would you?'

I nodded. I sat there, staring at the books on the wall, until I heard the trapdoor in the basement click shut, then I got up and stood in the middle of the room.

I imagined being like Marian, older, grey-haired, hard-eyed, the face of death and all that came after it. I imagined the crushing weight of that responsibility, the terrible loneliness. When she was dead they would stop throwing stones at me in the street and simply refuse to meet my eyes. Awe and ignorance would keep them away from me, as they kept away from her. When Marian was gone I would have no one at all who did not fear me.

Panic engulfed me, sudden and strong, the terror of having my life laid out before me, dark and inescapable as the tunnels that led down to the underworld. I felt trapped and helpless, like I was seven years old again and newly abandoned, locked in a bedroom and clawing at the walls—

Someone rapped on the door.

I stood still for a moment, as if nothing had happened. Then, still lightheaded, I went to answer it. I unlatched the door and let it swing open in the wind.

A woman stood there, tall and brutally thin, her hair white-gold, her eyes ice-blue, wearing a jacket and gloves of dark leather. She looked about twenty-five. I had never seen her before.

'You're not the witchling,' she said.

'I'm her girl. What do you want?'

The woman studied me for a moment, her tongue pressed against her lower lip. 'I heard a boy was brought to you yesterday, very sick. Can I talk to him?'

'No,' I said dully. 'He died.'

The woman nodded slowly, considering.

'I'm very sorry for that,' she said. 'Give my condolences to his family.'

'All right.'

She walked away. I closed the door and thought nothing of it for the next two years. That was the first time I met Leah.

# CHAPTER SIX

Elior would have died anyway, once we lost the war. I think his was the easier way out.

If you knew what to look for, the end was very close by then: in the east, the front we had long maintained in the mountains was crumbling, raiding parties breaking through our defences by night and slaughtering whole towns as they slept. The promises of our Lord Claire's descendants were dissolving. A year or so after Elior died the front would break entirely, the enemy would advance, and soldiers of our Lord Claire would come to our town seeking any man or woman willing to fight, promising riches and land and glory. If he had lived, Elior would have been seventeen when they came – young, strong, full of anger and hope. He would have gone with them, and he would not have returned.

It had been a very long war. It started around the time I was born, a quiet, relatively bloodless skirmish between the Houses of the lords Claire and Jonathan, over land across the mountains to the east that divided our country and theirs. By the time I was given to Marian, it had caught alight, pulling in young bodies and metal and wood from all over the country— even from our town, a hundred miles from the front. *Samen katoria,* they called the war in the lands of the Lord Jonathan, *the eater of sons,* and they were the ones winning it.

I'm no real authority on it, anyway; I wasn't there. Witchlings were forbidden from fighting because we were too important to lose: without us, there would be no one to carry the fallen to their afterlife. There were war-witchlings, conscripted from declining cities whose populations were now too scant to need them, men and women who travelled with the armies to heal their wounded and lay their dead to rest, but they were kept far back from the fighting itself, only allowed onto the battle-field afterwards to pick through corpses for the injured and the intact dead. If she had had a mind to do it, and I had been old enough to take her place, Marian could have volunteered for the front. But even if I had been old enough, I would never have gone to war. I had no one to fight for anymore; it didn't matter to me whether we won or lost. Or so I thought, in those days.

The year I was eleven, the eastern front broke and the forces of the Lord Jonathan crossed the mountains and invaded at last. They wanted our land, we knew that. They were not content with the line of rich-soiled hills the war had started over; they wanted our dark forests, our golden fields, our white western coastlines. And they would kill whoever resisted them. They had lost too much in the last ten years to spare lives now for the sake of mercy.

In the streets, everyone was quieter. We were scared, though we did not admit it. There was nothing else to talk about, so we did not talk at all.

When the army was fifty miles away, the soldiers of the Lord Claire, our patron and protector, came to our town asking for any help they could find. They needed people to meet the army that even now was dragging its caravans over the hills towards us – to kill the tired, iron-faced men clambering down the sloped valleys with swords in their hands. They were too late, of course. If the Lord Jonathan's soldiers were this far west, nothing could stop them now.

I heard they were bringing the lord herself through the towns, to gather men to fight. It was the only thing spoken of at market, and I had long since acquired the orphan's affinity for listening at doors. Our Lord Claire herself, coming, they said, to galvanise us and reinspire our loyalty. I came home and told Marian, and she raised her eyebrows and said, 'Well, I suppose you'll want to see her,' and so I went alone, disgruntled by her lack of excitement. I could not understand why Marian was not captivated by the lord, as I was. I think now that she might have been afraid.

I was standing in the crowd when they brought the lord past us. She was in a carriage more beautiful than any I had ever seen, all red velvet and gold embroidery. I was skinny and nimble, and pushed my way through the crowd. Some of the children tried to elbow me, but I was faster by then. I climbed up onto the bridge to get a better look. There was a statue at the edge of the bridge, of a warrior whose name I can't remember anymore – elegant and austere, staring out over our town with an unblinking gaze like Marian's – and I hung into the tip of her sword, feeling the river-breeze on my cheeks, watching the carriage. I could barely hear my own breaths over the cheering. From here, I could see the rolling hills and the moorlands stretching for miles into the unknown distance. The houses of our small town seem to thin out and disperse too quickly, as if the heather was creeping up on us, growing over and through us like tree roots through a corpse. I understood for the first time, in that moment, how tiny we were. I remember that bird-flutter longing to escape.

I could never leave. Not even for a week. When Marian died, I would be the witchling of this town, and their dead would need me. I felt suddenly trapped. I could not breathe. I saw for a moment the hugeness of the world, and understood for the first time that I would never see it. The brightness of witchling-magic dulled in my head, and old resentment welled in me. I was chained forever to these people who did not love me.

The crowd were trying to swarm the carriage, but the lord's

men were unyielding and did not allow anyone within a few yards of it. Their swords glinted in the dim light through the clouds. The carriage parted the horde and touched the edge of the bridge beneath me, and then I saw her.

She was beautiful in the way that mountains are beautiful, or statues. She was too pale, almost translucent, her bones sharp and bird-thin, as if she were shaped from crystal; I knew somehow that her touch would draw blood. Her hair and eyes were glass-blue, her long fingers curled over the carriage windows, her eyes sliding over us, her people. She looked about forty, the age she had been when she had died. She was very clearly not human – she took everything elegant and graceful about a human woman and stretched it until it was frightening. You could not look, and you could not look away.

She had chosen to be judged in the underworld, and she had been found good, and that had changed everything. Claire had lived her life with her hand on her heart. She was neither thief nor murderer. She had not cheated her friends, betrayed her lovers, or beaten her children. She had been kind when she could afford to be, and sometimes when she could not. Hers had been an ordinary kind of goodness, but it was more deserving of reward than punishment, and so she had been sent *up* – not back to the living world, but to the world above, where those who have lived charitable, selfless lives are sent to enjoy eternity.

And then Claire, for her own reasons, having obtained eternity in paradise, chose to forego it and come back to us. She lived for the first few decades of her immortality in the freezing woods to the south, where she'd grown up, performing minor miracles for the people of the surrounding towns – healing the sick and the injured, restoring a couple of decades of youth to the ageing, ensuring good harvests, that kind of thing. There are stories of lords like that in Marian's books, recorded by the witchlings who knew them – lords living quiet lives of uncorrupted obscurity, beloved by those around them, bestowing healing and good fortune by their presence. It takes a truly good person, an unblemished soul, to give up eternal joy in the world of the blessed for that. It's rare, say the books, but it happens.

That kind of life must have been Claire's intention in the beginning – and that of the eastern Lord Jonathan, I imagine. I don't know what made him stray from that path. I do know that after fifty years Claire fell in love and bore children, and those children grew into strong young men and women – mortal, but with her lordly beauty, her surety, her shining grace. They were worshipped, too, but they lacked her goodness, her restraint. They gathered riches, and then armies, and began to build an empire in her name. They settled her in a palace in Arbakin, the great city in the north, and there she lived quietly for two hundred years. I can understand that, in a sense: she did as her children asked, what she thought would make them happiest. For centuries, her sprawling web of descendants held our land in the palms of their smooth, strong hands. We sang hymns to her.

And then from across the mountains came the armies of Lord Jonathan, and everything fell apart.

A lord cannot die, at least not the way humans die. Lock them up in a cell, starve them, deny them water or sleep, leave them for a thousand years, and when you return they will be waiting for you, watching calmly through the bars, unchanged.

But, as Marian could have told me, not even lords are completely invincible. Everything can be destroyed if you try hard enough.

The visit to our town – as I'm sure you have worked out faster than I did at the age of eleven – was not a gesture of good-heartedness or good faith by the lord's men. They knew it was a matter of time before the palace at Arbakin fell, and they could not stay there. Lords cannot move air or earth, or break the charge of foreign armies. Jonathan's men were coming for Claire, and so her descendants took her away.

She passed through our town, heading west, away from the mountains and the advancing armies. When they found her, six months later, they say she was hidden in a woodland tavern, dressed as a barmaid. They cut off her head, boiled off the flesh, and crushed her skull underneath a rock. The rest of her they burned. By then, of course, the war was over.

Not long after the lord's visit, when Jonathan's men had fought their way to the hills east of our village, Daniel knocked on our door.

He did not acknowledge me. His eyes were on his mother beside him, and the woman in her arms. It took me a moment to recognise her, bloody and rasping, her hair matted, one hand a cauterised stump. Then I realised who she was, with a dull thud. Niamh.

I did not even know she had volunteered. I had thought her too young, but in that first frantic scramble – as Marian guided them to the living room, as they lay Niamh down and I lit the fire with shaking hands – I realised that she must be seventeen by now. There was no trace left of the girl who had shown me mercy years ago. This was a haggard woman, her face made gaunt by pain and hunger. She trembled violently on the rug as blood seeped from the stump of her left hand.

Marian gave me orders. I do not remember them. I had been with her long enough by then that I responded instinctively to the sound of her words, without having to consciously understand their meaning. I watched myself descend into the pantry, pull amaranth, mace and thyme down from the bundles of herbs that swung from the ceiling. I could hear the commotion upstairs: Marian's low urgent voice, Daniel's rough sobs, his mother's keening wail. I balanced fennel seeds in the palm of my hand and tried to calm myself.

When I returned, everything was quieter. Daniel was kneeling at his sister's side, rocking slowly backwards and forwards. I gave the herbs to Marian and she turned at once to their mother, who stood beside her, staring down at Niamh on the floor.

'Anya,' Marian said quietly, 'I need you to take Daniel into the living room. All right?'

Anya shook her head wildly. 'No. No. I'm not leaving her.'

Marian took Anya's chin in her hand and tilted her head up gently, so that the woman was forced to look her in the face. 'Listen to me. I will do everything I can for your daughter, Anya. But I need to be able to work. Let me have this room. Haley will get you if anything – if we need you.'

'Mama,' said Daniel hoarsely, beside her. 'Mama. Come on. Let's get out of her way.'

Anya was very still, her eyes empty. He had to tug at her wrist several times. I looked at him, hoping to catch his eye, but his eyes were on his mother. 'Mama. We have to go. Please.'

At last, she let him pull her away. I heard her choked sobs move down the corridor until the living-room door clicked shut behind them.

Niamh's eyes followed them down the corridor. Her hand was at her chest, at the wound that Daniel and Anya had not seen in their panic. She could feel the broken rib and the torn lung beneath. She had lost more blood than our magic could replace in the time she had. We all felt it, the gathering dark in the air around her.

Marian knelt beside her. She took the girl's undamaged hand and held it. I had never seen her so tender. I don't think either of them realised I was still there. 'Oh, child,' she said softly. 'You've been so brave.'

Niamh's gaze fixed on Marian's. She swallowed. It seemed to take her several attempts to speak.

'*Don't – bring me—*'

She coughed, then convulsed in pain. I knew what to do before Marian had to tell me. I went to the cupboard for the laudanum and the soothing tea. The kettle was already on the fire. I could feel Niamh watching me. She tried to speak again.

'*Don't bring me – to the underworld.*'

Silence from the living room. I couldn't see Marian through the dimness of smoke and fading sunlight. I poured two drops of laudanum into the tea.

'Child,' said Marian softly, 'do you know what you're asking me?'

'Yes,' whispered Niamh, vehemently. She coughed again. 'I don't – want – to be judged.'

'You don't have to be.'

She made a soft hissing noise that might have been pain or laughter. 'And wander around – down there – until I fade away? I'd rather— I'd rather be nothing. Less than nothing. I'd rather be *gone.*'

My hands were shaking now. I stood there, waiting for them to steady so I could carry the tea through to Niamh. She eyed it, bloodshot and suspicious. I tried not to look at the blackened sinew where her hand had been.

'It's tea,' said Marian. 'It will help with the pain.' When Niamh reached for it with her good hand, Marian pushed her hand down gently. 'Let Haley do it.'

Niamh's eyes focused on me for the first time, then widened. 'Haley? Yes, of course.' She tried to smile. There was bloody darkness where some of her teeth should have been. 'Are you all right?'

I could not answer that. I guided the tea wordlessly to her mouth and she drank, wincing slightly at the heat. I heard the shivering rasp of her swallowing, the muscles moving under the blood and dirt of her neck. When her eyes focused on Marian again they were brighter, her voice clearer.

'I mean it. Burn me after. Tell Daniel and my parents . . . whatever you want. I'm not going down there.'

Marian's face was impassive. After a moment she said, 'Why are you so frightened of being judged?'

'Why do you think? I was—' Niamh winced and closed her eyes. 'At the front. I did things . . . I killed . . . I—'

'Were you cruel? Did you torture or rape? Did you take life when you didn't have to? Did you do more than you needed to, to survive?'

'I . . .' Tears welled in her bloodshot eyes. 'I did everything I could, but I . . . I had friends, they . . . they did things, and I went with them . . .'

'Hush. You're not evil, child.'

'You don't know that,' said Niamh. She was trembling now. 'You don't.'

'I do,' said Marian softly. 'I know more than you think. You were born here, on this floor. I remember you. You are not evil. Look at me.' Niamh turned her bloodstained face to Marian's through the candlelight. It was only the two of them in that moment, and the silence was as thick as new-fallen snow. 'Look at me, child. Do you trust me?'

Niamh was shuddering so violently I thought she would break apart on the floor. Marian placed her hands either side of her face, and held her.

'Do you trust me?'

Niamh nodded very slowly and closed her eyes. She was calmer after that, her breathing softer and quieter.

Marian stroked her hair in the flickering candlelight until she died.

I was the one who had to go into the living room to tell Daniel and Anya while Marian burned herbs in the grate and prepared blood-ink for the rites. Daniel flinched when I came into the room. I think he already knew. When I tried to comfort him, he pulled away from me.

'*She said she'd do everything she could!*' was amongst the many, many things Anya screamed at me when I told her Niamh was dead. I did not know how to tell her that Marian had not lied. From the moment she had come through our door, there had been nothing anyone could do.

Later, much later, after they were gone and the house was quiet, I found Marian sitting at the table, a cup steaming on the table in front of her, staring into the darkness of the hall.

'Did you take her down?'

Marian nodded. She looked for a moment like she was about to say something, but stopped herself.

'What?'

'Haley—' She hesitated. She never said *you wouldn't understand,* not to me, ever. She raised the cup to her lips and then put it down again.

'Sometimes,' she said, 'if someone dies too young, they've never really felt guilt before. Not the way you feel it at the end. It hits them too hard. They act . . . rashly. You have to be careful. You have to soothe them. If they won't be moved, if they really don't want to survive death, then you have to honour that. But if you can, you stop them. You understand?'

She was watching me very intently.

'Yes,' I said, though of course I didn't.

Marian nodded and took another sip from the cup. Then she looked at me again, differently. 'Are you all right?'

She had come to find me when I fled to Daniel's house. She must have known what Niamh was to me, or part of it. I had thought she had forgotten.

'I'm fine,' I said. 'We need more amaranth.'

'I'll go and get it from the market tomorrow. Go to sleep, Haley.'

I shook my head very slowly. Marian looked at me and understood.

'All right,' she said, 'you can start *On the Development of the Infant,* then,' and so we sat there together for a long time, me staring unseeingly into the book, her into the grey dark of the hall, until the world outside began to wake again.

A few months later, just after my twelfth birthday, Lord Jonathan's army came to our town. Their approach over the hills to the east had been very slow; if we'd wanted to fight, we would have had time to prepare. No one did. A few fled, those with parents or children in other towns, but those of us with no safer harbour stayed where our livelihoods were and waited. It was a greater risk to flee, anyway; we had heard rumours of the advancing enemy finding and killing everyone travelling alone, assuming they were Claire's soldiers. We might, I suppose, have gathered weapons, destroyed the bridge, dug trenches between the town and the hills and thrown hot oil at Lord Jonathan's men as they approached – but we were all so tired. Anyone with a mind to resist had gone to the front long ago, and we were left with grieving mothers and dead-eyed fathers, squalling babies and silent children.

They came for us first, as Marian had warned me they would. She had me waiting by the window, looking down the street. Everyone was quiet, hidden in their houses, trying not to be seen. In the last months of the war, our lord's generals had decided that even if the army of the Lord Jonathan outnumbered us two to one then we would halve them before we fell, match them death for death. We succeeded in that much, at least, and in revenge, their army wiped out one town in every ten. They set the buildings alight and chased the children into the burning woods, put their parents to the sword and left the corpses to crumble to ash in the flames. They used fire, of course, because it meant the bodies could not be brought down to the underworld or resurrected. Their ghosts were destroyed when their bodies burned, and they were lost forever.

We did not know if we were doomed. So we stayed quiet, and prayed to our lord. We did not know then that she was dead, too.

I saw the Lord Jonathan's men coming around the corner as I sat by the barred window of my bedroom. They were easy to make out: paler-skinned than us and older, more haggard. They carried swords and walked down our street with purpose. There were half a dozen of them. How many men did they need to burn us? If they killed Marian and me, there would be no one to carry our dead to their next lives. They would condemn the whole place to evanescence and oblivion, a slow death. There would be less sport in it, of course, than running us down as we fled; no legend in it, to scare the next village west into terrified submission. But it would be more efficient. Perhaps they wanted that, by then, I thought. Perhaps they too were tired.

I ran down the stairs, leaping over the one that creaked. Marian was sitting at the kitchen table, her hands pressed together. She stood up when I entered.

'They're here?'

I nodded. Marian sucked in a breath. She curled one long-fingered hand around the back of her chair, staring at the door.

'They'll want to separate us,' she said. 'They fear what will happen if we are together, if we're allowed to plan. You remember what I did the night that man hurt you?'

I nodded.

'When you raise something, you give them your life, you take in their death. You keep it in you. Can you feel it?'

For a second I had no idea what she meant. Then a memory flickered: the cat and the mouse, dead in my hands, and the warmth that had trickled from me into them, and the death-cold they had given me in return. Marian was right, I realised with a start: it was still there. At her words I felt it ripple, like a stone had been dropped into a clear black lake. I stared at her.

'You can take it,' she said. There was anguish in her face I'd never seen before; I knew she didn't want to have to tell me this. 'Release it into them. You need to touch them, skin to skin.'

'I can do that?'

'Only if they try to hurt you. Haley—'

A rap on the door. I turned, but Marian's eyes stayed on me.

'Haley, look at me – do *not* hurt them unless you have no choice. If they want you dead, do not give them any excuse—'

'*Witchling!*' A rough shout from the front. '*Open up!*'

Marian's hand tightened on the back of the chair. Then she pushed her greying hair out of her eyes, composed herself and walked slowly towards the entrance. I stayed behind, watching, terrified.

The door swung open.

A woman stood at the threshold, half an inch taller than Marian, with a sword at her hip. She had a roughened, scarred face, dark hair. She did not smile.

'We would like,' she said, 'to come in.'

'Why?'

'We will discuss that inside. Not out here.'

If they had wanted to kill her, they would have done it on the doorstep. More visible, a better example to the town – blood in the hallway, on the cobbled street. Marian's eyes moved over the woman's face, the faces of the men behind her.

'Be careful with my books,' she said, and opened it wider.

They filed into the house. Marian did not usually allow more than a couple of grieving relatives with a body, and the soldiers felt too big in the darkened room. I could feel their warmth, their tight, quick breaths. They did not belong here, in this house of death-magic, and they knew it. I could feel the house reaching into me, strengthening me. I stared at the branches that curled through the walls of the kitchen, tried to see again the gnarled fingers that had terrified me when I was younger. I imagined them twining slowly around the necks of the soldiers, tightening.

The woman looked at me coolly. I tried to seem very calm.

'This is your girl?'

'Yes,' said Marian.

'Interesting,' said the woman, lightly. 'In all the towns we've come through, all the witchlings have been women. I'd never noticed that before.'

Marian said nothing. In our books, it said that death-magic showed itself in girls over boys nineteen times in twenty; there were male witchlings, especially in the warm north where people clustered thickly and each bustling town had ten Houses of the Dead, but they were rare out here. That was our knowledge, though, and Marian was not going to give it away. She was not going to give this woman anything if not directly asked for it. I saw that, and was strengthened.

'My name is Esther,' said the woman, after a moment. 'I am a general of the lord's army. We require your assistance.'

There was a silence.

'You require,' said Marian at last, '*my* assistance?'

'Yes. The Lord Jonathan's granddaughter is ill.'

Another pause. Everyone was still. I could feel the tension in the man next to me, his fixed gaze, his hand on the hilt of his sword. He could chop off my head in one smooth movement, before I could move.

'What ails her?'

'You will help?' said the general.

'I asked what ailed her.'

'And *I* asked—'

'I know what you asked,' said Marian, and for the first time there was an edge to her voice. 'I know how this works. I help or you kill me, and leave my girl to tend to this town, twelve years old and alone and not yet trained. I understand threats, General. You don't need to condescend to me.'

There was no movement from the soldiers behind the general. I tried to imagine carrying Marian's body down to the monsters in the underworld. Waiting alone in the House of the Dead for someone to break a leg and be brought to me. Rifling through our books for her words, her advice. The looks the people would give me.

The general said, 'We have orders not to kill you.'

'And I have whose word for that?'

'Mine.'

Marian gave a harsh, cold laugh. It was so unlike her that it frightened me.

'Your *word*. Very well.' She ran a hand through her hair, tried to calm herself, failed. I had never seen her this angry. 'You killed my brother, did you know that? I hadn't seen him in years, I didn't even know he'd gone to the front, and the next thing I heard about him was that you had killed him. He had a husband and two children.'

'What was his name?'

'Aron.'

I stared at Marian. A man called Aron had come to this house a year ago, the worried father of a small girl with a fever. Marian had soothed him, healed his daughter, sent him home. Had that been her brother? She had shown no sign of love or fear for him or the child – just her usual calm reassurance. Had Aron known who she was? How old had he been when she was taken away? When had Marian found out about his death? Why hadn't she told me?

'I did not kill him,' said Esther. 'I know the name of every man I have killed.'

Marian's voice was low and furious. 'Your men, then. One of you. He's dead, and that's on your conscience, you and every man you stand with, and your damned *lord*—'

One of the men moved suddenly, hand on his sword, but Esther shot him a quelling look and he stopped. Marian considered him with contempt. I had never seen her like that. It frightened me.

'Don't you dare dirty his name,' said Esther, at last.

'Or what?'

'Or we will show you what blasphemy deserves.'

'You mean you'll kill me,' said Marian, with dark scorn. 'You see? That took thirty seconds. I understand the value of your *word*, general.'

They looked at each other.

'You will help us,' said Esther at last, and it was no longer a question.

'I have conditions.'

A slight pause. I could sense Esther gathering her patience. She pursed her lips and released the handle of her sword with what looked like some effort.

'You will bring his granddaughter here,' said Marian

'Absolutely not,' said Esther.

'I need this house. I need my books, my ink, my knives—'

'We can bring them with us.'

'They are my blood and bone,' said Marian. 'They are the things by which I live. You will not take them from this house.'

'We will,' said Esther, 'if it is required.'

Another pause. I could see the tightness in Marian's jaw, her short, angry breaths, her fists opening and closing at her side. I knew it was all an act. She must have known that the lord would never allow his kin to be taken into the house of an enemy witchling. If they had to use us, they would do it

somewhere we did not know, amongst their men, with knives
to our throats. Marian knew that and so did the general. This
was just a bargaining tactic.

'I want my girl with me.'

'Is she necessary?' said Esther.

'She helps me. I will be more effective if I have her.'

It would be easier for Marian to protect me if I was at her
side. Esther looked at Marian for a moment, then nodded.

'And I want payment.'

Esther's eyebrows rose. '*Payment?* You took vows, witchling—'

'Not in *bronze*,' said Marian. Her tone was clipped and
even again, but I could see her white knuckles. 'How do you
think I feed myself and my girl? We live off gratitude. The
fisherman brings us a trout in thanks for laying his mother
to rest. The farmer delivers a sack of flour in return for healing
his son. But now the fishermen are dead, and all the flour
sent east to feed the soldiers you slaughtered. We have no
food. I have supplies for a week and a half, no more. I want
food and water, I want paper and ink, and I want your word
that so long as your lord has power in this country, we will
not want for either. We are your responsibility now.'

Esther seemed uncertain. Her eyes moved slowly over the
jars on the walls, the flasks of blood and thinning bundles of
rosemary and sage. Our pantry was in the back; I salted the
meat every week and had seen how little there was.

'Very well,' said Esther, at last. 'You have our word.'

Marian gave that rasping laugh again, but the general
ignored her.

'You will come with us now.'

A pause.

'Yes,' Marian said at last, 'I suppose we will.'

And that was it. We belonged to the enemy.

*

The air outside was thick and dark, and smelled of rain. They put us in a cart and the soldiers surrounded us like a guard of honour. They carried torches, so our faces were clearly illuminated. The townsfolk would see us from their windows and think we were being taken away for execution, or that we had defected, and then they would panic – and that, of course, was the point.

Marian seemed perfectly calm as they led us to the cart. I tried to copy her, though I was terrified. It wasn't impossible that this was all a trick, some pretext to make us leave the House of the Dead without a fight, and they were going to drag us into a ditch and stab us and leave us to bleed out. I had seen people die of wounds like that. My hand was tight on the edge of the cart. Marian would not look at me.

We were in the cart for an hour, trundling over the moors between dark hills. I could see the lights of the town, its glittering fires, lamplights from windows. That comforted me slightly. If I had to run, I could find my way back.

And then the hills gave way and we were on the other side, into a field a thousand acres wide, covered in tents and camp-fires. I gasped. I had never seen so many people before. Their voices rose like smoke into the cold air.

'This is your *army*?'

I had not meant to speak, and cursed myself for it. Esther looked at me properly for the first time, and I stared furiously at the bottom of the cart, waiting for her to look away.

'A division of it,' she said, at last.

How much was a division? A tenth? A hundredth? I stared around at the mass of people, heaving and swirling like river water. Rough soldiers laughing around campfires, cooking meat on spits. The childish part of my brain remembered the rumours we had heard years ago, that Lord Jonathan's army ate the people they killed and carried a store of salted corpses with them to feast on after battles. The more rational part of me was simply awed. So many of them. No wonder we had lost the war.

I wondered whether there were more of them back in the lands of the Lord Jonathan, or if the war had drained them as it had drained us. If their towns were bereft of young men and women, too; if their children had been orphaned. I hoped so.

We shuddered to a halt before a tent made of soft grey silk, guarded by impassive soldiers. Marian made to get out of the cart but Esther put out a hand to stop her.

'You must be invited.'

'What?'

The look in Esther's eyes was reverent. I had never seen that kind of light in anyone's face before. 'She is holy. You cannot enter without invitation.'

Marian looked disgusted.

One of the guards went into the tent. I heard voices. Two minutes passed, and then the flap opened again and there was the lord's granddaughter.

From the delicate silk, and Esther's air of protective devotion, I had expected a child younger than me, but the woman on the soldier's arm was at least nineteen or twenty. Something was quite obviously wrong with her – there was a childlike blankness in her face, and she clung to the soldier's arm with fearful strength. He leaned over to her and whispered in her ear. She spoke haltingly, as if in an unfamiliar language.

'You may enter.'

Marian nodded and climbed out of the cart, and I followed her. Esther's face was carefully expressionless.

Inside, the tent was warm as a brazier. The lord's granddaughter lay down on the couch and gazed up at the silk that shielded her from the stars. The soldier whose arm she had clutched stood above her, looking into her face with a worried tenderness. I would have said they were lovers, except she did not look at *him* at all.

Esther came after us into the tent with another soldier, carrying a crate full of Marian's books and inks. The second soldier bowed and left, and then it was just the five of us. The granddaughter did not move.

Marian turned back to Esther.

'What ails her?'

It seemed to take the general some time to speak. 'You tell me.'

Marian stared at her for a moment, then looked back at the girl. Finally, she turned her whole body to face Esther, and crossed her arms.

'You're her mother,' she said.

Esther looked back at her, her expression quite empty.

'I guard her,' she said softly. 'I keep her safe.'

'Clearly not.'

I thought for one heart-stopping moment that Esther was going to draw her sword then and run Marian through. At last, she resumed her dead-eyed composure, and said nothing.

Marian turned back to the girl, studying her. 'She doesn't look sick.'

There was impatience in Esther's voice now. 'You've been a witchling for twenty years. Surely you can do more than *look*.'

That stilled Marian for a moment, her hands on the girl's wrist for her pulse. 'What do you know about me?'

'The lord himself directed me to find a healer. Better than our own witchlings. I asked our prisoners. They said you're the best witchling within a hundred miles of here.'

'You came to this town because of *me*?'

'We came to this town to heal my daughter. I was told you could do it.'

There was a silence. The girl had not moved throughout any of this. There was a certain sheen of holiness about her, I thought. She had a warm, dark-haired beauty, not as ancient and unnerving as Claire's, but more human, compelling. You wanted to trust her. There were strands of gold in her wide eyes, and her body was long-limbed and lean and muscular; she had been raised as a soldier. She would have looked like a queen, or a general herself, someone people would follow, if she had not been marred by her strange blankness. She lay on her back on the velvet couch, staring up at the tent. Her soldier-lover watched her anxiously. I observed her curiously. I did not know what could sicken the grandchildren of lords.

'What's your name?' asked Marian.

'Cor—'

Marian held up a hand to silence Esther. 'What's your name, child?' she said to the girl.

The granddaughter gave no sign that she had heard Marian at all. She stared unseeingly up at the silk ceiling.

'Her name is Cora,' said Esther, at last, 'but she does not know it. She does not speak. She barely eats. All she hears is *him.*'

Her voice was full of bitter anguish. I thought of my mother, who had given up her child willingly. This was a different kind of loss. My mother had not felt pain like this.

'Give me a torch.'

'You will not bring fire into this tent. I will not let you hurt her.'

Marian twitched her head slightly in irritation. 'Something bright, then. Anything.'

After a moment's hesitation Esther gave the order. A flat stone, its surface polished smooth, was brought in by a soldier and placed in Marian's hand. She knelt beside Cora and held the stone over the girl's face, angling it so that the flat, polished face caught the light outside and sharpened it. The girl blinked. Marian nodded, and clicked her fingers beside Cora's left ear. She twitched.

'She sees and hears,' said Esther. 'She knows *his* voice, but no one else's.' She jerked her head towards the soldier, who in all this time had not looked away from the girl's face.

Marian looked at him for the first time. 'Who are you?'

He looked up, then got to his feet and saluted. Marian looked taken aback.

'My name is Emyln. Sir.' It was what they called all their commanders in the east.

'I mean,' said Marian curtly, 'who are you to *her*.'

'Her husband,' he said. 'In a month.' Out of the corner of my eye I saw Esther look away in disgust.

Marian tilted her head towards the girl. 'Talk to her.'

The soldier moved forwards, taking the girl's hand. 'Cora,' he said gently. 'Cora, it's me. Look at me.'

She turned her head, and for a moment her eyes seemed to focus. 'Emlyn,' she whispered. Her hand twitched, and he grasped it.

'Cora, there's a woman here to make you better.'

'Am I . . .?' She spoke haltingly again, her mouth clumsy around the words. 'Am I sick?'

He looked as though he was about to break down. 'Yes, love,' he said. 'You've been ill. But you're going to get better.'

Marian got to her feet. She spoke quickly and quietly to Esther.

'He's the only one she remembers?'

Esther nodded. 'Not me, not her brothers, not her father. Not even the lord. Just him. She sounds— She can barely speak. She doesn't eat. She can barely walk. It's as if – as if she's been taken away.'

Marian looked over at the girl staring into the eyes of her beloved.

'Let me think,' she said finally. 'I need to go outside.'

Esther nodded tightly.

'My girl will come with me.'

A slight pause. 'You will be guarded,' said Esther.

Marian's expression flickered almost imperceptibly. 'Fine.'

I followed Marian out of the tent. The night air felt cool and clear after the stuffy warmth inside. Marian walked unseeingly through the lines of tents and campfires, and I followed her, and so did the soldiers behind us. I had the sense that Marian was trying to escape the camp, to shake the soldiers off, but after a while she seemed to realise it was impossible, and sat down on the grass. I stood uncertainly and she gestured impatiently for me to sit opposite her.

'I've never seen this before,' she said. 'Not in people so young. Sometimes the old fade as they age, but not like this.'

I said nothing. I knew what she was talking about. There was no cure for this kind of ailment. Rune-magic could hold together and animate what was already there, but could not regrow what was not: spilled blood, sawed-off hands, memories. It could stop a dead man's rot and hold the fading heartbeat of a child, but it could not save Niamh, and it could not bring back this girl's mind.

I imagined what Esther might do to us if we could not prevent her daughter from sickening further. I thought again unwillingly of my mother, and the time our cat had scratched the baby's face. She had kicked the animal into a wall in her fury, and bandaged the baby's wounds carefully, with cloth torn from her best shirt.

I pushed the memory away. I hadn't thought of my mother this much in years. I had promised myself never to think of her again, but tonight had returned her to me.

'What would you do, if you were here alone?' said Marian at last.

'I don't know,' I said. It was the wrong answer, but it was the truth. 'What are you going to do?'

Marian looked at me. 'We'll work it out,' she said after a little while. 'I'll work something out.'

There was a silence – and then suddenly, from the tent, a cry of anguish.

We all turned towards it, the soldiers drawing their blades. Something was wrong. There was commotion inside the tent, the violent flickering of shadows. A man's voice raised in terror.

Marian ran towards the tent, and I scrambled to follow her, slipping on the dewy grass. From inside the grey silk there came a terrible wail.

'*Cora!*'

Marian ripped open the tent flap. Inside, all was chaos. Esther had drawn her sword and was brandishing it at nothing. Her daughter flailed around on her couch like a fish drowning in air, spasming violently, bloody foam drooling from her open mouth. Emyln was trying desperately to hold her down.

'*Cora!*' He looked up, and saw us. '*Help me!*'

'Hot water,' said Marian to the soldiers behind us. 'Get it now.'

One of them turned and ran out of the tent. Marian grasped my wrist. The shock of it was almost more than that of seeing the girl.

'You remember?' she said, soft and urgent. 'You know what to do?'

I nodded. I could see it before me: Michael with his blind tearless eyes and Elior spasming on the wooden floor. We could not help him, and he had died, but for a little while the laudanum had seemed to calm him. If we could stop this seizure, maybe then she would live, and we could think of something else—

Marian looked down at me. Her eyes were bright. For the first time in my life, I saw that she was afraid.

'Do the best you can,' she said.

I ran out of the tent. There were soldiers guarding it. They moved to grab me, a runaway child, but faltered when they

realised who I was. I stood for a few seconds, staring at them.
I could not think.

'The hot water,' I said at last. I was surprised to hear the
authority in my voice. I sounded like a witchling, like Marian.
'And the crate.'

They brought it to me and I kneeled beside it, moving
through the bottles. I knew every one of them by touch. I
was not looking for the tea leaves now – tea was for soothing,
and we were past that. I brought out the brandy and laudanum,
and closed my eyes.

The girl was dying. We could no more save her than we
had Elior. This was the illness we could not name or cure.
His memory had been addled too, at the end. *Yara,* he had
whispered to me, but there was no one by that name in this
town. He had imagined her. And then he had died.

I knelt in the dirt, breathing too fast. The hopelessness of
the brandy and laudanum felt suddenly clear to me. It hadn't
saved Elior, and it wouldn't save the girl. I could hear the
soldier's shouts inside the tent, Marian's snapped orders, the
girl's strangled breaths, her spasming thuds. Panic had seized
me.

*Breathe.* Slow breaths, in and out. If I calmed down I might
be able to think. I pressed my hands into the dirt.

Then, at last, I raised my head.

The world had frozen.

The soldiers around me were blurred. If I looked away from
them they were not there. The firelight no longer flickered. I
tried to turn my head but could not. Time slowed like honey,
and then stopped. The sky above me was silent. Everything
had stopped.

'Look at me,' said a voice at my back. 'Kid. It's all right.
Look at me.'

I turned, slow in the thick air. It was difficult to breathe
and the world had turned suddenly colder.

A woman stood beside me. Her hair was cropped white-blond, her hands in the pockets of her black leather jacket, and her gaze was steady. She seemed the only real thing in this unholy darkness. I knew I had seen her somewhere before.

'This will heal her,' she said quietly. 'Take my hand.'

I did as she said, mesmerised. Her skin was cold and I felt something pass from her into me, a shivering pulse, deeper than witchling-magic and colder than resurrection. It lay in the bloodless cavity beneath my heart.

'Give that to her,' said the woman. Her eyes were ice-blue, and did not leave me. 'You hear me?'

I nodded, staring at her. I could not do anything else. The woman turned and vanished into the darkness.

And then suddenly everything began moving again. I was near the soldiers gathered around the fire, and the flasks of brandy, laudanum and rue were warm in my hands. The screaming from the tent was glass-clear in the blue dark.

I was frozen. I did not understand what had just happened. It was like falling awake: like the moment where you lie in the numb daze of half-sleep and everything drops away from you, and when you wake the stillness and the falling clash in your head for a moment before everything fades.

The girl gave another choked scream. I turned, and everything seemed to condense. The girl was dying. I had the flask of rue in my hand. I breathed to steady myself, and pushed my way into the tent.

Marian and the soldier were holding the girl down. Esther was cradling her head, trying to keep her airway open. She was not crying, but her face was full of pain. Cora had stopped shaking and was turning blue.

'Cora,' Esther whispered, 'Cora—'

The girl's breaths were hoarse and rattling, and her eyes had rolled back into her head. I uncorked the flask, and with Marian's help, I started to pour the warm golden liquid into her mouth. A soft unearthly calm had settled over my mind, and I saw, half-surprised, that my hands were quite steady.

'Not too quickly,' said Marian sharply to me. 'Don't choke her.'

Esther gave a soft, dry sob.

I poured it in a warm trickle down the girl's throat, watching the flickers of the muscles in her neck. Slowly, she began to fall still. Her betrothed was not blinking or breathing. He stared at her fixedly, like a blind man at the sun.

After all the liquid was gone there was a silence of perhaps a minute. The girl had stopped struggling and her breaths were almost inaudible now. She looked years older, sweating, emaciated. Her limbs were slack.

Her soldier's eyes were full of tears. 'Cora,' he whispered, and pressed his palms to her cheeks. 'Cora, sweetheart.'

I knew, numbly, that she was dying. My rue had not worked. She was still, and her eyes would not open, and there was no movement in her but the slow, almost-exhausted rise and fall of her chest. I remembered the seconds between Elior's his last seizure and his last breath. Perhaps she would cling on for hours like this.

She was going to die. She could not die.

There was no panic left in me. I was floating, suspended in a dream. I knew what I had to do. I took the girl's wrist and closed my eyes.

The spell the woman had given to me was so delicate and subtle that I don't think even Marian sensed it. I felt a silvery prickle down the nerves of my arm, and then it was gone. It is important that I remember that – it did not leave me when I touched her, uncontrollably. *I* did it. I did as the strange woman had told me. I took the spell she had given to me and I pushed it into the girl.

There was another silence, longer.

I watched it dazedly. I could see the spell, though I knew

no one else could: a shadow under the girl's skin, spreading through her to her brain and heart, her veins blackening. I watched it move – slowly at first, and then rapidly, like the quickening of flame.

Something was being burnt out of her.

I realised it very slowly, a rising darkness in my numb brain. The woman had lied to me. The spell was not meant to heal her at all.

My grip was too tight on Cora's wrist. Panic rose within me at last but could find no way out. Her skin was reddening, and in it I could see the flow of blood and the spell to her heart. Her breath was hitched and rapid.

I saw hope light up in her betrothed's eyes. He grabbed her other wrist and whispered, 'Cora—'

Her muscles clenched and her chest lifted off the couch. Every muscle stood out in her neck. Her mouth opened. She knew what was happening to her, I could see it in her blood-shot eyes.

'No—' Marian said quietly, 'no, no—'

A last shuddering gasp through half-open lips, a slackening release. Her betrothed's hands tightened on her other wrist. And then it was over.

Esther gave a terrible scream.

I just sat there, and after a few seconds I let go of the arm I was still holding. The girl slumped on the couch, still and dead, and we were alone with the silence and Esther's awful cries.

# CHAPTER SEVEN

At first I thought they were burying us, but it was just a hole in the ground. Everywhere they went, I learned later, in every camp they made, they dug cells for their rapists and murderers, twelve feet deep on the outskirts of the tents. If the crime was heinous enough, sometimes they'd just leave people there when they moved, their cries fading against the empty hills.

For a while, I thought that was what they were going to do to us. Then I thought they were just going to kill us outright. Then I didn't know anymore.

They'd separated me from Marian in the tent, and I had no idea where she was. I cried out her name and heard no answer. I was alone in the pit. I stayed awake for three nights, clutching a shard of rock I'd prised from the walls of my cell, waiting for Esther to descend on me in the night. If the woman who had stopped time had come to me again, I would have stabbed her too. She had lied. She had given me a spell to kill the girl and told me it would heal her. It was *her* fault the girl had died, not ours. Not that Esther would believe me, if I told her that.

The camp seemed oddly quiet. Guilt and terror ate away at me until I threw up in the dirt. Then I just sat, watching and waiting.

A couple of times a day the guards would throw down a flask of water or a hunk of bread. My heart sank the first time: it meant they were keeping us alive for some worse punishment, and whatever that was, it would certainly be worse than starvation. I ate the food anyway. I was twelve years old, and witchling's girl or not, I still feared death.

I got used to the rhythms of the camp, the soft whispers and sharp cries of night, the rough shouts and metallic clashes of daylight. They were training, this army, even now, with the war over. They were bored and restless. I think I knew then that there would be another war. You could not send people like this back to their old lives, on boats and in fields, and expect them to forget what they had become out here. An army this large would demand another country to chew and spit out again.

Once, many years later, Adrienne asked me why lords started wars. They were the best souls humanity had borne, after all; they had been judged worthy and sent to the world above, and then they had given up eternity in that paradise to return and do good here. And yet Claire and Jonathan had ended with empires at their feet, and in command of wars burning in foreign hills. Why had they let their children do this, in their names?

If someone had asked me that question then – when I was twelve years old and waiting to die in a pit on the orders of a lord – I would not have had an answer. Now I am older and more cynical, and I understand. I remember the empty eyes of the Lord Claire in her carriage. You would fade, I think, after six hundred years. You would grow bored of the world – of miracles, of alleviating pain with a touch. You would be worn to exhaustion by love and grief, watching your children, your friends, your lovers, grow old and die before you, until eventually you stopped feeling anything at all. You would stop, and the world would simply pass before your eyes. You would fade away. And then how would it concern you if your descendants, their hearts corrupted by privilege and worship, started wars and conquered lands in your name? What could you do about it with your heart burned away?

You would not care anymore, if they used you to feed their mortal hungers and vices. You would turn away, and close your ears, and try to sleep.

I never saw the Lord Jonathan. I heard later he spent the war away from the frontline, watching as his sons and grand-daughters and great-grandchildren gave orders. He was thin and frail and motionless, and he never spoke a word.

I told Adrienne: if you end up in paradise, sweetheart, never come back.

At night in my cell, I heard the voices of those who guarded me and learned to recognise them. Two men, a younger and a woman. It astonished me that they even kept a guard on my cell. Did they think I could climb up twelve feet of solid earth? What did they think witchlings were?

Sometimes, in the dark, I thought I saw the glint of their eyes peering down at me. Maybe that was just sleep-deprived delirium. I don't know.

After those three first days I could no longer stay awake, so I curled up on the cold earth and prayed that it would not rain. Marian and I had treated the kinds of sicknesses that came from exposure; it was a terrible way to die. I prayed to my Lord Claire, but when I closed my eyes I saw Cora inside my head, her terrible stillness. I thought I could still feel the flutter of the spell inside me, beneath my heart. I had been so stupid. Her wrist, in my hand—

And the woman. The woman who had stopped time.

I did not understand her. Time was not a viscous liquid to be thickened and slowed. Marian had once mentioned that in the higher and lower worlds, time moved differently. Was the woman a lord, then? She had not looked like one. I had seen Claire in her carriage, beautiful, chiselled and cold. This woman had been beautiful, too, but strange and unholy.

She made me kill the girl. Fury and hurt welled inside me, although I did not understand why it felt like a betrayal. The woman was a stranger, and owed no loyalty to me. But she had stopped time to come to me as if in a dream, and because of that, I had trusted her. I had felt special, chosen.

I had been so naïve. Not for the first time, I ached to be grown up. Childhood had never helped me – it had made me helpless cargo, property to be traded and delivered. And now it had put me here, in this pit. Because I had trusted too easily.

I sat in the dirt, staring up at the sky, clutching my sharp rock. Day blurred to night, voices rose and fell like waves, hunger throbbed insistently in my stomach. I could not tell if I was awake or asleep. I lived in a miasma of cold and anger and fear. The only thing I can remember thinking clearly is: the girl had been dying anyway. If the woman had simply wanted the girl dead, all she had needed to do was wait. The spell hadn't just killed her. It must have done something else, too.

'Haley.'

I awoke slowly. My mouth felt full of dirt and I ached everywhere. I was curled up in the pit. The stone dug sharply into the inside of my clenched fist, but I did not open my hand.

It took me a few moments to realise that someone was crouching over me.

'Haley. Come on.'

The voice settled into the base of my stomach. Marian.

I scrambled up, breathing fast. She was next to me, grey-eyed and sombre, the lines on her face deeper, but she was unharmed. I stared at her. I had thought she was dead, that if I was alive they must surely have killed her. I wanted to collapse, to cry out with joy and relief, but I knew we were being watched. It was not over. I could not show weakness yet.

'Haley. Come on. We have to go.'

The words took a long time to make sense in my head. 'We can go?'

'Yes. They have a cart for us.'

I just looked at her. There was no relief in her face. I did not believe it.

There was a rope ladder dangling into the pit. Marian climbed up first – the better, I think, to protect me if Esther was waiting at the top with a knife. It was just dawn, or dusk; it took me a while to work out which. The hills were east of the town, and so west of us, and the sun nestled in them, white and blind like a corpse's eye. Dusk then, yes. The light was fading.

The soldiers remained expressionless as they loaded us into the waiting cart. With a shock I realised that Emlyn, Cora's betrothed, was holding the reins. He kept his eyes fixed on the horses as they snorted and stamped at the ground, and did not look at me. I wondered where we were going. Surely they would not allow us to go home after we had let the girl die.

The camp was oddly quiet as we rode through it, with the five of Esther's soldiers who had brought us here in the back of the cart. It felt like we were the only ones awake, and I recognised the heavy blanketing silence of mourning.

We juddered towards the hills until at last the cart pulled north, out of the way, and I thought: at last, the trick. I had an odd feeling of relief. But it was only to take us past the headstone. Esther must have ordered it.

The place was quiet, on the riverbank at the outskirts of the camp, and the stone was beautifully carved, and bore her name. I have never seen a memorial site so covered in flowers in my life. I thought, surely they can't actually have *buried* her there. The idea was barbaric. They must have given her body to another witchling, to take down to the underworld. But how? There was only one entrance to the underworld within twenty miles of here, the one our House of the Dead was built over. The whole town was built around it.

So where had they taken Cora? Back to her home country, to the witchling who had delivered her? The thought was oddly comforting. If she was far away, I wouldn't have to see her dead face ever again.

The hills swallowed us, and everything became a shadow in the shiver of the twilight wind. I watched Marian's face, impassive in the thin light, and clutched the side of the cart for strength, and waited.

Then the hills gave way, and at last I could see the town again. Firelight was just sparking in its windows, gold and green in the fading sun. I had never loved my town so much. I wondered who had fallen ill in our absence, who had died. They would be so angry with us. And what would we say to them? That we had been taken to help the enemy, and had failed?

They would like that, at least, that Cora had died.

The thought unsettled me. Marian had taught me, long ago, that there was sanctity in death. It was to be treated with respect, but not reverence. There should be no pleasure in it, no victory. I thought of the woman who had stopped time, with the now-familiar wince of fury and guilt. She had pursued the girl's death, but she had seemed to take no joy in it.

The horses crossed the bridge and we turned left towards the House of the Dead. I knew the town was watching us from their windows and I lowered my head. Shame overtook me suddenly. I could not look at Marian or the soldiers beside me.

The cart stopped.

'Get out,' said Emlyn. Something had changed in his voice, deadened it. I looked up. We were in front of the House of the Dead.

Marian did not move. She was looking at him. 'Are you leaving us here?'

'Get out,' he said.

Marian looked at each of them in turn, then slowly got out of the cart.

'Your girl, too.'

I looked to Marian. After a moment she nodded, and I climbed down to stand beside her.

The soldier gestured to the door. 'Go in.'

'Are you coming after us?'

'No,' he said. 'You're home now.'

There is a reason you have to knock to enter the House of the Dead. There is old magic in the door, runes carved into the ancient wood that called to the tattoos on Marian's arms. I did not have marks then, but the house knew who I was, and if Marian was inside, the door would usually open for me without her having to answer it. Nobody else could open it without the witchling's permission. That was why the grieving brother, five years beforehand, had broken in through the window. The soldiers would have done that too in the end, I think, if Marian had refused to let them in. She knew there was no point in resisting.

She looked between them, and nobody moved. Their hands were on the hilts of their swords.

At last she pressed her hand to the door and it swung open. I could see the grief already in her face.

They divided at once. Two soldiers grabbed Marian and threw her to her knees; another two strode inside the house. One seized me, though I screamed and fought to escape. I could feel her arms tightening around my chest, suffocating me, and I believed for a second she was going to kill me. I thought of the grieving brother, long ago, and my mind went blank with terror.

Only Emlyn remained. He was very calm, and his face was expressionless. He took a flask of blood-ink from the crate of our supplies in the cart, and smashed it over Marian's head.

She did not cry out, but I did. Shards of glass glinted in her hair and blood-ink trickled down her face. There were dark, open lacerations in her forehead and cheeks, and new, bright blood in with the old. I watched in horror as she lay curled where they had thrown her, knees pressed against her chin, her hands over her head, trying to protect herself. They pulled her out of that position, Emlyn taking one of her arms to stretch her out on the ground. He stomped on her hand when she tried to put it over her face. I heard the sickening crunch of bone, and at last she screamed.

The other soldiers came out of the House of the Dead, carrying books from Marian's shelves. They had raided the parlour, too, taken all of our herbs and inks and essences, and they smashed them over the books. I watched a year's worth of distilled rue soak into *On the Development of the Infant Skull*.

They had ripped a branch from the ancient tree that grew around the house, and as I watched they dipped it in our phosphor, lit it with flint, and dropped it onto the pile of books. It caught it at once. I saw Marian's face in the greenish firelight. There were many kinds of pain there, and old grief. She cradled her shattered hand against her chest.

'You let her die,' said the soldier who had broken her hand. His voice was cold and empty, and there was no pity in it. 'You killed her.'

Marian looked up at him. *You let her die!* I wondered how many times she must have heard those words.

'Don't kill Haley,' she whispered. Her voice was hoarse with smoke. 'Please. Don't hurt Haley.'

They started kicking her, all five of them. She curled up, crying out when her bones cracked under their blows, falling silent when the agony rose beyond the reach of her voice. I was half out of my mind, struggling as hard as I could against the woman holding me, barely aware of my own sobbing. I could feel the pale lake of death at the base of my skull but could not reach it; it was beyond me, hidden beneath pain and panic. The terrified child in me overwhelmed the witchling. I hated myself for that, afterwards.

The other soldier kept me crushed against her. I screamed and swore and kicked at her knees, trying to break them. The smoke was in my eyes, in my throat, and I choked on my sobs. All I could see was Marian, the way she held herself, and the blood staining her shirt. The light going out of her eyes with the last blow to her head.

They did not lay a hand on me. For reasons known only to themselves they had decided that the town was valuable enough not to burn, and that meant they needed me alive to care for its people, if they killed Marian. The brutality of that, the cold calculation of it.

I wanted them to hurt me. I wanted with all my heart to suffer with her, to fight and be kicked apart and die with her. I could not bear the sight of her being broken while I was trapped and unharmed. I screamed and kicked and wished a thousand deaths on the woman holding me, but she did not hit me, and she did not let me go.

Eventually, after minutes or years, it ended. They grew tired of beating her, and then everything grew quiet but for the crackling of the flames. I knew people were watching from windows of the surrounding houses, but nobody came out to help us. They were too frightened.

The woman released me at last, and I collapsed, sobbing, as they filed into the cart. I considered running after them, killing them all one by one. Emlyn first, with his empty dark eyes. I would find a knife somewhere.

But no, Marian. Marian needed me.

They had left her there covered in blood, half-dead in the ash and the smoke. They did not burn down the house, though they could have done; they needed it unharmed too, for the town. They had thought this all through very carefully.

I ran to Marian and knelt beside her as the cart trundled off into the distance. I pushed her hair from her face and pressed my fingers into her neck for the slow beat of her heart. She was unconscious, her mouth slightly open, blood trickling into her eyes. Her grey hair was matted with it. They had broken her left hand and most of her ribs, and her left leg bent horribly in two places; who knew what kind of internal injury they had inflicted. I was breathless at the sight of it all. I had seen corpses less badly damaged than this. She could easily have been dead.

But she was still breathing.

I felt her kneeling beside me, spectral as my mother. *What would you do if I weren't here?*

I closed my eyes and tried to breathe with her.

The first thing I did was to take her inside. I had to haul her onto a bed sheet and pull her along the floor as carefully as I could. By the way her chest folded in on itself, I knew I was worsening the damage to her ribs, but there was no helping that; she would die out there in the cold, and there was no one to help me carry her. Her blood smeared across the varnished wood of the hallway.

I laid her down on the floor of the kitchen, like we did with all our patients. Then I stood in the wreckage of the house. Ruined books lay scattered across the floor in piles of broken glass. All her hard work destroyed.

I went to the door and closed it. There was no one coming to help me. I breathed out, trembling.

Everything was quiet. The sound of the soldiers' cart had long faded. I could already feel the bruises of the woman's grip across my arms and my chest. I stood for a moment with my forehead pressed against the cold wood and felt the magic thrumming gently through the door. I tried to put myself into it, imagining Esther's face, the soldiers', the camp. I said to the house, *Don't let them come back. Don't let them come in, please. Help me keep her safe.*

I waited for an answer, but none came.

I went back to Marian.

I had barely slept or eaten in a week, and the emptiness in my body silenced any panicked thoughts. I was very calm; the world was two steps away, unreal. I moved slowly and deliberately in the darkness of the house. Without supplies, I was helpless. I put away the remaining books, first, and cleared away the glass; Marian would never have allowed the kitchen to be so filthy when she was treating a patient in it. I lit the gas lamps and the fire. Everything had the too-quiet, stark air of midnight, and I thought again of the night Elior had died.

They had not burned our bandages, and for that I was grateful. I cleaned the blood from her skin, set her broken bones and bound the cuts made by boots and broken glass. For the deeper wounds I had no remedy. Marian might have used magic to seal the set bones and stop the internal bleeding, but I had no runes of my own yet; she always said I was too young. All I could do was pray, and hope desperately that whatever witchling-magic I had would seep into her, like it had when I had resurrected the cat, and knit her flesh together somehow. I did not know if that was possible. I did not know anything.

It occurred to me that if she died, I would have to carry her down to the underworld, to watch her be ripped apart by monsters. She would not want to be resurrected. I knew that for certain. But I had no marks to protect me from the underworld, and what lay beneath the trapdoor in the basement would kill me. *It will eat you alive,* she had said. At that moment I was not entirely sure I cared.

She breathed slowly and gently, her chest not quite moving. I watched her in the silence.

After perhaps a quarter of an hour, I went to the parlour with a torch and found a crate in a corner, full of things so commonplace the soldiers hadn't bothered to burn them: a bundle of sage and rosemary, a lemon, a half-empty jar of honey. I burned the herbs in the grate, breathing more easily in the familiar smoke. I dissolved the honey in hot water and poured it carefully down Marian's throat, thinking it might strengthen her. I did not dare try to drag her upstairs, but I brought the pillow and blankets down from her bed, and wrapped her in them.

By then it was almost dawn. I put out the torches but not the fire. I sat in my chair at the kitchen table, watching her breathe. I kept thinking, *This one's going to be the last one*, but her chest kept rising and falling, slower and weaker with every breath. Second by second, she stilled.

I felt lightheaded. I was back in the pit again, half-gone from my body, drifting in terror and guilt. There were a thousand voices in the silence of the room, and Marian's breathing was hoarse and rasping, the rattle that traced the slow descent to death. The air swam around me. Cora rose from the varnished floorboards, pointing her finger into my face, saying in the voice of the grieving brother, *You let her die!* Esther was kneeling above me, smashing my head into the floor, while my mother stood by and watched, holding the baby. I knelt beside my barred window and stared as the strange woman with ice-blue eyes walked into the darkness of the alleyway, and then turned around and saw the dead cat on my bedroom floor, who blinked at me and said, *Please, don't hurt Haley—*

I woke suddenly. I had slid onto the floor and was lying beside Marian, my hand on her wrist, feeling her fading pulse beneath my fingers.

The fire had gone out. The air was clearer, and through the windows I could see that night had fallen again.

Slowly, I got to my feet. My thoughts were sharper now. I was possessed of a slow, glassy certainty, like the night I had tried to escape. I pulled the blanket over Marian's shoulders and lit the fire again, so she wouldn't grow cold. We were almost out of wood, too.

I pulled on my coat and walked out into the darkness, and after a few minutes I reached the bridge, where the woman with ice-blue eyes sat waiting for me.

The starlight glittered off the water, and as I came closer I saw her silhouette crouched beneath the statue I had climbed to watch Claire's carriage cross the river. She got to her feet when she saw me. I could see the knife she had been cleaning in her left hand.

For a moment we just looked at each other. I spoke quietly, so my voice would not carry to the surrounding houses.

'Who are you?'

She seemed unsure how to answer. 'Leah,' she said finally.

'Leah?'

'Yes.'

A silence.

'I'm Haley.'

'I know.'

Another, longer silence.

'What did you do? When you talked to me before?'

'What do you think I did?'

I was so sick of being taught, of being tested and guided. My voice cracked. 'Just tell me.'

She looked me up and down so swiftly I almost didn't see it.

'I slowed time,' she said. 'Or I . . . made it look like I had. I needed to talk to you without being seen.'

'How did you do that?'

'Magic,' she said, as though it were obvious. Which, in fairness, it was.

She wore the same leather jacket, breeches and boots that covered her skin perfectly, without gaps or seams. I knew again, through the same quiet well of intuition that had led me here, that they concealed tattoos like Marian's, carved with a hot knife and darkened with blood-ink. Runes that controlled and directed the magic of the woman who bore them.

'Are you a witchling?'

The woman shook her head slowly and said nothing.

'Are you lying? Don't lie to me.'

She just watched me. I was suddenly very aware of my own childishness, the high-pitched ridiculousness of my anger. I was smaller than her, alone in the darkness, and she had a knife and magic unknown to me. Why was I trying to threaten her? What good would it do?

'No,' said Leah evenly, at last. 'I'm not a witchling.'

She was not human, either. That was obvious. She was too unearthly, ethereal – but too warm and solid to be a lord, either. There was colour in her cheeks, and her hands were callused. She did not make sense. But Marian was dying, so I cut to the essentials.

'Can you heal people?'

'In theory.'

My heart sank. 'You've never healed anyone?'

'I know how to. I know the spells.'

It was better than nothing, better than anything I could do. I tried to moderate my tone, to make it plaintive, humble. 'Will you come with me? Please?'

'Who's been hurt?'

I stared at her. 'Marian. The witchling. Because of the girl you killed.'

It came out more accusatorily than I had meant it to, but she did not seem angry.

'She was dying anyway.'

'Then why did you make me kill her?'

'Because if she'd died like that . . .' She trailed off, lost. At last she found the words. 'She would have hurt other people too.'

'*How?*'

She shook her head. 'You wouldn't understand.'

Fury flared in me, and despite myself I snapped at her. 'Stop saying that. Stop it. I *would*.'

Leah studied me, infuriatingly calm. I was angry enough to hit her. And then at once, in a lightheaded rush, I remembered where I'd seen her before.

'You came to our house. After Elior died.'

She was quite still. Then she nodded, slowly.

I stepped forward, suddenly excited. 'The sickness. You know what it is. It killed Elior. It was killing the girl.'

She did not move.

'You know what it is. *Tell me.*'

Silence. She folded her arms.

I took a deep breath. I had a thousand questions, each more urgent than the last, but before I could speak, Leah said, 'Take me to the witchling.'

'Elior—'

Leah was suddenly sharp. 'You want her healed? Take me to her.'

I knew that steel. I had heard it in Marian's voice. I hesitated for a moment, thinking of the camp, of the way Leah had slowed time, of her impossible magic. I wanted so much to be angry, to stand my ground. But I held my tongue. If she was Marian's only chance of survival, I was not going to push her away. I gathered myself, and then turned back towards the town.

She walked slightly ahead of me, moving at the turnings before I did, and reached the house three seconds before me. I broke into a run, thinking that the door would not open for her, but when she laid her palm upon it it swung inwards at once.

I stopped in the doorway, panting, staring after her. I felt the magic thrumming in the house. It knew her as it knew me. If she was not a witchling, she was something like it.

She moved through the hallway without hesitation, and I followed her to the parlour and the dying fire. Marian seemed so small, wrapped in the blankets from her bed, barely breathing. Leah winced at the sight of her. Her chest still looked wrong; you could see the bulges of splintered bone beneath the skin, the horror of the bruised flesh.

'Can you help?' My voice echoed strangely in the silence of the house.

Leah studied Marian, running her fingertips over the broken bones so gently that the skin did not yield at her touch. At last she looked up at me.

'I'm not allowed to heal the living,' she said. 'By law.'

'What law?'

She did not answer that, just ran a hand across her forehead and stared at Marian.

'I can give you a spell,' she said finally. 'But you have to wait until I'm gone to use it. Do you understand? And you can't follow me.'

I scrambled to my feet at once. 'No,' I said. 'Not a spell. Not again.' I remembered how the death-spell had felt, lodged underneath my heart, prickling as it fluttered down the nerves of my arm. 'Some other way.'

Leah sat up on her knees and looked up at me. 'Listen to me, Haley,' she said. 'I promise I won't hurt her.'

'Oh yeah?'

'Yes.'

We stared at each other across Marian's body.

Leah ran her tongue over her teeth. 'The girl had to die,' she said, 'because she was possessed.'

I did not understand; for a second I did not even recognise the word. 'Possessed?'

'Possessed.'

'By what?'

'By a ghost,' said Leah.

I stared at her, then shook my head uncertainly. 'Ghosts are in the underworld.'

'Not always,' she said. 'Sometimes, they escape.'

This settled over me for a moment, but I shook it away before the implications of it could touch me. 'No, they don't,' I said, as if by denying it I could shake her surety. 'They can't.'

'They escape,' said Leah relentlessly, holding my eyes, 'but they can't last long up here, in the living world. They dissipate, and they're destroyed. So they find a living body to crawl into and hide. But there's already a ghost in there, the living person's ghost, and there's not room for both of them in one body. They fight. Sometimes they're both destroyed. Sometimes one overwhelms the other.'

I just looked at her. I did not know what to say, how to prove to her that what she was saying could not be true. She had taken off her gloves and laid them carefully on the wooden floor beside Marian's head. Her hands were covered in intricate, black-line tattoos. She moved them gently over Marian, an inch above her skin, and I thought I saw a shimmer in the air between them. She kept talking, not looking up at me.

'Whatever happens, the body starts to fail. There are seizures, and then death. But if the person dies with both ghosts trapped in it, then they'll both be released when the body is taken down to the underworld. If the escaped ghost is intact, and escapes again, someone else will die.' She looked up at me at last. 'You have to scour the ghost from the body, while it's still alive. In the underworld it's impossible to destroy, but in the living world, in a body, it's weak. You have to get rid of it then, before it can possess anyone else. Once the body dies, the ghost goes back to the underworld, and you can't touch it till it comes back up.' She glanced at me. 'There was a boy who died here – well. I suppose you remember. But I got here too late for that.'

It took me a while to find the words. 'So that's what your spell did? To the girl?'

'That's what it did.'

'It destroyed the evil ghost. The one that possessed her.'

Leah looked back down at Marian. 'It destroyed them both,' she said. 'It couldn't tell them apart. There was no other way.'

I could not speak. I thought of Esther, many miles east now, carrying Cora's body back across the sea to the witchling who had birthed her. Believing that she was giving her child an afterlife, unaware that it was impossible now. All trace of her daughter was gone forever, obliterated from the worlds. It was an act far more terrible than murder. And but for a few hours' delay she would have done the same to Elior. I remembered Michael's horror, his sobs through the floor-boards. At least he had the comfort of knowing some part of his son still lived, in the world beneath the earth.

'She was already too far gone,' said Leah. 'I heard them talking. She didn't know her own mother anymore. The other ghost had . . . strangled her. There was barely anything left. I just finished her off.' She looked up at me. 'It was mercy. You don't understand that, but you will.'

I just stared at her, gripped by a horror too deep to voice.

Leah sighed, got up and went to the kitchen. I heard the rattling boil of water in the kettle, though I had not put it anywhere near the fire, and she came back a minute later with a steaming mug. She handed it to me. I peered into it and saw only dark water.

'What's in it?' I spoke hesitantly. I was terrified now of this cold woman who wiped ghosts from the worlds and moulded time.

'The spell,' said Leah. 'I put it in the hot water, instead of in you. Make her drink that, every drop of it. *After* I'm gone. I can't have this tied to me, you understand?'

'Or what?'

She pulled her gloves back on and did not look at me. I sniffed the steam suspiciously. 'There's nothing in it.'

'There is.'

'But it doesn't smell of—'

'Herbs and spices,' said Leah, with a flicker of contempt, 'are for your kind. True magic doesn't rely on *leaves.*'

She glanced up at me, and smiled a little tiredly at my expression.

'What do you mean *true magic?* What are you?'

She tilted my chin, then took her gloved hand away and considered me. For an instant she looked younger – less certain, less callous, more *human.*

'Come on, kid,' she said softly. 'You're clever. You can work it out.'

I stood there staring. She turned in a sweep of leather and strode down the hall.

'Wait,' I called, 'no, *wait*—' I had to put the steaming mug carefully on the table and make sure it was completely stable before I could run after her.

The lock on the front door clicked shut as I drew level with the stairs. I pulled it open and stared down the street, but it was completely empty, the darkness thick and still. The shadows had eaten her alive, and I was alone again.

# CHAPTER EIGHT

Let me tell you Marian's story, which I did not find out in its entirety until much later.

She was born to a fisherman who lived three miles out from the edge of town, where the river widens and teems with salmon and trout. She was the eldest of seven, and most of her life was taken up with the care of the little ones, especially after her mother died giving birth to the youngest. She died in the House of the Dead when Marian was ten. Marian watched the witchling try to save her and fail.

The witchling at that time was called Dora, and she was already forty years old by then. Marian was haunted later by the slowness of the woman's movements, her sluggish reflexes. Her mother could have lived, Marian knew, if the witchling had been younger, cleverer, more devoted to her craft. But Dora was worn out and growing lazy, six years out from death, and had no girl to inherit from her. The air of the town was thick with worry. If she died without an heir they would all be cursed to oblivion.

After her mother died, Marian began to feel the gift of death-magic stir inside her, drawn to the stillness of dead bodies, itching to try to raise them. But she was cleverer than me, and hid it well. She was determined not be taken to the witchling – without her, the babies would be left alone, with their father and his sudden rages. She had to stay, and take care of them.

By the time she Marian was fourteen, it had become clear to

everyone that Dora was dying, and the town's gaze sharpened. There were searches, examinations of every child under ten. No one, they were sure, could hide their gift longer than that.

Marian kept quiet. She snuck out at night, crossed the river to the woods, stirred dead foxes and deer into milky-eyed life again. She felt brilliant, alive. Once the babies were older and safe, she would run away, far from this dying town, and become something wonderful – she did not know what yet – a travelling magician, a scholar in the Lord Claire's city in the north. A woman of power and ambition. Surely, if you could raise the dead, everyone would want you to be theirs.

Behind her, a boy was waiting in the reeds by the river, watching.

One night he revealed himself. He was older than her, with a slow smile. I know what you can do, he said. I know what you are.

No you don't, said Marian, but already she was panicking. If he said anything, Dora would take her and the babies would be left alone.

Bet the witchling would love to know about you, said the boy. Bet *everyone* would love to know. D'you want me to tell them?

No, said Marian quickly. No. You can't.

Can, said the boy softly. Will.

A silence.

What do you want? said Marian.

He wanted the obvious thing. Night after night he came and took it, holding her down, his hand over her mouth. The price of his silence. Marian saw him in the village when she went there with her father. He was the woodcutter's son, the youngest of five strong brothers. When he saw her, he smiled and raised a finger to his lips. Marian hated him with a trembling, violent loathing. When evening drew in, she had to ball her fists to stop shaking.

Her eldest brother Aron, a boy of thirteen, saw her grow sallow and thin. He asked her what was wrong, and when she could not tell him, he held her as she sobbed.

That night, she waited until he was asleep and went out to the river again. She had no choice. She could not lose him and the babies. If she became the witchling's girl, she would never see them again.

By the time she felt the child begin to grow inside her, she had become so thin she could not hide it. Her father asked questions. She claimed sickness, and with a heavy heart and churning stomach, she went to the witchling.

Dora gave her iris and rue and sent her home to bleed. But the witchling was old and bleary-eyed, and her treatment was imperfect. Marian bled for days, until her lips turned blue and she was grey and delirious. Her brother Aron, terrified, carried her back to the House of the Dead and said, Please, help.

The woodcutter's son grew angry when Marian did not appear that night by the river. He went to her house, as he had promised; he was a man of his word. Your daughter's a monster, he said to Marian's father. She wants you to die and rot in your corpse. She's lied to you.

Marian's father flew into a rage, as the woodcutter's son had known he would. Under the boy's satisfied gaze, he left the babies alone in the house and ran to the House of the Dead, a bottle in his hand, and hammered on the door. Dora refused to let him in; she knew him and his furies.

My daughter's a bitch, he yelled through the window. Give her back to me, let me deal with her.

You will not harm her in this house, said Dora. What has she done?

He told her all that the woodcutter's son had told him. Dora listened calmly, and then went back into the room where Marian lay. Her bleeding had stopped, and some of the colour had returned to her. Aron stood when she entered. Is she going to be all right? he said. She looks better.

Dora looked at Marian for a long time, and Marian understood and laid her head back on the pillow. She held Aron's hand, so tightly it hurt, and Aron looked between her and Dora in bewilderment and said, Mari? What's wrong? What's going on?

She's going to be fine, said Dora. You have to go now, son. She's not your sister anymore.

Ten years later, when Dora was dead and Marian was the witchling, a woman of around thirty knocked on the door in great distress. You have to come, she said. My husband's horse kicked him in the chest. Please, he's hurt.

Marian followed her to the edge of the town and into a small house where the woman lived with her husband and two young sons. Marian looked at them. Eight and six, she thought, not *too* young. If he dies they will survive. Then she examined the injured man.

The woodcutter's son had aged much more than she had, despite her calling. His hair was gone and drink had worn lines into his flushed cheeks. The horse had broken five of his ribs and he was coughing up blood. When he saw her, his eyes widened, but he could not speak.

Bring him to my house, Marian said. I will do what I can for him.

They carried him in a cart to the House of the Dead. After his family left she lay him down on the kitchen floor and locked the door, and they were alone together for the first time since the riverbank. His eyes followed her around the room. She sat down on the chair and watched him. She watched him for hours.

The ribs had punctured his lungs and his breaths were rattling and agonised. He stared at her, pleading with his eyes.

Are you expecting me to talk to you? she said. What do you think I'd want to say?

His throat was full of blood and he could not reply.

After another hour or so, when it became apparent he was not near death, she went into the kitchen and made tea. Drink, she said, and poured it down his throat. He tried to refuse and it splashed over his face. He howled when it burned him. Drink, she said again, and after that he did.

She had poured a whole vial of laudanum into the tea and he was dead in an hour.

She gave him the rites, called his wife and sons to weep by his side, carved the runes of protection into his skin with smoke and blood-ink, and carried him down to the underworld. She was a woman of honour, and merciful. But it's like she said to me. Some things cannot be saved.

By morning Marian's bones had righted themselves, and the twisted red bulges in her skin had smoothed over. It took another two days for the deep-black bruises to blossom, yellow and fade, and another three for her colour to fully return. I left the house maybe twice in that whole week. I was manic. At first I was terrified that it was another trick, that Leah was using me for another murder; that this spell was a slower-acting version of the last, and that at any moment Marian was going to take a slow rattling breath and go terribly still. And this time it would be my fault entirely, for entrusting her life to a known murderer. I would never have forgiven myself.

But the hours passed, and kept passing, and I saw strength begin to return to her. I could see her moving up through layers of unconsciousness, from the murky cold waters that preceded death to the gentle mist of living sleep. I breathed more easily.

I took nothing for granted. I slept beside her every night, and dripped water and honey down her throat. I learned exactly, without the muffle of a wall between us, the cadences of her breathing. Her silences began to wake me, and I lay there, listening with my heartbeat in my ears, until I heard her move. If she didn't, I would take her wrist and feel for her pulse. If she died now I would not bear it. My time in the pit had made me quietly, unshakeably certain of it. I could not live alone in this house, a twelve-year-old witchling, without her to guide me. Her death would break me, and then the town would be doomed.

Every cart, every noise outside frightened me. I thought Esther was trying to trick us – three days' reprieve, until the soldiers came back to drive a sword through Marian's heart. I was sleepless, always on guard; and when, at dawn on the fourth day, someone rapped on the door, I almost did not answer it. But I knew Marian would not have been afraid, and that was what made me at last haul myself to my feet.

I climbed down the stairs warily and opened the door a crack, then swung it back further when I saw it was Ira.

'Haley,' she said. I was slightly surprised; I hadn't realised she knew my name. I was used to being just *the witchling's girl,* or occasionally *that damn child* when I got under people's feet at market. I hadn't been Haley to anyone but Marian for years.

I let her in and offered her a seat at the table. I had no tea to give her. There was food somewhere in the parlour, a couple of salted joints and some stale bread and cheese, but I needed those for Marian and me. Ira looked concerned. I can only imagine how I looked, exhausted and still grime-coated from days in the pit.

'What do you need?' I tried to use Marian's patient-voice, at once brisk and reassuring. I knew all the voices she used when people came to see her. I had sat in the corner and watched this happen a thousand times. Sitting in her chair instead of my own was a strange, slightly out-of-body experience.

Ira, of course, ignored this completely. 'Haley, what *happened* to you?'

'Nothing,' I said, too quickly. Ira ignored this too. It occurred to me that I was younger than most of her children.

'They took you away in a cart.'

'We didn't want to go—'

'I know that, Haley. Where's Marian?'

I hesitated again, and Ira looked suddenly scared. 'Haley, she's not—'

'She's not dead. I—' I didn't know what to say, how to explain it all: Cora, Esther, Leah, the terrible swell of Marian's shattered chest. 'She's ill. She's getting better. She'll be all right.'

Ira looked at me searchingly for a moment. I was almost indignant – did she think I would lie to her about something like this? At last she looked away, up at the ceiling.

'She's getting better?'

'Yes,' I said, earnestly. I needed her to believe me.

Ira pursed her lips and nodded. Then she looked around at the empty room – the books missing from the shelves, the stained floor where the soldiers had smashed bottles of our essences on the varnished wood. I had scrubbed at them for hours, but could not get the marks out.

'Listen,' I said, hastily, so that Ira was forced to look back at me, 'what did you come here for?'

'Michael's medicine,' she said. 'But you don't have it.'

It was not a question. She could see the empty cupboards, the open drawers. Michael needed medicine every month, to slow the rot that was consuming his body. I cursed myself for forgetting that. Some part of me had believed that the world would stop needing things from us while Marian was healing.

Ira got to her feet. 'Right,' she said briskly. 'What do you need?'

I stared at her. 'What?'

'I've seen you at market. You need things. Herbs, and plants, and – no, what am I thinking, you need *food*, child, you'll starve to death. Give me a list.'

'No, I—' The things we used were secrets of the witchling's arts, and I could not give them away, not to anyone, not even to Ira. 'I can get it. Give me a day—'

'No, you can't. You need to stay and look after her. Give me a list, and I'll go to market.'

Panic rose in me. I was shaking; exhaustion was clouding my brain again. 'I can't – you don't have any money.'

She put her hand on my shoulder, and I almost flinched away.

'Haley. No one will ask for money if I tell them it's for the witchling. They'll understand.' She saw my face, and her expression softened. 'I don't know what Marian's told you, but you can't do everything yourself. No one's going to hurt you. Tell me what you need.'

*No one's going to hurt you.* I thought of Cora and her last rattling breath; Marian and her slow healing; Leah and her quick smile. I took a slow, steadying breath. This was Ira, kind and firm, whose son I had held as he died. I could trust Ira.

'You won't tell anyone? You won't give anyone the list?'

'On my life,' said Ira gently.

I nodded slowly, and then when the silence stretched into long seconds I turned and walked into the kitchen to search the empty drawers for pen and paper.

Ira was the second person I ever trusted. By the time I died, there were five.

In the depths of that winter, the eldest living son of the Lord Jonathan emerged into the sunlight from his palace, in the great city to the north where our Lord Claire had lived until she was murdered, and declared that the war was not over. His army would march west and further west, to the edge of the known world, and conquer all in its path. They would follow the slow track of the sun to the place where it dropped into the sea, so that everyone who lived in its light would know Jonathan's name and worship him and his children. Their scholars and holy men had found new maps and signs from the stars that promised a land across the unknown ocean, full of rich dark soil and plentiful cattle and endless summer, a paradise that would make our country seem shrivelled and barren by comparison. The glorious land across the sea had few inhabitants, they told us. The war there would be quick. But there would still be a war.

Of course, that meant conscription. That was why they had not burned our town when Cora had died: they needed us to die a thousand miles away, sacrificed to their depthless hunger. We were their soldiers now.

This news filtered slowly south to our town and caused a soft, despairing quiet to settle over the streets for at least a week. There was little true resistance, though. One young man attacked a soldier in Jonathan's army, crying a prayer to the Lord Claire, and was hung from the court entrance three days later with a thin steel wire. A woman who had kept a shrine to the dead lord was reported to Jonathan's men by her own husband, out of fear of what would happen to him and their children if it was found in their house. They took her from her house in the night and we never saw her again.

The only useful consequence of the new war was that the army camp on the other side of the hills packed up and marched west as soon as it could, in the first shivering light of spring, leaving a force of a couple of dozen men to watch over our town. None of them were the soldiers who had almost killed Marian, for which I was deeply thankful. It might have taken months or years, but one day one of them would have fallen sick and been brought to our house, and then I would have killed them. And what would have happened to me then, after I died? Those soldiers weren't worth an eternity in the world of the damned. So I told myself, but still sometimes at night I would wake from a dream of smoke and crushed bone, and lie in bed burning with helpless rage. I wished they were in front of me so I could tear out their throats, instead of miles west across unreachable mountains, gone to conquer the world.

Marian never knew how close she had come to dying that night. Most of the damage had been done after she had been knocked unconscious, so she had no way of knowing that her ribs had been broken and her lungs torn, that she had almost bled to death. Leah's spell had left no scars, and when the opportunity came, I could not bring myself to tell her. I said she had been concussed and weak, and that she had woken many times in the days after, spoken slurringly, and fallen asleep again. I knew what concussion looked like; I could feign the signs.

If Marian suspected anything was amiss in my story she did not tell me. She was busy, attending to the sick and the dead and rebuilding the trust that had been broken when the people of our town saw her going away to the camp of the enemy lord in a cart. I hung around in the corners of the House of the Dead, watching and learning, with secrets burning in my heart.

And Leah. I never told Marian about her, either. That is harder to explain, except that I did not have the words to talk about her – the things she had done, the look in her eyes as she had given me the spell that killed the girl, her soft fingertip-touch over Marian's skin and her broken bones. More than that, I did not *have* to tell Marian, and at heart I was a coward. The story of our captivity, of Cora's death, of Marian's injury and recovery, made more sense without Leah's involvement, and as the weeks stretched into months it became harder and harder to imagine sitting Marian down and unveiling the truth. I wondered whether she would even believe me. It was much easier to bury Leah inside my mind, let her burn there, obsessive fuel for my dreams. What *was* she?

I took down every book that remained on our shelves and scoured them. Marian was impressed with my studiousness. I barely spoke or ate. I was in my own world of mystery and wonder. Time was my inroad: stopping time, slowing it as Leah had done, was so wildly beyond the realms of the possible that if someone had encountered it before, they *had* to have written it down. But the soldiers had burned half our books, and most of what remained had been written either by Marian or by one of her predecessors – witchlings who had all lived and died here, in our sleepy, stupid town. Their cloistered, blinkered lives. I hated them all, the books and their authors, for their fanatical devotion to the possible and the mundane. Anatomy, rune-magic, blood and humours. Not one of them mentioned the flow of time, or spells that could be hidden inside the body and crackle through your nerves like lightning, or possession, or the workings of escaped ghosts. None of them talked about Leah.

She was a mystery, a terrible thing. A spirit who had come out of the night to set my mind on fire and then vanished again. I did not understand her. I wanted desperately to see her again, to unpeel her, make sense of her. I walked the woods beyond the House of the Dead every twilight I could, even scoured the hills where the army of the enemy lord had made its camp, the grass still trodden and crushed beneath their thousand boots, but I could not find her. I did not expect to. Part of me started to believe that I had dreamed her, but the other part still remembered the flicker of the spell down my arm, the terrible rattle of Marian's breath, her blood on the cobblestones. *I* could not have saved Marian. Her survival was proof enough of Leah's existence. I was not mad.

The world seemed a shade duller than it had been before

the night Cora had died. I spoke less, slept less. My voice deepened with disuse; I pretended to be normal and unchanged, but everything I said felt like a lie, and at night I lay staring out of the window at the stars. I knew the secret to the world. I had seen the crack in the firmament. The laws of nature could be broken and I had seen it done, and everything else was nothing. All that mattered was finding Leah again, understanding what she meant.

The stars flew over our heads, once and then twice. I turned fourteen. Leah did not come back.

One night, the spring after the second war was declared, Marian called me down to the kitchen to look at a dead woman.

I had watched her die that morning. She had been very old, and sickness had got into her lungs; even her son, who had brought her to us, had been unsurprised. 'I just want her to be comfortable,' he had said quietly to Marian as they stood in the living room, out of his mother's earshot, and Marian had nodded and laid a hand on his shoulder. 'I understand,' she said.

Marian had aged rapidly in the two years since Cora's death. She was only forty-three, but looked nearer sixty. The skin around her face seemed tighter and her touch, in the rare moments I felt it, was colder. She had acquired some of that skeletal thinness that laid the bone open to the eye. I knew that the soldiers' attack had left marks on her deeper than either of us could see. Her frailty scared me, somewhere deep and dark in my stomach. I wonder now if she might have been frightened too.

When I came down to the kitchen, the dead woman was laid in a corner, in the shadows of the branches that curled through the ceiling above her. Her body had been cleaned and wrapped in its shroud, and there were herbs on the fire. These were usually my duties. I looked at Marian, surprised and a little suspicious.

She held up a rust-stained flask on the table in front of her. 'What is this?'

I looked between her and the flask. Surely this was a trick question. She raised her eyebrows at me.

'Blood-ink.'

'Deeper than that, Haley.'

I felt a twinge of irritation. I had thought we were past this, past testing and tricks and mysteries. I was not a child anymore.

'Your blood.'

'And?'

'And what?'

Marian gave me a steady, hard look. I pressed my tongue against my lower lip and tried to control my anger. 'I don't know. You haven't told me.'

'I haven't told you because you've never asked.'

I stared at her, outraged. 'You always said I was too young!'

'You were,' said Marian. 'And now you're not.'

We stared at each other for a moment. Marian sighed, then sat back in her chair and put the flask on the table. 'Sit down, Haley.'

I didn't, for three whole seconds. Then, slowly, I pulled back the chair. Marian watched me levelly. There was a new tension between us these days. Age was wearing thin her patience, and youth was not doing wonders for mine.

'You have to be able to make this,' she said quietly. 'In a couple of years—'

'You're not going to die,' I said. I tried to be scathing, but even I could hear the crack in my voice. 'Don't try that with me. You're fine.'

A slight pause.

'You have to be able to make it yourself,' said Marian again.

I did not let myself look away from her. Gone were the days where she could scare me into submission with a glare and some talk of death.

'Tell me how, then.'

'I can't. There's no how.'

'What do you mean, there's—'

'I know how *I* make it,' said Marian, with steady patience, 'but that's not how *you'll* make it. Magic doesn't work like that. If you try to copy my work, it will poison you. Magic is born in you. It lives in you. It speaks to you. Listen to it.'

I stared at her. This was not how Marian usually talked at all. I was used to crisp instruction, gentle correction, exactitude.

'You're not going to teach me?'

'No.'

I stared at her, half-angry and half-afraid. I was looking at the tattoos on her arms, thinking of what they had cost her in blood and smoke and pain, the hours of careful design they must each have required. The ink and the hot knife. I had known I would have to do that, one day. I hadn't realised she would not help me.

'Haley, look at me.'

I looked up. Marian's expression was grave and intent. Clearly we weren't done. I waited apprehensively, refusing to give her the satisfaction of asking.

'What do you think happens when you die?'

I was about to lose it. 'You tell me.'

She raised her eyebrows, and I gritted my teeth.

'You get taken down to the underworld and you get judged.'

'Not quite.'

'Look, you know what I – you can *ask* to be judged.'

She ignored my tone. 'Better. By who?'

I stopped tapping my quill against the table. 'What do you mean, by who?'

'Who judges you?'

I had never really thought about it, or at least not for a very long time. My mental picture of the underworld ended at the staircase that led down into the basement, where Marian disappeared with the dead. *Monsters*, was the answer that came instinctively from my childhood, the voice of the seven-year-old who had lain awake in her bedroom and imagined them plotting downstairs with Marian to kill me. But now the idea seemed foolish. 'It's a person?'

'People,' said Marian. 'Witches.'

I stared at her. 'What?'

She smiled slightly. In that moment I hated her.

'You're taken down by a witchling, then a witch pulls your ghost out of your body—'

'Wait, wait.' I had dropped the quill now and was leaning across the table, staring at her. '*Pulls?*'

'Yes,' said Marian calmly, 'through the mouth. Once you leave your body, you can ask the witch to judge you, if you want, and if not, as you know, you wander the underworld forever.'

She paused, then gestured to me to ask questions. There so many I couldn't breathe with them. My mind was on fire. 'There are *people* who judge you? Witches are people?'

'Yes, in a way.'

'People *live* in the underworld?'

'Well,' said Marian lightly, 'I don't know that you could say *live*. They walk and talk, they don't rot, but . . . I wouldn't say they were alive, in the sense that we are. They can't die, for one thing, and I suppose that's as good a definition as any of living.'

I could not have cared less in that moment. 'What are they? Where do they come from? Are they like us? Do they come up here?'

'They are people, I suppose,' said Marian. Her voice was

hoarse; she coughed and took a sip of water. 'They look human. I don't know where they come from. I see them when I give them a body. We don't speak much.' I tried to ask another question, but she held up a hand to silence me this time. 'They have magic. Deeper and stronger than ours. And they don't come up to the living world.'

'Why not?'

'They take vows. Like us. They call it *natural law*. They're bound to stay in the underworld. They don't associate with the living.'

I started tapping my quill on the table. I was tense with excitement, consequences uncoiling across my mind like spools of wire. 'What kind of magic do they have?'

'I don't know exactly,' said Marian, gently. 'What they have, they use on the dead. This won't matter much to you, Haley. I'm just telling you now so you're not surprised.'

'I am surprised!'

She smiled wearily. 'Well. Better now than when I die.'

I pushed that aside. For once, there were more important things on my mind. 'Why aren't they in your books? Why didn't you tell me about them? Why don't people know?'

'One question at a time, Haley.'

I took a deep, effortful breath.

'They are in the books. They're in *On the Giving of Rites*—'

'Esther's men burned it.'

Marian grimaced. 'Of course they did.'

'Do *people* know? About witches?'

'No.'

'Why not? Who wouldn't want to know?'

'No one wants to know,' said Marian, and gave me that tired smile again. 'Don't you understand people, Haley? No one wants to think about death. No one wants to ask about the mechanics of judgement. They fear it too much. They ask on their deathbeds, sometimes, and then I might tell them.'

'You *might?*'

'It's not a comfort. It scares people to know that there are living beings with that kind of power over them. And my job is to comfort them.'

I rubbed my face, lost. '*You* have that kind of power. You can resurrect them.'

'Yes,' said Marian. 'And they're scared of me, too.'

A silence. I was still seething, my mind alight with questions, but there was only one that seemed truly important. 'Why didn't you *tell* me?'

'At first because you were too young. And then because you didn't ask.'

I burned with fury. 'Because I didn't – how would I even know to ask? It's your *job* to tell me things.'

'It was,' she said. 'And now you know everything.'

I stared at her as she stood up.

'You've got the whole kitchen,' she said. 'All my supplies. Work on it until it feels right. I'll come down and do the runes, but next time it'll be your turn.'

I sprang to my feet. This was insane – she couldn't just lay the world out to me like this and then leave me here, with no instructions and no guidance. Panic rose in me, the kind that tasted like smoke and blood. 'What happens if I get it wrong?'

Marian studied me. 'That depends,' she said. 'Maybe the witch won't be able to pull the ghost from the body. Maybe she will, but the ghost will get mutilated on the way out. Maybe it'll be stunted forever. I don't know.' She shrugged again. 'Magic is capricious.'

I was stunned with terror, trying to decide whether or not to say *don't leave me*. I heard it in my head, plaintive and pathetic, and decided against it. Instead, I said, 'I don't need to do this now.'

'Better now than later.'

'But I—' I was suddenly angry. 'You're not *dying!* Why do

you – stop being dramatic, I'm not going to – I mean, you're not going to—'

I trailed off as she looked at me, a little pityingly.

'Everyone dies, Haley,' she said. 'Sometimes it happens sooner than you think. You should know that by now.'

I couldn't think of anything to say to that. She left me there and climbed the stairs to her room. Her footsteps were slower than they had been, and I could hear every slow *creak*.

I will spare you the tears, the blood, the exhaustion. I will tell you that my blood-ink is made with boiled-down brandy, essence of lavender, and sage oil, among other things. You have to take the blood from the elbow, not the wrist – much easier there to cut too deep, and wound yourself in some irreparable way – and apply salve at once with a wet cloth, to prevent infection.

I have a single, raised purple scar now in the crook of each elbow, in exactly the same place as Marian did. It is the mark of a witchling, more than any tattoo. In the parlour behind the kitchen, stored within a dozen flasks, is six pints of my blood, boiled and stirred and carefully manipulated into something deeper: something that tastes of rust and salt and flowers, something that sings to my heart.

Magic, as Marian told me later, is not so much an art as a language, one you are born fluent in. That first time, when I was fourteen, I knelt in sweat and exhaustion as blood dripped from my arms and the dead woman lay still and cold next to me. A storm swirled around the house, but I could not hear it: the world had lifted away from me, and all I could feel was my own simmering blood, my senses vanished into my shaking hand on the bottle of sage oil. And as the last drop gathered at the edge of the vial and pooled there, something built inside me, a soft release.

The drop fell into the blood, and everything broke. I fell

to my knees and breathed for what felt like the first time in hours. I felt like a stonemason collapsed before a finished temple. I felt complete.

That state of mind, in which reason releases you and the world aligns itself with something higher, in which instruction comes from the slow certainty of the heart instead of the shallow cold of the brain, is called *transcendence*. That was the first time I felt it after I knew what it was called. Like the instinctive resurrections I performed as a child, it is born into a witchling and cannot be taught. So say Marian's books, anyway, and I have never met another witchling, so I have no way of knowing if she was wrong. It comes more easily with practice, and more easily still if you deprive yourself of food and sleep, and yet more if you are in great distress or confusion – although the combination of all of these things will make you all but useless to anyone else who needs your assitance, so it is unwise for a witchling to rely too much on starvation and anguish as roads to transcendence. You have to build the path within your own mind, with practice and peace and slow mastery, so that it is always there if you need it.

That first time was a revelation. I lost myself entirely in it, and could no longer feel my own body, kneeling there for hours in the cold night. In the bloodstained, light-headed daze of transcendence, the stars moved slowly above my head, and I could feel them, a steel cord that tied each of them to my heart. I could hear the worlds above and below me, the earth beneath my feet that shaded slowly to a cold amethyst sky, the teeming billion hordes of ghosts.

I saw Leah's magic, in my memory. Like a cloud of living smoke, a fluttering scrap of ether, it surrounded and shielded her. She was not of this world, but her magic protected her from the air, just as Marian's tattoos kept her safe as she walked in the underworld.

Inside my head, I saw Leah in the camp, turning towards me. I could see the spell within her arm, dark and glowing, like a clot of blood in her veins. I saw the way time flowed around her, how it tumbled and slowed. And I saw her magic gathering around her, gaseous and dark, the tendrils of it that wrapped around her chest and reached down, digging into the ground, tying her to the earth. To the world *beneath* the earth.

Marian was wrong. Witches did not all stay in the underworld. The laws she understood were false. One of them had appeared to me.

# CHAPTER NINE

After that I was careful. Never again did I leave a question unasked, and I dug at her answers, trying to bore through them to the truth. I had spent two years in thrall to a question she could have answered in a second, and now I was suspicious. What else did she think I didn't need to know yet? Did she know what Leah had told me, about ghosts and possession and witches who walked above the earth? It would have been a terrible betrayal; in all my life with her, she had never looked me in the eye and lied to me, or so I then believed.

I was so angry. I could have repaid her trust with my own and told her the truth about Leah, I could have bound us together with honesty, but I was young, and a coward. I was terrified of her disappointment in me, of losing her trust forever, and so instead I spun my guilt into fury. I slammed doors and snapped at her, pushed her further and further, believing that if she would not tell me the truth when I asked her, I could get her to shout it at me in anger. But she remained calm and impassive, and at last I was forced into acceptance: she truly did not know about possession, about Leah. If she did, she would have told me. I had to believe that.

That did not assuage me. I tended my rage assiduously, found ways to keep it alive. Why hadn't she told me this years ago, I asked her days later, voice full of curt fury. When had she decided I was stupid? Who was she to decide I was *too young* to know something? I had seen more death, knew more healing, than anyone of my age in this town— more than she had herself, at my age. Why didn't she trust me?

Marian sitting at the kitchen table. She looked at me and very slowly took off her glasses. The year before she had saved the glassmaker's son from lung disease, and the woman had made them for her in gratitude. Marian had refused to use them for months, but now her vision had deteriorated past the point of denial.

'Do you hate me?' she said at last.

That took me aback. There was no anger in her voice at all, only deep sadness. I had not bargained on this. I struggled for an answer, tried to find a tone of dismissive scorn.

'Of course I don't *hate* you. That's not what I—'

'You used to,' said Marian. She spoke quietly, and she was looking past me, at the dead man on the floor. 'I worried. When you were very young.'

I had no idea what to say. We had never talked about this. I had never seen this unveiled anguish in her before. I could not maintain my fury in the face of it. It took me a moment to speak.

'You took me from my mother. I was—' I tried to find the words. The terror and the grief, the hole my mother had left in me, the barred window. 'I was scared.'

'Of me?'

'You hit me.'

'Yes,' said Marian. 'Yes, I did.' She was still looking at the dead man's face. I was completely disoriented now. I could not remember her ever being unable to look me in the eye. 'That was . . . one of the worst moments of my life. I was very frightened, Haley. I was worried about what this would do to you. What *I* would have to do to you. And I was afraid for Lysa.'

The sound of my mother's name was impossibly jarring; I could not speak. When my voice returned, I was suddenly furious again. It was exhausting being so angry all the time, but I did not know how to stop. 'You were afraid for *her?*'

'Yes,' said Marian, evenly. 'I thought losing you would destroy her. I thought she would hate me. She's avoided me for years. She never comes to market when I might be there. She fears me even more than she does you.'

She stopped and looked at me. I had gone very still, staring unseeingly at the table beneath my hands. It was all I could do not to put my hands over my ears.

'I'm sorry,' she said, after a moment.

'Just don't,' I said tightly. 'Don't. Please.'

I had tried to believe my mother was dead. That she had died the day she turned into the alleyway and so there was no point thinking about her. The thought now forced into my brain – of her alive, years older, living in this town and avoiding me – was more than I could bear.

'I'm sorry,' said Marian again, and there was genuine anguish in her voice. 'I am.'

*It doesn't matter.* I tried to say it and couldn't.

There was a long silence.

'I know I scared you,' said Marian softly, 'when you were very young. I know I hurt you. I had to break you, Haley.'

I raised my head to stare at her.

'I could not teach you,' she said, steadily, 'if you still had hope. The longer you thought there was a chance you might escape this life, the worse it would be for you when you realised you couldn't. It was the easiest way.'

I stayed silent. I understood, but I could not bring myself to absolve her. I couldn't believe there had been no easier way, when the memories still hurt so much. I could not call that a kindness.

'I tried to protect you, Haley. I never believed you were stupid. I believed you were young, and I believed that meant you could be hurt. I have tried to keep you safe and happy, as much as I could. I wanted you to be a child for as long as you were able. I hope one day you understand that.'

'I do,' I said. My throat was tight, but I was not lying. 'I do understand.'

I'm not sure she believed me. She watched me for a while, her lips tight, and then put her glasses back on and returned to her book. Neither of us spoke again for a very long time.

What did I know, then, about witches? I knew that they judged the dead, but I did not know how. I knew they were women – sometimes men, but usually women – of terrible power, more than any witchling, but I did not know the form or extent of that power. I knew they swore oaths, and that those oaths bound them to the underworld, and forbade them from talking to any mortals bar the witchlings who came down to give them corpses. I did not know what force kept them to those oaths, or what happened to a witch who broke them. I did not even know how witches were born, or what happened if they died. *If* they died. Maybe Marian was wrong about that too. Did they have ghosts, like mortals? Did they walk for all eternity in the underworld? Were they subject, after death, to their own judgement?

I knew almost nothing. And of the little I did know, none of it allowed for Leah. A witch who walked the living world, talking about escaped ghosts and killing the granddaughters of lords. Nothing could make her make sense.

I had to find her again. It was the only way to soothe the burning ache in my chest. I would find her and ask her everything and then I would know the secrets of the worlds. But even if I had known where she was, there was no way I could leave the House of the Dead now, even for a day. Marian was dying, we both knew it, and I was bound more tightly to my town than I had ever been. Now I answered the door when the sick and dead were brought to us, I set broken bones and brewed salves, and Marian sat at the table watching me, offering gentle advice. Marian was a scholar and a genius, and her mind was crackling and undimmed, but now her hands shook on the needle when she tried to sew up a wound, and she no longer had the strength to pull a tourniquet. I did those things, the easy, menial tasks, while Marian spoke to the anxious and bereaved, explained sicknesses and healing and the mechanics of death. She confessed to me once, bitterly, that she felt like a puppeteer now, more than a healer. I asked half-jokingly if that made me a puppet.

By then I was sixteen, a woman grown, or so I thought. My arms were marked with tattoos I had sketched on paper, lost in transcendence, then carved into my own arms with blood-ink and a hot knife, biting down on a strap of leather. The pain was part of the magic, Marian said, and I could not dull it to save myself. And I looked like a witchling. My hair was longer and darker, I was taller, and no one treated me like a child anymore. Daring boys approached me, and if I liked them I would promise to meet them at midnight by the bridge, and sometimes I even did. I walked out of the House of the Dead quite openly at night and closed the door behind me, and if Marian heard she did not talk to me about it. I lay on the riverbank under the stars with some beautiful idiot boy and talked as if I were some mysterious envoy of the dead, as if I knew secrets he could only dream of – which I did, of course, but none I would ever really give away. Sometimes I kissed him, and sometimes I let him touch me, but never more than that. It was a kind of game I played with myself, to see how far I could make myself go without succumbing to my own revulsion. I could make myself like it, up to a point – but if they got too close to me I suddenly remembered who I was and who they were, and the strangeness of it all, and felt afraid. I would get up, pull on my jacket, say something flip-pant and walk away, leaving them bemused on the grass.

It made me bitter, and angry with myself. This should have been the easiest kind of power to take for myself, but I could not do it. I could not quiet the voice in my head that woke as they got closer, as their hands slid over me, that said, *no, I don't want this – no, get away from me—*

There was a hole in my heart. I was restless. I walked the streets at dusk, trying to pull myself out from the shadow of the House of the Dead, when I knew there was no way out, that I was trapped there forever. I could get up one morning and run, follow the river to the sea, but even there anyone who saw me would look at my arms and know immediately what I was. I would be captured and brought back by the lord's men.

Leah was my way out, my release from the strictures of my own life. If I could find her perhaps I could avert the decades of unending bleakness that stretched in front of me. She had a meaning I did not understand. She was the key to the world, the break in the clouds. If I could just *find* her again . . .

If I could go down into the underworld, I thought, I could find a witch and ask them about her and what she meant, but that was another thing Marian insisted I was too young for. I tried, once I had all my tattoos, drawn out in a transcendent haze and cut into my arms with ink and the cauterising knife. I was sixteen, that was old enough, I told Marian. I was ready to go down to the underworld, the next time we had a corpse.

'No,' she said.

We were sitting at the table. I had made braised pork with fennel for dinner, and the plates were not yet empty. Marian ate much less these days than she used to. I sat back in my chair and folded my arms.

'Why not?'

'Because you don't have to,' she said. 'I'm still the witchling, Haley. It's my duty, not yours.'

'You can barely even carry the bodies!'

Marian raised her eyebrows and at last I looked away, ashamed. I had not meant to throw her frailty in her face like that. Neither of us usually acknowledged it.

'The marks do not protect you entirely,' said Marian. 'They just stop the underworld killing you *quickly*. It will still kill you in the end. It might take thirty years'— she raised her veined, trembling hands— 'but it will kill you. I will not allow you to start that process before you have to.'

'But one visit—'

'Is that what you want?' she said, shrewdly. 'One visit? Ten minutes down there and you'll be satisfied?'

I glared at her. I could not tell her about Leah. But I wanted, for just a moment, to take the secret I had kept for four years and throw it at her. I wanted to show her what I was capable of – how much I had lied to her, and for how long. I wanted her to know I was not hers anymore, not in any way that mattered.

That impulse sickens me to remember. I am so very, very glad that it passed, and that I said nothing.

That night, I lay in bed awake, staring at the ceiling. I had spent too many years waiting for something to happen to me. I needed to *do* something. I could not let Marian keep me here any longer. I was free, I was my own—

Hours passed. The night darkened. I lay there, fuming, sleepless, steeped in my own indecision.

Then madness seized me at last.

I got up, and as quietly as I could I crept down the stairs into the basement. I have no doubt, thinking about it now, that Marian heard me. The house had been a part of her for thirty years, and she knew its every creak and sigh. It hid nothing from her. I wonder now why she did not follow me. Perhaps she knew this was a lesson I could not learn through her instruction. I had to be allowed to try, to test myself.

In the parlour there was a flight of stone stairs, moulded by the feet of eight hundred years of witchlings. I stared down them, crouched on the top step. I had been into the basement before, when Elior died and many times since, carrying bodies out of sight. The children were the worst. Small soft lumps, so still under their shrouds.

It hit me suddenly that I would never have a child of my own. I don't know why that mattered to me in that moment. I had always glossed over that part of the vows in my head; I had felt too much like a child myself for the idea of motherhood to touch me. But I felt it acutely, then, the loss of that future, taken from me before I could decide whether or not I wanted it. It ached for a moment – a chord struck in my heart – and then it was gone, faded into the darkness.

I felt cold and empty. I walked down the stairs.

There were three corpses in the basement, as I had expected. A mother and baby, struck by sickness that raised a yellow-white pox on their mouths and ears – I stayed well away from them – and an old man. His shroud was little more than a bed sheet, but his wife had brought it to us, weeping silently, and had kissed it before handing it over to Marian, so we used it. Everything given to us was a token of love too deep for expression; everything had a terrible significance I could never understand. The ring on his finger, his wife had told us, spoke of forty years of marriage. That, too, was closed to me. I could never love someone like that. Certainly, they could never love me.

My thoughts were bleak and numb. I turned to the entrance of the underworld.

It looked innocuous enough: a hole in the wall carved from stone, sloping into impenetrable darkness. It took Marian half an hour, usually, to take a corpse down to the underworld and return to the House of the Dead. But the tunnels were deep and dangerous, and I did not know the way. I knew time moved faster there; minutes here were hours in the world below. If I got lost, it might take until morning for Marian to realise, and by then I could have been down there for days.

I stood there for long minutes, defiance and foolhardiness fighting quiet reason in my brain. I was still there ten minutes later, when, from above me, there came a knock at the door.

If you live for long enough in the House of the Dead, you become very adept at translating knocks. There is the slow, heavy knock that means a loved one bringing a corpse after a long, expected death. There is the panicked hammer of those carrying the terribly injured, or the weak rapping of the sick and half-collapsed. This knock was none of those.

The person at the door tapped very lightly, almost as though they wished not to be heard. It was the sound Kavana had made when she had come to Marian two years previously, her eye swollen blue-black from her husband's drunken swing. You could see the marks of his knuckles in the bruise. That kind of knock, the quiet, ashamed kind, speaks of true, deep terror.

I did not hesitate. I scrambled back up the stairs and into the parlour. By the time I got to the kitchen Marian was making her way down. Age had slowed her; a year before this she would have beaten me to the door.

'Let me get it,' she said when she saw me. I stood back at once. The people of our town knew her better than they knew me. She was comfort to those in distress.

The door opened at her touch. A woman stood there, unbruised but trembling. She was older than I remembered, but I knew her eyes.

'Anya,' said Marian, quietly. I had not seen her since the day her daughter Niamh had died. She was grey-faced and trembling. She tried to speak, once and then twice, but could not get out the words.

Marian pulled the door wider. 'Come inside,' she said, and

Anya stumbled forward. I caught and steadied her, knowing that Marian would not have the strength, and put my arm around her shoulders.

'Come on, Anya. Come inside. It's all right.'

It was not all right. After twenty minutes, when we had wrapped her in a soft woollen blanket and I made her tea – camomile, for grieving; I don't know how I knew, it was just something in her face – we got her to talk.

She couldn't even say it, but had to write it out, in shaking ink-scrawled hand on Marian's parchment.

*Daniel killed someone.*

Marian stared at the note, then back up at Anya. 'Daniel?' she said, blankly. '*Daniel* killed someone? Who?'

I could not speak. I did not believe it. Daniel, who had played lords with me and tried to guard me until he found out I was the witchling's, whose sister had died at my feet. Who had flinched in disgust as I tried to comfort him. Whom I had loved, long ago, with a child's untroubled adoration. I tried to imagine him, seventeen now, a grown man, but all I could feel were his wrists in my terrified grip as we hid in his bedroom, Marian knocking at the door below us. *Daniel*. No, no.

Slowly their voices came back to me, slipping over my head like eels.

'I – I don't know who it was.'

'You don't—'

'I haven't seen her before. Maybe she's a traveller.'

'Anya,' said Marian suddenly. 'Anya. She's not a soldier, is she? She's not with Jonathan?'

'No,' said Anya, shakily. 'No, no, she's . . . I would know.'

A brief, shivering silence descended. We were all imagining what terrible revenge the remaining soldiers of the Lord Jonathan would wreak if one of ours killed one of theirs. The whole town would burn, with us locked inside our houses. At the least. I cut off my thoughts there.

'He, uh,' said Anya, and her voice shook and died. She pressed a hand to her forehead. 'He cut off . . . parts of her. After she died. I walked in on him doing it. I tried to get the knife off him, but he waved it at me, and I thought . . . for a moment . . . but he would *never* hurt me, not ever . . .'

Marian was very pale, but her expression had hardened. 'Is he still in the house?'

Anya looked up at her, afraid. 'Don't hurt him. Please.'

'I will try not to hurt him,' said Marian evenly, 'but if he's going to kill anyone else—'

Anya shook her head. 'I got Imran and the baby to my sister's house and then sent word not to come home – and, uh—' She swallowed. 'I, uh – I locked him inside. They think he's sick. They don't know.'

'You say he wouldn't hurt you,' said Marian quietly, 'but you're keeping his father and the baby away from the house. You know you're lying to yourself, Anya. You came to me.'

She did not look afraid. The silence in the house had congealed, and Marian's eyes were flint-hard. I was numb again.

'Does he still have the knife?'

Anya nodded slowly.

'Does anyone else know about this?'

'N – no. I came straight to you.'

'I'm glad,' said Marian. 'That was good of you, Anya.'

I remembered the woman who had been betrayed by her husband for worshipping Claire. If the people of our town thought Daniel was dangerous, or that he might bring danger to their houses, they would not hesitate to give him up to the Lord Jonathan's men.

Marian got to her feet slowly. I watched her. Anya was still trembling. She said again, very quietly, 'Please don't hurt him. He's my son.'

'I know,' Marian said. 'Take me to the house.'

*

Anya lived about a mile and a half from the House of the
Dead, along the river. I had not walked that path in many
years, but I remembered it well. That terrible day, cold in the
winter dawn, trying to escape Marian, falling and Niamh
pulling me up and taking me inside. Daniel's smile at the
sight of me. I tried to forget again, but his face was too bright
in the darkness. I closed my eyes, but it didn't go away.

I did not know Anya well. Was it not more likely that this
was all in her mind, some twisted hallucination? I did not
know what to believe. I wished I still had someone to pray
to.

It was very quiet, a dark listening silence broken only by
the gurgling of the river. I had the sudden feeling I was being
watched, and turned to look into the trees on the other bank,
alert for leather gloves, pale hair, quick ice-blue eyes. But I
saw nothing, and after a moment I turned back to Marian
and Anya. Some older, soured part of me knew that Leah
had long since forgotten about me, that she was never coming
back, but another part, still twelve years old and half-buried,
remembered her and burned.

The lights in Anya's house were out. Inside, Daniel might
have been dead. That possibility flashed briefly across my
numb brain: that this was a last lashing out, a spasm of pain
in a dying mind. It was no more impossible than anything
else Anya had said.

Marian held up a hand at the sight of the black windows.
'Stay back, Haley.'

'Only if you do.'

I was not staying outside with Anya. I would not let Marian
hurt Daniel, if he was alive – he was mine to protect, the
ghost of the eight-year-old with soulful eyes. I would not let
her harm him for the sake of the town, for some stupid abstract
purpose, like Leah had killed Cora. I did not truly believe he
was a danger to anyone, not yet. I thought this was a bad

dream of Anya's, and any moment now she would turn around and say, I'm sorry, I think I imagined it—

Marian turned around and looked at me. Her eyes were suddenly cold. 'Haley,' she said, 'do as I say.'

I could feel Anya behind me, twitching and anxious. It must have looked so strange to her to see us at odds. I had been a part of Marian for so many years, her obedient right hand, silent and watchful. I took a deep breath. We did not bring our own conflicts under the eyes of the town. She was the witchling and I was her girl, and if we were united in purpose and will, the town was safe.

'I want,' I said steadily, 'to help. None of us should go in there alone.'

'I should go in,' said Anya from behind me. 'I'm his mother. I can talk to him.'

Marian looked between us.

'We go together,' she said at last. 'Haley, guard Anya. I'll go ahead.'

I could not argue with her further, not in front of Anya. I nodded and clenched my fists.

The doorway was dark. Anya trembled as she handed the key to Marian, whose hands were steady as she pushed open the door. Marian held no knife; she was a witchling, and did not arm herself. She walked into the hall calmly and did not try to silence her footsteps.

At the foot of the stairs she stopped and called up into the darkness. 'Daniel,' she said. 'Daniel, child. I'm here to help you.'

Silence. I could feel Anya trembling behind me.

'Daniel,' said Marian again, coaxingly. 'Let me help y—'

From above us there came a high, joyous scream of laughter, and Marian threw herself backwards. I did not see why for a second, and then there was a ripple of golden light and a *thud*. Daniel had dropped a torch from the landing right over the place where Marian had been standing. It lay there on the wooden floor, the flame blue at its heart, terribly bright in the darkness.

I moved to cover it with my cloak, but for once Marian was faster. She pulled hers off in one smooth motion and dropped it over the torch. I stomped on it until the flame went out and then looked up into the darkness, panting. The laugh had been like nothing I'd ever heard – that of a wild animal, not a boy.

Marian was very calm. 'Daniel,' she said, 'you don't need to hurt me. I'm not here to do anything to you.'

That high, cackling laugh from above. It sounded like evil. It *hurt*. Anya's hand was at her throat, her eyes wide and glassy-gold in the candlelight. I couldn't breathe.

'Daniel,' she whispered. 'Daniel, love, please . . .'

At the sound of his mother's voice, his laugh rose to a shriek, and suddenly there was movement on the stairs, flailing limbs and the glint of a knife. I could not breathe, and for a moment the world flickered inside my head – I was seven years old again, standing in the doorway of my bedroom, the grieving brother lunging towards me—

Marian stumbled backwards and I saw with horror that Daniel's knife was covered in blood. He threw himself at her, and he was screaming, a high ululation in a language I had never heard, raising the knife, his eyes on Marian's exposed throat. Suddenly, I remembered I could move. I lunged for him, wrapped my arms around his chest and pulled him backwards, away from Marian's frailty and Anya's sobbing screams. His knife-hand flailed wildly, trying to find me.

Something moved within me, the twinge of an old scar. I felt a prickling pain down the nerves of my arm, the mark of something that had happened long ago. The residue of Leah's spell within me, the one she had given me to destroy the ghosts in Cora's body. It felt Daniel, and it remembered.

And then the pain intensified, suddenly hot and inescapable. I heard him scream in my arms and knew he could feel it too. The lightning in my nerves brightened. His shrieking was my own, we were joined in agony and I could not let him go—

'*Haley!*'

Someone's hand on mine. Marian's, pulling me away. The darkness around me formed shapes, shadows on faces. I released Daniel and he collapsed, pathetic. The knife clattered to the floor. I stumbled back and felt Marian steady me.

He looked up at me, and I could see him, right there, the eight year old in the seventeen-year-old's face, but there was no recognition there at all, nothing human – only murderous hatred in his eyes, purer than language. There was blood on Marian's hand, on my face.

'Haley, come *on* – come with me—'

Anya was still screaming. It took both of us to pull her out of the house. As we retreated through the doorway I could see her son scrabbling in the dark for the knife. My arm still burned. Marian's hand shook on the key as she turned it in the lock. On the other side, I could hear Daniel shrieking again, in a tongue I had never heard.

The words meant something in my head. The chime of a bell, buried deep in my brain. *Speaking in tongues.*

Marian was trembling. I saw the wound in her palm from when she had tried to grab Daniel's blade and stumbled towards her, tearing strips of cloth from my shirt. She was muttering something.

'Stupid,' I heard her say, as I bound her hand. She lifted the other to cover her eyes. I had never seen her do that before. '*Stupid.*'

Anya was sobbing on the grass behind us. 'My boy . . . my boy . . .'

Marian's hand was bound so tightly I could see the fingertips turning blue, and yet I was still rolling bandages. I made myself let her go, and sank to my knees on the grass. Anya's wails rose into the darkness and I could hear Daniel thumping on the front door, *thud thud thud*, trying to get out.

*Some things cannot be saved,* Marian told me long ago. She was right about that. Daniel was beyond saving. There was no Daniel anymore, and that was a terrible loss but also a swooning relief, because it meant the boy I had known was not a murderer. At least, at the very least, there was that.

Whatever inhabited Daniel's body now, the thing had called to the scar of Leah's spell inside me and cut women apart just to watch them bleed, was not the boy I had loved. It was something else entirely, and it had destroyed Daniel more thoroughly and completely than death. It had strangled his ghost in his own body.

Elior. Cora. Now Daniel.

When the others had been possessed, Leah had come for them. And in the dark, outside our house, I had seen something. A flicker in the trees. I had *felt* her watching me. This was the night, I knew it in my heart. Daniel's possession would bring her back to me.

Forgive me for this, in my obsession and my delirium. I had not slept and I was grieving. I was shaking as we trekked back through the dark, as I cleaned the blood from my hands, and Marian put Anya to bed in my room. Once she had cried herself to sleep we sat together in the darkness of the kitchen. Marian did not speak for a long time.

At last she said, 'I don't understand.' She clenched her fist over the bandage and winced; I had poured white spirits into the wound to keep out infection. 'I don't understand what's wrong with him. This isn't any kind of sickness I've ever seen.'

I understand, I wanted to say. I know exactly what's happened to him. I could feel the words on my lips. It was *right there,* the chance I could have taken, to explain to her about possession and the lord's granddaughter and Leah and escaped ghosts and what had really happened on the night she was attacked—

I let the silence stretch and deepen. Then I got up, stoked the fire, and put the kettle over it. Camomile tea for the grieving. I waited until Marian went upstairs to check on Anya, and then I reached up to the cupboard above the drawer of blood-ink. I felt the glass vial in my hand, so cold. Laudanum.

I stared at it for a few moments, waiting for my own revulsion to kick in. There was nothing. The inside of my brain was warm and numb.

I put a single drop in her mug. Enough to put someone to sleep for hours, to pull them into slumber so deep they could not struggle out of it. I stared down at it and tried to reason with myself, to still the motion of my hands, but all I could see was Daniel's twisted face. The last time he had really seen me he had turned away, cringed from my touch, but he had at least known who I was. Now even that was gone.

I pressed the cork back into the laudanum bottle and put it back in the cupboard.

Her tea was waiting for her, steaming on the table, when she came back downstairs. I watched her drink it, her bloody hands wrapped around the mug, staring sightlessly into the darkness. I was almost completely numb; my hands did not feel like my own. Sleep deprivation, the horror of what had happened to Daniel, and joy at the prospect of Leah's return had all broken something vital within me. I watched myself watch Marian from somewhere in the back of my own mind, wondering if I would have the courage to say something, to take it back, change course and apologise. But the minutes wore on and I did not move, and eventually Marian put down her empty mug and said quietly that she was going to bed.

I sat in that dark kitchen for a long, long time.

After half an hour I went upstairs to the bedrooms. Anya's face was red and swollen, I saw through her half-open door. I pitied her, trapped in her dreams.

Nearly a decade of deep-worn instinct stopped me opening Marian's door without permission, but I stood outside and pressed my ear to the wood. Slow, deep breathing. No movement. I considered locking her in, but the other part of myself, the younger part, recoiled. I was still afraid of her. Subterfuge and betrayal I could conscience, but open defiance . . .

I was a coward. That is what stands out most clearly to me now, after everything: the utter shamelessness of my cowardice.

Once I was sure she was asleep, I went back downstairs, took the knife we used for surgery, and left the house, closing the door very quietly. Before I returned to Anya's house, I stood outside the door in the airless silence, feeling the wind on my face. That feeling of being watched was back again, and joy surged in my heart.

For years I dreamed of this moment, over and over, and awoke shivering. It lives in me still, in the depths of my brain.

In my dream I am on the bridge. I have been trying to find Daniel for half an hour; his house is empty, the door ajar. My head is cool and full of light. I feel as though I have been sent a miracle. I see the warrior standing above me and rest my hand on her stone foot.

My arm prickles, and I turn, and Daniel is standing behind me.

I see him, covered in blood. He does not lunge for me. It hurts to look at that familiar face, its terrible new blankness.

I want to say, how did you get out of the house? I want to ask where he has been. When he escaped, did he come straight here to find me? The pain that links us throbs below my heart;

it calls him to me and draws him here. Did he follow it? Or did he go somewhere else? Whose blood is on him, on the knife?

In the dream I cannot speak, not in any way that matters. My lips move, I feel them, I *fight* them, but I cannot control the words. I say what I said in real life, when I was sixteen: 'Can you understand me?'

Something changes in his eyes. The ghost is pushing through Daniel's brain, trying to find the part of him that knew our tongue. Recognition flickers briefly in his eyes and then dies again.

I raise my hands. 'I don't want to hurt you,' I say, slowly. 'I just want to talk.'

He stares at me with blank eyes. We are alien to each other. I wonder what the ghost was before it died. I wonder what sin kept it from asking for judgement in the world below, kept it wandering around until it escaped. How long was it there? How did it get out? The questions are burned into me by years of obsession. It hurts, how much I want to know the answers.

I do not ask those questions. I restrain myself. Instead I say, 'Follow me.'

I turn my back on him. Trapped in my body, dreaming, I scream at myself in the memory. *What are you doing?* I try to halt my steps, to turn and throw myself at the no-longer-a-boy behind me. Anything but take him to the house. *Please, don't – don't make me – go away—*

I walk through the darkness. I can feel Daniel behind me. It is a strange buzz, the feel of my life in my hands. If he wants to kill me, he could do it. But I feel no fear. I know I fascinate him, just as he fascinates me, a witchling's girl who knows what he is. Perhaps he even remembers me, in some way he does not understand. He will not snuff me out just yet.

The dream ends at the door of the House of the Dead, the boy's breath behind me. I lay my hand on the door. I wake crying, filled with a terrible, useless dread.

In the dream I just walk him to the house. I dream of that, and not anything that came after, because that was the moment I could have gone back.

I had tea waiting for him on the table: laudanum-tainted, like Marian's. I gestured to it when he entered the front room. 'Drink.'

He looked at it and then back at me. He was not going to drink it. I had not really expected him to.

I waited. One second, three, eight. He was staring at me. His eyes were terrifyingly bright. It was a horror to look at, this corruption of a boy.

I turned away and opened the doorway to the basement. 'Come with me.'

He hissed at the doorway. I knew he could feel the under-world through it, its song, the thing the ghost within him had wanted so desperately to escape. I shook my head.

'No,' I said, slowly and clearly. 'Not that. Something else.'

He looked at me suspiciously. I shook my head more vigor-ously. 'Not that. *Listen*. Something *else*.'

He took a step forward, his eyes on the doorway. I wonder if he thought the tentacles of the world below would reach up and pull him back down. When it did not, he took another step.

'Down the steps,' I said. 'It's down there.'

I had measured it carefully. Six steps from the bottom, he turned and looked at me. I think he knew, but I had confused him. I urged him on. 'Another step,' I said. Six steps was too many.

Three steps from the bottom, I kicked him in the head.

He fell gracelessly, with a sickening crunch.

I descended the stairs lightly and knelt beside him. He was unconscious, but nothing was broken; he was not dead. I stood above him for a while, watching him breathe.

Then I sat beside him in the darkness and waited for Leah to find us.

I thought I had covered all possibilities. I was sure I had felt Leah watching me through the trees as we walked to Anya's house. If I was right and she was here already, she would come into the house and find us here. And if I was wrong, and she was in the underworld, she would come up through the tunnels, and we would be the first thing she saw. I thrummed with excitement. Tonight, all my questions would be answered. Tonight I would see her again.

I stared into the tunnels. Their darkness soaked through my brain and mesmerised me, deeper and purer than the darkness of the cellar. Daniel lay bleeding beside me, and I was full of silence and purpose. I had never felt more awake.

And then, at last, I heard something moving in the tunnels. A single soft thud, like a footstep.

I scrambled to my feet, but the sound faded. I waited for a long moment, watching for her. Could it be that she didn't trust me, after everything?

I kept very still, but there was nothing. 'Leah?' I whispered.

At my feet Daniel twitched. I watched him for a moment, fearing he would wake, ready to kick him again, but he did not move. Upstairs Marian and Anya slept like the dead.

'Leah?'

No answer. I stepped forward. My stomach was tight and sick. I could not bear the thought that she was there, out of sight, that I had come so far and done so much and was so *close* to knowing everything and she might walk away. That Daniel had been destroyed for nothing. I felt the stare of the darkness, and stepped into the tunnel entrance, trying to see her.

'Leah?'

She had gone. Vanished into the dark again. No, no, please, no. She was close, I could feel it, and so I clambered into the tunnel, my hands slipping on the smooth rock. I called out into the dark, but the echoes came back to me unadorned. I walked slowly, hoping she would hear my footsteps, but I was alone with the echoing drip of groundwater and the cold unyielding rock.

For one terrified moment I thought I would die down there. The tunnel, possessed by the ethereal witch-magic of the underworld, would know I was not Marian and would swallow me into its blackness. I was completely at its mercy. It brought a feeling like the one I had had when I turned my back on the ghost-boy: I could feel the spirit in my hands, my own pulsing lifeblood. I understood, in a flash of light, my own precariousness.

But I did not die. I stood there in the dark and listened to the murmur of the streams of soft water and I knew there was no one there with me.

My heartbeat slowed.

Something in me understood, then. The frenzy that had gripped me faded, and I saw more clearly the contours of my own mind. The sense that I was being watched, the presence at my back, paled slowly into the dark.

I gripped the wall to steady myself and twisted to look over my shoulder, back the way I had come. Behind me there was only darkness. Unease pulled at me, raising the hairs on my arms. Without quite deciding to do it, without even consciously acknowledging it, I started to move slowly backwards. Perhaps she was up there, in the basement. Surely that was the greater danger: that I had imagined only the footstep in the darkness, and she had come into the house, and found Daniel already, and killed him, and left without a word.

At last I turned completely and clambered back through

the darkness along the wet stone, and with every step my panic grew. Minutes in echoing blackness, my brain buzzing nervously, and then the light changed and I was in the basement again. I fell to the floor, panting and graceless.

It was almost dawn. The grey light fell in dusty slats through the floorboards above my head. It fell on the stone floor, the mother and child, the dead old man. On Daniel's blood, on the floor.

Daniel was gone.

I could not breathe. Fear and a terrible dread lit up my mind. I froze and then ran, slipping in the still-wet blood, up into the silent kitchen. No. *No.* Marian rose early, always. Perhaps with the laudanum – but no, that had to have worn off by now.

'Marian!'

No answer. Not even from Anya, upstairs. The house, *this house*, whose every creak and movement I knew intimately, this house would not talk to me. Everything was still and quiet.

My voice rose. '*Marian!*'

Nothing. I ran up the stairs, my hands sweat-slippery on the banister. I could hear movement on the landing, breathing. Anya's door, which had been ajar when I left, was wide open. I grabbed the edge of it and looked inside, then doubled over.

The bed – *my* bed – was soaked in blood. Anya was cowled in it, the dark sheets wrapped around her arms. Her eyes were open and glassy, and she did not move.

I tried to speak, to say her name or Marian's, but the breath would not come to me.

*Marian.* I pushed myself, queasy with panic, away from Anya's door, towards Marian's. It too was open.

When I threw myself inside, Daniel looked up at me. His eyes had a kind of bright intelligence to them, a cold curiosity. His shirt was covered in blood. His knife was still in Marian's stomach, and as he drew it out, she gasped, convulsing. Her eyes found mine.

I had no breath to scream. My brain was white noise, a blankness of horror.

I lunged for Daniel, and he raised the knife. My hand found his wrist. I slipped, and we fell together onto our knees. I could feel the cold of his skin, half-corpse already. I wondered if he knew he was dying – if this was anger, his last terrible revenge. He bared his teeth at me. I had no strength left. He gripped the knife.

And something in my brain clicked. Lying on the bedroom floor, the brother's strong hands slamming me into the wood, Marian behind him—

My mind knew it, and my body understood. I opened the part of my mind that knew resurrection, the pool of venom at the base of my skull where death-magic accumulated. I felt it move into my hand like a black flood, and then I grasped his wrist tighter and released it into him, his skin to mine, a surge of death into his trembling body.

He gasped. We could both feel it, the weight leaving me, and some instinctive hollow joy rose in my brain. Below me, I was watching him sicken and age, his skin tighten and turn sallow, and his eyes sink into his head, more and more the longer I held him. If I did not let him go he would die, in my grip—

I let him go, and he fell and did not move again.

I was on my knees, panting. My hands were covered in Marian's blood. It dripped from the bed onto the wooden floor, slowly, like rainwater from a windowsill. *Tap. Tap.*

She blinked slowly. I could not breathe. I scrambled to my feet and pressed the blankets into her wounds. So many of them, dark and clean. I was trying to stop the bleeding, but my hands were soaked with blood, so much of it I couldn't feel where the flesh gave way. She reached up to me, trying to brush my face with her fingertips. I could hear the slow rattling of her breath, but her eyes were bright.

'*Haley . . .*'

I stopped trying to bandage her stomach and looked up at her. I burned with guilt and horror. I did not have the words for the terrible silence within me.

I think she could see it. She put her hand in my hair. Blessing, absolution, condemnation. Her touch was so frail, so cold already. I covered her hand with my own. I could feel the tears in my eyes. 'I'm so sorry,' I said, 'I'm sorry, I'm sorry, oh, Marian, I'm – I'm *sorry*, I'm sorry . . .'

She died three hours later, and that was it. I was alone.

# CHAPTER TEN

That first month was a sickness. I remember it only in flashes, everything out of order.

The mourning ceremony was the worst of it, all those people gathered at her memorial stone. The winter sunlight unforgiving, a thin white knife in my brain. She had given up her family name when she took her oaths, so the stone just said *Marian, witchling, 7481-7526*. I only know that because I used to go back there every month or so to talk to her. My vision at the ceremony was blurry, a swimming haze.

They asked me to give a eulogy. I tried, I swear. I don't recall what I said. After a while someone – Ira, I think – pulled me gently aside, and I choked into silence. I did not cry in front of them, at least.

Then, later, I remember kneeling in the basement. Hauling her body with Anya's into leather bags so I could carry them through the trapdoor. I know that there were tattoos carved into her ruined stomach and forehead and sage-smoke in the air, which means I gave her the rites, and I know that the next morning their bodies were gone, which means I carried them down to the underworld. But I don't remember any of that. All I have left is that memory, standing over leather bags in the dark stone and dimness of the basement.

Anya was already inside hers, a tangle of limbs and blood. Marian lay open-eyed and motionless on the stone floor, with her twisted muscles and her blood-matted clothes, and I stared at the dark veins in her neck, and I thought blankly: this is

absurd. I can't pick her up and drop her in this bag like a
dead cat. She'd kill me.

Then I laughed until I fell down and wept.


I know I killed her. She and Anya would still be alive if not
for my obsession. I deluded myself into imagining Leah had
returned, and for that they died. For years I went to sleep
under the weight of it, and woke staring at it.

If I were a coward, I could say Daniel did it, but he was
not really alive anymore, and the ghost inside him was not a
person either, to be assigned blame and motivation. It was
half-destroyed by possession, torn and stripped down to its
very worst essences – panic, terror, bloodlust. You might as
well blame a thunderstorm. You cannot rage at wind and
rain. Blame instead the person who draws down the lightning
upon you.

I lured him to the house in the desperate hope of bringing
Leah to us. I left him alone with Marian and Anya to chase
noises in the dark. I killed them both. It is better, usually, to
look these things in the face. For years I said it to myself
every night, like a devotional. *I killed them*.

I did not kill Daniel, though I watched him die. I put him
in the basement and locked the door, threw food down the
steps every few hours. I knew what I was waiting for.

Three days after he killed his mother, he started having
seizures. I sat at the top of the stairs and watched the blood
froth at his mouth. When he died I took him down to the
underworld like Marian and Anya, though there was little of
Daniel left in him to judge. I should have buried him in the
back garden and let trees grow up through his body. But I didn't
think of that, then. I could not think of anything at all.


A few days after the memorial, I blinked slowly awake on the
floor at the foot of my bed. Anya's blood was dried into the

sheets. The sunlight was cold on my face again. After a moment, I realised what had woken me. Someone was knocking at the door.

I stumbled clumsily downstairs to answer it. I had not expected anyone. For a moment I could not remember why anyone would come to the house.

My fingers slipped on the latch. A man and a woman stood in the doorway, looking at me. I vaguely remembered the man's name. Malik. The woman, his sister, was holding an old man in her arms. He was too thin. I stared at him. His breathing was a soft rattle and there was bloody foam at his mouth.

'Help us,' said the woman desperately. 'Please.'

His name was Nathan, and he was dying. He was old – seventy-five, eighty, I forget. He had been ailing slowly for months, and eventually he had taken to his bed half-conscious and coughing up blood, and then that morning he had not woken at all. He still breathed, though, and they thought that meant there was hope. So they had brought him to me.

They laid him on the floor so I could examine him. Blood trickled onto his cheeks when he coughed. I remembered the name vaguely from *A Discussion of the Pulmonary Ailments* – *svasarakta,* a corrosion of the blood vessels around the lungs. That was immaterial, though, just a name to guide them through their grief. He was dying and he had been dying for a long time.

His son, Malik, did not take this well. He raged and swore at me, even as his trembling sister put a hand on his arm; he called me murderer, lazy bitch, fraud. I stared back at him from where I sat at the table. He could not hate me more than I hated myself.

At last he turned and stormed out of the house. His sister cast one frightened look back at her father dying on my floor, murmured something about him not wanting resurrection, and followed. Then there was silence.

I sat there at the table after the door closed and looked up at the ceiling, at my room through the floorboards, and the truth settled over me.

If Marian was dead, that meant I was the witchling.

It seemed unimaginable, a horrific perversion, like the ghost in Daniel's body. I could not replace her. I was her killer – how could I take over her duties, assume her title? I was pathetic, worthless, I should have been buried with her, I should have—

No. I tried to push my grief and guilt away for a second and clear my mind.

*Look at the task at hand*, said a voice in my mind. *You are the witchling now.*

I put my head in my hands, trying to block out Nathan's rattling breaths in the empty parlour. I had not eaten in days and my head pulsed from crying. The terrible silence of the house was its own accusation. I looked up and stared at the trapdoor, thinking dully that at any moment Marian's ghost would stride through it to admonish me, to tell me I disgusted her, that I was the disappointment of her life. Leah had said only the most cunning and resourceful ghosts escaped the underworld, and Marian was both. If she wanted to come back, I knew not even natural law could stop her.

But she wouldn't. She was beyond me now.

And Leah. My thoughts turned to her again, as they had almost every day since I was twelve, but the obsession that had fuelled me had died with Marian. I saw myself quite clearly now: a stupid, reckless child, careless of my duties or of the people I could hurt by neglecting them, following dripping water into dark tunnels and imagining eyes in the trees, desperately searching for a way out of a life I had not chosen. And for what? What would I do with that freedom? I could not leave this town, which would rot and die without me. Nor, even if another witchling miraculously arrived to lift the burden from me, could I leave my name and my calling and walk into another life. Witchlings could not abandon their duties, it was ancient law. I was one girl, alone and marked.

And Leah herself. The witch who walked the living world in defiance of all that was possible. I would never see her again; that, too, was suddenly, dully clear to me, as it should have been long ago. I was nothing to her. I did not know why she had come for Elior and Cora but not for Daniel, and I could not care anymore. Whatever she meant, it was no concern of mine. I was the witchling of a small town, and nothing more.

I closed my eyes. The terrible decades-long weight of it loomed above me. How could I do this? I did not deserve to be a witchling. If they knew what had happened to Marian, through my recklessness and my stupidity, they would never trust me.

*Then don't tell them*, said the voice inside my head, calmly. *You know what happens now.*

I was the witchling. That was the fact of it, whether I was ready for it or not, whether I had killed Marian or not. Whether I could do it or not. It was what duty required of me, and I would never ignore my duty again.

I gathered my shattered strength, and closed my eyes.

Marian often talked about the witchling's vows: never to take husband or wife, never to bear a child, never to demand payment in exchange for care, never to refuse healing or death rites out of personal dislike. *You treat the person in front of you*, she had told me countless times, *you do what is required, and you do not ask questions.* Now she was dead I was bound by these laws, as she had been. I would be watched by the town and the lord's men, and if I ever broke them I would be tried and punished. I wondered what the sentence might be; they could not lock me away or their people would sicken and die. But then I thought of Esther. There were other ways to punish someone.

It would never happen. I swore that to myself, steeped in a fog of grief and guilt and hunger so deep it edged transcendence. I forswore love and hatred and judgement, anything that could corrupt my heart and sway me from my calling. I would be as perfect, as trusted, as all-knowing as Marian had been, and I would never try to escape again.

I sat there with my head in my hands for minutes that might have been hours, lost in my grim thoughts with the old man dying at my feet, until someone knocked on the door again.

It took all the effort I had to pull myself out of my chair and walk to the door. Ira stood there, concerned and expectant. I tried to smile at her and failed.

'Haley,' she said. 'I had an appointment with Marian, before . . . I wasn't sure if . . .'

'Sure,' I said. 'Sure. Come in.'

Nathan was still on the floor when I brought her into the kitchen. Ira looked down at him. 'Is he all right?'

'No,' I said flatly. 'He's dying.'

'Oh, darling.' Ira put a hand on Nathan's cheek. 'He was always such a kind man.'

I was so tired it took effort to find words, to sort and orient them. 'There's some . . . treatment I should give him. It'll just take me a moment. Please, sit down.'

'Of course.'

Ira settled in her usual chair and watched me grind herbs for the salves that would dull Nathan's painful cough and thicken his sleep. She must have seen Marian do this a hundred times. I tried to mimic the surety of Marian's movements, but my hands were shaking again.

Michael was gone now, of course. One day, a month or so after the lord's army had first arrived in our town, the decay had spread so far that his body could no longer contain the soul bound to it. Ira had come upstairs to find him lying motionless in his bed and sent for me and Marian at once, but there was nothing we could do. His empty eye sockets were fixed on the ceiling, skin rotted away, his empty ribcage with its mould-furred heart half-covered with stained bedsheets. Truly dead at last.

Ira had wept all over again at the kitchen table, and we had helped her burn his empty body in the woods behind the House of the Dead, in secret, so that their friends and children would never see what he had become behind his locked bedroom door. His remains were buried in my back garden where no one could desecrate them, and Ira and her children came often to visit him. And now her new husband came with them, a kind man from two villages away, who was a hunter and the reason Ira was sitting in my chair now with her belly six months swollen with child.

'Forty years old,' she had said when Marian had explained to her two months ago why she could not stop throwing up, 'I didn't know I still had it in me.' And Marian had smiled and said, 'I've found experience helps these things, don't you think?'

I stopped with my hands shaking on the pestle, closed my eyes, and steadied myself.

Anyway. Ira had to come to the House of the Dead every week now, until the baby came. Forty was not dangerously old, as these things went, but it meant extra care needed to be taken. And so here she was. The world still moved, even though Marian was dead.

I let the hot salve cool on the table and lay Nathan down on the blankets in the corner. He weighed as little as a child. If he had even a few hours left I would be surprised. There was no magic that could pull him back from this, no injured part of him to be held together and helped to heal. Witchling-runes could not restore youth. All I could do was ease his passing.

Ira said gently, 'Malik's an idiot. I saw him leave. I'm sorry if he upset you.'

I shrugged, unable to speak, and rubbed the salve gently around his mouth and into the sunken blue skin under his eyes. I felt him slow and go still. I could feel Marian's shade watching me, noting my mistakes, and corrected them quickly before she could point them out. A shadow of the grief and guilt that had bedridden me for days was gathering at the base of my skull, pulling my thoughts into darkness. I tried to shake it off. I needed to concentrate.

'I'm sorry,' I said, getting to my feet. I could hear my voice crack, and so could she. I closed my eyes and tried it again. 'I'm sorry. I'm all yours now. Sit down, please.'

Ira looked up at me with concern, and I knew I could dispel it if I gave her something to do, an instruction, but when I reached for the list of checks for pregnant women in my head there was nothing, nothing, my mind was empty.

'Haley? Haley, sit down. Come on.'

I let her guide me into a chair. Everything was clamour and shadow in my head. All that mattered to me now was keeping my composure, I was the witchling and she was in my care, I could not cry in front of her, but all I could see was Malik and his fury and *murderer* and Daniel on the bridge and Marian's eyes on my face as he drew the knife out of her and *I'm sorry, I'm so sorry*—

Ira stroked my head as I sat there, staring unseeingly at the wood, every muscle in my body tense with the effort of keeping myself together, trying to force myself to calm down. 'Haley,' she said again, softly. 'Talk to me.'

I think she knew. She must have done.

'It's my fault,' I said, thickly, and I heard my voice break. 'It's my fault she's dead. I made – a mistake.'

A silence. I had not really meant to tell her. I had not meant to tell anyone.

I thought she would slap me, or get up and walk away and leave me in the silent house. But her eyes were full of pity. 'Oh, sweetheart,' she said, and drew me to her. 'Oh, darling, I'm so sorry,' and I cried until thought I would shake apart in her arms. After that, things got a little easier.

Take a walk with me through this terrible house. Come with me, the old man in your arms, still and dead, down to the basement where Marian and Daniel and Anya and Elior and Niamh and how many thousands of others have lain before him. You have given him the rites, carved marks into his skin with blood-ink and herb-smoke so that they look many years old. They will keep him calm, so that the shock of his own death does not tear him apart. You have fulfilled your duties. You have done well.

Climb through the doorway and walk down to the under-world, through the dark passages, the dripping water and the slowly thinning air. You need have no fear of darkness now. It knows you, and it will not hurt you. The old man becomes heavier as you walk, and just when you think his weight will break you, the darkness yields and you stand above the entrance to the underworld.

It looks, to the uninitiated, like a thousand feet of empty sky below you. You are not the uninitiated. Haul the old man over your shoulder, kneel, and reach through the hole between worlds until your fingers feel the rope. Cling to it as hard as you can, close your eyes and let yourself drop through the opening, and then – this is the worst of it – you must hang by your fingers above the dizzying world, clinging to the hard chipped-amethyst sky, and then take a breath and swing forward and clamber onto the wooden bridge with one hand, the other on the old man's ankle to stop him falling.

Don't look down. When you see the thousand-thousand ghosts below you, the teeming forests and the slow rivers, you will think about the infinity of death, and stare and stare until you are lost. It has been known to happen, even to witchlings. We are not immune to the slow forgetting of the underworld; we are still vulnerable, still human, even with our tattoos. So fix your eyes on the mountaintop ahead of you, take the old man in your arms again – don't carry him over your shoulder if you don't have to, give him his dignity – and walk straight ahead. Your balance is perfect. You were born for this.

As you get closer, the wooden slats of the bridge creaking and swaying beneath you, you see a figure ahead of you. She is dressed in the skins of underworld-creatures, huge silken bats and gentle furred aurochs. Never the same witch twice. She is waiting for you, though you will never discover how she knows you are coming. Witches disdain witchlings; your magic is a pale copy of theirs, mutated and diluted. They do not reveal their secrets to you, and you do not ask.

She keeps your eyes on you as you approach. She does not help you take the final, most dangerous step from the bridge to the mountaintop – wider than a human footstep, difficult with a corpse in your arms, the slopes of the mountain cold and endless below you – and when you slip a little and straighten up and look at her, she does not greet you. You are an envoy from your world and she from hers, and you are nothing to each other beyond that.

You look her in the face and quell the rising swell of hope in your heart again. She is not Leah, of course, and that more than anything is the confirmation you need: surely, if Leah wanted to find you, this would be the way. But you are not Haley, you are just the witchling now, and so you lay the body down in the snow and say, 'He died a few hours ago.'

'What of?'

'Svasarakta.'

You are almost certain she asks this just to test you, but

she sees no flaw in your diagnosis. She kneels in the snow – it never melts against the heat of her skin, and you have felt the warm touch of a witch, so you're almost sure now that it's not true snow, but a billion tiny fragments of glass – and examines the body. She strips the clothes off the body, and part of you wants to flinch, to look away at the sight of him shrivelled and naked on the mountaintop. But you are the witchling now, and this is all nothing to you, and so you watch.

The witch says, 'What was his name?'

'Nathan. He was seventy-nine.'

'Did he confess?'

They ask this every time you come down to the underworld they ask it. Did he confess, on his deathbed, to some terrible sin? People do, in their last moments – murders, cheated lovers, abandoned children. But Nathan was half-dead by the time he came to you, and could not speak; his secrets died with him.

So you say, 'No,' and the witch seems satisfied, but you are thinking of Niamh now, and her anguish. You almost look down, to try to see her in amongst the throng of ghosts. Is she still here? She has been dead five years now. Did she ask to be judged, or was she too afraid, for all Marian's reassurances?

But you steady yourself. Don't look down, remember. You might never look up again.

The witch nods and closes her eyes. You sense, though you cannot see, what happens next. Something reaches from her into the body, tendrils of smoke through the skin, searching and finding and wrapping around something deep and internal. The witch, with nothing at all in her eyes, reaches and tilts the old man's head back and opens his mouth. Again the desperate, visceral instinct to look away rises in you, but you have to fight it, because you are the witchling.

And then you see the fingertips at the edge of his mouth.

They are translucent – not grey, but utterly colourless. They do not look like they have substance, but they scrabble and pull at the corpse's lips, trying to find purchase: just fingertips at first, and then, with a twisting wrench, a wrist. The hand reaches blindly across the man's face, spiderlike.

The witch grabs it, and pulls.

The ghost's arm comes out up to the elbow with a *crunch*. There's blood and broken teeth in the corpse's slack mouth. She pulls again, and you're desperately glad they didn't let you stay when they did this to Marian, you couldn't have borne it. Nobody is allowed to talk to those they love after they are dead, not even witchlings. *Natural law,* again. They saw that you loved her and they sent you away.

Marian was the last person you will ever be allowed to love. Now that you are the witchling, you are bound by impartiality. If a man confesses to you, dying, that he killed a child, you are still bound to try to save him. You are nothing now but hands to tie bandages, carve runes, stroke feverish foreheads; you are the bones that make the blood you will one day brew into ink. You are nothing.

You stand on the mountain and watch as the ghost of the old man pulls his foot from the mouth of his corpse, looks down at his own ruined face, and screams.

When you brought Daniel's body here, you did not recognise the ghost they pulled from him, but you saw a wisp of something else, grey and soft, escape and drift away over the mountains. It's a calming thought, that whatever is left of him can fly.

Over the blubbering and whimpering, the witchling gives you a look, and dutifully you turn and climb the bridge again towards the living world. Your work is done.

That first year was appalling, swooning dimness and the shadow of grief. I have tried very hard to forget most of it.

I have vague impressions: the empty house, bodies in the parlour, women giving birth in my smoky kitchen. They still came to me, of course. A seventeen-year-old witchling was better than no witching at all, and no one was fool enough to try to give birth alone, or to treat blood poisoning and infections with their own scraps of wisdom. After Nathan died, his son spread rumours about me – that I was lazy, stupid, careless, more interested in killing than healing – but there I was lucky, because Malik was known as a drunk and a brute, and his animosity did me more favours than his respect would have done.

Ira defended me, as well. I owe much of my tenuous survival that year to her. She was liked and trusted, as were her new husband and her elder children, and when her baby was born she made a point of telling anyone who asked that the health of her rosy-cheeked little girl was down entirely to me. She named the child Elia, after the son who had died seven years before. Ira came with her to visit me under the pretence of check-ups, and after I performed the formalities of weight and pulse we would sit at the table and talk. It was months before I could say more than a few words without wanting to curl up under the table and sleep again. The terrible guilt-grief beat in my head – *you killed Marian, you killed Marian* – had congealed into an unyielding lethargy. It clouded my thoughts and kept me sitting alone at the table, not eating, unable to sleep.

But Ira knew that. She came and she stayed and she talked to me, she kept me functioning and alive. She never asked more questions about Marian's death; she knew everything she needed to. Sometimes she brought her husband to fletch arrows at my table, and her younger children to play on my floor, and then warmth and living voices were in the house again, and I was so grateful to her for that. Her visits brought pulse and rhythm to my loneliness, brightened it, and when she thought I was ready she came with me to market, to get the food and herbs I needed.

And there was my second relief. I thought the people at market would challenge me, try to charge me bronze or favours for what I needed, without Marian's calm authority to protect me. But nobody asked, not even when I went alone. That was the only blessing of becoming the witchling's girl so young: they had known me for ten years, and though they would have preferred Marian, they knew I was her heir and the product of her training. It was as if she walked behind me. Nobody threw things at me; nobody sneered at me in the street. I walked unharmed, and when they needed me they came to my door, and that was all I could have asked for.

One day I poured the last of Marian's blood-ink into the river, and that was another way in which she was gone. Somewhere around the nine-month mark I cried for the last time.

My world had mechanics and order. People came to me sick and I cured them; they came to me dying, and with effort I comforted them. My grief did not lessen, but its grip on me weakened; I could put it in the back of my mind for minutes, sometimes hours at a time, long enough to heal, to perform rites with a clear mind, to go down to the underworld. My life assumed a new kind of normality. I lay alone in my bed and listened to the silence, and knew that if I needed to I could get up in the morning, and the morning after. I could survive months and years and decades if I had to. I could exist in grey suspension for as long as they needed me.

## CHAPTER ELEVEN

I met Callum in the second winter after Marian's death. Those months were bleak: corpses thronged the basement, and worried loved ones of the ailing paced the hallway of the House of the Dead. Half the time the people who came to me only had minor infections, chills and the like, and I treated them in ten minutes and sent them briskly home. I didn't blame them, of course – who would risk not going to the witchling when their child was sick? We had all heard stories about mothers and fathers who waited a day too late, had just a little too much faith, and lost their child to sleeping-sickness or a fever.

Still, there were worse afflictions hidden amongst the throng of coughing children, and it took careful attention to sort through them. Before Marian's death we could have divided them up, worked twice as fast, but now that she was gone it was just me, sleepless and numb-fingered in the cold. And one day, in amongst them was Callum, with his son.

I had heard of him, though I don't think we had ever met. He was maybe thirty-five, a scholar of law who officiated at the court in our small town. He had maintained subtle control after the army of Jonathan came, making sure that the soldiers left behind to watch over us believed themselves in charge of the verdicts and sentences handed down by Callum and his officials, without ever actually allowing them any real power. It was a delicate job, and Callum did it discreetly and well. I learned all of this from Marian, who had known everything about everyone. Since her death I had been cut off from the comings and goings of the town. I did not know, for instance, that Callum's wife had got up one morning three weeks ago with nothing but the clothes on her back and walked away, into the woods, leaving him a note and the sole care of their two-year-old son.

'Oh, yes,' whispered Rina, his neighbour, as I measured out the tea I prescribed for her coughing sickness, 'just left – *I can't live here anymore,* she said, and walked right out. And their little boy, too. Disgusting.'

I kept my eyes on the tea leaves. Callum and his little boy were sitting in the hallway, and I could feel his gaze on Rina and me. I wondered exactly where Rina had heard this version of the story. Somehow I doubted that he had told her.

There was some debate over where his wife had gone. Before we lost the war, you could walk freely between villages, change your name and take up a new life with impunity; it happened all the time. In the year or so afterwards no one had dared do it for fear of being found in the woods and slaughtered as an enemy combatant by the soldiers of the new lord. But now things were easier. Jonathan's army was far away on the west coast, the last rebellions in our land had long since been crushed, and the descendants he had left behind to rule us were surer of their control, less inclined to kill a woman travelling alone in the forest. Callum's wife might have made it.

I wrapped Rina's medicines in brown paper, told her when and how to take them, and sent her away. She gave Callum an appraising look as she walked past him. He had probably heard her gossiping to me. But it didn't matter if he had, I reminded myself. I had listened with a witchling's implacability and had not offered judgement. Still, there was a little coldness in the way he looked at me.

He lifted his son up and put him on the chair. The boy

looked up at me plaintively, and I crouched down beside him. 'What's wrong?'

Always speak to the child before the parent, that was an old rule of Marian's. It made them both like you better. The boy opened his mouth, birdlike, and pointed sadly at his neck. I could see the white swelling of infection at the back of his throat.

'It's been sore for days,' said Callum, 'but today he woke up and he couldn't speak.' His voice sounded very low after Rina's chattering. I looked up at him. His gaze was piercing and oddly familiar. It awoke an old, sheepish instinct in me.

'I can make him something for that.'

'Thank you,' he said, and then, as I moved to the kitchen, he nudged his son's shoulder. 'Come on. Say thank you to Haley. She's going to make you better.'

I came back into the kitchen with the medicines I needed and a long needle to pierce the swelling at the back of the boy's throat. This was always the hardest part. I held it behind my back and smiled at the boy.

'What's your name?' I asked him brightly, and though I knew he could not answer I kept my eyes on him as Callum said, 'Aron.'

'Aron. Wonderful. We're going to play a game. We have to play it right, or it won't fix your throat. Are you all right with that?'

He nodded. He barely resembled Callum at all. Except the eyes, maybe.

'Okay, Aron. What I need you to do is open your mouth as wide as you can, hold very, very still and close your eyes really tight. For as long as you possibly can, okay? The longer you do it, the faster it will make you better. Does that sound good?'

He nodded again, hope in his eyes. Yes, they were definitely Callum's. They were bright and grey, hawk-like, with the same steadiness.

'All right. You hold your papa's hand, and open your mouth
– wider, that's good, well done – and close your eyes – very,
very still now—'

I glanced up at Callum before I revealed the needle. He
tensed a little at the sight of it but did not move to stop me.

'I'm just going to touch the back of your neck now, okay,
Aron? Stay very still . . . that's good . . .'

I took a breath, aimed, reached in with the needle and
pierced the swelling. The boy screamed, and Callum winced.

'Aron – Aron, come on, now—'

It was no use; he sobbed and kept screaming. It took about
ten minutes for Callum to calm him down and get him to
drink the vial of dittany I gave him. I busied myself with
making the fire while Callum murmured soft soothing words
and Aron's cries faded to sniffles. When I turned around Callum
looked exhausted, and the little boy was staring at me, red-
faced and accusatory.

'It *hurt*.'

'It had to hurt,' I said to him gently, 'or you wouldn't get
better.'

I handed the brown paper of tea leaves to Callum, who
took it, watching me with an intensity that made me want
to look away. I didn't know what he thought I was going to
do.

'Take this. He should drink it every night to stop the infection coming back.'

'Thank you,' he said. But he kept his eyes on me and didn't
turn away. I resented that – there was no one else in the
corridor, and I was exhausted and hungry, three women in
the town were almost due to give birth, and I knew of two
elderly townsfolk at home in their beds who might not last
the night, so I couldn't expect more than a few hours' rest
before someone else knocked on my door.

I took a deliberate step back, and he seemed to come back

to himself. He rubbed his face and turned to the door, then realised there was no one else there.

'Is there anything else I can help with?' I said.

'No, no,' he murmured. He didn't want to meet my eyes now. 'Thank you, you've been so kind.'

I watched him move to leave, standing alone in the parlour. He was halfway to the door before something snapped into place in my brain. It was his son's eyes that did it, I think, so steady and grey and familiar, and that gaze; how many times had I been stared at like that, been read and examined at this table? I knew him. I *knew* him.

'Callum,' I said.

He turned back to me, his eyes guarded.

'Did you . . . did you happen to know Marian? The witchling before me?'

He regarded me, and hesitated for only a moment.

'I did,' he said at last. 'She was my sister.'

Joy rose in me, so powerful I could not speak. Her *brother*, right in front of me. I had thought of her as irretrievable, and of course she was, but there was a kind of redemption in the idea that people of her blood still lived, right here in our town. A little boy with her eyes.

He saw the emotion in my face and put his son down on the floor. Aron climbed halfway up the stairs and sat there, staring suspiciously at me through the banisters.

'She told me about you,' he said, 'but I never met you. I never got sick enough to come here. She was very proud of you. I can see why.'

I just stood there, trying to find words. My throat was tight. All I could say, eventually, was, 'You talked?'

He nodded, slowly. 'She used to come to my house. When Vira was pregnant, she . . . she would make weekly visits.'

I tried to imagine Marian walking out of the house, telling me she was going to market or to the river, and then turning away towards where her brother lived. It was against the witchling's vows, of course. She had broken them, retained the family she was meant to have given up, and concealed it from the lord's men for years without discovery or punishment. It was glorious to think about. I smiled for the first time in months.

Callum's little son stared through the staircase bars at me. Then, at last, his father ushered him back down into the hallway.

'Aron,' he said softly. 'Come on. We should leave Haley in peace now.'

'No. Don't.'

I had said it too suddenly, too loudly. Callum and the boy looked at me.

'I, uh . . .' The words wouldn't come to me. I coughed. 'Do you want to . . . would you like some tea? I have bread, I can make . . . soup, if you want it.'

He regarded me for a moment, with that familiar piercing gaze. Then at last he smiled.

'That sounds wonderful,' he said. 'What can I do to help?'

After that, Callum and Aron came almost as often as Ira. I had carved toys for the children during my long months alone in the house, and the little boy played with them happily in the corner while Callum and I talked.

I was delighted to find that he had known Marian – not just distantly, as the older sister who had vanished into the House of the Dead when he was a small child, but *really* known her, had talked to her right up until the week she had died. She had never told me about it, had hidden her connections with her siblings from me when they came to the House of the Dead – not wanting to draw me into the conspiracy, or, I thought, to rub salt into an unhealed wound. Her siblings had held onto her, even in defiance of the lord's men; my mother had left me without a second thought, when her baby was too young to remember me. Marian didn't want that to hurt more than it had to.

It had not been easy, Callum told me. After she became the witchling's girl their father swore that he would beat her to death if she ever came to their house again, but he was dead of drink before Callum turned fifteen, and after that Marian visited as often as she could. Callum told me the circumstances of Marian's deliverance, how she had discovered what she was after their mother's death, what the woodcutter's son had done to her, her slow patient revenge. I was sorry she had got there first. I would have killed him in a heartbeat if he had ever come to my door.

That was why she never told you, said Callum. She didn't want you to want that.

We were nourishment to each other. He had carried her secrets alone for years, and could never talk about them – could not talk about *her*, really, because nobody else in this town really knew Marian, except as the witchling. But we remembered her, and we mourned her together.

I told him I had taken her body down to the underworld, though that should have been his decision really, as her next of kin. He would have done the same thing, he said. Although strictly speaking he wasn't any kin of hers, hadn't been from the moment she took her vows. I was her girl, her only real family. Bullshit, I said. Never mind technicalities. She loved you.

She had loved him. It was wonderful to think of, a crack in my terrible loneliness. My carelessness had not completely erased Marian from the world.

Callum had not really known her when he was a child. He was only four when she left, too young to really understand what witchlings were, why she was no longer allowed to see him. He was the baby their mother had died giving birth to, and his father had hated him for that. He hated everyone and everything, of course, but he loathed Callum especially, almost as much as he hated Marian for leaving and their brother Aron for taking over as the babies' protector once she was gone. Callum grew up in the unyielding glare of that hatred. I'm glad he died when he did, he said. I worry what I might have done.

On his deathbed, four years after Marian became the witchling, their father asked Callum to take him to the woods behind the house and bury him there after he died. Please, son, he said. It's what I want.

Why? said Callum. Are you afraid of her?

His father fixed him with bloodshot eyes and did not answer. Please, he said after a long time. Do you want me to beg? I'll beg.

Yes, said Callum.

Please. I'm begging you.

Callum sat there in silence until his father shuddered into stillness, then carried him over his shoulder to the House of the Dead.

His father, like the grieving brother who had attacked me so many years before, had preferred oblivion to the prospect of judgment or eternity in the underworld. Tough luck, Callum said to me. He should have arranged to die alone if he wanted that. Concealing a corpse from a witchling, intentionally letting the ghost in it rot away without giving it a chance at an afterlife, was a crime more serious than murder. Callum would have died for it, if the lord's men had ever found out. There are people I'd do that for, he said to me, but my father wasn't one of them.

At least he knew what he'd done, I said, at least he knew he would be damned for it.

Callum laughed bitterly. Yeah, he said. Sure. At least there's that.

After their father died Marian began to visit their house, at night and in secret. Callum remembered the door clicking open, the children rushing to embrace her. She brought them food, treated their cuts and bruises, listened to their stories. She would only have been twenty-two by then. It was Aron she was closest to, and Callum, a boy of fourteen, used to sit around the table with them at night when the others had gone to bed and listen eagerly as they reminisced about a past he could not remember – before their mother's death and their father's rages, when they had been children together in a world without war.

Marian, said Callum, had left behind six younger siblings. Alba had died at the age of nine, just after Marian was given up, of the sleeping sickness. It took a dozen children that winter, and you could not move in the House of the Dead for shivering infants and pale, tense parents. Dora and Marian were desperately overworked, trying to sort through and prioritise, unable to treat everyone. That had been the hardest thing, Marian had told him, measuring out laudanum and rue for a little blue-skinned boy as Alba lay dying in the corner, being forbidden from shoving all the other patients into the corridor and coax her sister slowly back from the edge of death. Witchlings' girls had no sisters, said Dora, and to Marian, every life had to be equal. She could not sacrifice others for the sake of one girl; she belonged to the town now. She had to watch as Dora worked Alba's body into a sack with two other corpses and vanished through the trapdoor into the underworld.

That left five siblings. When he was eighteen, Indra built a boat with his own hands and sailed down the river to the coast to become a merchant sailor; Callum had not heard from him in years. Another brother, Edwun, had married a scholar and moved to the city in the north to raise their children – his letters had stopped abruptly when Lord Jonathan's army reached the battlements. Dana and Aron had gone to war and died there, out in the eastern hills, and their husbands and children had moved away after that. And now Marian was gone, and Callum's wife too. Other than his son, he was alone.

I broke down when he told me that. I told him it was my fault she had died, that I had made a mistake.

He watched me intently. 'What kind of mistake?' he said, at last.

I did not know what to tell him. I could not explain Leah – I had never been able to explain her, she was a dream I did not speak of, she would die with me. Instead I told him of a boy who had gone mad and killed a woman in his house. I had thought in my arrogance that I could treat him if he came to the House of the Dead, but he escaped me and murdered Marian and Anya.

Afterwards, I questioned myself anxiously. Was that as close to the truth as I could get? Had I tried to make myself look better, more virtuous than I had been? I wanted to be honest with him; if he hated me, I would accept it. I didn't want his mercy unearned.

He considered me for a long time, and then got up and went to the kitchen. I sat at the table, staring at my hands. All my instincts told me firmly he was not allowed there, to get up and pull him back, protect my secrets, but I stayed where I was. I could hear him rifling through the cupboards.

He came back with two cups. I peered into mine. It looked like dark wine. He saw the hesitation in my face and smiled without mirth.

'Don't worry,' he said. 'I wouldn't know how to poison you if I wanted to.'

'You'd have the right.'

'No, I wouldn't.' He sipped the wine and stared down at Aron, playing in the corner. 'Marian used to talk to me about Connor.'

'The woodcutter's son?'

He glanced at me. 'Yes. She worried what the witches would think, when she was judged. She killed him. She was sure she wouldn't get sent to the world above after that.'

'He deserved it,' I said, at once. There was not a doubt in my mind about that.

'Yes, but it wasn't her place. The witches would have judged him, if he'd asked for it. She didn't have the right to take revenge. That's not how it works.'

'But—' I was aghast. 'She didn't go out looking for him. She would have left him alone. She *did* leave him alone, for years. He was brought to her. Was she meant to save his life?'

Callum looked at me bleakly over his cup. 'She was the witchling. That's exactly what she was meant to do.'

'You can't ask that of someone,' I said. 'No one can, not a witch, not anyone. She was human.'

'I know. That's what I told her.' He took another sip, staring at his son playing beside the fire. 'But she wouldn't listen to me.'

'You work at the court. You judge people all the time. Did she think the witches would damn you for that?'

'I told her that, too.' He smiled and glanced at me. 'She said it was different. I put them in prison, I take away their money. I don't kill them.'

'It's still judgement. It's still justice.'

'I know.'

Callum was sitting in Marian's chair; sometimes when he was here I'd turn absently and his silhouette and his greying hair would strike me dumb. It was so easy to let myself believe he was her, that she was alive. So difficult to remember when I had taken her presence for granted. The stupid, obsessed girl who had stood on the bridge with Daniel seemed a thousand years away, her thoughts impenetrable. It was impossible to imagine ever having been her.

Callum was watching me. 'You're worried she wouldn't forgive you,' he said, 'and I'm saying, she wouldn't consider it her place to do that.'

'She was human,' I said. 'I killed her. You can't say she wouldn't hate me for it.'

He shook his head and put down his cup. 'Absolutely I can. For one thing, you didn't kill her.'

'As good as—'

'I do this for a living, Haley. You made a mistake and she died, which is terrible, I understand that, but it's not *killing*.'

'It doesn't matter.'

'It does to me,' he said, 'and it would to her.'

I didn't have anything to say to that. I drank the wine and watched Aron try to build a tower out of the tiny wooden horses I had carved for baby Elia. I had worried about making them. I thought it might look like I was breaking my oaths, developing too much affection for Ira and her family. If they knew I wrought toys for little children they might think me soft and pathetic.

I had voiced this to Ira and she had sat for a while, stricken, watching her daughter play. Then she said, 'You think Marian was completely alone? That no one trusted her, no one ever talked to her? She never asked any of us for advice? Never cared for our children? You think that's what your vows mean?'

'No,' I said, 'no, of course not, that's not what I—'

'You think they would have respected her more if she had been? If she'd been cruel, if she'd locked herself away?'

'No,' I said, frustrated, 'no, I don't mean—'

'You're not Marian,' said Ira. 'Stop trying to be. You're eighteen, Haley. You'll never convince them you're her, and you don't have to. They know you're the witchling and that's what matters. And they won't think more of you if you shut them out.'

That had been a week before. With Callum at the end of the table, I sat in silence and watched his son build his tower and tried to imagine what the town would think of me in twenty years, when I was old. I could not picture them holding a memorial to me.

With the third horse, the whole tower collapsed and Aron started crying. Callum put down the cup, got out of his chair and picked him up. The little boy sobbed and beat his tiny fists against his father's shoulder.

'There, there,' Callum murmured, rocking him. I was reminded of Eve with newborn Grace, the first child I had ever delivered, whispering exhaustedly in this kitchen, a lifetime ago. *It's okay. It's all right.*

'*Bad horse! Bad horse!*'

'Don't worry. You'll build a big tower with them.' He stroked Aron's forehead. 'You just have to be patient.'

'*Want Mama!*'

Callum stopped dead at that. I looked down, and took a sip of the wine.

'I know,' he said at last. 'I know, sweetheart.'

It took almost ten minutes to calm Aron down, and by then I could hear rain pattering on the roof. Callum put on his coat and glanced out of the window, but I said, 'You can sleep here if you want. It's a long way back.'

He hesitated. 'Really?'

'Yeah. You can take my room, if you like. I have to . . .' I indicated the basement, vaguely.

He watched me as I got up, gathered my gloves and coat. When I turned back there was new determination in his face. I watched him apprehensively.

'Can I see it?'

'The underworld?'

He shook his head, made a hand gesture like swatting away a fly. 'No, I know I can't – the tunnel, I mean.'

I hesitated.

'It's just a tunnel, Callum.'

'No it's not. I'd like to see it.'

There was a childlike courage in his face, one I recognised from a long time ago, from the life I tried not to remember – running into the forbidden woods with Daniel, giggling, fear fluttering in my chest, playing at lords. My heart still ached at the thought of him.

He saw my reticence. 'What's the matter?'

I chose my words carefully. 'You must have asked Marian this. Before.'

'She wouldn't let me come to the house. It would be too obvious if I stayed too long, if someone came and saw us talking. The lord's men would have noticed.' He smiled without feeling. 'I'm not going to run after her, Haley.'

'I know. I know that.'

'Well, then.'

There was a strange defiance in his face. I couldn't think of anything to dissuade him. I wouldn't have done it for anyone else, not even for Ira, but my instincts told me the underworld was not as dangerous to Callum as it might have been to a stranger. He was a witchling's brother, kin to its kin. It might hesitate before it hurt him.

'You can't take Aron,' I said at last. 'It's too dangerous for children. Even the air can poison them.'

'He'll be okay up here. You can see him from the bottom of the stairs.'

Aron wasn't listening to us at all – he was beside the fire, trying to build his tower again. Callum was watching me expectantly, daring me to refuse him. 'All right,' I said, because I couldn't think of anything else. 'This way.'

We went down into the basement together. He behind me on the sixth step, as the chill set in and everything darkened suddenly. No lamplight came through the floorboards. Death lived here, you could breathe it. The stone was cold on my bare feet.

There was only one corpse here tonight – an old woman in the corner, tiny under her blanket. She had refused to see me, had been adamant when the sickness took her that this was her time and no witchling would be allowed to prolong it. Her daughter had brought her to me afterwards, weeping. The woman whispered prayers to the Lord Claire as she knelt beside her dead mother in the kitchen, and I waited tensely until she came out into the hall. A few years ago, if you had done that in the street, you would have been killed for it. The soldiers of the Lord Jonathan would raid homes, take hands for blasphemy or disrespect. Once a man had been killed at market for failing to bow to one of the lord's descendants. But that was a couple of years ago now, and the horror of it had faded in our minds.

I was glad the daughter had prayed in my earshot, though. It meant she trusted me.

I glanced up the stairs to make sure Aron was safely away from the fire, then bent in the darkness to find the old woman's body, wrapped in the shroud her daughter had brought, and hauled it over my shoulder. I turned back to Callum. He was peering into the tunnel from the other side of the room, one hand stretched towards it, as if he could touch it from twenty yards away.

'That's it?'

'That's it.'

He stepped closer. I slipped ahead of him, wary, and stood in the doorway. My tattoos glowed, a gentle luminosity you could not see unless you knew to look for it. But Callum's eyes went straight to my arms.

'They don't look like hers.'

'Every witchling's are different. You have to make them yourself.'

'Or what?'

His gaze was intent. It unnerved me a little. 'Or they don't work.'

'What would happen if I tried to use them?'

'Maybe nothing,' I said. 'With no magic maybe they'd just be marks. Or maybe they would kill you. I don't know.'

He nodded slowly, then looked into the dripping darkness of the tunnel. 'I thought it would look different,' he said.

There was silence. For a while, I thought something was about to happen. I could see the yearning in his eyes, the ache – for his mother, his dead siblings, his vanished wife. Waiting for him amongst the teeming billions in the dark.

I saw his knuckles white on the stone, the way he leaned towards it, and I was ready to drop the woman in my arms, hear the crunch of bone, lunge for him and pin him down as he fought to pull free—

'All right,' he said, and took a deep breath. 'All right.'

He looked at me a second, and then turned and went back upstairs to look after his son. I stood alone in the tunnel entrance for a while, the dead woman in my arms, hearing them talk and play above me.

Then I gathered myself and walked down into the darkness again.

He visited me every week for a year, and so on the day he failed to knock on my door I knew something was terribly wrong and I went straight to his house. It was the first time I broke my vows.

## CHAPTER TWELVE

I swore to myself this time would be different. Marian and Daniel walked behind me through the darkened streets towards the house beside the river where Callum lived alone with his son. I had my medicines in my bag, everything I could need, and I wore leather gloves and my bearskin coat. In my pocket, I carried the knives I used for surgery and the air-thin blade Marian had given me on the day I turned twelve to protect me from the soldiers of the Lord Jonathan if they decided that the town no longer needed witchlings. I would make no mistakes this time.

Everything was quiet. I was ready to meet the lord's soldiers if they stopped me – I had rehearsed a story about a boy who had broken his leg and couldn't walk to the House of the Dead to see me, I had the right equipment in my bag to set bone – but nobody challenged me. It was winter, and the town was silent. Everyone was huddled behind gold-lit windows, beside roaring fires. I hadn't seen a patrol in months. The army out west drew more and more of the remaining soldiers away, like moths to a sunset, to help them in their conquest of the world. They were not needed here anymore; they were confident now in our fear of them, in our passivity. Even now that awoke a simmering anger in me. I remembered Marian, singing hymns to Claire under her breath as she ran her hands over a child's fevered skin. She would have hated them, still, and I carried that hatred in my heart for her.

I had never been to Callum's house, but I knew where it was.

I guided myself by starlight and the murmur of the river until I saw it, built of slate and timber, in the shelter of the trees on the edge of the woods. It was set back slightly from the fishermen's houses around it, to give its occupants some privacy. I could see how easy it would have been for Callum's wife to simply walk out of the back door and vanish into the forest.

There were lights on in the window, silence inside. I hesitated, trying to hear its quality. I couldn't feel death inside the house, nothing as palpable and obvious as that, but there was something off about the air, like the creeping cold of the basement. Something was wrong inside the house. I hesitated, and then hammered on the door.

Scrabbling from inside, frantic. Then absolute silence.

Callum, or whoever was in the house, was trying to hide from me. I knocked again, harder. My other hand, inside my coat, grasped the hilt of the knife.

Still silence.

I breathed out, then pulled off my shoes and walked around the side of the house. The soil was dark and cold between my toes. I could smell the grass. I was tense, aware of how alone I was, listening for voices of guidance at my back that weren't there anymore. I clutched the knife in my hand.

At the back of the house there was a small door set into the wall. I pushed it very gently, and it swung inwards. Dread bubbled in my stomach. Callum never left his door unlocked.

I walked forwards slowly, knife in my hand. Inside there was darkness, pale lamplight under the doorway of the front room. I could hear scuffling ahead, and – I thought – the murmur of voices. There were doors beside me, locked, and in front of me—

I slipped in something wet and dark, and fell hard. I hissed in pain, and then tried to be quiet.

Ahead of me everything went suddenly silent again. I scrambled onto my knees, glancing down at the hand I had fallen on. No cut, but there was blood on the timber, not yet dry. I grasped in the dimness for something to help me up—

And something threw itself out of the shadows.

I moved at once, scrabbling back, but my fear did not paralyse me this time. My hand found the wall and I got to my feet, the knife in my other hand aimed upwards at the throat of the cloaked figure – three feet closer, and I would bury it in its face – come at me—

And then it stumbled, too. I thought for a second it had slipped on the blood, and I watched for it to fall. But it turned, and now there was someone behind it, two people struggling, cloak and muscle and gritted teeth.

*Callum*. Callum was trying to restrain it.

I moved around the wall, careful of the blood on the floor, and then lunged at the figure. I grabbed it round the throat and felt slick blood on its skin. It released Callum and flailed wildly, nails sharp on my thigh, but I pressed the knife into its stomach and it fell still.

'Don't move,' I said, 'I don't want to kill you,' and it growled at me, growled with its teeth bared. *She* growled at me.

Callum stepped back, panting. His eyes found my face and for a moment there was no recognition there, but then they widened. 'Haley?'

I felt the woman's attention shift back to him at the sound of his voice. I let go with one hand and slammed the hilt of the knife right into the back of her head. *Straight to sleep,* said Marian distantly as she fell.

Callum winced at the *thud*. He stared down at her, breathing hard. I looked at him properly, through the dimness, and saw that he was covered in blood.

'Callum—'

'I'm all right,' he said, 'I'm all right.' He was still looking at the woman, but then he came back to himself. 'Are you hurt?'

'No, I'm—'

'How did you know to come here? Did someone—'

'I was worried about you. You were meant to visit.'

'Oh,' he said, 'yes, we were.' He stared down at the woman again. He looked lost. I could see the cuts on his arms where she had slashed at him.

'Is Aron okay?'

'He's asleep.'

The woman stirred on the floor, and I tensed. Callum flinched again.

'Who is she?'

He looked up at me at last. 'She's my wife,' he said.

We tied her limbs with rope and laid Vira on the couch in their front room. I bound Callum's wounds and treated them with salt and strong wine. She had come through the back door, he said, just walked right in. She was covered in blood and her clothes were torn. When she saw him she lunged at him, grabbed a knife from his kitchen and attacked him with it, and he managed to restrain her and lock her in the front room but she escaped just as I came in. 'I'm so sorry,' he kept saying, and I recognised the helplessness in his voice from memories I tried not to touch and said sharply, 'Stop it. It's not your fault.'

His wounds were not deep, I told him, but they were painful and some of them might scar. 'Fine,' he said. 'I'll tell people someone at court did it. I've made plenty of enemies there.' He smiled, a thin smile that broke my heart. We watched Vira, bound and unconscious on the sofa. Even asleep I could see the animal wildness in her.

'I don't understand,' he said softly. 'I just – I don't understand.'

'Was she like this when she left?'

I had never asked him about his wife. I had figured, like Ira, that I knew all I needed to know. Callum did not answer for a moment.

'No.'

'Why did she leave?'

I asked it flatly, without delicacy. I thought he would appreciate that more than artificial trepidation. He didn't look at me.

'I don't know,' he said. 'I came back and she was gone. No note, nothing.'

'I thought she—'

'If you're about to tell me about something you heard from Rina,' he said tightly, 'I will lose it, Haley, I swear.'

I fell silent.

He closed his eyes. 'I didn't think she would leave me. And even if she wanted to, she wouldn't leave Aron. She didn't even take her clothes. No sign of a struggle, nothing broken. Everyone believed she left us, but I . . .' He rubbed his face, smiled without mirth. 'I thought she might have been taken. What a terrible thing to hope for.'

'It's understandable.'

'No, it isn't.'

His voice was tense. He had never snapped at me before. I stayed calm. He had Marian's gift for quiet disappointment; I feared his anger as I had hers. But now I had to be the witchling, and so I kept going.

'If you thought there was a chance she'd been taken, why didn't you tell anyone?'

'Who would I tell, Haley?' His voice was clipped. I could see how difficult it was for him to keep himself in check. 'You think Jonathan's men would help me? I looked myself, in the forests behind the house, but I couldn't – well. I couldn't even see a trail. I thought she must have walked away, covered her tracks. Maybe she did.' He looked down at her, bleakly. 'She came back of her own accord, so far as I can tell. And now she wants to kill me.'

'No she doesn't. She's ill.'

'You've seen this before?'

'Yes,' I said, 'I have.'

I laid my hand on her forehead. Vira did not stir at my touch.

'Does she have a fever?' said Callum, behind me. I could hear the anxiousness in his voice and knew that he still adored her, after everything. I could not imagine that kind of love.

'No,' I said. 'She's cold.'

I did consider telling him the truth. She was not completely gone, after all. Something in her had recognised him – I had seen the way she shifted at the sound of his voice. And she had known where the house was, too. She had known the back door, and where the knives were kept. She was not completely obliterated, as the others had been.

But what did I gain by telling him? Callum was not Marian, and he had no expertise I could draw upon here. There was nothing he could tell me that I did not already know, and dealing with his shock and his disbelief would waste valuable time. I did not know how long we had before she woke up. And I admit: I did not want to hurt him. Telling him that his wife was nearly gone, that her ghost was being destroyed within her body and her spirit mutilated, that she would never have an afterlife – that he would never know whether she had left him willingly or been stolen away – was crueller than I could countenance being to him.

So I just told him she was sick. I had seen it before, I said, but it was dangerous and – I laid a hand on his shoulder – sometimes fatal. It impeded memory. It led to unpredictable behaviour, and often violence. It caused seizures, I said. That was the dangerous part.

'Seizures,' he said hollowly, and put his face in his hands. 'Right.'

'We should take her to my house,' I said. 'If she's violent, we need to keep her away from Aron.'

He nodded, and then hesitated. 'What if she attacks you?'

I was touched by his concern. 'I'll be all right. I can look after myself.'

'How long will – will you need? How long will it be?'

*Until she dies? A day, maybe two. This is quite advanced.* I heard myself say it inside my head and winced. 'I'll do everything I can,' I said, 'but it might take a while before she's stable.'

He nodded. Then he hesitated, looking at me.

'What?'

'Aron's only asleep because I drugged him,' he said. 'We had some tea left over from that infection and I gave him all of it. I couldn't let him see his mother like this. Is he going to be okay? Did I – Should you take a look at him?' He said it baldly, unadorned. That was one of the things I admired about him. He never feared seeing what I thought of him.

I hesitated. 'I'll take a look at him, but he should be all right. I wouldn't have given you enough to harm him.'

He nodded. Some of the colour returned to his face, and I breathed more easily.

So this is where I was. At sixteen I had lured a half-mad, possessed boy to my house to try to show him to a witch. At nineteen, when Callum's wife returned with her mind ruined and the life-heat gone from her skin, I bound her and took her back to the House of the Dead to let her die in the basement. And I was proud of myself for that. I was already, as you see, quite far gone.

I didn't want anyone else to get hurt. That is the truth, I swear. I didn't want anyone else to get hurt.

# CHAPTER THIRTEEN

Vira sat in my basement for three days, by which time she should have been dead. I remembered Daniel and his seizures, the violent snapping of his joints, the frothing blood at his mouth. I sat at my kitchen table and listened closely to the silence below me, but I never heard anything.

I had chained her to the floor, real steel chains, the kind used to transport cattle and convicts. No risks this time, no overlooked contingencies. There were two places she could escape to, assuming she didn't try to dig her way out through the walls of the cellar: she could climb up the stairs or into the tunnel. I wasn't sure which was worse. If she got into the house, of course, she could kill me and any patients under my care, but if she managed to clamber down into the underworld . . . I could not imagine going back to Callum, telling him his wife was dead, but that there was no body, and I could not tell him why, he could not see her, I had not saved her. I paid careful attention to that instinct, because I knew now how dangerous it was. I should not have cared in the least about Callum and his broken heart. Affection swayed judgement, and was therefore against my vows.

Still, though. Little Aron, and his plaintive eyes . . .

I would not let his mother vanish into the underworld, half-mad and possessed. I would give her a better death than that. She was not as cleanly obliterated as Daniel had been. Perhaps when she died some fragments of her ghost would remain and she could have a peaceful afterlife. Perhaps there would even be something to judge.

So I chained her to the wall and waited. Patients trudged in and out of the house, and I treated them, and kept them away from the stairs in case they heard her. The cold rose through the cellar with the slow creep of winter, and I fed her three times a day and waited for her to die.

But she didn't.

I listened in the dead of night for thuds from below me, cries, the slow tread of footsteps. But there was nothing. She sat there and waited.

On the third day, I went down to speak to her.

Vira must have heard my footsteps, because she was sitting upright waiting for me when I got to the bottom of the stairs. She was quite beautiful, or had been; her beauty was a ravaged, feral thing now, made rough by filth and starvation. She had a strong jaw, dark matted hair down to her shoulders, and dark staring eyes that I was very glad Aron had not inherited. They had a kind of madness in them.

I sank into a crouch on the other side of the cellar. Her eyes followed me and she did not blink. I spoke quietly so as not to provoke her.

'Can you understand me?'

She knew the sounds of the words. I saw familiarity spark in her eyes, but no comprehension. I tried again. 'Do you know where you are?'

Her mouth opened to reveal yellowing teeth. They clenched around words, chewing them, and then with effort she spoke.

'You're . . . not . . . the witchling.'

'The old witchling is dead. I'm the witchling now.'

She just stared. I could not tell if she understood. I leaned in a little closer despite myself.

'You remember Marian?'

She looked around at the walls, the stone floor. Her eyes

lighted on the tunnel entrance, the darkness that was more liquid than light, and stayed there. The ghost in her knew what it meant, I could tell.

'This . . . is . . . her . . . house.'

I waited until she looked back at me.

'Yes.'

'I . . .' She put her hand to her stomach. I knew she was remembering the same thing I was, the day almost four years ago when she had lain on the floorboards and screamed as Marian pulled her son from her in a gush of blood. He had been born yellowed, for which the cure was sunlight. On Marian's orders I had cleaned him, swaddled him in linen and stood barefoot on the grass outside the House of the Dead, holding him in the soft breeze as he wailed. Inside I could hear Vira's cries and Marian's soft comforting whispers in answer – he was close, he would be all right. I wonder if Vira remembered that now, that raw terrified adoration. Perhaps not. She had abandoned her son, after all, in the end.

'What's your name?'

She almost answered. I could feel it there, on the tip of her tongue, sense her confusion. She wrapped herself around the word, clumsy.

'Im . . .ogen.' She hesitated, then said it again with more confidence. 'Imogen.'

My heart lay still for a moment.

'Imogen?'

'Yes.' She spoke more easily now. I could see something coming back to her. Her hands were clenched around her chains, the dirt and blood underneath her fingernails. 'Yes. I . . . lived here. In this town. My daughter . . .'

'Your *daughter?*'

She looked at me. Her eyes narrowed. 'You were – the witchling's girl?'

'Yes. Until a couple of years ago. Now I'm the witchling.'

She shook her head. 'The witchling – no, no. The witchling had a boy.' She looked around. Fear was returning to her. 'Who are you? Where am I?' She struggled, pulling at the chains. She bared her teeth at me. 'Let me go! *Let me go!*'

*Treat the patient in front of you.* I recalled my vows and summoned my strength and stayed calm until eventually her writhing passed and she sat heaving, blood on her wrists where the cuffs had rubbed away the skin. A lifetime of instinct called me to healing, but I stayed where I was. Her ailments were too deep for cleaning spirits and bandages.

'You attacked your husband,' I said. 'You attacked me too, with a knife. Why?'

'Husband?' She looked at me, confused and angry. 'I don't have a husband. I – my daughter—'

Her daughter. In the days when the witchling had a boy, she had lived in this town with her daughter. Now, dully, I saw what a terrible mistake it had been to leave her here in the cellar and wait for death to claim her. I should have killed her that first night. She had still been Vira then – Callum had seen it, I had seen it. Now she was Imogen. The ghost had taken her completely, and Aron's mother was destroyed. I let my anger wash over me and fade, and breathed.

'Imogen, do you remember dying?'

'*Dying?*' She stared at me.

'You died. You lived in this town a long time ago, you died, and now you're back. Do you remember any of that?'

She raised her hand to her face. The shape of it must have been unfamiliar to her, the veins and nails. Then she lowered it again.

'I'm not dead,' she said. 'How can you say that? I'm not dead.'

And of course, there was nothing I could say to that.

*

I didn't sleep that night. I didn't go anywhere without a knife in my hand. At some point she would try to escape, surely, she would break her chains and come through the house to kill me, and then I would feel no guilt in drugging her tea with laudanum and she would be finally dead. I *shouldn't* have felt guilty, anyway, I should have been able to do it then. I didn't know why I was hesitating. Vira was long gone, and Imogen should have been dead anyway. She was an abomination, and by killing her I would restore the world to rightness. All I was taking was a pulse, and I had done that before anyway, to those in pain without help of salvation, when it had to be done. Marian had taught me well. *Some things cannot be saved.*

And yet I couldn't. To take a living body, a soul intact, not even in pain, and stop her heart . . . I couldn't do it. I was a witchling, it was against my vows. It would be worse than what Marian had done to the woodcutter's son, and with far less cause. I was not a murderer.

So I waited. I had not eaten in a day and a night. Hunger lightened my mind and lifted me towards the buzzing brightness of transcendence. I was the closest to my nature like this, deprived and alone; I was what I needed to be. I sat there with the knife, curled on the wooden floor of the kitchen, burned herbs in the grate and waited for Imogen to doom herself.

Hours passed. Darkness stained the air. Beneath me, all was silent.

I stared into the white-charred logs in the fireplace. I wanted to go down to the basement and speak to her again. I wanted to break her chains and see what she did, to scour her mind and understand how she had escaped, to see if any part of Vira still lived there. I wanted answers.

I stayed where I was. My fingernails dug into my arms, into the floor.

I stayed and stared and waited.

*

In the small hours of the morning there came a knock on the door, and I knew it was Callum. It took all my energy to get up and walk to the end of the hall. The hallway spun and I clutched at the walls. I closed my eyes and opened the door. Aron was curled in his arms.

'How is she?' asked Callum, anxiously. And then, at the sight of me: 'Oh, dear lord, Haley.'

'She's ill,' I said. My voice sounded strange and weak. 'She's still very ill.'

'Haley.' He set Aron down on the floor gently – the little boy was half-asleep, and stumbled towards the kitchen without thinking. 'Come with me.'

Part of me rebelled at the sight of the living room – the chairs, the tea-stained floorboards, the cushions I had sewn when I was a child. It was a place to sit grieving relatives and tell them everything was going to be all right, or that it would never be all right again. I hated that place. But I let Callum sit me down and look at me with concern. He looked exhausted, too. There were lines on his face I could have sworn hadn't been there before.

'Are you OK?' he said. 'You look sick, Haley. Have you got – is it contagious?'

That made me laugh, long and hoarse. He watched me in alarm, hands hovering in the air, wanting to touch my shoulder to steady me but unsure if he had the right. He was so kind.

'Haley, tell me what's going on.'

I couldn't stop laughing. I fell to my knees on the wooden floor, and then it became coughing, and I could feel him watching me, and I could taste blood, but what could I say, what could I possibly tell him? *Your wife isn't your wife, your wife is worse than dead and I have to kill her so could you please leave my house?* The words flitted through my mind, ridiculous in their blank horror. I could hear Marian's blood dripping from the bedframe again. His hand was on my shoulder—

And then from beneath us came a child's terrible scream.

Have you ever heard a child screaming? Adults, when confronted with danger, give short sharp yelps of fear, the sound of the breath leaving them. It is followed by adrenaline, by windedness, by the urge to fight. Children, if they're young enough, have no such instinct. They scream long and loud, a scream that is half a sob, a scream that will get them killed, because what use is it trying to defend themselves, when they are so small and weak? It is as much lament as terror. It goes straight to your heart and lights you up.

We ran. That terribly familiar white noise was rising in my brain, sweaty hands on the staircase railing. I was faster than Callum because I knew where I was going. Imogen was waiting for us in the basement, and she was bound by her torso but her hands were free. She held Aron against her with one hand, small and terrified and uncomprehending, and the other was around his throat. There was dirt under her fingernails and her eyes were wide and wild.

'Let me go,' she said. There was a tremor in her voice, and she spoke only to me.

Behind me, Callum had stopped dead. He did not try to speak, to plead. He did not need telling that this woman was no longer his wife. I could feel his gaze over my shoulder, on his son, a cordon of terror that linked them. Neither of them moved or spoke.

I wanted to kill her. I loved that little boy. But I kept my voice low and soft, my eyes on Imogen's.

'You were dead. Now you're not. Do you understand that?'

She nodded stiffly. I saw Aron jerk at the movement, his little chest rising and falling. He whispered, 'Mama?'

Imogen looked at me, stricken.

'This was . . .' The words did not come easily to her. 'I was – this was—'

'Yes,' I said. 'He thinks you're his mother. Please let him go. You're hurting him.'

She looked at me. I did not expect her to listen to me; I thought possession eroded all compassion. But something clicked in her eyes. I think she heard the terror in the too-quick breathing of the boy she held captive. He said, '*Mama,*' again, and over his fear and confusion there was joy at seeing her again, and I don't think she could bear that. Her grip slackened and she let him go. And then I knew I could not kill her.

'Mama.' Aron put his hands to his throat and coughed. He turned around and tried to smile. 'Mama!'

She pushed him away, clumsy in her chains. The boy stumbled, and I felt Callum flinch behind me.

'Go,' she said hoarsely. 'Go.'

He stared at her, not understanding.

'Come to me, sweetheart,' said Callum quietly from behind me. 'Come on.'

Aron turned to his father, confused. 'But *Mama*—'

'Come to me. Now.'

Aron stood frozen for a moment, torn between his father and the woman he thought was his mother, but Imogen couldn't look at him, and after a few moments he turned and stumbled towards us. I breathed again.

As soon as he was within reach Callum snatched his son from the ground and pressed him against his chest. His eyes were on Imogen – utter disbelief, and a vicious kind of hatred. It did not suit him. It twisted him.

'Vira?' he said, and it was not her but me who answered him. 'No.'

He looked at me, then turned with Aron in his arms and fled up the stairs into the kitchen. I stood there with my hand on the banister and watched him go. There was a long, long silence.

'I had a daughter,' Imogen said behind me, hoarsely. 'I would have – I would have died sooner than hurt her. I . . . I did.'

'I know.'

We stood there for a while in the quiet. The world seemed absurd, and I was entirely alone within it.

'I thought I had to kill you,' I said. 'I do have to kill you. But I don't want to.'

Imogen looked aghast. 'Why would you kill me?'

I didn't know what to say to that. I felt the cold at my back and turned away, then climbed slowly up into the candlelit darkness of my house.

'Let me go,' she called, behind me. Her voice was a croon, a low moan, but all I could see were Aron's terrified eyes. 'Please. Let me go. I just want to live. Please . . .'

I closed the basement door, but I could still hear her.

Callum had left the front door ajar. I walked towards it, fearing that the cold wind would fan the fire, imagining the spreading of sparks and the catching of ancient timber. Everything lengthened and darkened as I took slow steps, the world rose and spun above my head. I was on my knees, staring at the floorboards beneath me. I could sense the rock under the wood, and the tunnels beneath that, and then the opening of an amethyst sky, the fathomless underworld beneath my hands. I ached with hunger and exhaustion. Death-magic was in the house, it was in the walls, it was in the air, next to me. Kneeling in front of me, hand on my chin, raising my head. 'Haley,' it said.

I blinked. Callum was back, come to save me. But he could not save me from what I had to do, I was his guardian and I was as powerless as he was, and I laughed and tasted blood and spat. The grip on my chin tightened. 'Haley,' the voice said again, more urgently. 'Haley, look at me.'

A woman. Not Callum. I blinked, trying to get my eyes to

focus. *Imogen*, I thought wildly, and then even more wildly, *Marian*. Marian was here again, back from the dead, the worlds had split and returned her to me.

'I'm sorry,' I said, but the words wouldn't come out right. I tried again. I needed to say it, I had promised myself I would say it if I ever saw her again. 'I'm so sorry.'

'It's all right,' she said. 'It's all going to be all right.' She drew me towards her, into her arms. I felt the warmth of limbs. Someone was stroking my hair. No one had done that to me for a long time, maybe not ever, and I shrank from her touch. She caught and steadied me. I could see the black tattoos on her hands. Until I saw them again I didn't realise I had copied mine from her.

'You're sick, kid,' she said softly, and pressed her palm to my burning forehead. 'I'm so sorry. I should have got here sooner.'

# CHAPTER FOURTEEN

I woke much later. Sunlight on my face.

I tried to get up, and I felt the throb of unassuaged hunger in my stomach. My body was disappearing beneath me. I thought I had dreamed everything for a moment – Callum, Vira, Imogen. Then the aches seized me, twisting and warm, in my legs and my chest. That was how I knew everything was real.

I lay there and closed my eyes. Was she still in my house? Had she left me, again? I had to be ready for it.

I hauled myself to my feet, wincing, and pulled on my clothes, dirty and sweat-soaked. Then I stood looking down at the hilt of the knife sticking out from under my pillow. She did not want to hurt me, I was almost sure of it, and if she did no knife would protect me. I closed my eyes and breathed.

I went downstairs very slowly. Midway down I almost slipped. I caught myself and breathed deeply to calm my thundering heart.

I knew the silences of the house acutely, and so heard her before I saw her, her soft breathing, her stillness. She was sitting at the table waiting for me. She made to get to her feet.

'No,' I said. 'Stay where you are.'

Leah did, watching me.

I was taller than her now, or maybe it only seemed that way from here. I considered her from the doorway. I had tried desperately to bury the childish part of me that had spent years waiting for her to return, but now that she was here it was in me again, whole and undamaged. I found myself completely unsurprised by her. She looked exactly as I remembered. She should have looked at least thirty by now, but she had not aged a day.

She was here. She had come back. I stared and stared, until I came back to myself. 'Where's Imogen?'

She just looked at me, darkly and a little pityingly.

'Where is she?'

Leah inclined her head slightly towards the basement.

Panic gripped me. I moved to the staircase at the back of the room and stumbled; the world spun and I caught myself on a chair. Leah had started to catch me, and stopped herself. I saw the look on her face – confusion, restraint. The instinct to help was unfamiliar to her, I think. She was not used to weakness.

Now she was between me and the basement. We looked at each other.

'You're still sick,' said Leah, in an oddly flat voice.

'No I'm not. Get out of my way.'

She did not even flinch. Hostility was unfamiliar to her, too, or unexpected. What had she expected, a joyful welcome?

'You don't need to go down there.'

'Get fucked,' I said. 'It's my house.'

She blinked at me.

I pushed forwards, straight at her, and for a moment I think she considered catching me and pushing me back. She could have done it, of course. I was nothing against her. She hesitated, but then she stepped out of the way. I felt her tense, watchful presence behind me as I stumbled clumsily down into the dark.

Imogen was dead. I knew before I saw her, felt the soft presence of death in my stomach, roiling and heavy like storm clouds. She lay pale and silent on the floor, pallor already creeping into her cheeks, and the symmetry of her pose was a shock, the way Leah had laid her out. All the danger in her gone. Leah had taken off her cuffs, and her wrists were bloody.

I leaned against the wall and wept. I was too tired and hungry for dignity, too scoured by shock to maintain my composure against this grey horror. Over my own sobbing I heard footsteps behind me. I did not turn.

'Get out,' I said, and was almost surprised to hear the fury in my voice. 'Get out of my house.'

She didn't move. I turned to glare at her. I knew how I must look, tattered and filthy and tired, face swollen by weeping, pathetic, but I didn't care. She looked back at me and there was nothing at all in her eyes and I hated her so, so much.

'Get *out!*'

'You were going to kill her,' said Leah. 'You know that. Or you would have released her.'

'You don't know that. You don't know what I—'

'I do. You know how this works. You were going to kill her, but you couldn't do it. So I did.'

I wanted to fly at her, to hit her. '*You had no right!*'

'I had every right. She was going to die anyway, Haley.'

'Don't—' *Don't use my name,* I wanted to say. 'She wasn't! She lived – she was going to live, you know that—'

She did, I could see it. She knew that Imogen would have survived. It had not been mercy, just murder.

'She was an abomination.'

'*So are you!*'

A ringing silence. Leah looked at me expressionlessly, and for one wild and singing moment I thought, good, fight me, come on, but of course she was too pitilessly controlled for that. Instead she said, 'Take my hand.'

'Fuck off.'

'Take my hand,' she said again. Her right hand was outstretched.

I stared at her, panting. I remembered the camp, the flicker of the spell beneath her skin. *Take my hand, kid.*

'I don't trust you.'

'I'm not asking you to trust me. Just take my hand.'

'So you can kill me?'

She looked so tired. 'Why would I kill you, Haley?'

'Why are you here?'

Something passed across her face and was gone. Then she was hatefully calm and restrained again.

'Why do you think?'

'Don't fucking test me.'

'Stop swearing at me.'

'You killed someone in my house. I can say what I fucking want to you.' She tried to speak again, but I cut her off. 'You would have left after you killed her. You wanted to leave while I was asleep. You're only still here because you need my help.'

Leah looked at me levelly.

'Yes,' she said.

I laughed, low and cruel.

'Listen to me, Haley,' she said. 'Take my hand. Things will make more sense.'

'I don't want answers from you.'

Leah looked at me, and all the laughter in me died. 'Yes, you do,' she said.

She was right, of course. I wanted explanations from her more than I had ever wanted anything, more than the resolve that kept me to my vows. I wanted to know her. I had wanted it for years, so much I had killed Marian for it. And now that she was back, finally, I only wanted her gone. I wished she had never happened to me.

'I hate you,' I said.

'No,' she said, 'you don't. You hate yourself. It will pass. Take my hand.'

I could not think of anything else to say. My head hurt. I

felt suddenly too tired to stand. I looked into her inscrutable face, and then recklessness seized me at last, and I stepped forward and took her outstretched hand.

The world vanished, and I was no longer myself.

I was kneeling in my daughter's bedroom. *Fiora.* Her toys were arrayed against the back wall. Some of them I had made for her; some were gifts from my father or my husband. We adored her, and we poured that adoration into woodwork, or the sewing of stuffed creatures, as if we could preserve our love in their whittled perfection. It was night, but the windows were open and the wind was too cold on my skin. I wanted to sink to my knees and weep.

She would be too cold if I didn't close the window. I needed to close it, but I couldn't move.

She was under the bed. Her eyes glittering in the darkness. 'You're safe,' I said, 'you're safe, sweetheart,' and I heard her indrawn breath and my own slurring speech. She was so afraid. I wanted to stop that. Nothing would hurt her, nothing would frighten her, not now. My darling.

Something was in my hand, something I couldn't look at. I stumbled to my feet, clumsy, turned and walked down the corridor. Outside it was starting to rain. I wanted to sleep, to lie curled in this feeling of new safety. It was all right at last, he could not take her, she was mine, and she would always be safe.

I walked with dreamlike slowness down the corridor. I stopped in the doorway of my bedroom and looked down at his body. My love. The nights I had lain awake to watch him sleep, the rise and fall of his breathing in the dark, before everything had broken. This strange stillness did not suit him. I wanted him to move, to rise and kiss me.

I put down the knife and sank to my knees and rolled him over. Blood-soaked shirt, wounds in his neck and chest. Open, terrified eyes. I wanted to take the fear from him, to calm him. Now we would never fight again. He would never scream at us, he could never put that terror in her heart. We were safe. I had fixed everything. We could be a family now.

I held him and wept, until I heard my daughter's footsteps behind me. She stopped in the doorway. I heard her breathing rise until she started to cry.

'Haley. *Haley.*'

'Let me go – let me *go*—'

'Haley. Come back to me.'

'No—'

Stone against my hands. I was staring into darkness. The air on my face was cold and I wanted to breathe it in, but someone had me trapped. Strong arms around my waist. The beautiful darkness.

'Haley.'

I had to find Fiora, she must still be in the house. She was crying and I had to soothe her. I couldn't bear the sound of her fear, but when I reached for it there was nothing, the air was silent. Where was she?

'Haley,' said a woman in my ear, and I realised I had stopped struggling. She was holding me up, my weight. 'Come on now.'

'Fiora,' I said dully, but the name was unfamiliar on my tongue, in this mouth.

'Tell me your name,' said Leah. *Leah*. I opened my mouth and had no answer, and then something came together. *Haley*, she had said.

And then I came back to myself. I was standing at the edge of the tunnel that led to the underworld, trying to clamber into it, and Leah was holding me back.

'I'm all right,' I said hoarsely. The words were strange and clumsy, and I tried again. 'I'm all right.'

She did not let me go. 'What's your name?'

'Haley.'

'How old are you?'

Again the response came after a beat, buried under someone else's instincts. *Thirty-eight,* came the answer, and then it faded and I knew myself again. 'Nineteen.'

She released me. I fell too sharply, unused to my own gravity. I caught myself, and pressed my body against the cool stone.

'Water,' I said hoarsely, and then time flickered and she was pushing a wooden cup into my hand. I drank and sat down slowly.

After a while I said, 'I killed my husband.' My voice sounded strange and low.

'*She* killed her husband,' said Leah. She was looking at the body on the floor. I stared at it.

'And then . . .' I lifted a hand to my throat. I felt the rough tightening rope around it, and wanted to cough and throw up, and then the sensation was gone.

'They hanged her,' said Leah.

'Yes.'

I stared at Vira's body, trying to sort through my own cluttered mind. That girl had never been my daughter. That was Imogen's heart breaking in my chest at the sound of her wails. And the man she killed had never been my husband. Those were not my memories, of his touch, the warmth of his body. His bloodied fists.

'He hurt her,' I said.

Leah inclined her head. 'And then she killed him.'

'Is that why you killed her?'

'It wouldn't matter what she'd done. She shouldn't be alive.'

I looked at her. Her face was expressionless, too pale in the blue dark. 'Then why did you show me?'

She didn't say anything for a moment, staring almost absently into the dark. Then she turned to me. 'What?'

'Why did you show me what she'd done? If it doesn't matter?'

'It matters to you.'

'What, and now you think I'm fine with you killing her? Are you trying to convince me?'

A pause. 'Yes,' she said.

The fact that it mattered to her what I thought struck me for a moment, but I shook it away. 'Well, I'm not. I don't.'

'She was a murderer, Haley.'

'He beat her. He beat their child.'

'And if he asks to be judged, he will suffer for it. But that is no excuse. She killed him.' She said it so flatly, nonchalantly.

'It's not that simple.'

'Yes, it is.'

'She wasn't dangerous. She didn't hurt the boy.'

'What boy?'

'The woman whose body she took,' I said. It was effort to find the words, to funnel the clamour of thoughts into my own hoarse voice. 'She was . . . the wife of someone I know. He came looking for her. He brought his son. Their son. The child ran to her. She threatened to hurt him if I didn't release her. Then she found out he thought she had been his mother. And she let him go.'

'And you think that means she shouldn't have been destroyed?'

'She said, *I had a daughter*. She wanted to find her again. She loved her.' I could feel it, the fading pulse of Imogen's love. 'She had mercy. There was goodness in her.'

'Everyone loves their children,' said Leah. 'That doesn't save them from death.'

'You would have damned her? If she'd asked to be judged?'

'But she *didn't* ask, Haley.' There was an edge to her voice now, and I was glad; I wanted her to be angry. I wanted her to be as upset as I was. 'She escaped. She left the underworld. She tried to cheat death. She knew it was against natural law and she did it anyway. The penalty for that is obliteration.'

'It's not that simple,' I said again. I felt clumsy, ineloquent.

'Yes it is,' said Leah.

'It is to you.'

She did not answer. I put my face in my hands. I could not believe this was happening, that after seven years I was arguing with Leah in the basement of the House of the Dead next to Callum's dead wife.

'Did you see if— was any of Vira still there? The woman she possessed?'

'A little,' said Leah indifferently. 'Her son's face, her mother's voice, things like that.'

'Did she remember leaving her husband? If she was taken, or just left, or—'

Leah shook her head. 'She didn't remember having a husband.'

I rubbed the inside of my wrist over my temples. I was so tired. Leah tilted her head, looking at me. 'Why? Does it matter to you?'

It shouldn't have, I knew that. I was the witchling, and Callum's broken heart was his own. 'Yes,' I said at last.

We sat in silence for a while, and I stared into Vira's dead eyes.

'You shouldn't have done it,' I said at last. 'This is my house. I don't care about your natural law. You should have shown me her memories and we should have – I mean—'
*Treat the patient in front of you.* Were there any circumstances, really, under which I would have allowed Leah to kill Imogen? Certainly my vows did not allow it. My affection for Callum and Ira and their children was one thing; I could live with that on my conscience, and hide it from the lord's men if they asked. But the murder in cold blood of a living woman . . . How could I look a witch in the eye and tell her I had done that, and expect not to be damned?

Or perhaps I was already lost. I had killed Marian, after

all. Perhaps when I found myself dying I would have to walk into the woods and rot away to nothing beside the river. And then everyone in the town would know I had done something terrible, and be shocked, and whisper about what had happened in my house. Everyone whose loved ones I had treated would be afraid of what my guilt might mean, what I had done to them. They might never trust a witchling again.

Leah was still watching me. I raised my head and tried to pull myself from my thoughts.

'What do you want?'

'I'm sorry?'

'Why are you here? What do you need from me?'

Leah did not answer for a moment. She ran her fingers over a tattoo on her wrist.

'It seems,' she said quietly, 'that I have been . . . exiled.'

'*Exiled?*' I stared at her. She did not look at me.

'Yes. My own kind have cast me out.'

'Cast—' I had not known witches did that. There was so much I did not know. 'Why? What did you do?'

'I have no idea,' she said. She raised her head and looked me in the eye. 'Haley, please believe me. I don't know why.'

I did not know what to believe. It was difficult to look away from her bright blue stare; I wanted instinctively to believe her, but I fought that. I was not twelve years old anymore. 'What does that mean, exiled?'

She smiled very tightly. 'I don't know. I've never seen it done before. I think they're hunting me. If I go back underground they'll find me. I need to stay here for a little while. Just a while, until they pass over here.'

I stared at Vira's body again. Leah wanted me to shelter her from other witches. The overwhelming terror of that hung above my head for a moment. 'Why did you come to me? Before?'

'You asked me to heal the witchling.' She looked up, at the floor of the parlour above us. 'Where is she?'

'She died. Three years ago.'

'I'm sorry to hear that.'

I doubted that. 'I meant, in the camp. Jonathan's camp. Why were you there?'

Leah looked at her wrists again. 'The girl was possessed,' she said levelly. 'My job is to find escaped ghosts and destroy them. I took vows.'

'Witches have vows?'

'Yes.'

'What happens if you break them?'

'Well,' said Leah with a grim little smile, 'I suppose I'm finding out.'

'How did you break them? By healing Marian?'

'They don't know about that. I promise. I covered my tracks—'

'Then how?'

'Nothing,' said Leah. She turned to me again, and her gaze burned with earnestness and intent. 'I promise you. There's nothing else. I was doing my job. The girl was possessed, so I killed her.'

'You made *me* kill her.'

She paused, and inclined her head again. 'Yes.'

She did not apologise. I gritted my teeth.

'Why did they exile you if you didn't do anything?'

'I really have no idea, Haley.'

'And you expect me to believe that?'

She looked at me for a moment and for the first time her expression was cool.

'Yes,' she said. 'I do.'

There was a silence.

'This doesn't make any sense,' I said at last. 'It doesn't, Leah.'

'I *know*,' she said. She was staring into the tunnel, but I could see anguish in her expression. 'I don't understand. Maybe they're planning something they don't want me to know about, or . . . I don't know.'

A conspiracy of witches. The thought was appalling. 'What do you need me for? You have magic. More than I do. You have power.'

'Over the dead, yes.'

I stared at her in disbelief. 'You stopped *time*.'

She shook her head. 'That was an illusion. Superficial. I came into your head and . . . I made the time seem longer to you than it was, shorter to everyone else. It was a blink. It wouldn't work on my own kind. Over the living, I can . . .' She smiled, without feeling. 'I can confuse them. With spells, I can heal them and kill them, but those take time and crafting. If those soldiers had seen me I would have been helpless.'

'Can you die?'

Leah thought about that for a moment.

'I can be torn apart,' she said at last. 'If you put a sword through my heart my spirit wouldn't dissipate. My body would rot, but I would be there in the earth forever. But my own kind . . . they could tear my soul into a thousand pieces and scatter them in the world of the damned.' She looked at me. 'I'm frightened of that, Haley.'

She said it baldly, honestly. I wanted to say something cutting, to try and make her beg for my mercy. But I couldn't. I couldn't tell her her death didn't scare me too. She was the secret that had lived in my heart since I was a child. I could not be the one to cast her out.

'If you let me stay,' she said quietly, as if she sensed the weakness in my heart, 'I'll never kill anyone again. If I find someone else who's possessed, I'll come to you. I'll help you in whatever you want to do. I—' Her voice did not break, but I heard the fear in it. 'I have no one else. Please don't send me away, Haley.'

I could not speak for a moment. I thought about Marian,

bleeding to death in the bedroom upstairs. I thought about Callum's terrified disgust, and the children who had thrown stones at me in the street when I was young. I thought about the emptiness of this house, and the dullness of my vows. I would be alone for decades, completely alone, but for the careful, distant respect of the thousands who depended on me. Even Callum and Ira would be brought to me bleeding, or sickened, one day. They were my patients before they were anything else.

I imagined watching Leah walk into the dark from my barred window, knowing I would never see her again. I would let her be destroyed, and I would have kept my word to the town, and I would never be able to tell anyone, ever. I would sit with the crackling fire and Marian's books and the memory of Leah's pleading eyes, and know that I had let her die, and the silence in the empty room would stretch for ever and ever.

I could be a coward, and abandon Leah, and keep my vows, and I and the town would be safer for it. If she died, I would be safer.

There was a long silence.

'If you break your word,' I said finally, quietly, 'even once, I will go down to the underworld and find the nearest witch and tell her where you are.'

'I understand,' she said. 'I won't lie to you.'

*Now.* Now I could go back. This was the last moment. But courage and a dark recklessness lit me up. I felt alive again for the first time since Marian's death. I held out my hand to her.

'All right,' I said. 'You can stay here until it's safe.'

She smiled with a blinding joy, and with that we were bound forever.

# CHAPTER FIFTEEN

Here is the world as I understand it, built largely around what Leah told me that cold and endless night.

Ghosts escape. That much I knew.

But they escape *all the time*. In every town and every village there is an entrance to the underworld, a dark and spiralling tunnel over which a House of the Dead is built, but there are more, too; in the thickets of impenetrable forests, set into the base of soaring cliffs, in marshy foothills and in endless slate deserts, places where no one can live, there are openings, unguarded. There are not enough witches in the underworld to watch all of them, to protect against the fading guile of nearly everyone who has ever died. So some escape, and those who do not dissipate survive to possess the living.

Natural law says that those in the underworld stay dead, unless they are judged and return to the living world as lords. There are no second chances. And so witches send some of their own kind here, to hunt down those ghosts who try to cheat their way into life again, to scour them away and destroy them.

This was, for countless years, Leah's duty. Often her problem was time. If the ghost was not strong enough to overwhelm the body's living spirit, or the body too weak to survive the torment of possession, the victim would sicken and die before Leah could destroy the ghost within. Then the body would be taken to the underworld by its loved ones, and the ghost might escape again, and justice would not be done.

You could talk to the witchling, I said, and explain what was happening. They might help you.

Leah said no. It was the great secret of witchkind. If the living ever discovered that death could be evaded, there would be panic and chaos. The uneasy layering of the worlds depended on natural law, on everyone knowing what they needed to know, and no more. The system of death was very delicate, she said, and if people stopped believing in it, it would break down.

Her job had grown much harder these last twenty years. The war had sent the dead flooding into the underworld, escorted by war-witchlings, and the trickles of ghosts emerging into the living world had become streams. Leah's jurisdiction, as a witch, stretched from this village a hundred miles west to the edge of the ocean, and now there were too many ghosts for her to attend to at once. For the last few years she had been with the lord's men on the coast, as they began to build the ships that would take them to their promised land across the ocean. Ghosts were drawn to the army, she said, its thronging mass of bodies and heat.

And then three weeks ago, as she wandered through the forest a little way north of here in search of another living ghost three towns over, she had received a message from her own kind in the world below, sent to every witch above ground. It was simply a picture of her face, and a single word: *jiolin*. It has no direct translation in my language, but then it meant *traitor* and *exiled* and *to be killed*, and when she saw it she ran and kept running. I was the only person in the world who she thought might help her, but when she came to the door she half-expected Marian, and a twelve-year-old girl waiting behind her. She had forgotten that I would have grown.

There is an art to harbouring a fugitive. It requires the capacity to withstand constant anxiety, a talent for deceit, and an obsessive attention to detail. How many cups have been left on the table? Can the soft breathing from upstairs be heard over the wind? The world closed in on us, airless, and everything was a threat. It was a different way of living.

Leah slept in the attic. I thought for a while of giving her Marian's bedroom, but something in me rebelled against it. It seemed a kind of betrayal. Concealing her existence from Marian had been my greatest mistake, the well of guilt that still lived beneath my heart. So I kept Marian's door closed and sent Leah upstairs to the attic, a single bare room with a glass window, full of warm sunlight and above the usual bustle of the house. In the years I had lived in the house that room had seen very few occupants, except in the deep winters when the town was clogged with sickness and every spare inch of wooden floor was taken up by patients. Leah slept on a straw mattress at first, and once I could gather together the materials I sewed her one of feather and cotton. It was not easy. I could not simply walk into the market and ask for a new bed without arousing questions, and there was no one I trusted when it came to Leah.

For the first few days we didn't talk much. Leah kept to the tiny attic room, while I treated patients at my kitchen table and recovered from the exhaustion that three sleepless days of panic had inflicted. I imagined Marian at the other end of the table, telling me I had been careless, that I could not allow myself to weaken like that again. I know, I said to her. I'm sorry.

You'll need to be better than that now, said Marian's shade. You'll need to stay more alert, if you want to keep a witch from her own kind. If they find her here, this town will be destroyed – you know that, yes? They'll never take your dead from you again. They'll deny everyone in this town an afterlife and leave you all to rot in your corpses. You're risking more than their lives.

They won't find her, I said. They can't know she's here.

She's told you that, said Marian's shade. Do you trust her?

That was a good question. I had made the decision to trust her by letting her stay. I believed what she said about the witches. She would have no reason to come here if they did know about me. This house would be the most dangerous place in the living world for her.

It would be better not to have her here at all, said the shadow at the end of the table. It would keep the town safer. That's what you're meant to do.

I can't let her die. It would wreck me. I can't do that to myself. They wouldn't do it for me.

I know they wouldn't, said Marian's shade. That's why you're the witchling.

Every third night or so I would wake and feel her watching me. I knew I was not the witchling she had been. I lived with a tight knot of guilt beneath my stomach, hot and unyielding. But it didn't matter, for those first few weeks, because I believed I could do it. I could keep the town safe and innocent, and Leah alive. I believed, and that was enough.

I buried Vira's body in the back of my garden, blisters on my hands from digging the grave. I had not done that since Michael's second death. The icy dawn air cleared my head a little. Vira was still and cold as I shovelled earth over her body. When I looked into her dead face, I still expected her to move.

Callum was undone by his wife's death. A brain tumour, I told him, surprised by the ease with which I could tell him this gentle lie. It caused terrible delusions, aggression. There was nothing that could be done, I said, so I had made her comfortable and given her the rites. He thanked me, tears in his eyes at the kitchen table, and my heart broke a little at the sight of his grief and his undeserved gratitude. I'm sorry you had to see her like that, I said. She would never have hurt Aron if she'd been in her right mind.

Maybe that's why she left, he said. Maybe she wasn't taken. Maybe it was the tumour, she was confused.

Yes, I said. That makes sense.

One night, a week later there came a knock at the door. I always slept with one hand resting against the wall next to my bed, and felt the rap in my fingertips, and woke. I rose and moved to the door. I slept fully clothed now, ready to deliver children, set blood-spattered wounds, hang my filthy clothes out by the river and slide into bed again.

I opened my bedroom door. There was a silhouette on the darkened landing. Something shifted in my brain; years fell away and I thought, *Marian,* but her silence and stillness were wrong, her hair too long, and at last she turned and became Leah, and I had to stand there for a moment until time made sense again.

Then I moved towards the staircase, and she moved too, to stand in my way.

I stopped. The knock came again below us.

I was angry. How dare she stop me from tending to my own patients, in my own house? I took two steps towards her, but she did not step back. I was so close I could see the strands of grey in her blue eyes. I waited for her to step back, to be ashamed, but her face was expressionless.

'Let me through.'

She looked at me. The knock at the door came again, and her eyes flickered towards it.

'Leah,' I whispered, 'if somebody dies—'

She breathed in through her nose, hesitated, and then moved aside. I shoved past her, down the stairs, and looked over my shoulder only when I reached the door, before I opened it to see Marya cradling her husband's body in her arms. By then, of course, Leah was gone from the landing.

Marya's husband was seventy-nine years old and already dead. I had seen him before at his house, heard the rattling of the infection in his lungs. *Svasarakta,* like Nathan. I had crushed medicine for him and prescribed salves for the pain, but I had seen the weakness in him and known he was past saving. His wife was crying when she brought him to me. I laid him down on the floor, wrapped him in a shawl, and sat her down.

I didn't even have to ask. 'Let him go,' she said, and wiped her eyes. I knew she hadn't been sure she would have the strength to say it. I held her hand and called her brave.

Her son came and walked her home, and then I was alone with a body again. The darkness was overwhelming. I breathed it in and leaned into my bleariness, kneeled on the floor until my feet went numb. I was falling. Everything was bright and the sky above me was endless. I found the runes in my head that meant safety from the underworld, solidity and safe passage, and my hand tightened on the blade. I moved unseeing, guided by touch, knife-fire-ink-cloth, carving the symbols slowly into his body.

When I came back to myself, Leah was standing on the other side of the kitchen, watching me, in the shadow of the gnarled branches that curled through the ceiling.

I flinched instinctively. Something came back to me, in the dawn half light – the figure of Esther in the doorway, and Marian bleeding on the cobblestones outside.

It took me a while to find words again. 'You can't be here.'

'I can,' she said calmly. 'Your magic won't hurt me.'

I had forgotten that. 'Well, you shouldn't.'

'Why?'

I wanted to explain how blind and vulnerable I was in the haze of transcendence, that her unseen presence, when I was that weak, was like a hand on my throat. But I was tired and angry, and so I just said, 'Because I don't want you to be.'

She nodded slowly and looked around at the darkened kitchen. Her hands were in her pockets.

'I'm sorry,' she said. 'I didn't . . . I wasn't thinking.'

I sat back on my knees, wiping the blood-ink from my hands on a cloth.

'Listen to me, Leah. I usually get to the door in twenty seconds. If that starts changing, people are going to ask questions. *Nothing* can change. You understand that, right? If someone gets suspicious—'

'I know,' she said. 'I know.' She rubbed her eyes. She hated being here. I could see it already.

'You have to trust me, Leah. This won't work if you don't trust me.'

'I do trust you,' she said, but she looked so tired, and I did not believe her.

We had no real plan. Leah believed, I think, that at some point we would see signs of witch-presence in the area, and then they would pass and she would be free to go – although go *where* was a good question. What kind of life could she live now, an exiled witch, feared by the living and dead alike and hunted by her own kind? Like a lord, she would not die of natural causes, or any but the cleverest poisons. She could go north across the great white-slate deserts, climb the mountain ridges and live under the relentless sun, until she dried out or starved. She could go east and live in the ashes of the towns devastated by Jonathan's forces, or west to follow their armies to the unknown sea. She could walk south, until the grass frost crunched beneath her feet and the world turned slowly white. But wherever she went, even if she evaded capture for a thousand years, she would have to stay in hiding. She would always be alone.

I think she feared that more than anything. She had lived her life above ground in shadow, in the constant presence of the living, watching them move and breathe and die. Total isolation was more than she could bear. The claustrophobia of my house, my discomfort and fear, the uneasy worry that she would be discovered, was better than that. I was better than nothing.

When the house was empty, I would sit at the kitchen table with her and drink tea and listen to her talk. She told me about her fellow witches, of the world beneath ours, of what might have happened to make them cast her out – of imagined conspiracies and grudges and wars amongst the dead. I thought she was looking for a way to make them take her back. I was doubtful. I had met witches beneath the earth, I had seen their cold faces and their dispassion, and I did not think they forgave.

As the months passed and no witch came through our town, Leah became less talkative again, retreating to her attic room for days at a time. I went about my duties downstairs, treating patients and brewing blood-ink, but I learned to keep one part of my mind on where she was at all times, listening for a nearly imperceptible footstep, a half-breath. If the witches ever did find her, I knew, they would not knock on my door and ask to come in. If they couldn't be bothered to kill me, I would simply wake one morning and find Leah gone.

When she was with me, she was curious, fascinated by my strange arts and how they differed from her own. Of course she couldn't be here when I treated living patients, but eventually I grew comfortable letting her in the room when I was transcendent, used to her presence in the back of my mind. She watched me brew medicines from essences and tattoo runes into the dead, and asked questions in moments when my concentration lightened and she knew she was not disturbing me. She had very good instincts for the way I worked; she learnt to read my expressions and my silences with unnerving speed. She asked the right questions, a step away from true understanding – she never needed to be guided through it. Once, I told her she would make a good witchling.

'You think?' she said. It was spring by then, and I had left the back door open. If anyone walked past and heard our voices drifting down to the river they would assume I was speaking to a patient.

'You have the right manner,' I said. 'You can be kind.'

'Well. I could learn to be.' She said it without self-recrimination, as a living person would have done. She was not used to human weakness and so had never learnt the practice of compassion. 'But you're forgetting. I can't go to the underworld.'

'You can,' I said. 'You just have to make sure you don't run into anyone else when you're there.'

I was unused to trusting anyone this completely. It took me a while to adjust to it. Slowly it became natural to have her there, to save up moments and anecdotes to tell her when the townspeople left and she could come down from the attic. They only felt real once she knew about them.

The hardest part of keeping her hidden was the supplies. I tried to vary the stalls I went to at market, but people talked, and it was very difficult to disguise that I suddenly needed more food. Leah knew that, of course. When she could, she went into the forest behind the house, brought back rabbits for me to cure and gathered wild berries, but those were the town's woods and the town's supplies, and if she wasn't careful it was almost certain she'd be noticed. In any case, it wasn't enough to live on. We rationed our food, planned weeks instead of days ahead. Leah needed less than me and could bear starvation more easily, but I wasn't going to let it come to that. She was under my protection.

We had strokes of luck. Sometimes people brought me gifts, if they were grateful for some act of care or healing. Long firelit winters always meant a spate of births in late summer, so that was a good season. For a few weeks the living room was stacked with gourds and ears of corn, loaves of sweet-baked bread, apples and berries, rope-nets of fish and squid, fillets of soft pink chicken and legs of cold beef, vines woven with garlic bulbs and bright red chillies. Leah was fascinated by this last offering – 'Why would you eat it if it burns?' – so I simmered the chillies into the stew I cooked that night with greens and pork, and she was so delighted by this she asked me to teach her how to cook.

How else do you want me to say it? I had someone to talk to, at last, someone from whom I kept no secrets and could discuss the glittering unknown vastness of the worlds. I was happy, really happy, for the first time in years. Each day differed from the last. I felt human again.

Then Grace came to see me.

Grace was thirteen, tall and lanky and awkward, with bright birdlike eyes. She was the baby I had drawn, bloody and wailing, from between teenaged Eve's legs a few weeks after I had been delivered to Marian. Eve was past thirty now, and I had watched Marian deliver Grace's three younger brothers years ago, but in my head Grace would always be *the baby*. I had not laid eyes on her properly since she had come down with pox when she was ten, and so it took me a moment to recognise her when I opened the door.

'Grace? Are you all right?'

She nodded shakily. She was barefoot and wearing only a nightshirt. It was almost midnight, the sky just deepening from blue to black. Leah and I had been up late, talking animatedly about some book from Marian's shelf – I think it was *An Examination of Decay in the Resurrected* – but when I turned around to beckon Grace inside I was unsurprised to find the kitchen table empty, the book back on the shelf, the pen and ink gone.

I gestured for Grace to sit on the chair next to mine – not Leah's, in case she found it warm. 'What's wrong?'

She couldn't say it immediately. 'I think . . . I'm sick.'

'How do you feel?'

She swallowed. I got up and lit the fire, filling the kettle from the barrel of water in the back room. Sometimes it was easier for patients to talk to you if they didn't have to look you in the eye.

'My stomach hurts. I feel like I'm going to be sick all the time but I don't. And I, uh . . .' Her voice shook. 'I'm bleeding.'

I sat back down on the chair next to her. 'Bleeding? From where?'

She kept her eyes firmly on the wall. 'From my . . . you know.'

'From your private parts?'

She nodded. I tried not to smile.

'You're not sick,' I said. 'Has your mother not talked to you?'

It was not the first time this had happened. In families where the particulars of adulthood were not discussed, parents could quite easily overlook how old their daughters were becoming, and girls would show up at my door scared they were bleeding to death. Marian had even told me a story about a sixteen-year-old who had been brought to her in labour, terrified by her own agony, and had burst into astonished tears when the baby was placed in her arms. Ever since then she had made a point of taking any girl Grace's age or older through the relevant chapter of *On the Development of Physical Maturity in the Body of the Child*, just in case. That was one of the books Esther's soldiers had burned, though, so I had to do the speech from memory. Grace's eyes widened.

'I could have a baby *now?*'

'If you wanted to,' I said. 'I don't think you do, though.'

Grace sat in her chair, absorbing this, while I fetched her ginger and fennel essence for the pain and fresh cotton to dress herself with. 'Do you want me to walk you home?'

She didn't answer for a moment. I turned. 'Grace?'

She shook her head mutely.

'Grace, what's wrong?'

She hesitated. 'Can I . . . sleep here?'

I saw the fear in her eyes. 'Yes, of course. Of course you can. What's wrong at home?'

'Nothing,' she said, with a child's guilty speed. 'Noth – I'm sorry, I can—'

'Grace,' I said, and was surprised when she fell silent. But then again, the authority of a twenty-year-old witchling must have seemed impossible for her to defy. I think I had already forgotten what it was to be a child.

She sat motionless in the chair, plainly terrified. I sat down again next to her.

'Grace, if there's something wrong, you have to tell me. If someone's ill—'

'He's not ill. It's – it's fine, I promise.'

'You are not helping anyone,' I said, as gently as I could, 'by keeping things from me, Grace. Do you understand that?'

A pause. Then she nodded, helplessly. 'All right,' I said. 'Tell me what's wrong.'


Upstairs, I knocked on Leah's door. She opened it at once. 'Is the kid OK?'

Leah's window had a good view of the front door, and she often crouched there watching when I sent her upstairs, watching the people outside as they spoke to me on the doorstep. She could not reveal herself to them, of course, but her helplessness made her all the more invested in the comings and goings that kept her trapped in the attic. She listened through the floors, helped me clean the bodies of the dead, asked me about every sick and injured person, what was wrong with them, how they were doing. They were her only markers of time.

'Yes,' I said. 'She's fine, she's asleep downstairs. Listen – can you make sure she stays here? Don't talk to her or anything, just – lock the door if you hear her moving.'

Leah was suddenly alert. 'Where are you going?'

'It's fine,' I said. I sounded so much like Grace I almost made myself laugh. Almost. 'It's fine.'

'Haley. What's wrong?'

It stunned me how well she knew me, how quickly. I could never lie to her. I moved inside and closed the door.

'Grace's father has been strange this week. Apparently.'

'Strange? What kind of strange?'

'Locking himself in the study. They hear crashing noises. And when he speaks, they've heard—'

'Different languages,' said Leah. 'Yes?'

'Yes.'

We looked at each other.

'I'm going to go and talk to him,' I said. 'You can't come with me, you'll be seen—'

'No, I won't.'

'We can't leave Grace alone.'

'She's asleep.'

'She's a child, she's scared—'

'Are there children in that house? More of them?'

Now there was a question she would not have asked a year ago. Or maybe she would have. She had broken witch-law, after all, and helped me when I was younger than Grace.

'Yes,' I said.

'Haley,' Leah said, very seriously, 'you can't honestly tell me you think it's a good idea to go there on your own.'

I couldn't, of course. It was just that I was so used to being alone.

I asked Leah once if she could make herself invisible, and she had said no, of course not. That was, I saw that night, *almost* a lie. She couldn't be truly invisible, but the darkness loved her, it caressed her like a child, and when she walked at night in the shadows of the town you would be hard-pressed to spot her even if you knew she was there. It was a strange feeling, half reassuring and half nerve-wracking, the feeling of someone always at your back.

I walked by candlelight, held under my face, in case the soldiers of the Lord Jonathan challenged me. A curfew had been imposed a few months after the war was lost, and only the witchling or those who needed her help were allowed to walk the streets after dark. Breaking curfew was, like most things, punishable by death, and although it had been years since anyone had been murdered in the streets – the soldiers had long since decided our town was too cowed to need much reminding – I still did not feel safe walking without my face illuminated. In days gone by it would not have been uncommon for one of the lord's men to come up behind you in the dark and slit your throat to make an example of you.

I did not know what I would say to Eve if we had to kill her husband. *Jorah.* I remembered his name – it was my duty to remember it, though he had not been in our house since the birth of his youngest son six years ago. It would be my job, if we had to scour his soul from his body, to bury him in our garden with Imogen and tell his family that I had brought him down to the underworld. But what if they didn't want that? What if they asked for resurrection? That was usually possible unless the body was not intact, and we could hardly – no. I winced at the thought.

They lived in the very centre of town. No privacy this time.

We would have to be very quiet in case the neighbours heard and asked questions. I closed my eyes. For a moment all I could think was: I don't want to do this. Why do I have to do this?

I almost knocked on her door, but Leah stayed my hand. She had a way of appearing from nowhere, subtly, like a shift in the air.

'If we have to kill him,' she said softly, 'we don't want to have been seen.'

'We're not going to kill him,' I said. Panic had lit in me again like struck flint. 'All right? We can't – I don't want to kill him.'

'Neither do I,' said Leah. 'But sometimes these things have to be done.'

She said it so callously it stunned me. I had thought she'd lost that, after a year in my house. I breathed in slowly. 'Let's find a window,' I said.

There was one around the side of the house, slightly ajar in the early autumn breeze. Inside, all was dark and silent. A study, with books lining the walls and a mahogany desk in the corner. Eve's or Jorah's? I tried to remember what either of them did for a living, but my mind was empty. Leah's hands were already on the windowsill and she slipped inside.

She held out a hand to help me inside but I did not take it, clambering over the sill myself instead. The room was empty. I looked for blood on the floor, the dark curl of a body in the corner. Nothing. *Yet*.

The corridor outside was silent. From upstairs I heard the low breathing of Eve and her three sons. Grace must have snuck out of bed to come see me once she was sure they were all asleep. If Jorah and Eve were in bed, there would be no way to get to him without waking her. I turned to whisper this to Leah but there was something in her posture that stopped me, a deep and listening stillness.

She held up a hand and in the silence I heard breathing from the kitchen.

She moved with inhuman speed, before I could stop her. I scrambled after her down the corridor. The kitchen was full of light, gleaming off the knives, the glasses in the open cupboard, the eyes of the man curled on the floor. Leah's tattoos were glowing, firelight in her veins, and a soft and pulsing glow hovered in her cupped hand. The man's face was wan and grey in the light. He was curled on the floorboards, his arms wrapped around his knees, taking long, sobbing breaths.

'Look at me,' said Leah, quietly. I saw power in her then as I had not seen it before, a magic like my own but fathoms deeper. I feared her as I had not in months.

But the man was not afraid. He sat up, and I saw that his eyes were red-raw from weeping, and when he saw Leah a look of such ecstasy came into his face that I knew he was not Jorah anymore.

'Please,' he said. 'Oh, please. Help me.'

## CHAPTER SIXTEEN

I lay in bed with my sister, dying. I could feel the sickness in my lungs, hear it in our breathing. My thoughts were warm and worn. I could feel them slowing.

My sister was four years old, tiny and thin and feverish. She curled against me, and when she stopped breathing I felt it, the shaking and then the stillness.

A howl rose in my throat, but I could not speak. My mouth was numb, my limbs were heavy and my eyes hurt to open. When the darkness came for me I went with it willingly, because I had nowhere else to go.

Everything was shadowy. I could feel my body turning cold, my own stilled heart. Beyond me there was movement, voices and flickers of light. I lay limp in the soft embrace of darkness.

And then suddenly, in a blaze of agony, my body returned to me again. Someone had a knife and was carving slow burning marks into me. I tried to scream but couldn't. I felt the trickling of blood, saw candlelight through reddened eyelids—

Then nothing. I was released. It was over, and everything went dark.

But something had changed. I felt it. I was real again.

Everything took a long time to solidify. I was lying on stone in a cellar, under a veil. I felt the fabric on my skin, sunlight on my face. Sensation was flickering; one moment I was here and the next floating in darkness again. Was this a dream? I could not move or speak. I waited for the terror to rise in me but there was nothing.

Above me I heard footsteps. Someone in the cellar. Soft humming. Words slid softly through my dulled brain, *witchling*, a woman with kind eyes. Hands on me, her touch velvety through deadened nerves. She lifted me up, over her shoulder, ready to carry me into the darkness – no, no, I want to stay here—

'Haley.' Leah's arm on my wrist. 'Haley, come back.'

Yes, I was here. I was not dead. I let go of Jorah's hand and pushed myself away from him. For a moment the girl's mind pulsed within my own, but when the connection was broken and it faded and slid again into half-memory. I recited the words, as Leah had told me to, to anchor myself in my own mind: *My name is Haley. I am twenty years old. I am the witchling. My mother was called Lysa, but I was raised by Marian. I am alive, I am alive, I am alive.*

'She was nine,' I said. I was surprised to find my voice shaking, and I swallowed. I had not known the dead could feel it when I carved runes into them. I felt again the shadow of that agony, and flinched. 'She died of the sleeping sickness.'

Leah raised a finger to her lips. I had forgotten we were still in Eve's kitchen, and she and her sons were asleep upstairs. The girl had lived a long time ago and far away from here. There was something strange about the air in her memory. Her mind worked in a different language, the melody fluid and alien.

'You were from the east,' I said. 'Across the hills. Right?'

'I don't understand,' said the little girl in Jorah's body. She was shaking, I could see it in his hands. 'Where am I?'

Leah was watching her silently. I could see something in her face, a buried and writhing confusion.

'You died,' I said. 'A long time ago. You were in the under-world, do you remember that?'

She nodded.

'How did you get out?'

'There was a tunnel. I climbed a mountain and found it.'

It was that simple. 'You didn't know you would come out here? In the living world?'

She shook her head, slowly. 'I . . . I couldn't breathe. It felt so horrible. Like the air was hurting me. And then I was awake, and I looked . . . like this.' She didn't want to look down at her own body. Her eyes were on Leah.

'This man was called Jorah,' I said. 'You possessed him. You don't remember doing that?'

But I could see the truth of it in her memories. A deep and endless darkness, an agony in the centre of her spirit as the living world began to destroy her. The trees and animals and the deep blue forest sky were blurry, as if glimpsed through dark water. And then there was Jorah. The sight of his face, and the feel of him. She had known instinctively that he meant warmth and safety and relief. But after that there had been no struggle, no grappling of spirits in which his soul was strangled, or if there had been she had not known of it. She had simply *taken* him, and woken up in his body, lying on the grass in the sweet summer air.

'Can I go back?' she said to Leah. She gravitated towards a witch's authority; she must have known witches in the under-world. 'I could find the tunnel again—'

Leah shook her head slowly. 'You're alive now,' she said. 'I'm sorry.'

'How are you talking to us?' I asked. She had not spoken our language when she died. She looked at me blankly.

'The man spoke it,' said Leah, still looking at the girl-who-had-been-Jorah. 'She has his mind. What else do you remember? About his life?'

The girl swallowed, looking between us. She clearly thought she was going to be punished, waiting for one of us to start shouting at her, and the impulse was so childlike it broke my heart.

'This is my house,' she said at last, as though the words did not come easily. '*His* house. And upstairs . . . his wife. His children.'

Leah spoke gently but firmly. 'What have you said to them?'

She shook her head frantically. 'I stayed here. I stayed under here.' She pointed to the desk. 'I didn't say anything, I promise. I'm sorry. Please help me.'

There was a pause. Leah glanced at me. 'We can't help you,' she said at last. 'Do you understand that?'

The girl looked between us, frantic. 'You're meant to help,' she said. 'You tried to help me. Before.'

Leah was blank. 'I did?'

'No, I mean – when I died – you – people like you—' She looked helplessly at the glowing light in Leah's hand.

'Witches,' I said. 'They're called witches.' I tried to imagine not knowing that, and couldn't anymore. *Don't you understand people, Haley? No one wants to think about death.* Marian would have done a much better job of comforting this girl than me.

'Sometimes,' said the girl haltingly, 'when I couldn't stop crying – I was trying to find my sister, I couldn't find her – a witch would help me. They said – they said I would find her soon.'

Leah and I both sat in silence for a moment. I was trying very hard not to imagine the little ghost-girl, wandering in the forest. The witches had lied to her, of course, but it was a kindness. She would never find her sister among the teeming billions of dead. How long had she been down there, alone?

'Why didn't you ask to be judged?' I asked, at last, but of course I knew the answer. The girl looked at me, confused.

'I was scared,' she said. 'I don't want to be damned.'

'No one would send you down there. You haven't done anything bad.'

She shook her head frantically. 'I stole it.'

'What?'

But I could see it, a memory sheathed in guilt at the back of her mind. A doll of her sister's, much-beloved, taken and hidden beneath the bed in anger. The sister had cried for a day until the girl had broken and given it back. *I'll never forgive you,* her sister had said, *never, never!*

'Oh, sweetheart,' I said. I wanted to take her in my arms and stroke her hair but something about Jorah, his threatening physique and his familiar eyes, stopped me. 'I promise you. You wouldn't be damned for that.'

'I stole it,' the girl repeated. For a moment I thought she didn't understand me, but then I saw she was looking at Leah.

Leah seemed unable to speak. When she did her voice was soft, hesitant.

'I can't speak for anyone else,' she said. 'But when I was underground, I never sent a child to the world of the damned. The youngest was . . . fifteen, I think.'

'What did he do?'

Leah shook her head and glanced towards the girl, and I asked no more questions.

'I don't understand,' whispered the girl. Her hands were shaking. 'I want to go home.'

It hurt, the aching pull in her voice. She had been dead for decades, maybe centuries. Where was home to her now?

'Let me talk to Leah,' I said, speaking softly and clearly, 'and then we'll come back and see what we can do, all right?'

She nodded and curled up beside the bookshelves, one hand against them to steady herself. Leah did not look at me but got to her feet too, her eyes still on the girl. We walked out into the corridor. Upstairs all was still silence and soft breathing.

Leah did not sit when we reached the study. She leaned against the table and folded her arms. I did not like the look she was giving me.

'What?'

'*See what we can do?*'

'What can we do?'

'Nothing,' said Leah, with such savagery I almost flinched. '*Nothing.* You know that, Haley.'

'You're a witch.'

'So?'

'You have powers I don't. You have ideas, you have *options*—'

'Not *here!*'

She made a fist and almost slammed it into the table, but then glanced up at the ceiling where Eve and her sons lay sleeping. She put her face in her hands. I don't think she saw my expression at all.

'Why do you send children down there so young?' she said at last. I wasn't sure if she was talking to me. 'She was, what, four? She wasn't going to go up to us and ask to be judged. She would have wandered around there forever if she hadn't escaped. What kind of parent does that?'

'What kind of parent buries their child in the woods and leaves their ghost to rot?'

Leah raised her head and opened her eyes. 'One who isn't squeamish,' she said.

I couldn't speak. I turned away.

'If she had died it would have been easier,' Leah said behind me, softly. 'She has a strong spirit. Normally they just seize and die, and I don't have to . . . But that happens in three days, and never if they can talk. She's not going anywhere.'

'Four days,' I said, to the empty corridor. I didn't want to look at her.

A pause. 'What?'

'There was one here, a few years ago. He died after four days.'

'You never told me about that.'

'He was a boy . . .' Was I really going to tell her this? I didn't turn, didn't want to see her face. 'A boy who was once – he was my friend. A long time ago. He was possessed. He, uh . . .' I swallowed. 'He killed Marian.'

'While she was trying to treat him?'

'No,' I said. *Say it*. 'I brought him to the house.'

'Why?'

'I thought you would come for him. I thought . . . I would find you again.'

Silence. At last, with effort, I turned around. Leah was staring at me. I met her eyes with diffiulty. It was a lot of effort to keep my voice low without letting it break, and I did not want to give Leah this. I did not want her to see this part of my heart.

'Why? Why did you – why did you want me to come back?'

I could not explain it, what she had done to me by appearing like lightning in the centre of my life, with her bright eyes and her infinite power and her flickering compassion. Instead I said, 'We can't kill her. She's a child.'

Leah closed her eyes and tilted her head slightly as if in pain. 'She *was* a child,' she said.

In the silence that followed, I saw Leah a year ago, turning to me in the cellar and shaking my hand. *I promise I'll never kill anyone*. She had never intended to keep her word to me. I had known it then, though I had tried not to think about it. I couldn't avoid it anymore.

She saw it in my eyes. 'Haley,' she said, 'don't get angry, now.'

*'Angry?'*

Now I heard the crack in my voice, but I didn't care. I was not as cold as her, not as heartless, but that did not make me weak. I wanted to hurt her in that moment, and the impulse scared me.

Something in her eyes went dark. 'I took vows, Haley.'

'So did I.'

My fist was closed on the table. She saw it. When she spoke, her voice was quite even.

'Listen to me. You don't understand what you're looking at, here.' She pulled up a chair and sat across it, leaning over the back, her gaze intent. I couldn't look away. 'The dead outnumber the living by more than you can imagine. There are a hundred thousand of them for every one of you. If nothing keeps them in, if I don't uphold natural law, they will take every single one of you until the underworld is empty. It'll be the same billion ghosts living and dying over and over. And if there are no ghosts left in the underworld, my kind will go extinct. We live off magic, and ghosts are raw spirit, pure magic. They're like a heat source, like a fire. They keep you and me alive, all creatures of death-magic. If they all realised they could escape, half of them would dissipate, and we would all die, and so would you, and there would be no one to protect any of you anymore.' Her voice grew tight and strained with the effort of not shouting. 'Don't you understand, Haley? You're letting it *happen* – I have a duty—'

'She is,' I said, trying very hard not to let my voice break again, 'a *child*.'

Leah made a growling noise of frustration, so sharp that I felt a blaze of power in the air. In the kitchen it shimmered and I felt again that profound powerlessness, my own death hanging in front of me. I wanted to run.

And then I heard shouting from outside.

Just one voice, at first. I thought instinctively they were calling for me, someone had been taken terribly ill in the middle of the night and could not be moved. They would have gone to the house and thought me tending to another patient. Which, I suppose, was true. I thought: Eve and the boys mustn't find me here.

Then the voices rose and multiplied, became five, ten, twenty, and I stopped thinking about anything at all.

The lord's men.

For a moment I was twelve years old again and trapped in the grip of the soldier, watching the blood drain from Marian's face in the flickering light from our burning books. I could not breathe. Then it passed, and I could move. I turned away from Leah, and ran out into the corridor. I heard Eve and her boys wake upstairs, call to each other and then fall silent. They knew they had to hide.

I opened the door and stepped out into the dark. The street was full of torchlight. I couldn't see the soldiers at first, but then I saw silhouettes at the end of alleyways, doors being pulled open, voices rising from behind the muffled wood, screaming. They would come here if they hadn't already. I could not be seen to be hiding from them.

I turned and began to run towards the House of the Dead. I did not have to look to know that Leah had vanished from my side. I could only hope that she was hidden as well as her power would allow, because as soon as I emerged from the alleyway into the square at the centre of the town, I understood the screaming.

This was a raid. There were fifty of them at least, far more than had travelled here with Esther, and they were pulling people from their houses and pushing past them, going into the houses, throwing aside possessions and breaking windows. They were searching us.

For what?

People were standing outside in their nightclothes, weeping and holding their children. One couple was naked, the man wrapping his body around the woman to cover her humiliation and protect her from the cold. From behind me I heard resistance – swearing, then a thud and a *crunch* and a scream of agony – and then it died down and there was only sobbing and the shouting of orders.

'*Where is the witch?*' roared a voice from behind me. I turned, as if through a dream, and saw the commanding officer standing beside the stall where Marya sold her wares in daylight hours.

Absolute silence.

'*Where is the witch?*'

Nobody answered. I was shivering. There was a soft buzzing in my brain.

I was not yet terrified, because this did not make sense. Why did *they* want her? They were the lord's men, and she had been outcast by her own. She was not their exile, this was not their fight. Why did they want Leah?

Then the fear came, overwhelming. Did they know she was here, or were they guessing? If they found her – no, no—

'*Where is she?*'

No one answered. It was as much confusion as terror. You would have had to ask Marian or me directly even to know what a witch was, and I couldn't remember anyone ever doing that unless they were dying. Jonathan's men might as well have been shouting in a different language.

I said nothing. Let me say in my defence: I considered it. I heard it in my head, my thin voice in the darkness: *Don't hurt them, please, I know where she is.* It did not occur to me that at that moment I did not actually know where Leah was, could not lead them to her if I wanted to. All I saw, in my head, was them tearing Leah apart, then making me watch as the town burned, killing me slowly and leaving me in the ashes of the town. Or if by some miracle they spared us, then word would get down to the witches in the underworld, through the dead, and then they would refuse to take our ghosts and I would be no use as a witchling at all. If they knew I had sheltered her this town would be destroyed, one way or the other.

So I stayed quiet, and watched as the commander lowered his torch to Marya's stall and set it alight.

I heard her wail from across the market square. Everyone else was silent, watching it burn. I thought: very clever. The commander had chosen Marya's stall, at the end of the street, twenty yards away from anything else that would burn. They did not want to destroy all our supplies or set the whole town on fire. They wanted us alive. It was terribly cold.

*'WHERE IS SHE?'*

From a couple of streets away I heard breaking glass. I backed slowly towards it, hoping to walk through the shadows and avoid the gazes of the soldiers. I needed to get back to the House of the Dead, if they burned more of the books, if they—

And then I remembered. *Grace.* I started running.

I came out into the street, too late. The soldiers had got there before me. She was outside, sobbing, wrapped in her nightshirt. I saw bloodstains on it. Vials of my medicines were broken on the cobblestones. She must have let them into the house when they shouted at her. When she saw me an ecstatic relief came into her face, and I realised with dull shock that she thought I could save her.

'Haley, please, I'm sorry, I'm sorry—'

*'Witchling!'*

Someone grabbed me from behind. I pulled away and there were more arms around me, trapping me. I should have taken it with dignity and stopped struggling, but I would not, I would *not* do this again. My whole being screamed against it, and in that singularity of focus something blazed within me, a pulse of death-magic wired into the tattoos up and down my body. Someone behind me cried out, and I was released.

I almost stumbled, but caught myself. I turned around. I thought, all right, they're definitely going to kill me now, but there were twenty or so soldiers arrayed against the ransacked houses behind and none of them were moving. Perhaps they thought swords could not kill me.

'I'm sorry,' I said quietly to Grace, behind me, keeping my eyes on the soldiers. 'I'm sorry, I shouldn't have left you alone.'

*'Where is the witch?'*

The commander pushed forwards, through his men. He was at least a foot taller than me and heavily armed, but I noticed, he stayed three steps away. I recognised the distaste in his eyes, and thought of the boy who had thrown a stone at me in this very street, so many years ago. *Dead girl.*

'Where is she?'

I felt Grace's trembling behind me and knew I held more than my own life in my hands. I spoke almost casually.

'What witch? What are you talking about?'

'A witch passed through here.'

'When?'

A little jerk of his head, and I knew he was working from second-hand information. This was not his fight. He was just following orders.

'A year or so ago.'

I paused, then shook my head slowly. 'I don't know what you're talking about. A *witch?*'

In my own memory I sound hollow, desperately unconvincing. The commander was expressionless. 'If you lie to me,' he said, 'you understand that you die, yes?'

I pressed my tongue against the roof of my mouth and tried to look afraid. I had long since stopped fearing death; there were worse things to feel than numbness, and in the bright light of danger I felt beautifully alive.

'Yes.'

'If the witch were here,' said the commander, 'she would have come to you.'

A jolt of horror – how did they *know?* – and then I remembered that to him a witch and witchling would seem as good as kin, devoted to each other's interests. Perhaps he thought that we all knew each other.

'There's no witch here,' I said. I tried to look annoyed and outraged, to look anything but guilty. I thought he would be able to see it in my face. He scrutinised me for a long time, his hand on the hilt of his sword.

'Where were you tonight?'

'Tending to a patient.'

'Who?'

I did not allow myself to hesitate. 'Jorah. The weaver's husband.'

He stared at me as I tried again to summon that fierce clarity of purpose: *leave me alone, go, believe me, please.*

'Take the girl,' he said, and the soldiers pushed past me and moved to grab Grace. Four men to tackle one thirteen-year-old girl. She did not even have the strength to scream; shock knocked the breath from her. One grabbed her around the waist, arm crooked around her mouth.

'When we find the witch,' said the commander to me, 'you can have her back.'

Horror silenced me. I waited for shouts of outrage from the crowd, for someone to protest, but everyone was quiet. They were all too terrified of the lord's men, who had burned towns and killed so many of their sons and daughters, to protest the taking of one girl. I waited for Eve's wail of horror, but of course she was not here. She was hiding in the house, trapped there while it was searched.

Then Grace screamed for her mother, and I broke.

I stepped towards the commander. 'You can't take her,' I said, clearly.

With horrific speed he pulled his sword from its sheath and levelled it at me, pressing its point against the centre of my chest. 'Not one step closer,' he whispered. 'You hear me, corpse-bitch? Stay where you are.'

I tried to summon Marian's shade to strengthen me, the memory of her arguing with Esther, but all I could think was: that's my rib you're trying to stab through, you idiot. You want my heart, move an inch to the left.

'You can't,' I repeated, 'take her.'

'Why not?'

It was the only thing I could think of. 'She's my girl.'

There was a moment of dizzying silence. If the soldiers had been watching the residents of our street, shivering in their nightclothes, they might have seen the truth in their expressions – confusion, then understanding, then a hasty blankness. Every man, woman and child in our town knew I was lying. Nobody spoke.

'I need to keep her,' I said to the commander. I kept my voice low and intent, holding his eyes, as I did with the dying. 'If you take her, you might as well burn the town. Burn all of us.'

The commander's gaze flickered behind me, to my house, where they had found Grace sleeping. He took a slow breath and then inclined his head.

Behind him, the soldiers released Grace. She fell to her knees, sobbing in terror. I was glad of that. It meant they could not see her face.

'We will need someone,' he said, 'as evidence of your word.'

If it had been in my power I would have volunteered. I had never hated myself so much for helping Leah, for being the witchling, for all my selfishness, as I did right then.

But then, from behind him, Marya said, 'Take me.'

There were still tears in her eyes, but her voice did not waver. Nobody moved to stop her. She was almost seventy, ailing, widowed, and with her stall burned down she had no trade left. She was choosing herself because she knew she was the one fewest people would mourn.

They took her at once. She was old, so they suspected no trick. Later we found out they killed her out west, after she tried to escape. She took two of them with her. I hope they did not burn her, that they gave her to the war-witchlings; I hope that she exists somewhere down in the dark. The underworld is the best she could hope for, I think. Those murders were not in self-defence.

She was the third person to be killed because I protected Leah. I kept her face in my mind and whispered her name with Marian's and Anya's as penitence, every night until the day I died. I have no day and night anymore, of course, but I guess at the passage of time and try to mark nightfall with their names. It feels good not to forget these things. I remember them, and so I am still myself.

# CHAPTER SEVENTEEN

Afterwards there was darkness and confusion. Grace was my first concern: I wrapped her in a blanket, cleared the shards of broken vials from the cuts in her knees, and hugged her until she stopped crying. She kept asking for her mother, and I comforted her – *she'll be here soon, just wait, I'm sure your mother's coming* – until I realised that she wasn't, and what that must mean.

When I got to Eve's house, I heard the weeping before I saw Eve or her three boys. In the general chaos no one else was paying much attention to them; under any other circumstances they would have drawn half the town with their sobbing, so in that sense I was lucky. I was the first to walk into the house, and find them gathered around Jorah's body.

The world went quiet around me. Everything shone very brightly. I felt everyone else's eyes on me and remembered I had no reason to look shocked: I was the witchling, and saw death all the time. I could not even press a hand to the door-frame to steady myself. All I could think was *Leah, no, no,* but I could not say that to them. They were grieving, and I had only been lied to.

'Grace said he was ill,' I told them once I'd brought his body to my basement and Eve's tears had finally dried. Her eyes were dead, her face bloodless. It was a strange, sleepless dawn; no one was speaking to each other, the streets were full of broken glass, people were sweeping the ashes of Marya's stall from the cobblestones. Ira's husband had taken three hunters and gone up into the western hills to watch, in case this was a feint and the lord's men were about to circle back and burn us. I did not sleep either, waiting in the kitchen for Leah to come through the door, but the house was silent.

I did not know what I would say to Leah now. I had let Marya be taken for her, and the moment I was gone she had killed the little girl in Jorah's body. I was furious, and there was a crack through my heart, but more than anything I was worried, because the lord's men had gone and she had not come back. I had to drink the camomile tea I usually reserved for the grieving, because I was shaking so badly I could not stand up. Before Leah came I could have borne this kind of fear alone, but now I was weak. This was my fault, all my fault, and I could not even apologise for it.

'It's a kind of sickness,' I told Eve, though I wasn't sure she was listening. 'It killed Ira's son, too. People forget who they are, they start having seizures, and then they die.' So many lies tonight. I had broken my vows a hundred times since the last sunrise.

'Take him to the underworld,' said Eve, dry-voiced and red-eyed, before she left. Grace and her brothers were inconsolable, weeping in the study. Grace blamed herself, though of course she had no reason to. Guilt, Marian had told me, was a child's natural response to death.

Eve sat staring into the fire for a while, listening to her children cry, then slowly, achingly, got up and left.

*Take him to the underworld.* Of course I could not do that: there was nothing left to take. But there was too much attention on me right now. Townsfolk were guarding the woods outside my house in case the lord's men came back, someone would notice me burying his body. So I kept him in the basement, and waited.

I couldn't make sense of anything; my thoughts were clamouring and there were too many things I had to do. More powerfully than I had in years, I longed to speak to Marian. And still Leah did not come back.

Why hadn't she told me the lord's men were after her? Had I been wrong to shelter her? Had everything been a lie? What could I do about it now? I had lost too much in her name to let her go. Or maybe I was just a coward, my vision too blurred to understand that the right thing to do was to turn her away if she came back, to look into her face and send her into the dark. Could I do that now?

I slept fitfully. There were knocks on my door every hour or so, bruises and broken bones from where the soldiers had been rough in their search for Leah. Not since the winter had the House of the Dead been so full, and it had never been so difficult for me to be the witchling, to bury my frantic heart and summon the voice in my head that spoke words of healing, the instincts that guided my hands. My patients asked me what a witch was, what Jonathan's men had been looking for, and I did not lie to them then, at least. They were as shocked and horrified as Marian had promised when they learned that their judgment after death rested on *people*, inhuman women and men with fallible hearts and brains. I did not have it in me to comfort them. I bound their wounds and sent them away.

When evening drew in, the chaos faded slightly and I curled up on the floor next to the kitchen table, too exhausted even to climb the stairs. I slept until I was woken by the next knock on the door, and walked dreamlike to answer it.

'Haley?'

'Callum.' The world condensed. 'Are you all right? Is Aron all right?'

'I'm fine. Can I come in?'

'Sure.' I thought of my patients and then realised the house was empty. 'Come in.'

He seemed very alert, his movements sharp and jerky, and

I knew he too had not slept. He pulled up a chair and sat down, looking at me very intently.

'Did the witch kill Vira?'

I stared at him. Of course, *he* would have asked Marian, he would know what witches were. 'What?'

'The sickness. It's not natural, I know that. Did she kill her? Is that why Jorah died? And Ira's son?'

'What?'

'Haley.' He leaned forward. I knew he was trying to see into me, like Marian had been able to, and I fought the urge to lean away. 'Are you hiding the witch?'

'No.'

'Tell me the truth. On her life.'

'Callum, what—'

'Tell me. I would understand. There are things . . .' He paused, struggling for the words, and so he missed my hesitation. What would it be like, being able to tell someone? I glimpsed the beautiful relief of it. He kept talking, gesturing at the air. 'There are things going on – this is beyond me, I know that. Witches and madness and the lord's men, I'm – look—'

He closed his eyes and gathered himself. I could not speak.

'If you told me,' he said eventually, 'that you were hiding her, and there was a reason for it, even if you couldn't tell me what it was, I would understand, but . . . I would need to know, Haley. Just – tell me.'

I might have done it. I had seen him less often since Leah had come to me; I cared for him too much to lie to him on a weekly basis, but now that he was here again I felt such relief. I felt younger. It seemed so natural to trust him, to confide in him. Perhaps he would not even hate me. Perhaps we could sit at this table and plan together, and wait for Leah to come back, and then I would not be alone in my distress and my fear. Perhaps if I let him he would lift my burden from me, as he had done when I was seventeen and over-whelmed.

Or perhaps I would tell him that I had failed and endan-gered the town where he lived with his son. Perhaps I would tell him that I had lied to him about how his wife had died, that Leah had in some sense killed her, and then he would walk out of the door and give me up to the lord's men. I had never seen him truly angry. I remembered the woman who had been betrayed by her own husband for worshipping Claire, years ago, in the days after the declaration of the second war. Fear could break people, and Callum was very afraid.

I breathed in and out, gathered my strength.

'No,' I said, 'I'm not.'

He got up and walked around, his hands in his hair. 'All right,' he said. 'All right.'

There was a silence. My heart was still beating too quickly. I leaned back in my chair and watched him pace my living room. He was maybe forty by then, but looked suddenly much younger. In that moment I envied him his carefree life, how light his responsibilities seemed compared to mine. All he had to contend with was his little son and his dead wife.

I heard the words in my head, and was disgusted at myself.

'Who was the girl?' he asked at last.

'What?'

'The girl in your house, last night.'

'Oh.' For a moment her name escaped me, in my exhaus-tion. 'Grace. Eve's daughter.'

'Right.' He was looking at me again. I could see his restraint.

'What?'

'Haley, what you did – saving the girl – it was very brave. It was admirable.'

'But?'

He sat down again, playing for time. I hated that knowing look, that gentleness.

'What, Callum?'

'They will come back,' he said gently. 'Jonathan's men. And if she's not still living here when they do—'

'I know, I know.'

'What are you going to do?'

'I don't know,' I said. I was exhausted. 'I really don't, Callum, I – it was the only thing I could think of to say.'

'It's all right, Haley. It was the right thing.' A pause. 'There's no chance she really *is* your girl, is there? Because that would make things—'

'Not easier,' I said sharply. 'Eve's just lost her husband, don't say *easier*.'

'I wasn't going to.'

'Then what?'

'Simpler.'

I got up and poked at the fire reflexively, set the kettle over it. I didn't want to look at him.

'Are you sure?' he said, at last. 'Absolutely sure?'

'Yes,' I said. When the girl with my gift stood before me, I would know her, I was sure of that. He gave up.

I stared into the fire. Outside, fading green-gold leaves fluttered past the open doorway and I heard faint birdsong from the woods. It was a callously beautiful day.

'Why does it scare you?' Callum said, at last. 'The idea of having a girl?'

'It doesn't scare me.'

'It upsets you.'

I inclined my head.

'Why?'

'Because I don't want to do that to someone, Callum. Is that wrong?'

'Do what?'

He seemed genuinely confused, and the idea of explaining it seemed almost impossible. I rubbed my face.

'I loved my mother. I hated Marian so much when she took me. It was like . . . it was a kidnapping, it felt like . . . everything tore apart. I didn't want to be a witchling. It took me years to make peace with it.'

There was a pause. When he spoke, his tone was carefully expressionless. 'Did you love her?'

I turned to him, horrified. 'Of course I did. Of course.'

'But?'

'There is no *but*.'

He kept watching me, curious, trying to read me. I hesitated, trying to reach for words I thought I had buried long ago. They came so quickly it alarmed me.

'When children are that young, they love who they're told to love. You know? They love who they have to. I would have liked to have been able to . . . to choose to love her. I would have liked to have been older.'

'Wouldn't that just have made it harder?'

'No.' I was sure of that. 'It was the worst thing that had ever happened to me. Being younger didn't make that better. I was just . . . more confused.'

He nodded. There was a long silence. He pushed his hair out of his eyes and sighed. 'We can spread the word,' he said. 'If anyone asks, Eve's daughter is your girl. She can move some of her things to your house. If we see them coming back, she'll run over here. We can make it work, until the real one turns up.'

His determination made me feel helpless. 'Callum, I'm twenty years old.'

'So?'

'So the real one might not be born for years. Marian was thirty-six when I showed up. Dora was older than that.'

'We'll make it work,' he said. When I tried to look away, he held my eyes. 'For as long as we need to. Listen to me, Haley. You don't have to do everything alone.'

We sat together in silence at the table until the fire died. I didn't know how to tell him he was wrong.

At the end of the second day Leah came back.

I was sitting at the kitchen table and looked up, and she was standing at the back door. I almost cried out. She raised a finger to her lips and stepped inside, and closed the door with such effortless grace that the hinges were silent. Something about her movement was so impossibly beautiful I was struck dumb.

'Are you all right?' she whispered.

I nodded. For the first time it frightened me, the depths of my joy at the sight of her. I feared that if I spoke, she would see it.

'Where's the girl?'

I tried to come back to myself. 'Home.'

Leah nodded. She stood and looked at me and there was that strange awkwardness again – of being in someone else's home, of being enclosed, as if she were waiting for me to sit down.

'Where were you?'

She hesitated. 'In the underworld.'

'How? I thought they'd catch you—'

'I know places to hide,' she said. 'At least down there, there wasn't a patrol looking for me. I didn't go far – you know the mountain across the bridge when you come through the tunnels? There's a cavern a half-mile down.'

'They didn't have the entrance guarded?'

'No.'

'How did you know they wouldn't?'

'I didn't,' said Leah. 'Why were Jonathan's men looking for me?'

'I don't know. They were following orders.'

'Whose?'

'A commander's. Maybe one of the lord's children, I don't know. Whoever they take orders from.'

Leah pulled her feet up into the chair and pressed her hands into her face. It was oddly childlike, and I longed to soothe her panic, the soft warmth of her despair.

'I don't understand,' she said. 'I don't understand. Why can't they – why would they want me dead?'

'Maybe they found out about Cora.'

'Who?'

She did not remember the name. The implications of that made me hesitate, how many she must have killed before the names had begun to fade. 'Esther's daughter. The one you had me kill.'

She shook her head. 'No. They couldn't have. I was careful. And it was what, eight years ago? Why would they find out now?'

I hesitated, full of dread. 'Leah.' It took her a moment to lower her hands and look me in the eye. There was an air of studied politeness in it, as if she did not see me at all. I tried to keep my voice reassuring. 'Have you told me everything?'

Something hardened in her eyes. 'Yes, Haley.'

'You killed the girl,' I said.

She turned her head to face me, resting on her knees. 'Yes.'

'*Why?*'

'Because it was kinder.'

I could not speak. She saw my stricken face and raised her head. 'You didn't find her?' she said.

'What?'

'The girl.'

I didn't understand. She got to her feet in one smooth unfurling movement, catlike, and I felt another electric pulse across my heart. It was disorienting.

'Come with me.'

I hesitated, but I followed. Despite everything, I still trusted her.

In the basement she uncovered Jorah's body, peaceful and bluish beneath his shroud, and lifted his wrist, offering it to me like a gift. 'Do you feel it?'

I touched him, so terribly cold, and through the stillness of his vanished pulse I felt something flutter beneath my fingers, like the struggle of lungs to breathe. A ghost trapped within the corpse.

I looked at her. I didn't dare say it for a moment, worried that naming it would make it untrue. 'You didn't destroy the girl.'

Leah smiled. 'Not everyone deserves a second chance,' she said. 'But she did. You can take her down the tunnels with you in the morning if you want.'

I stayed crouching beside the body as she got to her feet. I did not trust myself to speak, fearing the shaking of my hands, what I might say to her in my shining relief.

'I do listen to you, Haley,' she said. 'I know you think I don't, but I do.'

Long after she went upstairs to sleep I stayed there, in the basement, in the thrumming dim stillness, alone with the body.

# CHAPTER EIGHTEEN

After that, she could have left.

I brought it up once, a few days after she returned. I was cooking dinner and she was sitting at the table, and I said something like, I saw Callum today, he says the lord's men have retreated over the hills, the patrol's gone.

He had also told me they had put up posters asking for a witch in the town centre, on the wall of the chapel that used to be Claire's, but I did not say that.

Leah watched me for a little while.

'They don't think you're here,' I said, trying to keep my tone light. 'They've moved on.'

She continued to watch me. Then she said, with equal lightness, 'How far have they gone?'

'I don't know.'

'Are they going to come back looking for me?'

I turned to her. Something had hardened in her eyes. 'No,' I said, slowly. 'Not unless someone tells them to.'

'Then that makes here pretty safe, doesn't it?'

I didn't press it further. I like to think that I was never afraid of her, but sometimes I remember her look, how badly she wanted to stay here, of the power in her tattooed hands, and I wonder. It was a long time ago, and people remember what they want to.

Why did she want to stay after the immediate danger had passed, when she could have travelled east, away from the patrols, and lived in peace and quiet somewhere in the woods?

I should be clear: I did not particularly care why. I knew that *I* did not want her to leave, and so I did not think too hard about it. Some part of me – the part that had forced me to raise the subject of her departure – knew that she had to go, that I had taken too many risks to keep her safe, and crossed the line into a recklessness I could no longer justify. So long as she lived in this house, the town was in danger. Grace might see her on one of the nights she spent here; someone might spot her in the window, staring down into the street. No one would keep *that* secret for me. They would give me away in a moment, in the hope of saving themselves from greater punishment when she was discovered.

So she had to go. I knew that, but could not bring myself to act on it. What would I do, once she had gone? I would feel her absence acutely. I would dream of her, and hope desperately that she had not been caught and killed, and I would never know. I would die not knowing. I would not be able to bear the emptiness of the house, once she had gone.

And there was something else. The electric relief that had come over me when she returned had not passed: it had sunk into me, crackling blue in the meat of my heart, and now she *hurt* me, in a way she had not before. I watched the way she pushed her hair from her face, and the look in her eyes when she was absent-minded, and the way she pulled on a jacket. I treasured the moments when she looked at me. The part of me that cared about her had strengthened, fermented like bad wine, and now when I made her laugh I felt myself light up. In those moments— when we were alone in my kitchen, in the shadowy dark of lamplight and aromatic smoke, talking of witch-magic or witchling-magic, my past or hers – I lost myself. I followed those strange wants to their roots in the dark of my mind and saw what they were, with a fervour that scared me. I wanted those silences with her to stretch, moment to moment, and for her to kiss me. I wanted her to take me upstairs to her room, and lay me down, and take off my clothes in the dark. I dreamed of it when she wasn't there. It was an itch, an illness.

She had to leave. In clearer moments I could see that. It would hurt, but the pain of losing her would not actually kill me. I knew that, because I had read about this kind of love, the painful kind that grew in you like infection, but I did not quite believe it.

Once when I was eleven or twelve, Marian told me: never believe in the inevitability of the heart. People will tell you about it, but it is not true. They will say, when you love someone that's it, you're gone; you will have no choice but to follow them, to die for them. They will tell you that sometimes things *just happen,* that they are the way they are, and there's no fighting them. Marian had said to me gravely: there's always a choice. You cannot control love, but you can control how you act under it. You may tell yourself you have no choice, but that is weakness and cowardice. Everything you do, you choose to do.

Who had she loved, I wonder now, to know that?

I could have thrown Leah out of the house. I could have fought her about it, if she did not want to leave. I could have closed my heart to her and done what I knew was right.

Instead I found myself asking her, casually, one night at the dinner table, if she'd ever been in love.

Leah looked at me from under heavy-lidded eyes. I was deep into my sickness then, and the sight of that look, of her caught interest, was enough to harden the breath in my lungs. We had been talking for the hundredth time about the question, *the question,* around which both of our lives now revolved: why were Jonathan's men hunting her? Why were the witches hunting her, why had she been exiled? I did not care anymore, about any of it, though I tried to force myself. She talked intently to me of conspiracies and allegations, of pacts between lord's men and witches, old connections. All Leah's theories sounded slightly mad to me. I wondered idly if she would ever know if she was right.

'In *love?*' she said, after a moment. 'What do you mean?'

That should have put me off at once, but instead I leaned forward, hand on the stem of my wine glass, and pressed further. 'I mean – well—' I couldn't find any reference point between my life and hers. 'When you were young, I mean.'

'I was never young.'

'What do you mean?'

'I mean—' She spread her hands helplessly. 'I mean, I was never a child, I never grew up. I was how I am.'

'How?' I tried to take the idea apart. 'What's your first memory?'

'I don't have one.'

'You must.'

She shook her head. 'I was just . . . in the underworld. Walking around. Accepting ghosts, judging them. It never *starts.*'

'You don't remember a mother? A father?'

She shook her head again, a little ruefully. It did not seem to distress her at all, the fact that she did not make sense.

'There was no one you loved?'

She swilled her own wine in her glass, staring at it. 'You say *love,*' she said, then almost laughed. 'This sounds ineloquent. You say *love* and I know what you mean, I hear how you talk about Marian, I've seen it in the memories of ghosts, but I've never felt it. I could imitate how it looks if you asked me. I could describe it. But I don't understand it.'

'Never?'

'Not that I remember.' She looked up and met my eyes. 'I know you don't believe me.'

She was right. I didn't. 'Where do witches come from, if they don't have mothers?'

'I don't know.'

'You never asked?'

'I asked. No one ever told me.'

We sat in silence a while, contemplating that.

'I had a mother,' I said, after a while. 'Before Marian.'

'You've told me.'

'I know, but—' I struggled with the words. Talking to her was normally so easy, so natural, but this was different. 'There was a baby.'

Leah looked at me alertly. Alcohol never seemed to affect her like it did me. 'Another one?'

'Yes. My . . . sibling, I guess. I don't know if it was a boy or a girl.'

'What happened to it?'

'I don't know. I never saw them again after I was given up.'

Leah hesitated, with the air of a woman walking into a dark forest unarmed. 'You loved them.'

'Yes.' I said it too quickly, with too much feeling. I felt the seed of the memory opening in the dark mud at the centre of my brain: the house, the dead cat, the dim shroud of my mother's face, the baby crying from upstairs. My love for them: bright, solid, knife-sharp, unquestioned until the day my mother had drugged me and brought me to this house. And then after that – darkness, terrible grief.

'What was it like?' Leah spoke carefully. She could see in my face the strength of the emotions she was stirring, though she did not understand them. She was trying not to hurt me. I saw that and was grateful.

'With my mother . . .' How to describe that? 'I was safe when she was there. She was . . . Nothing was right, without her. When I lost her . . . it was the worst thing I could lose. And the baby . . .' I forced myself not to strain away from the memory. 'I would have died for them. Protecting it was why I existed. The baby meant I knew what was right, and what wasn't. Hurting it was the worst thing I could ever do, and every other wrong was a fraction of it. That kind of love . . . it's steadying.'

'You would have died for them,' said Leah, quietly.

'Yes.'

There was a silence.

'I can care about people,' she said after a while. 'I can want them to be well. I care about you.'

She said it so casually it almost slipped past me, but it was like a punch in the stomach. I did not know how to reply to it. But it didn't matter, because she wasn't looking at me; she was staring into the darkness of the hall.

'I can't *die,*' she said thoughtfully. 'I can be destroyed, spiritually, but I couldn't die for someone. If that's how you define love, then it makes sense that I can't do it.'

'Could you learn?'

'Maybe.' She was still looking into the hall. I did not trust myself to speak.

Leah looked back at me. 'I am sorry,' she said, at last. I heard a huskiness in her voice, a deep-felt emotion. My pain hurt her. I marvelled at that. 'About your mother. And the baby. I'm sorry I can't sympathise more.' She looked at her hands. 'I wonder what I'm missing. Do you think it's anatomical?'

I shrugged jaggedly, with a casualness I could not feel.

After that, after all hope was gone. I spent a lot of time lying awake, wrestling with myself. I was trying to scour the infection from myself, to clean the part of my head that wanted her. Sometimes it was easy to forget my feelings; sometimes they faded, and I could talk to her freely and joyfully, as if nothing had changed. Sometimes they overwhelmed me, and I tried to avoid her for as long as I could, from fear they would burst from me unprompted. As if I could not have controlled it. *You always have a choice.*

I could not tell her, of course. Confession would simply put the burden of my discomfort on her, and she could not possibly reciprocate my feelings. She cared about me, and that was all. That was fine. I resolved, with a witchling's practical determination, to make it fine. I would wait, and this fire in my nerves would pass. It would be all right.

Needless to say, I never asked her to leave. Do you blame me? I would understand if you did.

In the year before Adrienne came two things changed: Samuel came into my life, and Leah found her calling.

It began in the depths of that last terrible winter. The river froze quite early on, so I knew it was going to be bad: in my whole life the river had never frozen, dead fish trapped in the grey ice. We had thought we were too far north for that.

The winter lasted four months, and in that long darkness almost thirty people died. The house was always full, I barely slept, and Leah spent days at a time trapped in the freezing attic. I missed her terribly, though I could feel her through the floorboards and branches above me, shining at the edges of my consciousness. I consoled so many mourners that the words started to feel dull in my mouth. It drained me, and when I saw Leah we barely spoke, because we did not have to. She felt like truth now; only in her presence could I be myself, only to her did I not have to lie. Sometimes, on evenings when I was too exhausted to talk, I slept on her floor, wrapped in rugs, just to hear her breathing, to be not-alone.

And then one night I woke up beside her bed and she was gone.

I sat up, panic forcing its way through the soft bleariness of sleep. I scrambled to my feet and down the rickety stairs, past my own bedroom and Grace's empty bedroom – and then something stopped me. I could feel a heartbeat in the house, the little creaks and silences in the floorboards, living movement. There were no patients here, only bodies I had not yet given the rites to.

Leah looked up when I walked into the parlour. I stopped dead, catching my breath. For a moment I couldn't speak, weak with relief.

'What are you doing?'

'Helping,' she said.

'What?'

She got to her feet, watching me. I could see the sheepishness in her manner, the slight discomfort.

'Take my hand,' she said.

I still expected her touch to be cold, for death to linger physically within her. Even after years I still was not quite convinced she was real, and so it took a moment to feel the flickering light of the spell beneath her skin, the second living warmth beneath her own. It disarmed me.

'What does it mean?'

'Do you remember what happened to the girl?'

I felt it. The shiver of her mind, trapped in her skin. The half-sensation. And then, when the knife came, the searing agony of the tattoos, the rites.

'I want to take their pain,' said Leah, simply, and for a moment I thought she was hearing my thoughts through my touch and let go of her wrist abruptly. That was too dangerous to risk.

'So that it doesn't hurt?'

'Yeah.'

'What if they – I mean – can they hear you now?'

'She can't hear me,' said Leah. 'She won't know anything.'

*She,* I thought, and then looked down the body and winced. Yes. Alanna. I had been trying not to think about her. She was twenty-four years old, and nobody had known she was with child until the seizures had started. I had thought at once of possession, but it had been more mundane than that, the poisoning of the blood and nerves that sometimes came with pregnancy. She lay bluish on the floor at our feet.

'You're a healer,' said Leah earnestly. 'Isn't the risk worth it? To you?'

No, was the honest answer. Nothing is worth more than you. But I could not face saying it to her. If I said it aloud I would have to hear it and know I was past saving.

Three days later she came to me with a salve, a clove-and-willow paste I used to dull aches. She had distilled it, she said, purified it a little, it would help, and I saw in her a desperate desire to be useful. This, then, was why she wanted to stay here. Acting through me, she could have a duty and a cause. When she was exiled she had lost her purpose; with me she could regain it. She could decide to care about these people, my patients, and make their welfare her calling, as it was mine. Away from me, she could only ever be a woman hiding alone in the woods, fearing the sound of distant footsteps, purposeless and immortal.

How could I deny her that? I was always helpless in the face of her joy. So I took it, and used it, and that was the beginning of the end.

Then there was Samuel.

Callum was the one who came to me when Samuel's brother was arrested. He was one of the men who had dragged the brother off to jail, and there was still blood on him when I opened the door. I gasped.

'Callum—'

'I'm fine,' he said, more curtly than I think he meant to. I could see that he was shaken.

'What happened?'

'The, uh—' He closed his eyes, puffed out a breath and then spoke more calmly. 'The blacksmith's boy. You know him?'

'Yes.' This was Samuel's brother Luke. Twenty-one years old, newly married to one of Eve's apprentice weavers. I knew *of* him more than I knew him. I had treated his mother for an abscess a couple of years ago and had glimpsed him at the door. Slight, quick-eyed, with callused hands.

'He killed, uh – the wife. His wife.'

'What?'

'Don't make me say it again,' said Callum tightly. 'Come with me.'

No one else could have spoken to me like that. Respect, as Marian had told me long ago, was a witchling's living; if nobody listened to you, you could not heal them, and they would not believe you when you had to tell them things like *I'm afraid he's going to lose his arm* or *this is going to hurt but I swear it'll be better after* or *get out of my house*. But this was Callum and I trusted him, or had trusted him before Leah came and changed what trust meant to me, and so I followed him and I did not ask questions.

Samuel's brother lived in the middle of town, near the forge at which he was apprenticed, and so there was already an audience gathered around the house. They moved back when they saw Callum; they knew what he meant. Then they saw me, and all expression vanished from their faces.

'All right,' said Callum, but they were already scattering. He glanced back at me, but I was watching them retreat. It is hard for me now to remember how I bore it before Leah, before I had someone to whom I would never signify death and darkness.

The door of the house was ajar. I stepped inside and sensed the body at once: ahead of us, through wooden floor.

'Is there anyone else here?' I said, softly. Death lay over the house like dust, in thick soft layers, and I did not want to disturb it.

'No,' said Callum. 'I cleared it.'

'Why am I here?'

'I need you to tell me you can't help her. So I can convict the son of a bitch.'

I glanced back at him and he nodded towards the kitchen. I took a breath and kept going.

The room was dim and cluttered. There were dirty plates and knives everywhere, rotten food in the corner. The back door was open so I could feel the breeze on my face, but it did not help the stench. It came thick and foul from the middle of the room where a floorboard had been pulled up, and in the cavity below it—

I gritted my teeth, pressed a hand to my forehead, and looked again.

'How long has she been dead?' said Callum from behind me. His tone was carefully expressionless. 'Just tell me and then we can go.'

It took me a moment to collect myself. He had the advantage of having seen it before; he could brace himself. The woman's face was sunken and dark with mould. I could see the yellow of her teeth through her peeled-back lips.

'Two weeks,' I said. 'Maybe three.'

'Is there any chance her ghost is still there? Could you take her—'

'No. She's gone.'

Callum nodded. 'All right,' he said tightly. 'Thank you, Haley. I'll call in the boys and we'll bury her.'

He put a hand on my shoulder. He'd never done that before. I suppressed the urge to be sick, and walked out of the house with him. Nobody ever lived there again; traces of the woman's dissipated ghost hung over the place, or so people said, and they tore it down a few months later.

Outside, Callum looked at me. There was something odd in his expression.

'What?'

'You're too young for this,' he said.

'I'm twenty-one.'

'Exactly.'

I didn't like the way he was looking at me. It was like the way he looked at his son, and it made me want to stop talking and step away from him. I was not his daughter.

'I wish she'd lived longer,' he said at last. I knew he was talking about Marian. 'She would have been fifty by now.'

'No, she wouldn't,' I said. 'We don't live that long.'

I left him there, on the street. Ever since I had started lying to him I could not grieve with him anymore. Marian's death felt a long time ago now.

Anyway. Samuel's brother killed his wife, and waited long enough that her ghost was destroyed and I could not help her, and for that he was tried and convicted. He went to prison in Arbakin, the great city to the north, and was hanged a year later in a spurt of executions ordered by one of the Lord Jonathan's more whimsical grandsons. But I had to show up to the trial at our court to talk about what he had done, and that was where I met Samuel.

I had never met him, because he had not been sick in fifteen years. He was twenty-five, a fisherman with steady eyes. He greeted me politely and without fear, which of course warmed me to him instantly, and walked into the courtroom after me and spoke gravely about how his brother was a good man. I didn't blame him; if it had been my brother, I would have tried to defend him too. For the first time in months, since I had talked to Leah about it, I thought of my mother's baby. They would be almost grown by now. I wondered if I had passed them in the market and not realised, or whether they had been carefully avoiding me their whole life, like my mother.

I cut off the memory at once, forcefully. I had no brother or sister, and no mother. I was the witchling.

After Samuel's brother was pronounced guilty I found Samuel waiting outside the courtroom. I said goodbye to Callum and then hesitated. I should to go home. Leah would be waiting for me. Someone might need my help, and it was important they knew where I was.

I closed my eyes and tried to convince myself of it. I had to go home. I had to go *right now*.

After a few moments, I walked over and stood next to Samuel, leaning against the courtroom wall. He was smoking a cigarette. I said, 'That was horrific.'

He looked at me like he'd just seen me. 'Yeah,' he said. 'I'm sorry you had to deal with that. I'm . . .' He waved the cigarette, a vague hand gesture like he was trying to swat something away, and the smoke left a thin trail in the air. 'I'm sorry.'

'Not your fault,' I said.

'Isn't it?'

'No.'

He looked down at me. He was quite extraordinarily good-looking. I felt the thought pass through my mind and settle. It had been a long time since I let myself think like that.

We stood there for a while, leaning against the wall. Everyone had gone now. It was evening and the street was empty. I was so tired.

I looked up to find him watching me. I was standing just a little too close to him, but he did not move. Good. I think he was desperate, too.

'This is going to be embarrassing,' he said, 'but I don't think I know your name.'

I smiled.

'Haley.'

'Samuel.'

'All right.' I couldn't think of what else to say. We stood

looking at each other in the birdsong sunset, and I moved
very slightly towards him, and then he dropped his cigarette,
stamped it out carefully, turned and kissed me.

It was furious and mindless and beautiful. We stayed against
that wall for a long time, lost in each other, until I realised
he was touching me in ways I could not, as the witchling, be
seen to be touched, and broke away from him. He saw it in
my eyes, and understood. 'Let's go to my house,' he said, so
we did.

It was so easy and joyful. I wanted him, so I took him. It
was freedom.

He wanted me to stay with him, in that bed in the thickening night, but I told him I had to go home, and he understood that, too. He never asked anything of me.

When I got home I went up to the attic, because I knew that
if I didn't Leah would know something was wrong.

She was sitting on the floor, surrounded by herbs and pastes.
The air around her shimmered slightly. And there was that
expression of blankness again, as she drew herself out from
her own mind, until she recognised me.

'Haley. How was the trial?'

'All right,' I said. I thought of Samuel's brother's burning
eyes. 'He'll die in prison.'

'Good. Why did he do it?'

'I don't know,' I said. 'I don't care.'

She studied me gravely. I was convinced then that she did
not know, could not see him on me; I am convinced now that
she must have done.

'You're not sleeping,' she said softly. 'You should sleep more.'

I nodded curtly. Her concern was unbearable. There was a
moment's silence and then I turned and left her there, alone
in the attic.

*

Almost every other evening for the next three months, I knocked on Samuel's door. It was easy enough to disguise my visits: he wore a bandage around his left thigh and I always carried the right medicines for infection, and if either of us were asked that would have been our excuse. Only someone with an ear pressed against his bedroom door would have known we were lying, and the lord's men weren't going to do that. I was very nearly sure of it.

We didn't talk much. Once, he asked me about my tattoos and I told him what they were for, and he lay there tracing them for a while until I got up and left. Samuel was gentle and kind, and sometimes when I spoke to him there was something closed off in his eyes. I think he had someone else, too, someone he was trying to pull himself away from. It didn't matter to me.

Leah and I never spoke about it. There was nothing to say.

Samuel was another broken vow. If the lord's men ever *did* find out, through some neighbour with a grudge or our own carelessness, they would take me to trial and punish me – and maybe him, as well, though I didn't allow myself to feel guilty about that. He was a grown man, and perfectly aware of the risks he was taking. And the lord's men could not truly hurt me, because they did not know who I cared about: I had been very careful about that. And the risk of discovery for this, of trial and public humiliation, was nothing compared to what I was risking by keeping Leah in my house. I had hidden her for three years; I could hide this.

Anyway, I argued with myself, was this technically against my vows as they were written? Samuel was not my husband. I had forsworn love, but this wasn't love: this was trust, and shared escape. With him I could breathe, and I never had to lie to him, and that made him special to me amongst everyone else in the world. In his house I did not have to be the witchling; I lay in the sunlight, in his bed, and felt warm, and clean, and happy. I had him for three months, and then everything broke again.

One morning I was woken by shouting outside. It was spring, just before dawn. I thought for a second, wildly, that the search party of lord's men had returned, that they had found out about Leah, but then sleep lifted and I heard them. Two voices, sobbing, one of them a child. They were in the street. '*Help!*' one of them cried. '*Help us!*'

Some selfish part of me wanted to curl up in bed again, but I got blearily to my feet and pulled on my jacket. Whenever anyone cried *help*, they were always asking for me.

I saw Leah on the landing. We looked at each other for a moment, and I could see the thrumming frustration in her. She wanted to answer the call with me, hated being invisible to the people for whom she crafted medicines in her attic. I saw how it wore at her. After a few seconds she turned and climbed the stairs again.

I ran down the stairs and out of the door. In the middle of the street, a woman lay in a pool of blood. She was half-dead already, her skin a greyish brown. Her husband was dragging her towards the House of the Dead, which must have pulled at the wound in her stomach, but she was too far gone even to scream. Her daughter was at her feet, wailing.

'Get away from her,' I said sharply, and he dropped her immediately. The daughter looked maybe ten or eleven. She did not acknowledge me at all and instead knelt at her mother's stomach, trying to press her hands onto the wound to stop the bleeding. It was pointless trying to fight her.

'Kid. Go into the house, get me—' She wouldn't know what any of the herbs were. Damn it, *damn it*. 'Help me carry her.'

The girl did not look at me. I went to lift the woman by

the shoulders, and was half-surprised when she moved with me, to pick up her mother's feet.

'One – two—'

She was strong for a child that young. Together we moved her mother into the kitchen. The woman's face was too pale, I didn't like it at all – and where was the husband? I turned. He was in the parlour, panicked, hands covered in blood. The look in his eyes was wild. Instinctively, I locked the door.

'What should I do?' he said huskily, and I told him to sit in the living room. He did so at once, hunched, his hands over his face. The girl was sitting beside her mother when I got back into the kitchen, pressing two hands into the wound. I knew she wasn't going to leave.

'Go sit at the table. I need you out of the way.'

She glared up at me, tear-streaked and furious. 'I want to help.'

'I promise, this is how you help. I've been doing this a long time.'

She looked suspicious, but then retreated to Marian's chair, leaning over the back on her knees. Her eyes were on her mother.

I pulled myself back, focused on the woman at my feet. A single knife wound to the stomach. Horizontal, and nearer the hip than the waist, so not self-inflicted. Nobody tried to kill themselves like that. You had time to position and centre the knife if you were using it on yourself. Somebody had done this to her.

She was bleeding out, that was the first danger. I bound the wound tightly but the bandages were soaked as soon as I applied them. All right. Something else.

I went to the drawers. Blood ink and a knife, lavender and amaranth for the fire – damn it, the *fire* was out. I threw wood onto it, sparked it with flint. One of Leah's pastes was in my hand, to stop bleeding and slow infection. I put it down and breathed. The sleep was gone from my mind now, but I tried to call it back, sink into the brightness of transcendence. Magic could hold the skin together, hold the blood in her body, stop the slow seeping of her life into my hands. She was not yet too far gone.

The smoke thickened and curled around us. I gathered myself and cut off the woman's shirt. I held the knife in the fire, waited until I could feel pain flickering at the ends of my nerves. The blade was red-hot. I held it in the blood-ink, felt the hiss of steam, and then lowered my knife to the woman's stomach.

I traced the mark into her skin, sure and quick, and then something shifted and I was alight. There was a pulsing in my hand. I gave it to the woman, so she could take it and stop bleeding and heal. *Heal*.

Time passed. Seconds, minutes. The smoke began to clear again. I could hear my own hoarse breathing, and the girl's quickened gasps.

And nothing else.

The woman's eyes were open and unblinking, and her hands slack and covered in blood. Her chest had stilled. The magic had scoured the life from her; the shock had been too much for her weakened body. Marian had told me that happened sometimes. I had read about it, but I had never seen it before.

I closed my eyes and sat there until her daughter started screaming.

'Mama! *Mama!*'

'Shush,' I said wearily, and then when she wouldn't, 'Shush, come on. I'm sorry. I'm sorry.' I got up and tried to take her in my arms, but she pulled away from me. I don't blame her.

'Hey. *Hey.*' I knew we didn't have much time; I tried to keep her still. 'Listen to me. Did your father do this to her? Did they have a fight?'

She stopped struggling, and stared up at me. I saw the lightning-bolt of terror in her face and let her go.

Footsteps in the corridor. I turned. The husband – his name was Linas, I learned later – burst into the room. He saw his dead wife on the ground and stopped, panting.

'Amy,' he said, 'no. No. No.' He rounded on me, panicked and furious. He was a big man, six foot one, maybe six foot two.

'Bring her back,' he said.

My instincts were good. I put myself between the girl and her father, my back to the kitchen table. She was still sobbing uncontrollably.

His voice rose and he stepped forward. His face was blotchy-red. 'Bring her *back!*'

'Get back,' I said. 'Two steps back.'

I said it calmly, but his face contorted with rage. Another step towards me. I had left my knife beside his wife's body. I tried very hard not to look at it, in case he followed my eyes.

'Bring her back.'

'I can do that if you step back.'

'Give me my daughter.'

I did not want to say *no,* but I could feel her trembling fear, and I was not going to let him near her. I could feel his wife's staring eyes from the floor. 'Step back. Step away—'

He moved with brutal efficiency. I felt the blow across my face, and then the wall slammed into the back of my head. I fell to the ground, and the pain hit, and I was curled in on myself trying to hide from it, waves of it, buzzing and unbearable. I had fallen on top of the girl, and he pushed me aside, pulling her out from under me as she screamed for her mother. I put my hand out blindly, blood running over my face, but he was stronger than me. I felt her slip out of my grip and swore in my head as the pain throbbed and receded.

I tried to push myself up onto my feet, but the world was turning around me. I could feel his footsteps through the floor, thundering and painful. Any moment now he was going to find the door and realise it was locked, and then, oh no, I was going to die. I tried to find the gravity of the moment, but I couldn't get a hold on it.

My hands found the familiar grooves of the wall and I tried to pull myself upright. The footsteps had stopped. I could hear voices.

'Get out of my way, bitch.'

'Where's Haley?'

'Who the fuck is—'

And then silence.

The girl started screaming again. 'Mama! Mama!'

What was going on? I clambered around the corner, into the hall, holding onto the wall with all my strength, in case the swooning nausea claimed me and I fell again.

I blinked, not sure of what I was seeing.

The husband was on the floor in the corridor, unconscious, though he was not bleeding. The girl pushed past me to kneel beside her mother again. Leah had stepped over his body and was moving towards the parlour. She stopped when she saw me, horrified. I must have been covered in blood.

'Haley,' she whispered. 'I'm sorry – I heard—'

'Get Callum,' I said, and spat blood so I could say it more clearly. 'Don't . . . heal me. Get Callum.'

My hand slipped off the wall, and I knew with dull panic that I was going to fall. Leah caught me, held me up, cradled me against her. I could feel my blood soaking into her clothes. Her sure heartbeat against me. In her arms I felt calm, and completely safe.

'I'm sorry,' I tried to say. 'I'm sorry.'

But she wasn't looking at me. I felt her stillness, and tried to push myself to my feet. She stopped me, helped me to turn as I lay on the floor.

'Haley,' she said softly. 'Look.'

I tried, wiped the blood from my eyes. There was sunlight

in the hall and it was difficult to see into the dimness of the parlour. The girl was kneeling beside her dead mother, who was sitting up. She blinked at us, slow and unfeeling, and then collapsed.

Everything was swooning, blurred. The girl had started to wail again. I stared uncomprehendingly at her mother's twitching fingertips.

# CHAPTER NINETEEN

I remember what happened next only vaguely. He had hit me very hard, though I knew from the timbre of the pain that I would survive it. I did not feel in danger; I could feel Leah's presence just above me, waiting.

I was lying on the floor of the hall, the breeze on my face. Leah was gone. Then someone else was standing over me, trying to sit me up.

'Haley. Look at me, Haley – tell me what to do.'

Callum. I reached for his hand, and felt it covered in blood. His blood – no, that didn't make sense. My blood. I grasped him tightly, looked into his eyes and tried to speak.

'He – killed—' I pointed into the kitchen, where Adrienne's mother lay dead. 'Make sure – he can't—'

'All right. All right.'

He tried to let go but I held his hand tightly, pulled him down so I could whisper in his ear. *She's the girl.*

It was important that he knew. I saw him staring at me, and then the darkness tugged at my vision again until I was floating and alone.

I woke again in my own bed, later. The house was empty. Leah was sitting in the corner of my room. She got up at once when she saw my eyes open.

'Are you all right?'

'Yeah, I'm . . .' I put a hand to the back of my head. 'I'm fine. I feel fine.'

She nodded. 'I left you a scar. I figured you'd need one. In case anyone asked.'

I could feel it, under my hair. 'Thank you.' It seemed an odd thing to say. 'How long has it been?'

'Two days. You needed to sleep.'

Two days was fine. I was a witchling, and people would believe I had recovered on my own in two days. 'Was anyone sick?'

'People knocked on the door. No emergencies. Callum told them what happened, told them to come back.'

'Callum's been here?'

'All the time. He's been sleeping in the room next door every night, him and his little boy. And this woman – forties, tall, dark hair—'

'Ira.'

Leah nodded. 'She's been bringing you food and water.'

'And none of them have seen you?'

She gave me a tight, bleak smile. Of course not.

'The girl's father saw you,' I said, suddenly remembering. I sat up in horror, and the dizziness made me close my eyes. 'Leah, the *girl* saw you. Where are they?'

'It's fine, Haley. They won't remember me. Linas is in jail now anyway.'

'Linas?'

'The father.'

'How do you know that?'

She jerked her head towards the floor, a little bitterly. She was reduced to listening at floorboards now, this woman who had once judged the dead.

'You're sure they won't say anything? They won't remember?'

'I'm sure. Trust me.'

I tried again to sit up. 'What did you *do*, Leah?'

Below us, I heard the front door open – gently, so as not to wake me. Callum's soft voice in the hall.

'You should go talk to them,' said Leah. Her face was expressionless. 'Let them know you're okay.'

'Leah—'

She raised a finger to her lips. I could hear Callum's footsteps on the stairs. She got to her feet, stepped backwards into my cupboard, and closed it silently. I saw the flash of self-disgust in her face. The indignity of all of this. Was it still worth it to her, then, to be able to heal through me? And then I wondered, with a flash of fear: when would it stop being worth it? Would I wake up that day and find her gone?

The door edged open. I sat up, trying to clear my expression before Callum pushed his head tentatively around it.

'You're awake,' he said. 'Oh, Haley, thank— I was so worried.'

I was touched by his relief. I tried to keep my eyes from darting to the cupboard.

'How are you? Are you all right?'

'Yes.' I tried to get up and swooned. My throat was suddenly dry. 'No. I need water.'

'I'll get it for you.'

'No, I'll come downstairs. Help me balance.'

'Are you sure?'

'I'll be fine.' I took his arm and he guided me out of the room. As soon as he closed the door, the tension in my chest lessened.

Aron was waiting for us at the bottom of the stairs. He was seven now, and barely remembered the mother who had attacked him. When he saw me he ran over and hugged me, shouting my name. Callum had raised him not to fear me. I smiled down at him, stroking his dark hair.

'Haley! Haley!'

'Hey, Aron.' I kissed his head. His father said, 'Careful with Haley, now, she's just recovering.'

Aron looked up at me earnestly. 'Papa put the man who hurt you in jail.'

'Good,' I said to him. When he'd let me go and run into the parlour, I asked Callum quietly, 'Where's the girl?'

'Her aunt's looking after her. Come and sit down, Haley.'

He poured me water from the barrel in the corner. The mother's body was in the sitting room, covered by a sheet. Callum went into the corridor and pulled the door closed so his son wouldn't see it. Aron was sitting happily in a corner, under a curl of branches, playing with a little bird I had whittled for him.

'Did she leave any wishes?'

'Her sister says she wanted to be taken down.'

'Good. I'll do it today.'

He looked at me with concern. 'Are you going to be strong enough?'

'Yeah.' I said it offhand, like it was nothing. 'Is the girl all right?'

'No. But that's understandable, I suppose.'

I drank the water, felt the breeze on my face through the open back door. Suddenly I felt trapped; I wanted to be outside, to feel the fresh air. I tried to get up, but I stumbled again. Callum moved to catch me but I held the back of the chair. I tried to think of something to distract him from my weakness.

'How did you know to find me?'

He didn't answer.

'Callum?'

'I've been wondering about that,' he said. 'You should sit down.'

'Yes. Outside.'

He guided me into the sunlight and sat with me in the grass. It was a beautiful spring day, and the sky was a hard, chipped blue. I watched Callum for a while, his furrowed brow. He looked so much like Marian when he was anxious.

'I don't know how I knew to come here,' he said at last. 'I was just . . . I worried. I knew something was wrong.'

'Maybe you heard something.'

He grimaced. 'From a mile away? I don't think so.'

*That was an illusion,* she had told me once, when I had asked her how she had made time stop around me in the camp. *Superficial.* Perhaps that was what she had done to the girl and her father. I had to ask her.

'Haley?'

I came back to myself. 'Did you ever think about how you could get into the house?'

'What?'

'Before Linas attacked me, I locked the door. But you still got in.'

'It was locked?'

'Not for you.'

He looked at me, nonplussed. I reached behind me and laid a hand on the smooth wooden doorstep. It was reassuringly warm in the sunlight.

'The house knows you. It knew I wanted the door kept locked for Linas, so it didn't let him out. It knew you wanted to help me, so it let you in.'

'The *house* let me in?'

'Didn't Marian talk to you about this?'

'No,' he said. Then he smiled a little. 'I guess I never asked.'

'Yeah.'

I leant against his shoulder a little. Everything hurt. It felt strange and comforting to be near him again. With him, I felt lighter, and calm.

'What happened?' he asked me, after a while. 'How did you manage to knock him out?'

I stared into the whispering trees, the teeming forest. I was so tired. I didn't have the energy for an elaborate lie. 'I don't know. I don't remember.'

I wasn't afraid, really; I had been lying to him a long time. I trusted to his ignorance of witchling-magic and his faith in me, and I was right: he asked no more questions. I felt a strange, reckless disappointment. Part of me still wanted him to turn to me, tear apart my lies and half-deceptions, to be discovered.

We sat like that in silence for a while until Aron came running outside to join us. 'Can I go in the river?'

'Not on your own,' said Callum.

'I can swim!'

'You can paddle. It's a different thing.'

'I want to learn! I want to swim!'

'Give me a moment. I need to talk to Haley.'

Aron narrowed his eyes. 'Two minutes.'

'Five minutes.'

'Four.'

'Done.'

Aron shook his father's hand solemnly and then ran down to the riverbank, dangling his feet in the water and shooting us resentful looks.

Callum turned to me. 'So. The girl. What are you going to do about her?'

'I don't know,' I said, wearily. 'What am I supposed to do?'

He laid a hand on my shoulder. 'You'll be all right, Haley.'

'I know,' I said. 'And Grace can leave, now.' I would miss her. I would try not to miss her. She would be able to go north, to the great schools in Arbakin. She was smart enough to win a scholarship. I wanted to ask him if Marian had been frightened when I had been brought to her, fifteen years before, but I was too guarded for that now.

He got up after a while and played with his son in the river. and I watched them and felt Leah's thrumming, trapped presence in the house behind me, and then as he was leaving, pulling on his coat in the doorway, Callum turned to me and said, 'How did you know his name?'

'What?' I was sitting at the kitchen table.

'Linas. How did you know his name?'

Leah had told me. I reached for an excuse and felt only the sharp falling of panic in my stomach. A hesitation. I *know* he noticed.

'She said it.' I gestured with a slight jerk of the thumb towards the body in the parlour. 'She was calling to him. As she was . . . you know.' I did not want to say it in front of Aron.

It was a shameful lie, and for the first time since I had met them I felt relieved when they were gone.

Afterwards, I sat at the table with my head in my hands until Leah came downstairs. She sat opposite me at Marian's chair at the kitchen table.

'Haley,' she said softly. 'Listen to me. It's going to be all right.'

'No, it won't,' I said. 'It won't. She's going to live in the house with us, Leah. How are we going to hide you all the time?'

She didn't answer that. There was a silence.

'What did you do to them? The girl and her father?' She didn't answer. 'Leah—'

'A spell,' she said shortly. 'The girl won't remember me. She was in shock anyway, it didn't take much. If she sees me again, maybe, it might come back to her.'

'And the father?'

She shook her head. 'Don't worry about it, Haley.'

'Leah—'

Her tone hardened. 'Don't worry about it.'

I could not bring myself to fight with her, not then. We sat in silence for a while.

'We could tell her,' Leah said quietly, after a moment. 'The girl.'

'About you?'

'Yes.'

I shook my head. 'It's too big a risk. The first few weeks . . . she'll hate me, Leah. I'll be the monster who's taken her from her family. And she'll see other people coming into the house, she'll be with me. If Marian had given me a secret that big, early on . . . I would have told people, just to hurt her. Or to bargain with her, get her to give me back to my mother.'

'And after?'

'What do you mean after?'

'You loved Marian,' said Leah quietly. 'In the end. The girl will love you.'

'Maybe she will.' It was difficult to think about: the child would be so isolated she would have to love me, for want of anyone else. I didn't want that kind of love. 'Or maybe never. I don't know.'

We sat there for a while, and then Leah got up. 'If it takes a few weeks,' she said, 'then we wait a few weeks. I can do that. I have my work.'

'Are you sure?'

'I'll be fine,' she said, and at last she smiled. 'It'll be all right, Haley.'

I remember her so clearly in that moment – her soft smile, the candlelight on her pale face. I hold it to myself now when I think of her.


I allowed myself one day. I recovered, I ate, I slept, I took the corpse of Adrienne's mother down to the underworld, and then I lay in bed that night and looked at memories I usually tried to keep buried: those early days, the breaking of my spirit. There was no making it better, I knew that – no sheltering her from the fact she could never love her family as her family again, and until she understood that I would not be able to teach her what I needed to. All I could do was make it quicker.

The next day I went to Ira's house. She knew what had happened, of course, and fussed over me, looking at the scar at my temple. She tried to reassure me: I was safe now, Linas would spend the rest of his life in jail for attacking me and murdering his wife, he would never be able to hurt me again. She worried about me too much. She never asked me any questions about what had happened, not wanting to make me relive it.

Linas himself, as it turned out, had nothing at all to say about that morning. If you spoke to him all he would do was scream, bloodshot-eyed and gaunt with terror, as if trapped in a room with his nightmares. It made it almost impossible to hold a trial, and eventually the lord's men took him to the citadel in the north, where as far as I know he still resides, screaming every night until he coughs up blood.

Then there was the matter of the girl.

Ira knew Adrienne's aunt. It was all very coordinated. Grace came to collect her belongings that morning; she was elated to be able to leave in the autumn for the city in the north. She was going to be a historian, she told me excitedly. I kissed her head and told her to remember us.

Then we sat and waited.

Just after sunset, we heard a knock. Leah retreated upstairs and I walked into the hall. I wanted to be sick. I wanted to do anything but open the door. I breathed in and out, pressed my forehead to the cool wood, and before I wanted it to, it swung open.

Adrienne's aunt was trembling but otherwise composed. In some ways, I thought, the murder of Adrienne's mother was good cover; it had given her family space to look as though they were grieving without the girl realising they were mourning her as well. The child herself was dead-eyed, staring into space. She had followed her aunt here because she had been told to, and did not have the energy to disobey.

I saw her blink and realise where she was. She shook her head, slowly and then faster. 'No. No, no.'

'Come in,' said her aunt. Her lip was trembling. 'Come on, now. I just need to talk to the witchling.'

'No,' repeated Adrienne. 'I don't want to.' She started to back away. She was cleverer than I had been, or maybe just older; she knew that once she crossed the threshold she would never leave again. She stepped back, tried to run. Her aunt caught her but she struggled, fought, slipped away. 'No, *no*—'

She was a quick child, sure-footed and agile. And yet somehow, on that day when her life depended on it, she tripped on the cobblestones and slammed into the ground, hard enough that she cried out and laid still for a moment. She tried to get up, put her hand to her face and found blood.

I did not glance up at the attic window, though I wanted to. Instead, I picked her up and slung her over my shoulder. She fought, of course, and screamed, but I had been carrying bodies all my life.

Her aunt was crying now, hand over her mouth. I wanted to say something comforting to her but could not think of anything. 'Don't take her,' she whispered. 'Please. Just – give us a month. Please. Not now.'

I looked at her weeping helplessly in my doorway as I held her niece in my arms, and knew that my job here was to be the evil hard-faced bitch she had imagined. I walked through the doorway, Adrienne pounding against my back as hard as she could. '*No! No!*'

Her aunt sobbed, but I heard the door click behind me and knew it would not open. I carried Adrienne upstairs, away from her aunt's wails. When I let her down in the centre of Marian's bedroom, she charged at me, bloody and breathless. I held her back, an arm's length away, as she struggled.

'I know you hate me,' I said. 'I'm sorry this is happening to you. I really am.'

She spat in my face.

I remembered Marian slapping me when I was a little girl. I looked down at Adrienne's screwed-up face, her fury and grief, and could not do it. Marian had had years that I had not, to get used to this, to plan. I could not be her.

I left and locked Adrienne inside, and then I sat down in the corridor and listened to her beating against the door, screaming, for an hour until eventually she grew tired and sat against the door, sobbing. Then at last she stopped that too, and there was silence.

Hours later, in the darkness, I heard footsteps on the stairs.

'How are you?' said Leah softly. Her hands were dyed green from her work upstairs. Today she had been working on a salve for the drawing-out of pus from a wound, to prevent the deepening of infection. Leah went to great pains to conceal the traces of witch-magic in her work, so that I could take credit for it. Nobody seemed to suspect anything; I think they simply assumed I had inherited Marian's genius.

I shrugged. I didn't know how I was.

'Is she asleep?'

'I think so.'

Leah watched me. She had that look in her eyes again, focused and searching, like she was trying to read me but could not find anything to latch on to. 'Are you OK?'

I shook my head slowly.

She stared for a moment longer, then descended the rest of the stairs. She sat down beside me, next to the door.

'She'll get used to it,' she said, softly.

'That's not the point.' I rubbed my face, trying to keep the anger out of my voice. This was not Leah's fault. 'I don't want her to have to. I never thought . . .' I could feel the crushed little girl within me stirring again; the barred window, my shattered heart. Pounding on the door I was now sitting calmly on the other side of. I had sworn to myself that the second I got a chance I would sneak past Marian, run away, leave the house and go back to my family. The little girl I had been would not understand me now at all. It would be incomprehensible to her that Marian had now been dead for six years and yet here I was, in her house, with no one to keep me here, taking up the duties she had left to me. And in twenty years' time I would be dead and Adrienne would be here, a solemn young woman with tattooed arms and no dreams of freedom, as different from this furious little girl as anyone could imagine. I could not bear it.

Leah was still watching me. After a while, she seemed to realise she could not help, and looked away. We stared at the wall. I could feel Adrienne's fitful breathing through the door behind me. I was almost sure she was asleep.

'How're we going to hide you?'

Leah shook her head. 'Don't worry about that now.'

'No, we should worry.' I shook my head, trying to clear it. 'You can't do things like that – making her trip up, we have to be more subtle—'

'It's fine.'

'It's not.'

'I didn't want you to have to run after her,' she said quietly. 'If people saw they might think you can't control her. You always say, if they see weakness—'

'I'd rather they see that than see you.'

'It'll be fine, Haley.'

'You can't just say that.'

'I'm not just saying it. You have to trust me.'

I turned to look at her face in the fading candlelight, her sombre too-bright eyes.

'The thing you did to her,' I said, after a while. 'To make her forget you. Would it have worked on me? In the camp?'

'I don't know. I didn't try.'

'Why not?'

Leah thought about that for a while.

'Because it wasn't worth it,' she said. I could see her, years ago, merciless and untouched by the death around her, making the calculation in in her head. 'You would have remembered Marian being injured. You would have asked questions about how she'd survived. And . . .' She hesitated. 'Well. No one would have believed you.'

That was true. I thought again of the boy who had thrown a rock at me when I was young. *Dead girl.* I tried to stay steady-voiced, to stay calm. I looked at the wall on the landing, not at her. 'I'm so scared for her.' Once I said it, I felt laid open. 'I don't want to do this to her.'

Leah put her arm around me. I shivered.

'She'll be all right,' she whispered. 'You're all right.'

'I wasn't always.'

She looked at me. I think she saw how close I was to losing it and doing – *something*, anything to be not myself, to get away from here. She was too close in the warm darkness. I could not bear the familiar crackling pain. I made to get up.

She pulled me down and kissed me.

The first moment was wild and bright and full of shock. The second was electric. I was frozen, and then I wasn't; I was pushing back, hands in her hair, hungry. I felt opened, complete. She was hard and sweet and warm, and I was alight, and her hands were at the small of my back, pulling me closer—

And then I came back to myself.

I broke away. I could still see her lips, they were all I could see, soft and wet, and her hands were still on me. I wanted her to touch me more, closer, deeper, I wanted to be naked on the floorboards beneath her and her moving slow and soft down my body. I could *see* it, and it hurt.

I pulled back and got up, pressed myself against the wall

on the other side of the landing. I looked down the stairs at the street through the glass of the front door, looked anywhere but at her, still and ruffle-haired and uncomprehending, sitting with her knees up in the dark.

'Haley,' she said after a moment, very softly, almost plaintively, 'come back.'

I breathed out and walked slowly back towards her. I sank down the wall in front of Adrienne's room.

Leah put her face in her hands, then looked at me.

'I'm sorry,' she whispered. 'I'm sorry. I thought—'

'Don't apologise.'

'I should have – I should have asked—'

'Leah, it's fine.'

I touched her wrist, and she looked at me through her fingers. I had thought I was going to lose it, and maybe I still was, but in that moment my mind was cool and bright. Everything around me seemed very still. We looked at each other.

'I thought it was what you wanted,' said Leah, her voice a horse whisper. 'I thought—'

'It was. For a long time.'

'Not anymore?'

'Maybe. I don't know.' The window at the end of the landing was slightly ajar, and wavering in the warm spring wind; I wanted to get up and close it, but I was scared to break the moment. 'I never wanted to want it. I knew you didn't – you couldn't feel like that.'

'I could,' she said. 'If it would make you happy. I could teach myself to want it.'

I did not know what to say for a few long moments. When I spoke, I was slow and careful. 'That's not love, Leah.'

'Isn't it?'

'No. Look—' I tried to find the words, to untangle the thoughts that had lain for so long in my bruised mind. 'I didn't want to . . . to feel that way about you. It wasn't something I was ever going to act on. I was waiting for it to pass.'

'But I could—'

'Don't. Please.' I closed my eyes; if she offered it, said it aloud, I did not trust myself. 'This isn't your problem. You can't solve it. It's going to be all right. I'll be all right.'

'But if you want—'

'I *don't*,' I said, urgently. I couldn't find a way to explain it to her. 'Leah, how do you think I could live with myself? You in my attic, hidden from everyone, doing things that you don't *want*, just to assuage me—'

'Not to *assuage* you.' She cupped my face in her hand; my breathing hitched, despite myself. 'Haley, I want you to be happy. I don't care how. Isn't that what you mean by love?'

It was a genuine question. 'No. Not that kind.'

'I wouldn't mind—'

'Not *minding* isn't enough. It would – I would hate myself. It would be worse than nothing.'

She didn't understand, yet; she was intent. 'Do you love . . .' She gestured. 'Whoever it is?'

'Samuel? No.'

'What's the difference?'

'He wants me, and you're just being kind. I can't explain it, Leah.'

'Try harder.'

She was bright and focused again. I felt exhausted. I did not know how to explain how I felt to her, with words I had only just begun to allow myself to think, *love* or *passion* or *desire*: all these things that witches did not feel, that she had talked about with detached interest when they appeared in my patients but which had never affected her at all. It would be nothing at all to her to wake up beside me every morning, just a change of sleeping arrangements, and it would be the greatest joy in the world to me, and the knowledge of that disparity – that she was pretending to love me to make me happy, that everything was a lie – would hollow me out until I was nothing.

'I don't love him and he doesn't love me. We know where we stand. With you, I – I couldn't do it. I care too much. It wouldn't help.'

'Then what would?'

'What?'

'Help.'

I could feel her confusion, her guilt, her intense kindness. 'Nothing. It will pass. I'll be fine.'

'You're sure?'

She was so intense. She did care about me, I know it.

'Yes, Leah. Go to bed.'

She looked at me a while longer and then went obligingly upstairs. I stayed where I was, on the floor outside Adrienne's room. The house was silent around me. I could still hear Adrienne's soft breathing through the door.

What do you want me to say? It was fine. I was fine. It was a bad few months, but we got through it. Leah and I spoke less than we had done, and never touched, even casually. Adrienne fought and kept fighting.

She had no home to go back to, with one parent dead, the other imprisoned, and her aunt the traitor who had brought her here. That made it harder for her and easier for me, because it meant there was nowhere for her to run to – nowhere I knew about, anyway. She might still have a Daniel, though, some friendly house she thought would shelter her, so I made very sure she had no chance to escape. I did not want to have to do what Marian had done, to abandon her in an empty house in deepening silence. I hoped Adrienne would understand if I explained it to her: what

she was now, why her responsibilities as a healer and coun-
sellor meant she could not have a family again. But that
understanding would come gradually and painfully. She was
only eleven, after all.

She was a small child, with dark almond eyes and straggly
black hair. When I opened the door to bring her food she
would throw herself at me, all nails and fury. She could not
overwhelm me, of course, but what she lacked in physical
strength she made up for in fierce intelligence and cold artic-
ulacy. She would kick over her food, mutter insults and curses:
I was ugly, I was a bitch, I was stupid and dumb when I
wouldn't answer. Too stupid to be a witchling. Clumsy dumb
bitch, I had let her mother die. Murderer.

I would never have said these kinds of things to Marian, I
said to Leah. I would never have dared. Should I try to make
her scared of me?

She is scared of you, said Leah. That's why she says them.

Leah had not left the attic in daylight for two weeks by
then. She washed in darkness by the riverside, sneaking past
Adrienne's doorway in the middle of the night. I told myself
I needed distance from her, that it would be healthy, but on
the second day after Adrienne came I went upstairs at midnight
to talk to her the way I had always done. There could never
be any real distance, not the way we lived, and I could not
bear to leave her completely alone.

I sat in the chair beneath the window now, not at the end
of her bed. There was a new delicacy in the way she treated
me, like she was scared one wrong word would break me in
half. I wished I had never let her see her own capacity to hurt
me. I would much rather have dealt with her obliviousness
than her guilt.

It wasn't going to work, I said to Leah, hiding her in the
house. It could never work, not for years until Adrienne was
old enough to be trusted. It was insane.

It would, said Leah. We would make it work.

It was a mantra now and neither of us really believed it.

In the background of our lives something else was happening. Since the end of the war we had received a steady, if controlled, flow of information from the citadel in the north, the front-line, and the towns and villages down the river. Even in the early days, when it was too dangerous to even mention the names of relatives who had died fighting Jonathan, the lord's men would stand at the doors of the town hall every five days at sundown and read out the names of the cities his descendants had conquered. Now we didn't even have that. The world dried up to the heather in the eastern hills, and the air was silent.

We didn't know what was happening. There was no one we could ask, certainly not the soldiers, and the fishermen who sometimes drifted downriver selling their wares would not speak to us anymore. Eve was distraught when the letters from Grace stopped coming. She had been doing well as a student of history in one of the great schools in the citadel, sending weekly affirmations back home to her mother that she was all right, that she loved her, that she missed her brothers, that she still mourned her father. Now she too had vanished into the wide and open silence.

At the same time, strangers began to appear at the House of the Dead, frightened-looking young men and women who came complaining of some minor ailment or other. I did not know them, but I was bound to treat the patients in front of me, and so I did. I told them they were in good health and sent them on their way, wherever that was, and considered it only a minor imposition until Ira came round, furious, carrying little Elia, now six years old and covered in marks from some pox. 'Conscripts,' she said, before I could speak.

'What?'

'Conscripts. They're sending them through here on their way out west.'

'*What?*'

Elia coughed in Ira's arms. It was winter now, and bitingly cold. 'Come in,' I said hastily. 'What happened?'

Ira laid Elia out on the kitchen floor and talked while I examined her. 'They came round to ask for spare trappings from Neil.' Her husband, the hunter. 'We said yes at first, they looked hungry, and then once there were more of them we started saying no, and then the next one who showed up had a *military escort*.' Elia coughed again, and Ira's disgust turned at once to worry. I saw it in her face, like a struck match. I had never quite understood parental love. 'And now she's sick – is it contagious? Should I keep her away from the others?'

Some of Elia's sores were weeping pus, and her skin was cold. I could see the broken blood vessels in her eyes. I sat back on my knees. 'I think I'd like to keep her here, Ira.'

I saw her face go greyish-brown. 'Is it that bad?'

'Ira, listen—'

'I can't. Haley. I can't.' She got down on her knees and sat next to her daughter, stroking her hair, and lowered her voice to an anguished whisper. 'You have to tell me the truth. Do you understand me?'

'Mama?' Elia was half-conscious. She reached a hand out towards her mother. 'Mama?' Ira took her hand and pressed it to her lips. I remembered her son, years ago, convulsing on this floor in the darkness.

'Ira, she'll be fine. Listen to me.' I tried to hold her gaze with Marian's warm intensity. 'There are elderly people in this town, babies, people who are already sick. I'm keeping Elia here for their sake, not hers.'

Ira's hand was so tightly clenched in her daughter's that I worried she would hurt her.

'Listen to me, Ira. Do you trust me?'

The number of times I had asked that question. I don't know why anyone did. I couldn't say it to Callum anymore; I worried the guilt would show in my face. After a moment Ira nodded.

'I'll go get her things,' she said, but she didn't get up, so I did. I sat on the stairs for a while, as Ira said goodbye to her daughter. When she came back her face was taut with the effort of not crying. 'How's your girl?'

I smiled tightly. 'She's fine.'

She had stopped beating on the door and trying to hit me, is what I meant. Ira saw that in my face. 'It'll get better.'

'Everyone says that. How do you *know*?'

'Well,' said Ira, 'I remember you.'

I could not say anything to that. Ira looked at me tenderly, then kissed my forehead. She had never done that before. There was a moment when I let myself lean into it, the smell of her, her familiar embrace. Then I came back to myself.

'Look after my daughter,' she said softly.

'I will. I promise.'

She left.

Elia was shivering now. I covered her in blankets and laid her on the straw mattress I kept for patients. I rubbed one of Leah's dark salves against infection on her sores, and gave her a tonic for her fever. She cried for her mother, and then went to sleep.

I sat there for a while, poking at the fire, and then went upstairs to give Adrienne her food and to gather my own blankets. I would sleep beside Elia tonight. Leah was in the attic, but I could not risk going to talk to her while Adrienne was still awake to hear us. I leaned against the wall outside her bedroom, exhausted, trying to work out the last time I had eaten. Then I composed myself and knocked on her door.

There was no answer. I pushed it open, prepared for her to fly at me.

Adrienne was sitting on the bed, knees pulled up to her chin. She had been crying again. My heart cracked at the sight of it, but I just put down the food and made to retreat. I had trained myself well.

'Please let me go home,' she whispered, and I stopped despite myself. Her voice was hoarse with tears. 'I'm sorry I hit you. I'm sorry I said those things. I just want to go home. Please.'

I stood there with the door open. I wanted to look impassive, as Marian had with me. Instead I said, with unexpected feeling, 'I'd love to let you go home, Adrienne. You think I want to keep you here?'

She blinked at me, wiped more tears angrily away.

'Why won't you, then?'

'Because you're the witchling's girl.'

She shook her head. 'I'm not. I'm not. I promise.'

'You are. You think I wouldn't know?'

She glared at me, full of fury again, but did not answer.

I leaned back against the wall, pretend-casual. I could feel my heart thrumming in my chest. She would remember this conversation for the rest of her life; that was how it was with the first few months in captivity.

'Have you thought about where home is?'

'With my aunt.'

'She has three little ones, she can't afford to take you in.'

'I can work. I can earn money. I can—' Her voice broke again and I looked away so she could wipe her eyes. She looked angry with herself again, or with me. 'I want Mama back. Why didn't you bring her back?'

'She didn't want to be resurrected.'

'You don't know that!'

'I do. Your aunt told me.'

Adrienne shook her head again vigorously. 'She's wrong.

She was wrong. Mama would never leave me. She said she'd never leave me.'

A pause. I felt the burning light of her certainty, and considered my words very carefully.

'Do you know what happens when you get resurrected?'

Adrienne made a violent jerking motion that might have been a shrug.

'You walk around. You're *alive*.'

'You're not alive. You're just conscious. You don't breathe, you don't eat, you don't have a heartbeat. You're cold. Then, slowly, you rot. It takes years, but you rot to dust, and then you don't have a ghost, or any afterlife at all. Would you want that for her?'

Adrienne wrapped her hands around the back of her head and rocked backwards and forwards. 'I want her back,' she said, a soft moan. I wasn't sure she'd heard me at all. 'I want her *back*.'

I stayed there, but did not comfort her. I saw her anguish and knew there was no helping it. I saw my mother's face again, watched her turn into the dark. I think I would rather she had died. It would have been an cleaner grief.

Eventually Adrienne raised her head again and wiped her eyes. She swallowed. 'Where's Papa?'

'He's in jail.'

'He can't come here?'

I shook my head. Adrienne took a long slow breath. 'He's going to be so angry,' she whispered.

'It doesn't matter if he's angry,' I said. 'He can't get in here.' The back door was always locked now, and the window the grieving brother had broken fifteen years ago had been barred ever since. 'So long as you're here, no one can hurt you.'

It was a difficult tone to strike – soothing enough to reassure her, but not so transparent in that motive that she doubted my sincerity. She looked up at me. 'Do you promise?'.

I nodded, and Adrienne looked a little soothed. She leaned back on the bed, against the wall. 'What'll happen to him?'

'Well, there will be a trial, and he'll be convicted.'

'Will I have to go to court?'

'No. There's more than enough evidence without you. Callum saw it, and he's an officer of the court.'

'They'll find him guilty?'

I nodded again. I was watching her carefully. She loved him, but I supposed that wasn't her fault.

'Will they kill him?' she asked quietly.

'I don't know. I can't control that.'

'I don't want them to kill him.'

'You can't control it either.'

'Can I see him? Or Jacira?'

And there again, the difficulty of saying it firmly but not unkindly: 'No. You know that.'

'*Never?*' She looked horrified. 'No – you've made a mistake. I'm not the witchling's girl. I promise.'

'Your mother sat up,' I said softly. 'You made her sit up. You saw it, I saw it.'

'I—' She clenched her jaw, helpless and angry. 'I'm not! I'm not!'

'Kid, listen to me—'

'Don't call me that. I'm not a kid.'

A pause. I could tell she was trying to find my breaking point. So was I. 'Adrienne,' I said slowly. 'I'd like to trust you. I really would. Please don't start by lying to me. She *sat up*, and you did it.'

'I didn't!'

'Don't shout at me,' I said quietly. I was surprised by the speed with which she fell silent. Perhaps I had scared her.

I pushed the bread and cheese towards her. 'Eat,' I said. 'You won't starve yourself out of here.' I sounded so much like Marian, so painfully like the monster I had dreamed about during my early imprisonment, that it shocked me.

Adrienne crossed her arms. I couldn't blame her. Stubbornness was all she had left. I stood there in silence until she spoke.

'Will I see Mama again? When I die?'

Everything in me wanted to lie. But she was not a patient. She was my girl, and I owed her the truth.

'No,' I said. 'Even if you die, even if you both choose not to be judged, you could spend a million years down there and never find her. There are too many ghosts. It'd be like . . . two drops of water finding each other in an ocean.'

'But it *could* happen? It's not impossible?'

*Let her hope,* said Marian quietly in my head, and I relented. 'Yes.'

Adrienne closed her eyes. I could see the relief again in her face, and could not bear it. I made to leave again, but her eyes snapped open, and so I stopped.

'Why was Ira here?' she said.

That took me aback for a moment. But of course she knew Ira's voice, had heard it through the floorboards. Ira was how she had been brought here. 'Her daughter's sick.'

'Which daughter? Elia?'

I nodded, and real panic lit up in Adrienne's face. 'Is she going to be all right?'

'Yes, I think so.'

'Do you *know?*'

'No one ever knows,' I said. It was important that she understood this early. 'But I think so.'

'You won't let her die?'

'If it's in my power,' I said, patiently, 'and I think it is, she won't die.'

'Can I help? I want to help.'

Another hesitation. *Let her in,* said Marian. 'If you want.'

Adrienne scrambled to her feet at once, then stopped. 'Will I get sick?'

'No.' In fifteen years of daily contact with the desperately ill, I had never once fallen sick myself, except through exhaustion or grief. The gift of death-magic protected us from it, I was almost sure, though Marian's books did not talk about that. 'But be careful, and do exactly what I say.'

She nodded. I could see the light in her face, the excitement. I remembered being eleven years old, full of sombre dedication. That would come to her, in time. I had to believe it.

Elia was sleeping fitfully when we got downstairs. I lay between her and the fire in case she rolled over. 'Do you think you can stay awake?' I whispered to Adrienne.

She nodded again.

'Give her water every hour. One drop of lemon and one from the vial on the counter. Can you do that?'

She nodded yet again, tense and eager. I lay down to sleep with one hand around Elia's wrist, so I would wake if she stirred or grew cold. I felt Adrienne's footsteps around me, and for a moment I was gone again; I was a child curled by the fireplace as Marian tended to unknown labours, and then the fire-warmth and the blankets drew me into sleep.

When I woke, Adrienne was gone. The back door stood open in the dawn breeze. Elia had regained a little of her colour, and her sores no longer wept. I reapplied the salve carefully, then went to the water barrel.

Twelve cups gone, or thereabouts. She had been diligent in Elia's care, every hour on the hour until dawn had broken and she knew I was about to wake. She could not have gone far.

I went upstairs. Leah was curled at the end of her bed. When I came into the room she opened her eyes and got to her feet at once. She was always worried these days when she saw me.

'She's gone to the woods,' I said. 'There's a patient downstairs. Could you watch her for a while?'

'Of course,' said Leah. 'What if her mother comes?'

'Keep her out. Try to stop her knocking, if you can. If she realises I'm not here she'll lose it. I won't be long.'

Leah came downstairs with me, watched as I pulled on my coat. As I made to leave, she reached for me, brushed her fingertips with mine, a light electric touch. 'Are you going to be all right?'

'I'll be fine, Leah.'

I know she didn't believe me.

The woods were crunchy with frost, the grass furred white at my feet. I loved winter: the deep brightness of the silences, the cold crystal sky. Adrienne had grown up in these woods, but so had I, and I was older. I walked in quiet joy down unseen familiar paths, following her trace in the air, until the trees parted and I heard rustling ahead.

She fell silent as soon as she heard me. I stayed still, too. I was curious what she would do when she knew all was lost. It would be good to know early what panic inspired in her. I had seen it bring forth paralysis, wild viciousness, deep unearthly calm. What would she do?

More rustling. I thought for a moment that she might run.

Then something flew out of the trees towards me, earthy and *big,* and I pulled back in alarm and raised my hands to cover my face—

A doe stumbled in front of me, caught in thickly twisted vines. She had been dead several days and smelled foul, and now she was clumsy, unused to life again. There was panic about her. She was blind. I steadied myself against a tree, watching her.

'Here,' I whispered. 'Come here.' The deer heard my voice, turned her head and took a tentative step towards me. I held out my hand. Her fur was greasy with rot. The moment I touched her the life went out of her, and she collapsed.

I stood above her, heart still thundering. I thought for a

second that I had lost Adrienne. If she had wanted to run, now would have been the time, when I was still disoriented. But I couldn't hear footsteps.

When I had gathered myself, I pushed through the trees and found her sobbing in the clearing beyond. She was staring, astonished and horrified, at the gap in the shrubs the deer had pushed through. 'I didn't mean to,' she said, over and over. 'I'm sorry. I didn't mean to.'

'Hush, child,' I said, 'it's all right,' but she kept sobbing, and after a while she let me take her in my arms.

# CHAPTER TWENTY

The conscripts kept coming. They had been sent here by the lord's men, who expected me to check them over before sending them west to the endless war a hundred miles away. I did it without complaint. *Treat the patient in front of you.* I was still the witchling, no matter what vows I had broken, and I dared not openly risk the wrath of the Lord Jonathan's commanders. I had Adrienne to worry about now. She was as old as I had been when the lord's men had beaten Marian almost to death. I remembered her shattered bones, her blood on the cobblestones. I would not let Adrienne see me like that. I had not even visited Samuel since the day she had been brought to me.

Still, I had questions. Why were the conscripts being sent here? We were a smallish town in an insignificant backwater, fifty miles from the western coast.

'It's you,' said Ira, when she came to collect Elia. She was full of gratitude: the sores had cleared and the child's colour had returned. She played with the hem of her mother's shirt, sitting on the floor with bright, excited eyes. 'You're the best witchling outside the citadel.'

'I am?'

'Of course.'

'The lord's men have heard about me?'

'Haley—' Ira looked at me, half-sad and half-exasperated. 'How many people have died in your house in the last seven years?'

'Dozens, Ira.'

'I don't mean the elderly. People you could save.'

I had not thought about it. Adrienne's mother was the last person who had died in my house of anything but old age, and before that . . . Very few. Certainly no children. Leah's salves and tonics, infused with her spells, had seen to that.

Adrienne was sitting in Marian's chair at the kitchen table. I saw her eyes widen at Ira's words. She had thrown herself into her lessons after the initial shock of her captivity. It was something to fill the space in her heart that her parents had left. She had an easy instinct for compassion, a bright mind, and steady hands. She would replace me very well.

I went upstairs to talk to Leah after Adrienne was asleep. She was paler than usual, and thinner. It was hard work to siphon off enough food for her, refill the barrel of water in her corner, listen for Adrienne's breathing to ease so I could go and talk to her. For years her world had been this house, its walls and limitations, the branches that grew through her ceiling. She had chosen to be trapped here, to work and live with me, over the lonely purposelessness of the wider world. But now, after Adrienne's arrival, she could no longer even leave this room. Adrienne's respect and trust was too fragile to risk confiding in her quite yet. I saw the shadows under Leah's eyes, and she spoke to me less and less. But when I told her about the renown her medicine had brought me, her eyes widened, and she sat up.

'They're sending soldiers here because of you?' she asked.

'Because of *you*.'

She leapt to her feet at once. 'Then I should go.'

I sat up. 'What?'

I had meant it as a compliment, as a way to ease the burden of her imprisonment. But here she was, pulling on her coat, gathering her things. She had not come with much, years ago.

There was a bag full of clothes packed in the corner. I had never noticed that before.

'Leah?'

She turned to me. Her hair was down to her shoulders now. It did not suit her. She looked gaunt and wild and dirty. 'I can't stay here, Haley. I'm bringing them down on you—'

'Not like that! They don't suspect it's anything but witchling-magic – it's fine, Leah.'

'No it isn't. You've got a kid to worry about—'

I was on my feet, hands raised, as if calming a mad dog. 'It's fine. We're fine. Don't worry about it.'

'How do I not worry about it, Haley? I never expected this would— When I asked you to hide me . . . I mean, think about it, if they found me—'

'They won't find you, Leah.'

'You don't know that!'

'Nobody knows anything.' I caught her wrists. 'I have faith.'

'In what? Me?' She pulled away and laughed, so wildly I worried Adrienne would hear two floors below us. 'This is a sick joke, Haley. This is sick. I didn't— I wasn't thinking ahead, you were so young, you built your whole life around me, of course I was going to mark you – this is fucked up, this is so fucked up, I should never have—'

'*Mark* me?' I stared at her. 'What are you talking about?'

Leah stopped. She put her face in her hands, then looked up at me. 'I want you to be free, Haley,' she said. 'I want you not to live like this.'

'Is this about—? No, Leah, no. I'm not – I don't feel like that anymore.'

'Really?'

'Yes.' I didn't know if she believed me. I didn't quite know if I believed myself.

'You care about me too much,' she said, and there was a soft tenderness in her voice that verged on pity and that I could not bear to hear. 'I don't care in what way. You've built everything around hiding me. You care about me too much, and it's not healthy, and you'll never be free while I live here. I want you to be able to breathe. I don't want to make your life harder.' She took my hand, very gently. 'Is that love? I think it is.'

It took me a moment to find my voice. 'No,' I said, and my tone was too cold, too sharp, but I couldn't help it. 'If you loved me you wouldn't want to leave me.'

Leah looked exhausted. 'This can't work, Haley. You know it can't. Not anymore.'

'We'll tell Adrienne. Give it a few more weeks, it'll get easier—'

'No,' she said. 'Absolutely not. I won't do that to her. Look at yourself, Haley, look what I did to you. It's too big a secret, and she's a kid. I can't let you put that on her for me. It'll destroy her.'

'Leah—' I was terrified. Everything was breaking apart too suddenly for me to control. 'If you leave they'll find you.'

'Maybe. Maybe not. If they do, at least you won't die with me.'

'Don't be a fucking hero,' I said. I could hear how it sounded, but I couldn't stop myself. 'Don't leave me, Leah. Come on. Don't leave me alone.'

She looked at me, terribly sad, and then she laid a hand on my cheek. 'You weren't alone before I came. You won't be after I leave.'

'Don't act like you're doing this for me – like I don't know what I want—'

'I want you to be happy, Haley.'

'Then *stay*!'

She let me go and turned away. I think she thought I was beyond saving. She picked up her bag and looked towards the door. I was helpless, panicked. I could not believe she was going to leave me now, with no warning, end four years in as many minutes.

And then from beneath us came a rapid, frantic knock on the front door.

It meant *sick*, not *dead*. Leah hesitated and I saw my chance. 'Please,' I said, hoarsely. 'Give me ten minutes. Don't leave like this. Let me deal with it and then I'll come back.'

She knew it was a bad idea. But she could not bring herself to hurt me any more, and so she nodded.

I ran downstairs and opened the door at the third knock. A boy of about sixteen, dark-haired and sweating, stood wringing his hands in the twilight. It was too cold for his thin shirt. 'Please,' he said. 'My mother's ill. Really ill. You have to help. Please.'

'Bring her here, then. It'll be easier to—'

He shook his head frantically. 'She can't be moved. She can't. We tried. I'm sorry.'

'It's fine,' I said, but silently I cursed him. What if Leah left while I was gone? I stood on the step, thinking.

'Please,' said the boy, and I was so close to saying, *find someone to bring her here, I don't care how you do it,* but I could feel Marian's shade watching me and so I said, reluctantly, 'All right. I'll come. Let me bring my girl.'

Adrienne was already on the stairs. She had heard the conversation at the door. I wondered what else she had heard – but no, no, I could not worry about that now. 'Is somebody sick?'

'Yes. Get the bag.' There was a leather sack full of emergency supplies in the back kitchen – three knives, a vial of blood-ink, dried herbs – for exactly this occasion. Adrienne ran for it at once. She was a very quick learner.

The boy led us to a small house by the river. The tides had risen that spring and soaked the outside walls; you could see the marks of cut-away rot. He knocked on the door, and a man who did not look like him opened it. He was tall and looked frightened, shadows under his eyes and at his jaw.

'John?'

'I brought the witchling. And her girl.'

'Oh, thank the lord.' He opened the door wider. 'Come in, come in.'

The house smelled musty, but everything was clean. As soon as the boy's mother got ill they had closed off the world. I kept an eye on Adrienne. She had not yet learned to be comfortable in other people's homes, in the middle of the night. This man was roughly the same build and height as her father; he had the same air of coiled, efficient violence. I made sure to stay between them. My heart was in the House of the Dead, worried about open front doors and empty attics, but the voice in my head that belonged to Marian said, *Concentrate,* and I tried to obey it.

He ushered me into a darkened bedroom. Something about the smell hit me immediately, and I stopped in the doorway. It had unlocked something in the base of my brain; I wanted to pause and examine it, but the woman's husband and son were behind me, pushing past me, and Adrienne was watching me, and the husband was saying, 'Lysa, the witchling's here.'

She shook her head furiously. She was lying in bed, filthy, the tracks of tears and drool on her face. She had the distinctive look of the sometimes-lucid. 'No,' she said, hoarsely. '*No.* Not the witchling.'

I stopped dead. Our eyes met for a moment and I think something lit in hers, but then something deeper went out and she began to mutter in a language I did not understand. Then she started thrashing, covers flying everywhere, and a second later she started screaming, and her husband held her down.

I couldn't deal with it. I left the room and stood outside

the corridor with my head pressed against the wall. She was still screaming through the door.

I tried to breathe. I remembered so much suddenly, and in the rush of memories I tried to catch something I could hold onto. I lay drugged on a floor, staring at a wall, and Marian was singing under her breath at the table. A hymn to the Lord Claire. I listened to the memory of her voice and felt a scrap of calm for a moment, but then it evaporated and I was lost in panic again.

'What are you doing?' The husband was here, in the corridor, staring at me. 'Help her! What's wrong with you?'

Was this my father? I stared at him. No, surely not. We looked nothing alike, and I would remember the fear of living with a man like this. The boy, though, standing behind him, confused and terrified. His hair was coarse and dark, like mine. There was something in the wringing of his hands, a note in his voice at the base of his throat, the shape of his eyes. He was familiar to me, an echo from down a hall. I remembered the baby in my mother's arms. So it had been a boy, then.

It was Adrienne who shook me awake. She had followed me out of the room, and touched my shoulder tentatively. 'Are you all right?'

'Yes,' I heard myself say. 'Yes.' I tried to come back to myself. I was the witchling, they could not see me like this. 'What are her symptoms?'

'What are—' The husband stared at me, furious and dumbfounded. 'What do you think her fucking symptoms are?'

'Rory,' said my brother quietly, from behind him.

'She's not – she's not herself, she spits and speaks in *tongues* and doesn't know her own son – didn't you see her in there? She's *sick!*'

'I can see that.'

'Then heal her!'

Oh, lord. Not this, not now. Of all the people the ghost could have chosen to draw into darkness – why couldn't it have been *him*, this angry man she had chosen as her husband? But then I would have had to talk to her as she grieved, be the witchling to her. I could not have dealt with that either.

They were all still watching me, and I tried to gather myself.

'I'll need to take her to the House of the Dead,' I said. 'It's a very particular illness, and it can be dangerous. I'll need to keep her a few days.' *And by the end she'll be dead, or gone.* 'I can care for her better if she's there.'

*Care for her* seemed to reassure him. It implied devotion. 'I'll stay there with her.'

'No, I'm afraid you can't.'

He took a step towards me. 'You won't keep me from my wife, girl.'

I was so close to it. I could have said, *I'm her daughter, I have more right to her than you.* I could have waited for him to attack me and then got a hold of his wrist and drained the life from him. I wanted to start a fight with him, this man who did not know who I was and whose face I knew from somewhere I didn't like, but Adrienne was watching me and learning. So instead I said, as acerbically as I could, 'If you try to interfere with my work, she'll die. This is not about you.'

Fury twisted his face. But my brother laid a hand on his arm with a practised mixture of restraint and tentativeness, and after a moment Rory said through gritted teeth, 'You'll call me if anything happens.' It was not a question.

'Yes,' I said. 'Bring her to the house.'

'How?'

'Find someone to carry her,' I said. Not everything could be my problem.

\*

Adrienne walked with me back to the house, and we waited for them to arrive. I wanted so badly to run upstairs to the attic, to see if Leah had kept her word and stayed, but I could not with the girl watching me. I should have got my medicines, I should have got the chains from the basement if my mother was possessed and dangerous, but all I could do was sit in my chair at the kitchen table and stare into the unlit fire. After a while Adrienne said, tentatively, 'Are you all right?'

I hesitated. *Let her in.* How could I tell her about Leah if I couldn't trust her with this? 'No,' I said.

'Why?'

I breathed in and out. Knowing it was one thing, saying it was another. 'That sick woman, back there . . . she's my mother. Or she used to be.' I rubbed my face and looked up at her. 'She gave me up when I was younger than you.'

There was no pity or shock in her face. Her mother had died on my floor only months ago; mere abandonment must have seemed like nothing in comparison.

'You haven't seen her in all that time?'

*All that time?* How old did she think I was? 'No. I think she avoided me.'

'Why?'

'Because she felt guilty.'

'You never tried to see her?'

'No.'

'Why not?'

'Because I knew it would hurt. And because . . . I didn't know what I would say to her.'

She didn't understand that at all, I knew. She would have given anything to see her mother again. I saw her try to hide her confusion and was touched.

'And they don't know who you are?'

'No,' I said, and realised what that meant for the first time. 'She never told them about me.'

There seemed nothing more to say, and we sat for a while in silence until the knock came at the door.

Rory, my brother and three other men delivered my mother to me like a package and laid her out on my kitchen floor. She was unconscious. 'She fell asleep,' said her husband unconvincingly. I remembered how she had drugged me. She had kept that in her cupboard, then, whatever it was. Perhaps, in sixteen years, she had not changed at all.

'Thank you,' I made myself say, in the firm, reassuring tone Marian had drilled into me. It was very difficult; I could no longer quite hear my own voice. 'I'll get a message to you tomorrow.'

He looked at me suspiciously, but eventually he walked out with the rest of them. I wonder whether he loved her. Certainly he didn't like the idea of her life being in anyone else's hands.

Adrienne stayed in the kitchen with me while I stared down at my sleeping mother. Her hair was not my hair, and it was long and unkempt. She must have been, I don't know, fifty years old. I looked at her dirt-streaked face and felt no urge to clean it.

After five minutes I heard another knock. It was my brother. He had doubled back and lost the others. 'Please,' he said hoarsely, 'let me in. I want to help. I can help. Tell me what's wrong with her.'

I looked down at him and saw that he had been crying. I remembered the warm and trembling love I had felt for the baby in my mother's arms. I thought about how good it would feel to tell him everything – that this was possession, to explain to him what that meant, ask him what he wanted, what I should do. Sixteen was old enough to know, to be entrusted with someone's care. It was how old I had been when I had become the witchling.

It was how old I had been when I had killed Marian. At sixteen I had sat at the kitchen table under the crushing, terrible weight of that guilt. I had felt it change and warp me.

I looked at his trembling hands, his determination. 'No,' I said, 'it's not safe,' and I closed the door on him. It was my first and last act of sisterhood.

I did what I had to do. My hands knew the motions of cleaning, of making someone comfortable, so that I could do it unthinkingly and not have to really look at my mother's face. I tied her wrists and feet, and when Adrienne stared at me I said, 'If she wakes up she'll be confused, I don't want you to get hurt,' and she seemed to understand that. I didn't know how to explain possession to her. I was so tired.

My head was full of memories I did not want. I felt like a frightened child again, desperate to escape. Something in me recognised Lysa, something deep and visceral that I could not kill, and said to me that she meant warmth and safety and love, and the effort of keeping that instinct tamped down and controllable was exhausting.

I sat for a while with my head in my hands. It was very late.

'Go to bed,' I said to Adrienne, at last.

'Do you need my help?' She was concerned for me. I loved her for that.

'No,' I said, 'it's all right, I've seen this before. I'll tell you about it in the morning.' I did not know why I was promising that, but she turned and climbed the stairs without further protest.

Then I was alone in the silence.

I stared down at my unconscious mother, and another memory came to me. The bottom of a pit, and eyes in the darkness. Hunger and exhaustion. Voices in the twilight, the clash of swords and the empty hunger of conquerors. I was twelve years old and Cora had just died and I was imprisoned in the camp, and a guard was looking down on me, throwing bread as I waited to die. And I saw his face—

Rory.

Rory had been a soldier for the Lord Jonathan. He had been in the camp. He had stayed here when the rest of them had moved west, and he had married my mother.

I tried to be angry at her for that, but I did not have it in me. I was so tired. I could not look at her anymore. I lay on the floorboards and stayed beside her trying to sleep.

Then I went to the attic.

Leah was still there. I don't know what I would have done if she hadn't been. I imagine myself standing in the empty attic, falling.

She was sitting on the bed, waiting for me, holding the bag and tapping her leg against the floor. She got to her feet as soon as she saw me. 'What's wrong?'

'Nothing's wrong.'

'Haley, you look—' She couldn't find the words. 'Tell me what it is.'

'My . . .' It was so bizarre it was difficult to say it. How had I got here? 'My mother's possessed.' I wanted to laugh. I sank to my knees. 'My mother's possessed.'

Leah's eyes widened. She stared down at me, then knelt beside me. 'Oh, Haley,' she whispered. 'I'm sorry. I'm so sorry.'

She held me as I cried. I couldn't remember the last time I had wept, and afterwards I felt cleaner.

I brought Leah downstairs and we stood over my mother, watching her. I worried the drugs might wear off, but she seemed peaceful. I was still trying to find myself in her face. A hook for my compassion. I didn't know how I should feel, but I knew it wasn't like this.

'What do you want to do?'

'It's not about what I want.'

'I think it is,' said Leah quietly.

'She has a husband. And another child.' I caught myself. 'A child.'

'You're her daughter.'

I shook my head. 'Not anymore. Not for years.'

Leah absorbed that for a moment and did not speak. My mother made a small soft noise in her sleep. I winced.

'You have options.'

'I know.'

'You could let her go,' said Leah, after a moment. I could feel her watching me. 'If you did, I would understand.'

I stared at her. 'What do you mean, *let her go?*'

A pause. 'I mean,' said Leah, quite carefully, 'instead of killing her.'

It hurt when she said that, a sharp shock deep in my chest. 'No,' I said blankly, 'no, I mean – of course I won't kill her. Why would you say that?'

Leah looked away.

'Wait,' I said. 'Wait.' I was coming back to myself again. 'She's not dangerous. All she's been doing is screaming—'

Leah cut me off, very gently. 'She's confused, Haley. The ghost is taking over her body. She's losing her memories. If you let her wake up, she won't be there anymore. You know this.'

I did, but did not want to. 'You can't destroy her. Please.' Panic rose in me, though I didn't understand from where. I had thought I did not care about this woman. 'You can't *destroy* her.'

Leah caught my hands. 'Of course I won't do that, Haley. She's your mother.'

'Promise me.'

'I promise.'

I wanted to believe her, but I did not know how much I could trust her. I knew she would say anything to ease my guilt, to calm me down. I was wild and manic again. I did not know what I wanted, but I knew I could not let Leah wipe my mother's spirit from the face of the worlds. But if I let her lie there, asleep, while the ghost ate her from the inside, it would happen anyway.

I sat down in the chair and put my face in my hands.

'Listen to me,' said Leah, softly. 'It's going to be all right, Haley. You're going to be all right.'

'Stop telling me that,' I said, through gritted teeth. 'Just – please. Stop.' Silence for a while. I tried to settle myself. I could hear my mother's breathing.

'Could you look at her memories?' I said, at last. 'Could you . . .' *Could you see if she loved me?* I couldn't say it.

'I could,' Leah said. I could tell she was taking care to keep her tone expressionless. 'If you wanted me to.'

I imagined the memory. Standing at Marian's door in the rain with a drugged child in my arms. I imagined knowing the contents of my mother's heart with certainty, pulling it apart. I would know what she had been doing the last sixteen years, I would watch my brother grow up, I would know why she had defied decency and loyalty and married an enemy of our lord. And then I would stand with that knowledge in my heart and decide whether or not to save her soul.

I sat at that table for a long, long time.

*Treat the patient in front of you.*

I knew I did not have the right to her memories. I was not yet that corrupted. Using them to decide whether or not to let her live would be a violation so profoundly evil that my soul would not recover from it. I was the witchling. I healed and consoled. I did not hold grudges or ask for favours, and I had no family but Adrienne.

I took a deep breath and steadied myself.

'OK,' I said. 'Give me a moment.'

Leah left. I think she went to the living room; I didn't hear her climb the stairs. I went to the counter and pulled out my knives and herbs. I didn't know what for. To drink, she would have to be awake, and I couldn't stand that. I didn't want her to see my face. I think it would have hurt her as much as me. I remembered her standing in the alleyway, the tears in her eyes. I remembered her singing.

Because she had given me up, Elia and Aron and countless others were alive. Because she had given me up her husband and son would have an afterlife. I knew that. She had done what she had to do for the greater good.

I knew that, but I could not forgive her. Was that all right? Was it enough? She had not asked for my forgiveness, after all. She could have come to the house at any time since I was sixteen. She could have talked to me, explained why she had given me up, and then I could have looked into her eyes and forgiven her. But she hadn't. She had chosen to avoid me, and that was painful, too.

I wished that she had asked my forgiveness. Then I would have had peace. We could both have had peace.

I steadied myself. I did not need to forgive her to heal her. I was charged with the preservation of her spirit, and could not let it be corroded. That meant not letting her wake up.

I cradled her head. I could see the lines in her face. She did look like my brother.

I balanced the knife in my hand. I allowed myself one breath. I angled the point at the base of her skull, upwards.

Two breaths. Three.

Come on, now.

Four.

I got up. The knife was still in my hand. I did not know what to do.

I walked slowly into the hall, into the doorway of the living room, and saw Leah sitting on the sofa. Her eyes went from the bloodless knife to my face. 'I can't do it,' I said, blankly. 'I can't do it.'

Leah watched me for a moment. Then she walked towards me and laid her hand on my cheek. It did not hurt anymore. 'Of course you can't,' she said. 'Of course you can't, Haley. Why are you doing this to yourself?'

'It's my—' I couldn't say *duty*. 'I have to. If I don't she'll be – I have to—'

'No you don't,' said Leah, softly. 'You don't have to do everything. Sit down.'

I sat down, shaking, in the curtained dimness beside her. She put her arm around me and we sat there for a while in silence. I could feel her searching for something to say, but I could not tell you why she said what she did, then. Perhaps she thought it would comfort me.

'I had a mother,' she said.

I didn't turn to look at her, but something in my chest went cold. 'You said you didn't remember—'

'I know,' she said, quietly. 'I lied to you, Haley.'

I didn't say anything. I leaned against her shoulder, and closed my eyes, and I did not move.

'We lived in a village with a lord,' she said. 'The lord was . . . I can't even remember her name, now. She'd only just returned from above, she said she'd been dead about thirty years. She was very kind. When we were unhappy or unwell we went to her, and she'd bless us and calm us down, and we were happy again. She never married, she had no children, she was never corrupted.' Leah raised a trembling hand to rub her eyes; I felt it in the movements of her shoulder, leaving against her. 'The soldiers, Jonathan's soldiers, came and tore her apart. They killed my mother, too. I think I was about five years old. I know I loved her. I do remember that. I don't remember what it felt like, but I know I did.'

I sat up slowly. I was shaking again. She was looking straight ahead, at the wall. Her jaw was set, and all colour was gone from her face.

'If you're going to run away,' I said, 'just run. Don't try to make me tell you to go. I won't do it.'

There was a trembling silence. She turned to look at me with enormous effort. 'I lied to you, Haley,' she whispered. 'When I came to you and asked you for help, I said I didn't know why I'd been exiled. I lied.'

I nodded slowly. 'All right,' I said.

She stared at me. 'Haley—'

I was so tired. 'I *know*, Leah. You think it never occurred to me? All these years, you think I never considered that you might be lying?'

'But if you—'

'I care about you too much.' I expected to be angry, I waited for it, but all I felt was numb exhaustion. 'Don't you get that? I made my choice a long time ago. Whatever you did, I don't care. I don't care how much you lied to me. There's nothing you can say to me that would make me throw you out now. So don't make me hear it, all right?'

'Haley, I—'

'*Don't make me hear it.* I don't want to hear it.' I was on my feet now, pulling away from her. 'I can't do it, Leah. You're always so *guilty*, and now you want to come clean just so I can shout at you and kick you out and you can feel like you've been punished? Fuck you. Don't do that to me.'

There was a silence. I could see her shaking.

'I'm sorry,' she said, softly. 'I am.'

'I don't want to hear it. I don't, Leah.'

'Haley—'

I backed away, through the door into the corridor. I looked down the hall and saw my mother, sprawled and half-breathing on the kitchen floor, and then Leah was in front of me, in the doorway, with her desperate eyes—

I couldn't breathe. I turned and opened the front door, my hands fumbling on the latch, and stepped out into the street.

The door clicked softly shut in front of me: on her, reaching out, pleading. In the street everything was silent. I stood staring at the door, breathing hard. Just behind it, I knew she was standing there, shocked into silence.

And suddenly I realised: out here I was free. She could not follow me out into the open, and she could not shout after me, for fear of waking Adrienne.

I took a step back, then another.

The light was fading now. I wasn't even wearing shoes. I walked down the cobblestones, down my street, and sped up. I left her there inside the house and walked away from the House of the Dead, my hands over my face, trying to get myself to breathe. I whispered it to myself like a mantra. *I can't. I can't. I can't.*

In my head, I saw Leah's eyes as I closed the door in her face. She had been opening her mouth to say my name.

I walked for hours. I did not cry, because I might have been seen, and the instinct to hide weakness was too deeply ingrained. I walked the dark streets in long unthinking loops, and kept myself carefully away from the edges of town. I imagined for a few minutes just walking away, through the heather towards the hills, and leaving everything behind, but there was nowhere I could go. Once I left – *if* I left, the idea was insane – I could never come back; they would never trust me again. Adrienne, eleven years old and with no training but the few of Marian's books that remained, would be left to tend to the town. And Leah – what would happen to Leah?

I couldn't leave. But I could not go back to the house and hear Leah's confession, watch my mother dying on the floor. I did not have it in me.

I hated Leah for admitting her lies, for this too-late attempt at catharsis. I had chosen certainty long ago. In the cellar, next to the body of Callum's wife, I had taken Leah's hand

and chosen to believe her. For that certainty I had broken vows, I had lied, I had allowed Marya to be taken, I had risked the wrath of witches. And now she had ripped it from me, and I was wandering alone, with no one to ask for help or advice or consolation. I had nowhere to go.

She had lied to me and used me. In the beginning, at least, that had been her intent. Had she changed, in four years with me? She cared about me now, I was almost sure she did, in her clumsy, selfish way. It was why she wanted me to know the truth. Or at least why she thought she did. *I'm sorry,* she had said. But I could not forgive her until I knew what she had done to be exiled, and I did not, *did not* want to know.

I wanted to talk to Callum or Ira. I wanted to talk to Marian. I wanted to run away. Peel the skin from my arms, wash away the tattoos, stop being a witchling, stop being myself. Run somewhere else, anywhere—

'Haley?'

The world returned. I was standing in front of an open door. I did not remember knocking. Samuel blinked at me. His house lay open behind him, the warm oblivion of not being myself. I had not seen him in months. I had vanished from his life when Adrienne was brought to me, without saying a word, and he had not come after me, or told anyone, or sought retribution. He was so kind.

'I, uh,' I said, and swallowed. 'Could I sit down? Just for a moment, I just . . .' If I stayed outside I would break and run. I could not face my own house, and I could not let myself flee. I needed walls, and warmth, and shelter.

'Are you all right?'

I hesitated, then shook my head.

Samuel opened his door wider. 'Come in,' he said. 'Sit down, Haley. It's all right.'

I felt like a patient. I sat on his sofa and shook for a while, and he watched me and did not ask questions.

After a few moments he got up and came back with a blanket and a pillow and three apples, which he stacked neatly on the cushion beside me. He hesitated, looking down at me, then kissed my forehead and climbed the stairs to his bedroom.

After he was gone, I cried for an hour until steadiness returned to me. My head throbbed. I knew I had to get up, but I lay there in the thickening dark until my body gave out. I was so, so tired.

At first I thought I was dreaming.

'Samuel? Samuel?'

Quieter. 'She's not in there.'

'She *is*. I can feel it—'

'Check round the back, see if there's an answer.'

'All right.'

'Are you sure?'

'Yes. I'm sure. Keep trying.'

A hesitation, then another knock. 'Samuel?'

I opened my eyes. Samuel was curled asleep in blankets beside me. He had not wanted to leave me alone, in the end. I tried to reach out to stroke his unshaven cheek, but couldn't move my arm. I had fallen asleep on it. I tried to sit up.

More knocking. *'Samuel?'*

I could not remember where and when I was. Then I heard Adrienne's voice from outside, a lightning-bolt straight to my heart.

'Haley? Are you in there? I know you're in there.'

Then Ira's voice, gentle. 'I don't think she is, sweetheart.'

It was dawn. Oh, no. No, no. I had not meant to sleep this long. There was warm light draped across my face through the curtains.

Adrienne had woken and I had not been there, so she had gone to Ira to find me. I sat up, panicked. I had not meant to leave her alone, to make her afraid. I struggled out of my blankets to my feet. I could not be found here.

Samuel did not wake; he always was a heavy sleeper. I looked at him for a breathless moment, the light on his face. Was it better to wake him, and give him warning? But then if they found us awake together it might look too conspiratorial. He could fend for himself. He was a good liar, or we'd have been discovered already.

I gathered myself, wiped the sleep from my eyes and walked as softly as I could towards the back door. I didn't know his house well, just the hall and his bedroom. In the back I found a small kitchen and a wooden door. No windows, thank the Lord Claire.

Ira was still knocking on the front door, still calling Samuel's name. I could feel Adrienne's presence, her shivering fear, as I knew she could feel me. It hurt me to walk away from her.

I pressed myself against the back door. Silence. One, two— I pulled it open.

Callum stood there, his hand raised to knock. He stared at me. Too late, I remembered his voice in my half-dream, saying he would check round the back. Ira must have gone to him when Adrienne said I was missing. She knew how well he knew me.

He looked at me for a long, long time. His face was blank. He had not really believed I would be here. He had thought better of me.

I held his eyes. I would not plead. I would not try to stop him. He was a lawman, and my vows were law. It was his right to call out, to give me away, *here she is.*

His gaze moved slowly from my face, beyond me, into the darkness of the house. He stared fixedly at the front door as I took a step towards him. I took another, then another, moving slowly past him into the alleyway at the back of the house.

He did not move.

I walked more quickly. I would go to his house when all this was over, bring Aron a gift. I would apologise and explain. He knew the life of a witchling, he would understand. Marian had broken her vows, too. I would explain to him about Samuel, assuage the disappointment I had seen in his face.

Don't think about that now. Get home.

The street behind Samuel's house was full of people, all gathered around Ira and Adrienne. That took me by surprise for a moment, until I realised how alarming people would find my disappearance. It would have gone house to house in whispers. *The witchling's gone.* I had to get back to the House of the Dead, so they could find me sitting calmly in my chair at the kitchen table. I could say Adrienne had been asleep, lost, confused. And Leah—

Leah could have stopped Adrienne leaving the house. She had ways, illusions. She would never have let this happen. If Adrienne was here, that meant Leah had left.

My stomach dropped away at the thought. I stood staring into the street, trying to calm myself and gather my thoughts, to plan, and so almost did not notice the man in the corner of the opposite alleyway.

Rory. My mother's husband. Like Callum, he went very still at the sight of me. We stared at each other.

I understood how it must look to him. The feckless harlot witchling, abandoning the care of his wife to visit her lover. *Lover.* The word seemed insane. I tried to imagine explaining this to him, and couldn't. I had run out of explanations at last.

He began walking towards me, slowly at first and then faster. '*Witchling!*'

Everyone turned. Ira, Adrienne. I saw them out of the corner of my eye, felt the gaze of the crowd on me, and thought I would crumple under the weight of my own shame. I could not speak.

Rory was too close. I saw the rage in his face, stepped back and raised my arms to shield my face. He brushed them aside and grabbed me by the throat.

The sheer violation of it was the first shock, and then the paralysing terror. He pressed his thumb into the base of my throat and the world went grey at the edges. He lifted me off my feet, and the pain was blinding. I could feel the words in my head breaking into pieces. This is how I would die, then, my brain dissolving into incoherence, and then soon there would be noth—

There was pain in my knees. Every breath was an agonising rasp. The grey of my vision began to pop like bubbles, and I could see cobblestones. I was on the ground, kneeling. He had dropped me. Shouting above me.

'*Where's my wife?*'

Another voice. 'I don't know, Rory.'

'*She wasn't in the house, she was out fucking the fisherman, and my wife—*'

'What happened to her?'

'*She was sick!*' Another winding pain in my stomach. He had kicked me. I bent over, trying to shield myself. '*And I gave her to the witchling and now she's gone—*'

'Get away from her—'

Rory's hand was on my chin, trying to pull my head up. Then he grunted. I felt his presence lift. I looked up, breathing jaggedly, and saw him stumbling back. Callum was standing over me. His knuckles were bloody. The crowd was watching everything. I saw Adrienne, Ira's arm around her shoulder, her eyes full of terror.

'She'll be taken to the court,' said Callum. His voice was slightly raised and I knew he was addressing the assembled town, though his eyes were on Rory. 'If she's broken her vows she'll be tried for it—'

'You think I care about her fucking vows? *Where's my wife?*'

Callum looked back at me. 'What are you talking about?'

My brother, John, was standing behind Rory. He had my hair, cut short to his neck. So young. He spoke to Callum, eyeing Rory nervously. 'We went to the House of the Dead when they said the witchling was missing. The girl was talking to Ira, she let us in. We were worried about Mama—'

'And she was *gone!*' shouted Rory. He was incandescent with rage and fear; perhaps he did love her, then. 'Not even in the basement—'

They had gone into the basement?

'I'm sure she's all right,' said Callum. He sounded so much like Marian that some part of me felt reassured, despite myself. 'Haley will explain.'

He looked at me. Everyone looked at me. My brain was buzzing, and I tried to speak but could not. Where was my mother? Had she been fully possessed? Had she regained consciousness and escaped the house? Was she another Daniel, roaming the streets with a knife?

And if she had escaped – where was Leah?

'She's not right,' said Rory. He was staring at me, shaking his head slowly. 'She's not *right*, Callum. Things happen in that house—'

'What are you talking about?'

'How did the last witchling die?' It was an effort not to look away from him. Everyone watching would think I was guilty. I could feel the tension in the air; they were confused, afraid. 'Stabbed to death by some mad boy. Yeah? Is that it? And he died after, right? He killed his own mother, too, and died after? Is that her story?'

A silence. Ira was watching me. I looked back at her and tried to ask her silently to take Adrienne away, not to let her hear things like this. But there was an odd blankness in Ira's eyes, and she did not move.

'She's the best witchling in fifty miles, but every so often people go mad and die in her house. Does that sound right to you? You pompous bastard?' Rory took another step towards Callum, and then stopped. 'What did she say happened to *your* wife?'

Another, much colder silence.

'A brain tumour,' said Callum, his voice like cut glass, but I heard the doubt in it and it pierced me. I was on my knees, my throat swelling slowly against my voice. I wanted to plead with him. I wanted to tell him the truth. I would have confided in him in a moment, then, without them all there.

'Why's she so good? She's what, twenty-two, twenty-three? She's better than the last witchling and she's got time to go out breaking her vows with fishermen – and *what has she done with my wife?*'

A pause.

'Haley,' said Callum after a long moment, 'tell him where your mother is, please.'

Rory stared between him and me. 'Why do I care where—'

'She's Lysa's daughter, Rory,' said Callum wearily. 'Look at her eyes.'

That silenced Rory for a few seconds. I put one cold hand to my throat and tried to sit up. Everyone was staring at me, and it would not do to let them see me so weak.

'I took,' I said, and coughed and tried again. 'I took her down to the underworld.' It was the only lie I could think of. All the life went out of Rory at once. I saw the colour leave his face. It was as if I had stabbed him, and despite myself, I felt guilty.

'You *killed* her?'

'She died.'

'Of what?'

*A brain tumour*, would have been my answer if we were alone, but Callum was watching me. 'I don't know. It's a disease I haven't seen before— '

'Oh yeah?' I could see tears in his eyes. I hated him so much his grief angered me. 'Some strange disease? Like whatever killed Jorah? Killed the lord's granddaughter?'

I had forgotten he must have been there that night. 'I think so. I've been studying it— '

Rory gave a low, harsh laugh. Adrienne flinched in the crowd behind him. Callum did not move.

'The witch killed the lord's granddaughter,' he said, and spat on the ground. 'A murderer-witch. This fucking witchling is covering for it.'

'A *witch?*' said Callum, quietly. 'What are you talking about?'

'There was a search party, remember? They came here. The lord's men have been hunting it for four years.' Rory's eyes were on me, full of hate. 'Look at her. She knows.'

I could not speak for a moment. But they were all watching me, I could not hesitate. Pointless to outright deny it; I did not know what he knew about Leah.

'I didn't know that,' I said. 'I didn't know there was a – I didn't know there was a witch in the camp.'

'Oh yeah?'

'Yes.'

Rory took a step towards us. Then another. He went right up to Callum, who stood his ground, and so he knelt down to be eye level with me. He smiled. His teeth were yellow and there were fresh lines in his face and I knew my mother's death had destroyed him. There was at least that.

'There's nothing in that house, then. Nothing at all. You don't know about any witch.'

My voice was still hoarse and painful. 'I don't, Rory.'

He grinned wider, his mouth a horror, and then he leaned in close and rasped into Callum's ear, loudly enough that the silent crowd behind him could hear, '*I went into the attic.*'

There was a moment of silence.

'What?' said Callum. He was looking down warily at

Rory, worried he was about to leap at me. 'What does that mean?'

Rory's eyes were on me, and everyone was watching me. The ground had gone from beneath my knees, and I could not speak anymore.

'Go and look,' said Rory, still with that empty, awful grin. 'Let's all go see her attic, shall we?'

'No,' I said, rasping and weak. 'You can't—'

'Why not?'

Callum stared at me. I wanted to say *please*, but I couldn't with all of their eyes on me, so we just looked at each other until John handed him the rope to cuff me.

When we got to the House of the Dead the door was still open, as Rory and John had left it. My medicines were soaking into floorboards, in pools of dark liquid and shattered glass. They had bound my hands behind me, and Callum had to help me up both flights of stairs.

Leah's things were strewn across the floor – her salves and mortars, her herbs, her clothes, her mattress, her leather bag. She had not intended to leave forever, then. Looking around, I understood, dully and without relief. She had killed my mother and taken her down to the underworld. Her last gift to me. Oh, darling.

I should have let her go when she asked me to. I should have let her go months ago. I should never have taken her in.

The room smelled of her. You could tell someone had lived here for years. Callum stood and surveyed her things, the salves with their traces of witch-magic in them. I knew he could taste the air of the underworld here.

'You see?' said Rory, from behind me. 'You *see*?'

'Be quiet,' said Callum softly, and Rory fell silent reluctantly, his breathing still quick in my ear.

There was a silence.

'Haley,' said Callum, looking at Leah's pillow, 'when did the witch start living here?'

I couldn't give her up, not like this, not after everything. 'She doesn't.'

'Liar,' he said quietly, and he looked up at me. I flinched at the look in his eyes.

I wanted to plead again, but it was too late for that, and I was too proud. He took three steps towards me. I saw his eyes move over my face.

'Tell me how Vira died,' he said.

'A brain tumour. Callum. Please—'

He watched me for another second. He saw the desperation in my face. Then he stepped back and looked over my shoulder at Rory.

'All right,' he said. 'Call the lord's men.'

# CHAPTER TWENTY-ONE

They force-fed me some of my own laudanum, out of fear I would escape. For a long time I was in darkness, my mind empty. Then the world around me lifted to a soft blur of voices. I wondered for a moment if I was dead.

I blinked. I was lying on my back. I tried to sit up, but the pain throbbed in my arms and legs, the swell of bruising. I was sticky with blood. Rory had not been gentle when he had dragged me back down the stairs.

In the room there was silence, and inside that silence was breathing. Many people very close. And within it, shallow and terrified, the rasps of someone smaller, younger. *Adrienne.*

I steadied myself and tried to sit up again. The pain flared once more, but this time I was ready for it. I breathed, and then I took in the room.

Rory was standing above me, face contorted with fury. I knew his eyes had not left my face while I slept. He was not in uniform, but the rest of them were. Two dozen men and women, crammed into my parlour and hall, knives in their hands and swords on their waists. I did not recognise any of them from the search party that had come to our town three years ago. Perhaps those soldiers were on ships across the great western sea to their promised land. These were younger, harder-faced.

Leah had not come back, then, through the entrance in the basement. If she had they would have seen her and we would all have been killed already. Did she know what was happening, did she know it wasn't safe?

Adrienne was crouched in the corner underneath the bookshelves, hands around her knees to try and make herself small. Her eyes were wide and full of terror. Two soldiers stood between her and me, knives out. They did not trust us, wanted to keep us separated. But they had nothing to worry about. I had not taught Adrienne how to fight, to use the pool of venom in the dark of her mind. There had been no time.

Two minutes in silence, Rory's harsh, furious breathing and Adrienne's raspy terror. We were all waiting for something. I couldn't see Ira anywhere. Had she simply handed Adrienne over to the lord's men when they came? I couldn't imagine that, but there was no room left in my heart for more fear. I would choose to believe she was all right, for now.

Then at last, a figure appeared in the open front doorway.

I watched her draw closer. She was almost sixty now and she had cut off her hair, but her eyes still had the bright focus of diamond. She looked a little like Marian with the heart cut out of her. They parted to make space for her without even looking. They were attuned to her footsteps – her soldiers, bound by blood.

Esther walked into the parlour and knelt down to look me in the eye. She examined me for a second, taking my chin in her hand. Her skin was cool.

'Haley,' she said, quietly. 'Am I right?'

I nodded.

'What happened to the older one?'

'She died,' I said. I kept my voice as quiet as hers. 'Seven years ago.'

Esther nodded. She was still holding my chin. It was an oddly motherly gesture, though I was waiting for the awful strength, the twist, the snapping of my neck.

'Where is the witch?'

'I don't know,' I said. That was true, at least.

Esther nodded, then let go of my chin. She pulled out a

knife from her belt and placed the tip at the base of my throat, in the hollow above my collarbone, so I was forced to look up. If she pushed, I would choke on my own blood before I bled out. She turned around, still crouching, to look at Adrienne.

'Where is the witch?'

Adrienne's eyes were full of horror. I tried to catch her eye, past Esther, through the legs of the men guarding her. I was trying to tell her: it's all right, say whatever you want. You don't deserve any of this. Whatever happens now I don't blame you. Okay? This is my fault, all my fault.

But she wasn't looking at me. She was staring at Esther, and the knife.

'Where,' said Esther again, quite patiently, 'is the witch?'

Adrienne shook her head frantically.

'This is not a game you want to play with me, child. What has she told you?'

She dug the point of the knife a little further into my throat to make the point. I tried to control what little breath I had and felt a drop of blood trickle down my chest, under my clothes.

'Did she tell you what this witch did? She killed my daughter, many years ago. And Haley here helped.'

My mind was clouded with fear, but that shocked me. Who had told her that? Ten years ago, in the camp, no one had known about Leah. She thought it was me and Marian had failed to save Cora. She had not known about Leah.

Adrienne's eyes were burning. She did not know who to trust anymore. Why shouldn't she believe that I had helped a witch commit murder? It was even true, in a sense. I could not tell Adrienne about the history behind those words with a knife to my throat – of the soldiers in our town, Esther threatening Marian, Cora's possession, the endless seething camp. Adrienne was much too young to remember the war, the Lord Claire in our streets, the cheering, the prayers. Jonathan was the only lord she had ever known, and she did not understand the old hatreds in this room.

'If you don't tell me,' said Esther to her, gently, 'I will hurt her, very badly. Do you want that?'

'No witch,' said Adrienne. Her voice shook. 'I've never seen any witch.'

I tried to stay calm, but I could still feel the point of the knife, pressing deeper with my breathing. Another silence.

Then Esther got to her feet and brushed herself off. She put the knife back into its sheath and turned to her soldiers. 'She's telling the truth,' she said. 'Search the house.'

They ran upstairs in pairs, leaving her and Rory alone in the kitchen. Esther sat in Marian's chair at the table and looked up at the ceiling. There were crashes and thumping footsteps, the splintering of wood.

'Child,' she said to Adrienne without looking down, 'this witchling of yours has harboured this witch for years. Do you understand that? By doing that, she risked your life, and the lives of everyone here. She knew that. Everything she ever told you was a lie.'

Adrienne stared at her. Tears stood bright in her eyes but she did not speak.

'You know what a witch *is*, yes?'

Adrienne nodded slowly. Everyone had known, since Marya died. There had been more bodies found in the woods since then. Marian had shielded the town from knowing too much about the mechanics of judgement. I had failed to protect them from that, too.

'Witches take vows,' said Esther to Adrienne, still examining the table. How did she know all this? 'They can send people to hell forever, and that's an important power, so they promise never to abuse it. Well.' She ran her fingers over a burn mark in the table absently. 'This witch did. She followed our army west over the mountains, and when soldiers wandered, or got lost, she would kill them. If she was near an entrance to the underworld she would take them underground and damn them, and if not she would simply bury them and leave their ghosts to rot in their bodies. She killed innocent men and women in their hundreds. She followed our army for ten years and slaughtered us.'

Esther was watching me now. My fingertips had gone cold. She spoke very deliberately.

'When her own kind found out what she'd done, they cast her out, and then they came to us. They sent a message to us through one of our witchlings. They gave us a picture. They told us she had killed Cora. And so we set about looking for her.' Adrienne's eyes were fixed on Esther, who was still looking up at the ceiling. 'I did not know the witchling and her girl had helped,' she said mildly, after a moment. 'I thought my daughter *died* through their incompetence. I didn't think they would help a witch. But clearly . . .'

She walked around the table, knifepoint pressed into the wood. I felt sick. Leah had told me she stayed with the army because they attracted ghosts. No. I remembered her in the darkness of the camp, full of power. The way she had looked at Vira, dispassionate. I knew she had been a killer when she came to me.

She had killed soldiers, for the joy of it. She always knew why she was being hunted. She knew she had deserved it. She had used me.

I remembered sitting beside her in the basement. I was nineteen then, and the only vow I had broken was in my affection for Callum and Ira, the law against platonic love that every witchling broke in the end. I had forsworn my obsession with Leah. I had dedicated myself to my duty and to the town. I had not yet ruined everything. I remembered the grief of Cora's young husband, the way it had destroyed

him when she fell still. *Hundreds dead.* If I had known that
Jonathan's army were hunting her, if I had known why . . .

The witches had not told Esther about possession, clearly;
they had kept that to themselves. I imagined trying to explain
that her daughter had died for a reason, that Leah had only
been performing her duties as a witch then. It might be an
option, if I were trying to bring on a quick death.

Esther stopped pacing and turned to me. 'When did the
witch leave?'

There was a pause.

I could talk now. I could betray her. I saw Leah's plaintive
eyes as I shut the door in her face. I remembered her kissing
me – because she did not understand love, because she was
kind – and the salves on the floor of her attic, and crying in
her arms with my mother in the kitchen, and kneeling over
Marian on the floor before she needed my help, and sitting
at the kitchen table, lying to me . . .

When she had come to me she had told me she wanted to
be different. And she had done it; she had changed. I knew
her now. I had decided to believe that years ago, and now
there was no choice to make, not really. I loved her too deeply.

I shook my head, slowly.

Esther sat down and leaned forwards in her chair, staring
intently at me. 'Why are you protecting her?'

It still hurt to speak; I could feel the marks of Rory's fingers
on my neck, the hardening bruises. 'I'm not.'

'When did she leave?'

I just shook my head mutely. Esther sighed, got up, and
kicked me in the face.

I slammed backwards into the floor. My head pulsed and
Adrienne screamed. I thought of her father, and fury rose
inside me. I spat out blood and teeth and tried to stay calm.
Fury would not help me, and it might hurt Adrienne.

My skull throbbed. For a moment I could not see; the kick

had dislodged something. I was dizzy with fear. I remembered Marian on the cobblestones, beaten and bleeding, the bones glistening through her bloody skin, and my resolve strengthened. I would never submit to this woman, I would not give Leah to her, no matter what she had done. Not to her, not ever.

I clung to that rage, more powerful and invigorating than my love, and gathered myself through the pain, tried to sit back up. Esther was still watching me.

'When did she leave?'

Everything hurt. The inside of my mouth ached. I did not answer.

Esther took out the knife again. She crouched down beside Adrienne, who gave a helpless little cry of fear. She grabbed the girl's wrist and laid the knife across it. My heart jumped.

'She can work with one hand,' Esther said to me. 'When did she leave?'

A pause. My heart thumped too loudly. I could not think.

'Two days ago,' I said hoarsely. 'Let her go. Please.'

Two days gave them a fifty-mile radius to search. It would spread them out more thinly. Esther looked at me. 'She's lying,' she said to Rory. 'Get the others.'

Rory looked towards me, and when he spoke he sounded almost helpless. 'What about—'

'Get the others,' repeated Esther. I think she wanted to kill me alone.

Adrienne was curled and trembling on the ground. My mind burned feverishly. I spat out blood again, trying to think. I had admitted it now. If they never found Leah, how could I regain the trust of the town? Maybe I could lie, I could say she had manipulated me. It was not entirely untrue. I would disgust myself, but I could do it. Maybe after that they might forgive me.

But Adrienne would have to know the truth. I could not lie to her ever again.

I tried to pull myself back to the dim room through my own panic. Silence had fallen. Esther was looking up at the ceiling again, and so was Rory.

The silence was too deep. The breaking of glass had stopped. There were no footsteps. Esther looked at me. Something in her had closed. What, did she think my house was full of traps? What powers did she think I had, bound and beaten?

And then I realised. She thought perhaps Leah was still here, hidden in the darkness of the house, and she had sent her men up alone to meet her. But she wasn't, she wasn't. Leah was in the underworld. She had left me.

'What's up there?' said Esther quietly.

'Nothing.'

Esther looked at me for a moment. 'Watch the girl,' she said to Rory, and then to me: 'Get up.'

I did, slowly and achingly. She gestured towards the stairs, one hand on her sword hilt. I felt her sharp wariness. 'Go on,' she said. 'Walk ahead.'

I did, slowly. It took effort to haul myself up each stair. Behind me I could hear Adrienne crying. I did not want to leave her alone with him, I wanted to turn and run back and stand between them, but Esther would never let me make it two steps if I tried to push past her. Rory hated me, not Adrienne. He would not hurt her unless Esther told him to.

I took Esther upstairs, leaving bloody handprints on the banister. There were soldiers standing in the open front doorway, in case I tried to run. They were well-trained, standing with their backs turned to guard Esther from the eyes of the town. I saw her glance at them. She might have called them upstairs with her, but she did not. She was not that wary yet.

Upstairs, there was silence. The doors to mine and Adrienne's bedrooms were closed. I steadied myself on against the wall, trying to breathe. Something just behind my eyes had been damaged when she kicked me. The world was blurry now.

She strode past me and pulled at my bedroom door. It would not open. She paused, then turned to me. 'Open it.'

She did not call to the soldiers inside the room; she had to look in control. I stumbled to the door, trying not to throw up. I was so dizzy, and my head hurt. I tried to steady myself. I laid my hand against the wood of the door and said to the house, *Open up.*

And I swear – in the creaking of the wood, in the stirring of eight hundred years of memory and ancient magic, in the imperceptible breathing of the living tree woven through the walls and the stairs – I heard the house say back, in a voice I knew, *Are you sure?*

I think I understood then.

The door swung open. Silence inside. I stepped back, and Esther stepped forward, because she was not a witchling and so could not feel what I felt. There was no sign of them at first. My bedclothes were strewn over the floor, my mirror broken, but the window was intact. There were no scratches on the walls, no blood.

Esther looked around, and then she heard what I heard. A soft scratching. It came from the cupboard and under the bed.

Downstairs, Adrienne had stopped crying.

The scratching got louder, and then a hand emerged from under the bed, scrabbling for a hold in the ancient wood. It was ringed and scarred, a single puckered streak of purplish scarring across the stark bones of the back of his hand.

Esther looked down at it. 'Tomas,' she said quietly.

The man pulled himself slowly out from under the bed. His face was very pale, and his ankles above his boots were a deep purplish-red. His eyes were open and unblinking. I could see the whites already drying yellow in the summer heat.

He stepped towards Esther. Her hand went to her sword hilt and then stopped. She had seen the cupboard door creak slowly open.

She looked towards me. I stepped away, reaching backwards to steady myself against the landing banister. Everything was blurring again. I felt oddly light.

The door swung shut with sudden force.

I heard thuds from inside and sickening crunches, and turned away. I thought I would vomit. Under my hands I felt a thrumming in the wood. *Don't let me die like this*, I said to the house, *not like this, please. Let me fight.*

The world was spinning again. I could hear, behind me, through the closed door, a ripping sound and an awful, rising scream. I sank to my knees. 'Adrienne,' I said, hoarsely, and then, in a moment of true madness, 'Leah?'

'Commander?' The scream had cut off, but I heard Rory below me answering it, panicked. 'Commander?'

There was nothing I could say to him. Adrienne cried out and my heart tore open with terror. I tried to get to my feet, but then I saw him, dragging her by the hair towards the stairs. The front door was shut now, though no one had closed it. Rory did not notice that. He saw me and his face contorted with rage again.

'*Commander?*' he roared.

No answer. There was silence inside my bedroom now.

He ran up the stairs towards me, dragging a screaming Adrienne, and drew the knife from his belt. *My* knife, the one I had left on the kitchen table. Oh, the sword would be better, it would be quicker. I held onto the banister as he reached the top of the stairs.

Adrienne's bedroom door swung open silently, untouched.

Rory turned and saw three of his comrades standing there, swords drawn, in perfect order. 'Where's the commander?'

They did not answer. He stared at them, and then saw their wide black pupils and red fingertips and unseeing eyes.

'Fucking witchling,' he whispered. He took two steps back and put his knife to Adrienne's throat. She had stopped sobbing. Her eyes were red and she was shaking violently, but she did not scream again. I tried to tell her with my eyes that it would be all right.

'Call them off,' he said to me, quietly. 'Call them off. Do it.'

I couldn't, but I did not know how to tell him that. They stepped towards him, and he pressed his knife into Adrienne's throat. I saw blood well under the blade. 'I'll kill her, I swear by the lord. Get away from me, I—'

They stepped forward again. Rory moved back, put one foot on the top stair, and it gave way beneath him.

He toppled backwards, screaming, one snapped leg trapped in the splintered wood. There was blood spreading through his breeches, and shards of bone glistening in the skin. He was still holding onto Adrienne's hair, and she was screaming now too, holding onto the banister for her life. The knife clattered to the bottom of the stairs.

*'Witchling!'*

'Let her go,' I said quietly, and then one of his dead comrades stepped forward and put the tip of his sword through Rory's hand, so he did, and then the rest of the stairs collapsed and he fell until he hit the stone floor of the basement and did not move again.

Adrienne was sobbing. She ran to me, and I held her in my arms as the dead soldiers went back into her bedroom and lay down. The house had finished with them. The branches twisting through the wall creaked and were silent.

'I'm sorry,' I said. 'I'm so sorry.' It hurt to speak. I could feel my missing teeth.

'You're hurt,' she said. She laid a hand on my head, on my blood-matted hair, and the gesture was so kind I almost broke down.

'I'll be all right,' I said, but I know she didn't believe me.

Outside, the remaining soldiers were hammering on the

door. It was shut tight, and the house would not let them in. I took Adrienne upstairs to the attic, where there were no corpses. She stared at Leah's bed.

'She was sleeping here?'

I nodded.

'How long?'

'Four years.'

'*Why?*'

'She needed help,' I said. 'It's in our vows. You help people when they need it.' It was a cold answer. I tried to focus, though the world was spinning again. 'I loved her,' I said, 'and I didn't know why they wanted to kill her, and I didn't want to let them. I'm sorry it put you in danger. I'm sorry I didn't tell you. I'm sorry.'

If she answered I didn't hear it, or don't remember. My vision was blurry, my hearing dipping into a high-pitched hum. Esther's blow had broken something I could not heal.

I looked out of the window. The soldiers had stopped hammering on the door and were gathered in a circle, deliberating.

There was someone standing in the window opposite. Ira. She looked horrified at the sight of my face. She still loved me, I think. I wish I had been able to tell her why her son had died. I wish I could have thanked her. I stared at her and my thoughts spun and the world dimmed and brightened again.

Something was strange about her presence in that window, and it took me a moment to find it: oh yes, she did not live there. She had gone into that house to try to see into mine, if I was still alive. *Yes,* I tried to tell her with my eyes, *I'm all right.*

I don't know if she saw it. Her expression did not change.

The soldiers were spreading out across the street, disappearing into alleyways. Then they were gone. They had left. They were gone. They would leave, leave us alone.

No, no. I tried to clear my head. *Think*. Would they leave Esther in this house? Would they just go, if they thought she was dead or lost? Why would they not leave together?

I tried to imagine Esther – clever, ruthless, diamond-hard from years of grief. She had walked into my house to find the witch who had killed her daughter. She was not stupid; she must have known she might not come out again.

What would she say to her soldiers, knowing that? Would she have left them orders?

My heart was pulsing too loudly in my chest. I could hear Adrienne trying to talk to me from somewhere far away. Ira was still watching me. I knew that she knew, too.

*Run,* I mouthed to her.

She saw that, and she slipped away from the window and out of sight. I gathered Adrienne in my arms. She clung to me despite herself, and trembled against my chest.

'What happening?'

'It's all right,' I said. 'It's all right, darling. Don't look out of the window.'

After five minutes or so, the cry was raised in the centre of town. People came out of their houses carrying bags, children, each other. They spread out, too, ran through empty streets to the unguarded outskirts. They were clever. Some of the older ones had known to expect this ever since the lord's men had appeared in front of my house, or even since Esther had first come ten years ago, seeking Marian's aid – since before that, really. Since we had lost the war.

It was all I could do to keep sitting up. Adrienne was sobbing in my arms. There were soldiers in the streets beyond, and from the window I saw people run through, cut down, bodies left on the cobblestones. A man knelt beside his dead wife and the soldier who had killed her drew his sword out from her chest and ran her husband through with it.

There was nothing I could do. I promise. I felt every death,

I wept for them, but there was nothing. Some made it into the forest, ran downstream where dogs could not trace them, out into the eastern hills. I don't know how many. I pray for them all the time.

I saw smoke rising from the courthouse. That was where they were starting the fires. *Callum*, I thought, and then, with a jolt, *Samuel*. What had they done with him? I had to get to them.

I stumbled to my feet and tried to climb down the stairs onto the landing, but the world was blurring again. Adrienne was behind me, hand on my shoulder, trying to steady me. 'Haley,' she said, 'no, look,' and I did.

The staircase. Of course. The bottom staircase had collapsed. I sank down onto my knees at the top of the stairs and covered my face with my hands. Adrienne was terrified, and I couldn't tell her what was going to happen, couldn't tell her about the war, the villages razed to the ground. *One in ten.* I had thought we were safe, but no, we had just been given a little more time.

I could smell smoke through the window now. My bedroom door was open again. I imagined Esther rising with her men to stand beside us at the house's command. Then I remembered they had torn her apart. Her ghost would burn with ours, and we would be taken by darkness together.

I took Adrienne in my arms. It was good that we were in the attic. If we fell asleep, I thought, it would be fine, the smoke would suffocate us before the fire reached us. I stroked her hair.

'Sweetheart,' I said, thickly, 'I adore you.' I don't know if she heard me.

*Sleep*, I said to my deepest self, and the magic in my bones took pity on me and rose up to claim us both. I thought, *I'm sorry*, and then nothing.

*

This was it. Surely.

I was lying on a wooden floor. Everything still hurt.

The dead did not hurt.

I was alive, then. That did not make sense.

Adrienne. Where was Adrienne? I rolled over and found I could move; blinked, through swollen eyes, and realised I could see. I was lying on the landing floor. Adrienne was standing beside the window.

'Adrienne?'

She did not turn around. I got slowly, achingly to my feet. I bent over, coughing on acrid smoke. It felt like it had condensed in my lungs, hardened to grime. I clambered over to the window.

I could not understand it for a moment. Nothing. I was looking out over a charred and blackened field. Flaked-white stumps marked where houses had been. In the distance, the forest was still alight, and there were smoke stains on the blue crystal sky, far above us. I could see bodies charred on the cobblestones below. I heard the crackling of the trees, and our breathing, and the soft wind blowing the smoke westwards. Beyond that, absolute silence.

'Why did we live?' said Adrienne, after a while. Her voice was trembling. 'Why didn't the house burn?'

I knew the answer to that. I remembered Leah with her hands pressed against the floorboards, staring at her salves, and that shimmering power in the air around her. The house moulding itself around her, learning from her, absorbing her. Painkillers, she had told me she was making all those years, ointments against infection. I should have asked. I should not have trusted her. I should have trusted her more.

'We were protected,' I said.

'By who?'

'By someone who loved us.'

There was no way out down the stairs, so we clambered down the wall from the second-floor window. A hundred times I thought the dizziness in my brain or my sweating hands would kill me, but I was lucky, and I did not fall.

On the ash-covered ground, we looked around. Nothing had quite sunk in yet. Adrienne walked over to the stumps that marked the remains of Ira's house, and looked up at me. Her thin hair was flaked with ash.

'How many people died?'

'I don't know,' I said. 'Do you want to count them?' It was an honest question. If she did not already, someday she might blame herself for this, and though it was not her fault, it would help her to be able to quantify the loss. But she said, 'No.' She was only eleven, after all.

'What are we going to do?'

I got to my feet. I swayed when I stood, but I tried to hide it. I looked down at her with calm and purpose. I had put her through so much. I would not let her think I did not have a plan.

'We're going to into the forest,' I said, 'and then Leah will find us again.'

'The witch?' Her face was full of fear.

'She won't hurt you. She wanted to protect you. She always just wanted to help people.' Partly true.

'But she—' She wanted to believe me, I could see it, but she was scared and uncertain. 'Why did she kill all those people?'

'I don't know.' I laid a hand on her head. 'I'm sure there was a good reason.'

She seemed unconvinced, but she was as desperate as I was to believe it. 'She'll help us?'

'Yes.' That I was sure of.

'How do we find her?'

Leah was not coming back through our entrance to the

underworld. If she was going to do that, she would have already. I felt her absence keenly, through the ground and sky below us. If we stayed here, eventually the lord's men would come, following Esther's vanished men and the brownish smokestains on the sky. But if we left I did not know how Leah would find us again.

Adrienne's face was grey with grief and fear, but she burned with the belief that there were answers. I would not deny her that.

'We'll figure it out,' I said. 'You and I, we'll figure it out.'

At the outskirts of the town, where the forest melted away to marshland and river, we heard scurrying. Squirrels, I thought at first, and then, no. The squirrels would have run away. The grass was burned to dry black nothing, and there was nowhere to hide. There was too much sky, too much silence. Too many bodies. We kept our eyes straight ahead and did not look at them.

Another rustling. I raised my finger to my lips and stopped, and Adrienne stopped with me, and stayed silent. The scurrying stopped too, then coalesced into the hushed and frantic breathing of a child. I could not see him and I would not scare him, so instead I stayed exactly where I was until I saw the top of a head emerge above the riverbank, black and matted with mud and ash. He ducked at once, but I knew him.

'Aron?'

He raised his head again and saw me. An expression of profound relief came over his face, and my heart sank. I could not mean safety to him anymore.

'Haley! Help me – please – you have to help me—'

He had been crying, which is how I knew it was too late. Callum lay in the mud beneath the riverbank. His eyes were open. The soldier had stabbed him in the stomach with the tip of his sword, but that was only the first wound. I could see from the curl of his arms that he had fallen protecting Aron. The soldier had stood over him and pierced him through the heart. His shirt was soaked in blood.

I knelt beside him. I wanted to collapse and weep, but the two children were watching me with hope in their eyes, and so I kept my voice level and my eyes dry. 'He's dead,' I said to Aron.

He swallowed and nodded. 'I know. I—' He was trying so hard to be fierce, to be brave. His eyes were Marian's, blood-shot with grief. 'Bring him back,' he said. 'Please.'

'I'll do everything I can.'

That too was a lie. My materials for resurrection lay shattered and abandoned in the House of the Dead, but I would not bring Adrienne with me back through the silent town full of charred bodies, and I could not leave her alone. I told them both to stand back. I sat beside Callum and watched the water stream softly over the smooth grey stones of the riverbed, and I lay my hand on his still-warm skin and closed my eyes.

My head throbbed, my arms ached, my vision had points of grey numbness in it, but my heart was untouched. The air around me was shimmering and full of death. I breathed it in, and was full of it, and breathed it out again.

Callum opened his eyes. I saw the moment he realised he could not draw breath. I saw him feel his own pierced heart. His hand twitched, and went to his blood-soaked shirt. He looked at me and did not know me.

'Aron,' he said, and coughed. There was no moisture in his throat. Aron ran to him with a flask of water. A resourceful child. He might survive.

'I'm here,' he said. 'I'm here, Papa.'

Callum looked at me again. Something flickered again, and this time it took. 'Haley?'

'Callum, I'm sorry. I'm so sorry. It's all my fault.'

He looked at me for a long time. Then slowly he got to his feet. Blood dripped from his fingertips. He moved stiffly, a mockery of his living self. Here was what I had made.

He looked around at the razed earth where the town had been. 'I called them here,' he said, raspily. 'This is my fault.'

'It was your job, Callum. And someone would have done it if you hadn't. Rory would have.'

He looked at me with yellowing eyes, then behind me, at the charred town. In death his face was expressionless.

'Callum,' I said, 'listen to me. Leah – the witch – she didn't kill Vira. Neither did I. She was sick and I tried to save her, but there was nothing we could do. Please believe me.'

He looked at me and said nothing. When he spoke, his voice was rough with the dirt his throat.

'Are you asking for forgiveness?'

'I want you to understand.'

'I don't,' he said. 'I don't. But I didn't think they would kill you.'

I do not know if I believe him.

He wiped some of the mud from his eyes. He was watching me, his pupils wide in death. He walked slowly to me. How long would he have, without the proper rites? Weeks, months? Long enough to get Aron somewhere safe. Arbakin, the northern citadel, where no one knew his name.

He walked to me and took my face in his cold hands, and I felt like a child for the last time in my life.

'Haley . . .' I could tell he did not know what to say to me. 'Just live, all right?'

I nodded, and he let me go. I was so grateful that his vision was not good enough to see how the blood crusted at my scalp.

We watched them walk into the woods. Aron turned back to look at us, though his father did not, and then they were swallowed by the trees.

*

We went west, because it wasn't where they would expect us to go. I felt Leah's eyes on me, though maybe that was the throbbing pain at the base of my skull. She had lived in the house, taught it to save us. She would not have just run when she realised we had been discovered. She would find us again. I believed it fiercely.

The darkness within the forest was soft and cool. I heard the fire crackling in the distance but could not taste the smoke anymore. I did not know what lay on the other side of the forest, but I thought there might be a town, a sympathetic witchling who might hide us. Or perhaps they would cast me out. I was an abomination, a witchling without a town, but Adrienne was young and unmarked by tattoos. They might help her. Yes.

Sometimes when I lay down to rest, I felt the numb grey patches at the base of my skull crackling into my brain. The pain at the base of my neck had changed; it was deeper now, and hotter. The cuts on my arms and feet from the splintering wood had stopped bleeding and instead wept pale yellow. I tried to hide it from Adrienne, but it was no use, and there was nothing I could say to reassure her.

I should have taken food from the house. I cursed myself for not thinking about it, but thankfully Adrienne was good at laying traps to catch hares and squirrels. When I asked her how, she said her mother had been a hunter. I could not believe I had never asked her about that before. She had quick, sure hands. She would have made a good witchling.

I set little fires, though gathering wood was difficult. Sometimes if I got up too quickly the world would turn over. Adrienne found me lying on the ground, trying to find my way back up, the third time this happened. She helped me up. There was no expression in her face; she did not want to look scared in front of me.

'We shouldn't stop again,' she said, as we sat beside the

fire eating strips of meat with clumsy hands. 'We should keep walking.'

'All right,' I said, so we did.

I kept thinking of Samuel. What had they done with him after they found me at his house? If they had bound him and brought him to the courthouse, or kept him tied up in his own living room, then he would have burned. But he had broken no vows, after all. The crime was mine. Perhaps they had just left him there, the door unlocked, and he had scrambled down to the river when they set the fires and run.

I hope he made it out. Sometimes I think of him and my brother John, wandering in the western plains, safe and warm and alive.

As we walked, we spoke. Adrienne was steadier than me and more determined. When I flagged she urged me on, encouraged me. Sometimes the cool brightness would overwhelm me for whole seconds, and the world would spin slowly, and I would steady myself against a tree and hope she did not see me. I knew if I sat down I might never get up again, and I refused to leave Adrienne alone.

When she asked me about Leah, I was relieved, because it meant she thought I was strong enough to answer.

'Why didn't you tell me?'

'I wanted you to trust me first,' I said. My voice was cracked with thirst; we had been drinking the water from leaves, new-morning dew. 'I didn't want to scare you.'

'I wouldn't have been scared.' She said it with such confidence.

How old had she been during the raids? Seven years old, eight? In my mind she had appeared on my doorstop fully formed, clever and fierce and resentful. I had forgotten that she had lived before she became the witchling's girl.

'Did you know she killed all those people?'

'No.'

'She never told you?'

'She tried to, at the end,' I said. 'I didn't want to know.'

Adrienne paused for a moment, chewing her lip. I'm not sure she understood me.

'Don't you hate her? Aren't you angry?'

'Why?'

'For lying.'

'No,' I said, and as I did I realised it was true. 'I know her. I love her. I trust she did . . . she did what she thought was right. She did the best she could. She'll find us again, Adrienne.'

'What if she doesn't?'

'She will.'

'And she'll help us?'

'Yes.'

She stopped in the woods, turned to face me, her arms crossed. 'Don't you *care* why she killed them?'

'I do,' I said. 'And I love her. They're . . .' I couldn't think of the words. 'I can do both.'

'How?'

'I have faith in her.'

The way Adrienne looked at me was half-suspicious and half-pitying. We walked in silence for a while.

'I'm so sorry,' I said. 'I love you.'

She turned around and looked at me. She was so young, with quick dark eyes. I wish I had had more time to know her. Eventually she turned back and kept walking, but at least I can be certain now that she knows.

Eventually the trees parted and we saw a town of brick houses, at the edge of a river valley. I wondered if it was our river – winding silver-gold through the rock. Beyond that, there was only flat scrubland, as far as the eye could see.

'I thought the sea was west of here,' said Adrienne, behind me.

'It is. Much further.'

'How much?'

'I'm not sure, exactly. We'd have to walk for weeks.'

*Weeks.* The idea was so alien to her. It laid wonder wide open in her face, until she saw me looking and turned away.

She was worried for me, so she wanted to go straight to their House of the Dead, but I said no. I was too obviously a witchling, and if the lord's men were there they might realise who I was and kill me, and maybe Adrienne too, though neither of us said it. So we stayed back and watched.

It was a very quiet town. There seemed to be no market. The people spoke softly, subdued, and I heard no laughter or weeping. Down in the valley, beside the river, were four or five fishermen in small, rickety boats. I thought: if there are hunters in these woods, they might find us. But there was nothing we could do about that except go out into the open, into the wide gold scrubland where we could not hide, so we stayed where we were. There was no true safety anywhere.

Night began to fall and still the quiet did not break. 'Something's wrong,' said Adrienne.

'I know.' The crackling grey noise spreading through my brain made it difficult to hear my instincts, but there was darkness in this town, I could feel it. I was so tired.

'Where are the children?'

'What children?'

'I can't hear any,' said Adrienne. She was staring into the town intently, her brow creased. 'No babies, or anything.'

She was so clever.

'I don't *know*,' I said.

'Why wouldn't there be—'

'I really don't know, Adrienne.'

She wasn't used to that. I felt her unease. 'I can't see any soldiers,' I said, 'but that doesn't mean there aren't any.'

'I could go in first. They won't kill me.' She was so brave, her hair matted and her jaw set.

'Sweetheart,' I said, 'yes, they will.'

'Then what do we do?'

My exhaustion was suddenly overwhelming. 'I don't know,' I said. The burning in my arms was deeper now, at the edges of my chest, and the world would not stay still; I could see the sky drifting at the corners of my vision. 'Sleep, first.'

'All right.' She looked relieved.

We lay down in the damp brush. The nights were cold, I had learned, and often I woke up with her arms around me. I loved her so much. I could see her future in the distance, our shining hope.

'It's going to be fine,' I told her. I think she was already asleep.

I listened to her soft breathing. The air had changed and I knew it was going to rain. The earth smelled different now, and there was an edge to the wind. The darkness came until I could not see her in front of me anymore.

# CHAPTER TWENTY-TWO

*Haley! Haley, no—*

Somebody was shaking me. Sensation flickered in and out, dulled and then electric.

*Haley, no—*

Her voice was far away, through an attic door. Thought was lost to me, its sharpness and intricacy, but something primal crackled in my soul at her distress. I wanted so badly to comfort her. *It's all right,* I tried to tell her, but could not speak.

I felt her turn me over. She was trying to wake me up. *Haley! Haley! No, no . . .*

She collapsed sobbing. I wished I had died with my eyes open.

She built a fire. I felt its warmth through fading nerves at my feet. For an hour she sat with her hands on my face, trying to resurrect me, and I felt her fierce will, bolts of intention through my skin to the place below my heart where I lived now. But she had no runes, no practice, no path to transcendence, and she was too tired even to make me sit up. My body cooled slowly in the air.

I wanted to speak, to say, *it's okay*. I wanted her to leave me here and run. I could not be afraid anymore. My own stillness, my silent heart, could not distress me. I would fade under the sun and then be gone, and that would be all right, if she lived. I loved her, I felt it, a hard, condensed thing in my stomach, but I could not remember her name.

I felt the sun on my face, red through my eyelids, and then it faded again. She lay down beside me. She was still sobbing.

Dread, blunt and unnamed, formed at the base of my skull. No, don't die with me. No, sweetheart. You have to live.

I felt my fingertips in the damp soil. A mouse crawled over me. I waited for disgust, but none came.

Night. The cold lay across us. The girl slept beside me. Then, from the trees, footsteps.

*Kid*, said a voice from the darkness. *Kid, get away from her.*

I felt the girl struggle to her feet. Her sobbing had left her voice hoarse. *She was waiting for you*, she said to the woman. *She was waiting for you. Where were you?*

*I know. I know. I'm sorry.*

The woman knelt beside me, and touched my chin. I heard the break in her voice, the tears. *Haley*, she said, softly. *Come back to me.*

I strained towards her, but I was paralysed in the congealing stillness of my own body. I knew she could feel me there, though, burning with love.

She could have brought me back, of course, but she didn't. She was too kind. She sat in silence, stroking my hair, until she had made her peace with the sight of me. At last she got to her feet.

*Would you like to come with me?* she said to the girl.

*Where are you going?*

*To lay her to rest.*

*You won't take her*, said the girl fiercely. *You won't take her from me. I won't let you.*

A silence.

*Where are you going?* said the girl again.

*I'm not sure*, said the woman. *She wanted me to keep you safe, so I'm going to do that. Beyond that it's up to you.*

*I don't need keeping safe. And you're a murderer.*

*Ah,* said the woman, after a moment. *You know about that.*

*Yes. You killed hundreds—*

*Three hundred and thirty-eight.*

A horrified pause. *You kept count?*

*Would it be better if I hadn't?*

There was a scuffle. The girl had tried to run, but tripped. I heard her terrified panting.

*Please, Adrienne,* said the woman. *I'd like to explain.*

*I don't want to talk to you, witch.*

*I killed those people for a reason. They were soldiers in an army. I followed that army across mountains, more distance than you can imagine, and I watched—*

*I don't care what you—*

*Listen to me. You know they used to burn towns. One in every ten.*

The girl fell silent.

*Didn't your parents ever tell you?*

*The lord's army did that? The Lord Jonathan?*

*Yes.*

A longer silence.

*My parents were soldiers for him,* said the girl, a little bemusedly. *They settled here once the war was over.*

*I didn't know that.*

*Did they burn any towns?*

*I don't know,* said the woman.

A raindrop fell onto my face and trickled into my eye. I felt it against the jelly of my eyeball, cold and sharp, but could not blink it away.

*I killed the ones who set the fires,* said the woman. *I killed the ones who chased children into the woods. I waited until they were alone and I killed them with knives and rocks and spells. I wasn't meant to interfere, I had a different duty, and*

*when my people found out they exiled me. So I came to
Haley.*

*Why?*

*Because when she was your age I healed the woman who
raised her. I thought she owed me a debt. I was selfish.*

*Why didn't you tell her the truth?*

*I was selfish*, said the woman again, more quietly. *I wanted
her to think I was a true witch. I wanted to start over, I
wanted to keep to my vows and do my duty.*

*They're all dead*, said the girl, her voice tight. *They all burned.*

*I know*, said the woman softly.

A pause.

*Why aren't there any children in the town?*

*Which town?*

*The one back there.*

*We're only about forty miles from the coast.*

*So?*

*Sit down*, said the woman.

*No.*

A pause. Then the woman said slowly, *Do you want to
hear this?*

*Yes.*

*They took the children with them to the land across the sea.*

*Why?*

*They needed to populate it. Children are easier to feed and
store on a ship. They don't fight back. They can be more
easily converted. Adults have stronger loyalties, they're harder
to confuse.*

*But they must have*—The girl was confused. *They said they
were going years ago. They left when I was born.*

*They went in batches. It took a while to build the ships.
The first batch went ten years ago, the second seven, the third
five. They left a few thousand people behind to guard this
country. But most of them have been gone for years. They*

took all the food and the grain and the gold they could from this country. There were famines in the big cities. A lot of people fled east.

*And they took children?*

Yes. After the third time they came, most towns along the coast swore never to have children again.

*How do you know all this?* said the girl suspiciously.

*I've been in the underworld for three days.*

*So?*

*I've been talking to the dead.*

A long pause. I felt the girl's horror like a mist in the air. *How far away is the land over the sea?*

*Why?*

*So we could go and get them.*

No, said the woman. *It's too late.*

A silence.

*Adrienne, she'll rot if we leave her out here. Help me carry her.*

I lay in the soft, cool darkness, in the witch's arms. She did not need help, of course, she just wanted to make the girl feel useful, and that too was a kindness. There was a shimmering power in the air about her. I felt it in my slowly congealing blood, and the girl felt it, too, because she walked more quickly, with purpose and strength.

We moved through the forest. Something in me now pulsed to sensation darker and deeper than sight and sound. I sensed north and south, the brightening and fading of the sky. I could feel the world below me, its swirling mist. I ached for it.

Eventually when the sun came up the woman lay me down, and they built a fire together.

*What do I do if they try to possess me?*

*Don't say yes.*

They sat around the fire, eating roast hare. They had laid

me carefully a few feet away and I felt my skin slowly drying in the hot air. The witch had been teaching the girl how to skin dead things. I should have taught her that.

*What?*

*You'll be asleep. Someone will come to you in your dreams. You'll turn around and they'll be standing there. They'll ask to come in and talk to you. They'll want to touch you, in the dream. Lay their hands on yours. And that'll be it.*

*That's all it takes?*

*That's all it takes.*

*What if I forget, while I'm asleep?*

*Then they get you,* said the witch. *I can protect you against some of them, but not all. There are too many now, since the war.*

*Are they here now? Watching us?*

*Maybe. They can't survive more than a few hours up here, so they're probably waiting for you to fall asleep.*

*Then I won't sleep.*

*Everyone says that,* said the witch. *You don't have to be scared. You just have to be ready for them.*

The girl was silent for a moment.

*Are you going to stay here?*

*No. It's not safe here.*

*Where will you go?*

*North, I think,* said the witch. *It's warmer, and there are fewer people. Savannahs and scrubland. Land for hunting, not farming. There aren't a lot of people there. The walk will take a few months, and I'll have to avoid the cities. But after that it'll be safe.*

There was a quiet.

*I won't bind you or keep you,* said the witch, *but if you want to stay with me, you can.*

*I know.*

The girl did fall asleep. It took a long time.

The witch walked slowly around her and I felt the air change, a gathering and hardening, something that repelled me in the space beneath my heart. A spell to ward off ghosts. I heard the girl's soft breathing in the grass dark, and was calm.

Once the girl was protected, the witch took me in her arms and carried me through the forest. The night air was soft on my face, and I could feel myself retreating, sensation fading from my dead nerves. My hearing came and went like tide, but I know she did not speak to me.

At last the darkness gave way to something deeper. She put me across her shoulders, my hands and feet swaying limply, and climbed down into the tunnel.

At once everything sharpened. The air became cool in my dry mouth. I could feel an electricity in my own dead body, something sparking and rebounding: the draw of the world below me. It meant stillness and home and rest. So close.

The witch carried me for hours that could have been minutes or days through winding darkness, and then the light through my eyelids changed to the soft pulse of amethyst, and I knew that we were there.

I felt the wind on my face as she lowered me gently into the softness of the snow-glass. She opened my mouth and pulled open my shirt, and lay her hand on my chest, and breathed, and then something passed from her into me, into the space where I lived beneath my heart—

And everything changed.

I was alive again. Not alive, no, but I was *physical*, too small, trapped in rotting flesh and wet muscle. I could not breathe, I had to get out. I pushed and tried to expand through vein and lung and throat, until last I felt air and openness. I tried to reach and felt the soft flesh of throat and mouth, and broke through teeth, and then felt air.

*Freedom.* I dragged myself from my own body, slowly, and felt it rupture around me. At last I kneeled on the ground beside it. I did not look at its broken face.

Everything was real again. 'Haley,' said Leah from above me. 'Look at me.'

I did. She looked clean and unhurt, and stronger somehow than she had done in my attic. Freedom had revived her.

'I'm sorry,' she said. 'I'm so sorry I lied.'

'It's all right. I know—' My own voice reverberated in my ears; it sounded different, smoother, undamaged by the flaws of human throat and brain. It was disorienting. 'I know why you killed them. I understand.'

'You do?'

'Yes.'

It was not joy in her face, I think, but a kind of peace. A relief.

'I should have told you the truth,' she said. 'That night, after Imogen. I should have been honest with you from the start. I was so scared you wouldn't let me stay. I couldn't – I couldn't be cast out again.'

'I understand, Leah.'

We looked at each other. There was almost nothing left to say. I did not try to touch her; I did not want to know that I couldn't.

'I tried to find you,' she said, and her voice cracked. 'I didn't know where you'd gone. I thought – I didn't know how badly you were hurt—'

'Don't apologise,' I said again. My mind was very clear and bright. 'It's all right.'

She took my hand – she *could* take my hand, though I felt no sensation in the fingertips – and kissed my forehead tenderly. We stood there in silence for a while, taking each other in.

'Don't come back,' she said. 'I know you wouldn't, but—'

'I won't.'

'I'll look after her.'

'I know you will.

'Leah . . .' I couldn't think of the right words; my life lay stark behind me, and I could not voice it. 'I did the best I could. Or I tried to. Always. Tell her that.'

'She knows.'

'She'll forget.'

'I'll find you again,' she said. 'I promise.'

She could not let me go, she had never grieved before, so I turned away and walked down the mountain into the dark and seething forest. I did not look back, and I never saw her again.

It is very quiet here. I cannot sleep, of course, but over many years I have perfected a method of rest not unlike transcendence. I sit beneath the soft purple sky under something that in the living world might be called a pine tree, in tall grass, and I stay very still until my mind settles and I am at peace. It is not as complete as transcendence, of course, but it soothes my mind, and that's all I can ask for.

The rest of the time I walk, and I think. I have walked a hundred miles in every direction, along rivers of smoke and in soft grey canyons and through endless teeming forests. I have seen white wolves, and dark sharp-eyed birds that look like hawks but aren't, and velvety, scurrying mice. I don't think these creatures are alive, but they're not dead either. I wonder if any of them have ever escaped.

At the edge of every skyline, as far as I can see, are mountain ranges, snowy and jagged and unthinkably beautiful. At their summits are the entrances to the living world. Sometimes I find myself wanting to walk up there, to examine the hard sky. I know that impulse is a lie. If I follow it, the desire to live will overtake me, and I will walk up into the world and take a body, and then I will have defied the last, best thing Leah asked of me: *don't come back*.

So I stay here, and walk, and examine my life.

I pass other ghosts. We do not speak to each other. I have not spoken to anyone in many years. The mind of a ghost is not like a living brain, because this long a period of isolation would have driven me insane before I died. My mind now is still and quiet like lake water. But I am still myself, I think. Every time I see a woman with short grey hair, even far in the distance, my heart leaps.

Do I have a heart? My body is whole, my skin perfect and unveined. My hair does not grow. I feel discomfort, but not pain; I never cut or bruise myself. I do not age. Some part of me hopes that I never see Marian. It would upset her to know that I died at twenty-two.

There is another option, of course. I could walk out into the living world, with no witch to stop me, and simply wait for the wind and rain to dissolve me. If I wanted it to be over.

It took me a very long time to realise that I was waiting for something, and then what that something was.

And then – maybe hours later, maybe months – I saw you.

I don't know why I was surprised. Of course not all of you would wait on mountaintops; you must have leisure and freedom, to walk and speak with the dead. You were sitting beneath a tree, and you looked young. You look a little like Adrienne, and some part of me trusted you for that, so I came to you and asked to tell you my life.

And now you know, and can judge me. One last thing, though, I have a theory. Hear me out.

I have walked in this world for years, and I've never once seen an infant. Children of ten or twelve, but no infants or toddlers. Nor have I seen any ghosts with children in their arms. Can you tell me why that is?

No, all right, I thought not.

Here is my theory. My theory is that you don't release those ghosts into the underworld, if they're too young to remember their lives. I think you send some up to the world above, and keep the rest in their bodies, and raise them up, invest them with deep magic, and call them your own. I think that's where witches come from. Am I right about that?

But Leah remembered. Maybe she was a little too old, she was a mistake. She could remember being alive, the soldiers of Jonathan coming to kill her and her mother and her lord. She remembered, and when her duties took her to the edges of his army, when ghosts gathered in the shadow of his war, when she saw other children burning, she began to take revenge.

Am I right? You would know if I was right. You know everything. Please. It's all I want now. Just tell me.

I've told you everything, and now I'm dead, and it doesn't matter if I know. Tell me if I'm right.

Please.

# ACKNOWLEDGEMENTS

My thanks as ever to my agent, Meg Davis, and my editor, Thorne Ryan, who made this book possible and readable, respectively; I rely on you both more than I have a right to, and I'm very grateful for you. Thanks also to Emma Coode, who copyedited the book, for her hard work and insight. For very different reasons, thank you to Sarah Williams and Owen Saxton, who have helped me so much over the last three years, for their immense kindness.

Thank you to Lara Welch, the most gifted artist I have ever met, for reading this book and making me cry last Christmas, and to Callie, for making me laugh right after. Thank you to Cel, Tom, and Chris, my darling husbands, and Fliss and Emma, my beloved wives; thank you also to Nic, whose steadiness and wisdom have been invaluable this last year. Thank you to Hannah, and Charlie, and Sophie (I'm sorry I didn't manage to get George and the lighthouse in here; I did try), and to Emilie, the only genuine witch in my life. I adore you all; the condition of this book is the very least of what I owe to you.

To my parents: thank you, I love you. And to Catherine, always. Every year I want to be more like you.

# If you enjoyed *The Witchling's Girl*, you'll love

'A twisting story full of surprises and rich, complex characters. Helena has created a beautifully written world of injustice, bravery and friendship'

Claire North, author of
*The First Fifteen Lives of Harry August*

'Kept me riveted to the page. The plot pulses with action and the characters are beautifully complex. This is a book that sparks with adrenaline and longing, all the way to the final page'

Rebecca Ross, author of *The Queen's Rising*

**Available in paperback and ebook now**

HODDER &
STOUGHTON